Dychweler erbyn y dyddiad olaf uchod
Please return by the last date shown

LLYFRGELLOEDD POWYS LIBRARIES

www.powys.gov.uk/llyfrgell
www.powys.gov.uk/library

What Kitty Did Next

A novel

CARRIE KABLEAN

RedDoor

Published by RedDoor

www.reddoorpublishing.com

© 2018 Carrie Kablean

The right of Carrie Kablean to be identified as author of this
Work has been asserted by her in accordance
with sections 77 and 78 of the Copyright, Designs
and Patents Act 1988

ISBN 978-1-910453-61-2

A CIP catalogue record for this book is available
from the British Library

Cover design: Clare Connie Shepherd
www.clareconnieshepherd.com

Typesetting: Tutis Innovative E-Solutions Pte. Ltd

Printed and bound by Nørhaven, Denmark

For Annabelle xx

CHAPTER 1

Longbourn, January 1813

Matters matrimonial had long been the focus of Miss Catherine Bennet's world. How could it be otherwise? The absolute necessity of finding a husband – a respectable husband, of course, but one whose chief recommendation must be his wealth – was the very cornerstone of her education. Her tutor and adviser in this winsome endeavour was none other than her indefatigable mother, Mrs Bennet, a woman whose sole aim in life was to see her five daughters married, and married well.

Catherine had accepted this doctrine, taking it as her own. Now though, with three sisters all wed within half a year, mildly disturbing thoughts were forming in her nineteen-year-old mind. Those sisters had all three married for love. Catherine hoped – expected – to do likewise but, young and inexperienced as she was, even she had begun to see that love was an indefinable commodity and certainly not one that guaranteed a life without care. Inchoate questions clamoured for answers she did not have. What if she were not to find a suitable husband? Where would she live? What would she do? What would she like to do?

Mrs Bennet burst into the parlour, dispelling any possibility of further introspection. 'Oh Kitty, there you are. Where is Mary, where is your sister?'

If she wanted a reply, Mrs Bennet did not wait for one. Instead, she peered at Kitty. 'Really, what is to become of you?' she said, shaking her head and unwittingly echoing her daughter's unvoiced concerns. 'You don't look well, child. What is the matter with you? Are you unwell?'

'I am quite well thank you, Mama,' said Kitty, wondering what was wrong with her appearance now. It really was very hard to please her mother. 'I am just a little tired.'

'You are not lively these days,' declared Mrs Bennet, subsiding into a chair. 'You and Mary should walk into Meryton; it is days since we heard news. The day is bright, there is no rain. Perhaps the militia are returned? Aunt Phillips will be waiting to see you. She will know if the officers are back. How I long to hear from your dear sister Lydia. Not a word from her since Christmas. I am sure she will have much to tell us.'

'Mary is not given to walks into Meryton, Mama,' said Kitty. 'If you can persuade her then so much the better, but I fear she will not give up her books.'

'Books,' said Mrs Bennet, investing the word with disdain. Since the early days of their marriage, a somewhat disillusioned Mr Bennet had treated his library as a refuge, both from his wife and the clamour of family life. Mrs Bennet had become used to this arrangement and tolerated books insofar as they could provide some form of entertainment, but that they should be preferred to social intercourse was, to her, quite unnatural. Her husband must read his books, of course, but for her daughter Mary to shut herself away reading her sermons and treatises was not to be borne. It was not as if the girl was blessed with uncommon beauty; she really must learn to smile more and lose those dour expressions. In that, at least, she could learn from her younger sister, Kitty. Books, indeed!

Mrs Bennet contemplated these unpleasant traits for a few moments and then, with surprising rapidity, rose, collected her skirts and left the room, calling out for Mary to attend her. Kitty stared at the closed door, sat back in her own chair and let the silence surround her. Did she look tired? She got up and went to study herself in the glass over the mantel.

Like young women everywhere, Kitty found much to worry her. She was not fair like her sister Jane; her expressions were not as pert and pretty as Elizabeth's; she was not robust like Lydia; her features were not good enough... and so on and on. To anyone else – anyone, that is, not prone to measuring every attribute of womanhood against a supposed ideal of physical perfection so that it can be found wanting – Kitty's looks were very pleasing. Some young ladies attain their fullest bloom at fifteen or sixteen years, and often fade fast thereafter; others have features that slowly and subtly change to reach their fullest perfection at one and twenty or thereabouts. Kitty was one such. Slender, but without any loss of feminine form, her figure was graceful. She appeared delicate. Her face, framed by an abundance of dark brown hair, could, in repose, seem rather too serious but when animated threw off any melancholic or grave aspects. Her eyes were clear and blue; her nose was straight and unassuming; her mouth neither small nor large. Nature had given her all the necessary attributes of attractive womanhood and if, when she entered an assembly room, she did not command as much attention as others less fortunate physically, this was more to do with a lack of confidence in herself (and, of course, a lack of fortune).

There was no sign of Mary; presumably Mrs Bennet had not been successful in persuading her of the merit of exercise over books. Kitty settled back into her chair, wondering how to amuse herself for the next hour. It had been some time since she had read a book. She had suffered poor health as a child and spent weeks confined to her room and her bed. During those times, books had offered some solace but when she had recovered her health she had not wanted to stay seated, still less reading. How she had envied Lydia's energy and high spirits. It had not taken long before the older sister had been in thrall to the younger and anything Lydia did or wanted to do was endorsed by Kitty.

And now Lydia was Mrs Wickham, living in Newcastle and all but estranged from her family. Jane was become Mrs Bingley and removed to Netherfield House; and Elizabeth was Mrs Darcy, mistress of a fine estate in Derbyshire, and far away. A Christmas had come and gone without the accustomed noisy family cheer. For Kitty, left behind in Longbourn with only her parents and Mary for company, life was dull and not a little lonely.

She did not much feel like meeting any new officers either, an unusual admission for Miss Catherine Bennet and one which, if articulated, would have produced an incredulous tirade from her mother. Marriage and money, livings and love… what else was there for her to think about? Kitty's thoughts returned to her sisters.

That Jane, the beauty of the family with a character and disposition perfectly in harmony with her pleasing appearance, should be married to an amiable, handsome gentleman of good fortune was, without question, exactly as things should be. Kitty held Charles Bingley in high regard and was exceedingly ready to like and admire him. Not only was he in love with her eldest sister but his personality was such to find pleasure in, or at least tolerate with benign countenance, the company of all his wife's family. Kitty was not in the least afraid of him.

Elizabeth's husband was a different matter. Whilst unfailingly correct and polite, the taciturn Mr Darcy was a figure of some awe to Kitty. In truth, she had been amazed when Lizzy had announced her betrothal and still did not fully comprehend her sister's choice – though she was in no doubt that it was an excellent match. Who would argue against a man with ten thousand a year, especially one of sound body and mind? Certainly not Mrs Bennet! Even so, to choose to spend one's life with a man such as Fitzwilliam Darcy, rich though he was, seemed to Kitty something of a sacrifice, although she had to own that Lizzy seemed not to consider it so.

With regards to George Wickham, Kitty scarce knew what to think. The circumstances of Lydia's hasty marriage to the dashing Captain Wickham, who with his red coat and easy manners cut such a debonair figure, were no longer discussed in the Bennet household, as if silence could eradicate the taint of scandal the elopement had occasioned. This suited Kitty very well. While not complicit in the couple's infamous plan, some censure had fallen on Kitty who had been in correspondence with Lydia during her stay in Brighton from whence she and Wickham had fled – the one to escape his debts, the other to pursue an ideal of romantic love. Kitty pouted as she remembered her father's unspoken wrath. Long since derided by him as one of 'the silliest girls in England', she feigned indifference but felt aggrieved. She was not the only one to succumb to Captain Wickham's charm. Why, even Lizzy, her father's favourite, had enjoyed his company, and Lizzy could do no wrong in her father's eye.

A petulant sigh escaped Kitty. It really wasn't fair. They had all been deceived as to Wickham, and this was another of the unwelcome thoughts troubling Kitty. How could one ascertain another person's character? What if another handsome young officer presenting as a perfect gentleman should turn out to be a blackguard? Kitty's confidence in mankind had been severely shaken.

Meanwhile, she was dissatisfied with both her appearance and her plight. In the wake of Lydia's 'shameful and deplorable antics' (her father's words), Mr Bennet had, at last, sought to exercise his parental control: he expected nothing less than perfect behaviour; he saw no need for his daughters to be at every social gathering, at every ball; henceforth any young men showing even a passing interest in his daughters would be the subject of his careful scrutiny; he required at least two hours of useful study every day. Mr Bennet did not mean these instructions to be taken literally, although Kitty interpreted them so.

For Mary, ever studious and serious, quite uninterested in such frivolous pleasures as flirting and dancing, life continued unchanged, but Kitty felt the strictures keenly. Why should she suffer blame for Lydia's indiscretions? Why was it all *her* fault? Why did no one ever listen to *her*? It was all so unfair!

CHAPTER 2

'Ah, what delight,' announced Mr Bennet at breakfast the following morning. 'I do so enjoy receiving a letter from our dear cousin, Mr Collins.'

'I wish you would not vex me so, my dear,' replied his wife. 'What possible delight can Mr Collins afford us, pray?' Had he been one of the most eligible and well-mannered bachelors in England – and Mr Collins was neither – it would not have been enough to endear him to Mrs Bennet. Had his bearing been elegant, his fortune grand and his wit eloquent, nothing could overcome the man's impudence in being the heir to her family home on the demise of Mr Bennet. Nothing, moreover, could induce Mrs Bennet to understand the laws of entail; the subject had been explained to her and subsequently denounced by her on occasions too numerous to quantify and there was no point in further effort. Mr Bennet certainly saw no reason to try.

'I hope he is not coming here,' continued Mrs Bennet, who could foresee no reason for Mr Collins's attendance on them except to see himself the future master of Longbourn, estimating the placement of furniture and furnishings and demolishing her domestic felicity. Within an instant, her imagination had occasioned Mr Bennet's untimely death, swiftly followed by indignity, shame and destitution as the cruel Mr Collins ousted her from the comforts of her home. With a shudder of relief, she remembered she was fortunate in having three married daughters on whom she could rely for solace and accommodation. Happily for Mrs Bennet, her projections did not include predeceasing her husband.

'Well, my dear,' said Mr Bennet, recalling his wife to the present, 'I am sorry to cause you any unhappiness but I must inform you that we are to be blessed with Mr Collins's company within a se'nnight. He writes to say that he and his dear wife Charlotte will be paying a visit to Lucas Lodge – no need to worry, Mrs Bennet, the good people of Hunsford will not be left rudderless in his absence, he writes to assure us all that *"my most excellent and kind benefactress, the Right Honourable Lady Catherine de Bourgh, has once again graciously condescended to allow me this temporary absence, yet another instance of her ladyship's incomparable courtesy and grace, and I have, as you will no doubt surmise, spared no effort to alleviate my noble patroness of any inconvenience by engaging another clergyman ..."*

'There is more on this hapless replacement, I shall not burden you with it. Now, what else does he wish us to know?

'Ah, yes. He looks forward to enjoying the company and ascertaining the welfare of his most dear cousins, *"not forgetting of course, my dear cousin Elizabeth, now so fortuitously allied to the family of Lady Catherine herself. Were I able to be any of any service in ameliorating the difficult and unhappy situation between Mrs Darcy and her ladyship then, given my situation in life, I should be most happy to step into the breach and offer my services and advice..."*

'What a fine fellow he is! So willing to help. We could all learn from him. No doubt you agree, Mary?'

Mary pursed her lips and nodded in assent. Mrs Bennet tutted her irritation and Kitty hoped Mr Collins's visit would be brief.

Mr Bennet turned back to his letter. 'He will not trespass on our hospitality long but, given our close family connections, he would feel it remiss of him... He sends his *"most respectful compliments to your lady and the delightful Misses Bennet"*, etc. etc.

'So Mrs Bennet. There you have it. Are you not keen to hear news of the beneficent Lady Catherine? Mr Collins is sure to have the most minute intelligence of her ladyship's concerns. Why he is better placed than our own dear Lizzy and son-in-law to know how things stand with our illustrious relation.'

Conflicting emotions stirred within Mrs Bennet. On the one hand, it was gratifying to count Lady Catherine de Bourgh a relation, through Lizzy's most excellent marriage to her nephew Fitzwilliam Darcy; on the other hand, her ladyship was not disposed to think well of the new Mrs Darcy and her less than satisfactory family. Indeed, her displeasure was so keen and her communication so voluble that even Mrs Bennet could not fail to notice it.

'I know quite enough about Lady Catherine,' harrumphed his wife. 'Why, pray, should I want to know more about her doings? Really, Mr Bennet, you do perplex me.'

'Is Mr Collins come for the ball at Sir William's, do you think?' wondered Kitty aloud. 'I do not think he is fond of dancing.'

'He danced at the last ball,' observed Mary. 'He is of the opinion that dancing, in the correct company and with appropriate partners, is not evil. I am of the same opinion.'

'Are you indeed, Mary,' said her father. 'I am of the opinion that young ladies such as you and your sister derive no benefit from such events. What need have you to go to balls?'

'Oh, Mr Bennet, how can you say such things,' exclaimed Mrs Bennet at once. 'Of course Kitty and Mary must go the Lucas Lodge ball. What would people think if they did not? How will they come by suitable young men? You would have them shut up for ever.'

'No, my dear. I simply pose the question. Will there be eligible young men at the ball? Is that why they must go? I have three daughters married; am I to lose the remaining two by their attendance at this occasion? I had no idea the situation was so urgent.'

More than twenty-five years of marriage had not alerted Mrs Bennet to her husband's sardonic humour. In consequence, she railed against his lack of understanding and he professed not to understand her meaning. Kitty waited; she had no wish to try her father's patience or endanger her presence at the ball, the only diversion on her calendar at present. It would be too dreadful if she could not go; she could not bear the thought.

'Jane is calling for us tomorrow morning, Mama,' she ventured at last. 'She sent word that the new shoe-roses are in; she says she will take Mary and me into Meryton with her. We will call upon Aunt Phillips, too.'

'And I will call on Marianne and Mrs Gregory,' added Mary. The Gregorys were a family of good standing but little wealth, who had lived in Meryton for many years. Mary, who was of a solemn disposition and unfailingly disapproving of her younger sisters' perceived predilections for carefree and therefore unworthy pursuits, had found a friend in Marianne, who was fond of discussing 'matters of importance' and making extracts from worthy tracts.

'Well, my dears, I see all is settled. I shall look forward to seeing Jane again,' said Mr Bennet, excusing himself from the table. 'Meanwhile, I shall be in my library.'

Chapter 3

As expected, Mrs Charles Bingley arrived at Longbourn the following day, looking serenely happy and exuding contentment. Her presence was a source of delight to all her family – even Mr Bennet emerged from his library to embrace her, while Mary put down her books and Kitty danced attendance. All were outdone, of course, by Mrs Bennet's effusions of delight and concern, but within a very short while it was confirmed that Mr Bingley was in fine health; his wife, also; that the journey to Longbourn that morning had been unexceptionable; that no fault could be found in the running of the household at Netherfield; that the servants were everything they should be – indeed, even the livestock were thought to be content, although their welfare was not specifically inquired after.

Jane was eventually allowed to divest herself of cloak and bonnet, and the women of the family were soon seated in the parlour. It was but the second time Jane had been at Longbourn since her marriage the previous November. She and Mr Bingley had been obliged to visit his mother and aunts for the Christmas period, which, according to Jane, had passed delightfully for all parties, and a short sojourn in London had followed before the pair had returned to Netherfield.

'You are looking well, Kitty,' said Jane as the ladies made themselves comfortable and tea was brought in.

'Am I?' Kitty stood up to look at herself in the glass. She supposed she was. Her blue eyes were clear, there was some colour in her cheeks, she had arranged her hair so that her dark curls framed her face. It would all be for nothing, she thought; there is no one to see in Meryton. She turned back to her sister.

'How liked you London?' she asked. 'Where did you go? Who did you see?'

'I liked it very well, though I am pleased to be out of it for a while. There is much gaiety, to be sure. So many galleries and concerts, and we made so many new acquaintances that it was, I confess, a little too demanding at times.'

'One can have a surfeit of gaiety,' remarked Mary, her expression as sententious as her tone. 'It is as well to remember that time spent quietly—'

'I should adore London!' interrupted Kitty, causing no one surprise. 'Concerts and galleries! So much to do and see! And the shops, too! I adore that lace on your gown; it is so becoming. It is from London?'

Mary's advice was left unfinished as Jane allowed her finery to be examined by Kitty and there followed a sisterly discourse between the two on the latest fashions as worn in town and by whom and for what, augmented by tales of the best shops and milliners, the most sought-after invitations to the most exclusive salons, as well as the more egalitarian pleasures of the city, including visits to St Paul's, the Royal Academy and the new Drury Lane Theatre. That Jane and Mr Bingley were not blind devotees of the social set was of secondary importance to Kitty; she took vicarious pleasure from their proximity to it all and no talk of crowded pavements, dangerous roads and noisy environs could dampen her enthusiasm.

Mary, who was making a great show of reading the learned book she held, looked up and seemed about to share some observation on the evils of the capital but was once again interrupted, this time by her mother, who declared it the greatest shame that Mr Bennet would never take a house in London for the season, how ill-used she was in this respect and – for the moment – quite forgot how much she disliked travel and being removed from the milieu and hierarchy in which she felt comfortable and where her own opinions, even when disliked, were rarely challenged.

The journey back to Netherfield via London had afforded Jane and her husband the opportunity to spend a few days with her favourite aunt and uncle. Mrs Bennet's brother and his wife lived in Gracechurch Street and Jane was able to give good account of both Mr and Mrs Gardiner, and her four little cousins, all of whom she had seen the day before her departure for Longbourn. Both Jane and Elizabeth loved and respected this branch of the family, feelings that were reciprocated. The Gardiners, in fact, had spent Christmas at Pemberley and were therefore well placed to provide all manner of information as to the goings-on at that grand estate and of its principal inhabitants. Jane had been the eager recipient of their news. That all was perfectly well with the new Mrs Darcy and her husband was no great surprise but good news is most usually welcome among family, and it is as well to have such assurances confirmed and spoken aloud. Simply hearing the words 'Mrs Darcy' and 'Mrs Bingley' still sent a frisson of delight through Mrs Bennet and she never tired of speaking those words herself. Her neighbour Lady Lucas was the unwilling and unhappy beneficiary of much of Mrs Bennet's joy. 'Mrs Darcy has written to tell me that their new carriage has been delivered,' she would inform her. Or, 'My daughter Mrs Bingley will be in London for the season.' Lady Lucas, kindly and well-mannered, was not easily provoked, but a half-hour with Mrs Bennet on the heady subject of matrimony and well-married daughters was a test of patience even for the saintly. 'I have half a mind to call my new poodle Pemberley,' she had remarked to her husband, Sir William Lucas, after one such lecture. 'I would do so, but Mrs Bennet would most likely take it as a compliment.'

Jane, meanwhile, had her own account of Pemberley to pass on. 'Lizzy says she is becoming quite used to being mistress of so grand a house and takes the wrong direction and loses herself but once or twice a day!' she smiled.

'I long to see Pemberley,' declared Kitty. 'London and Pemberley are the places I most want to see in the world!'

'That is all very well, Kitty,' said her mother, 'but your sisters don't need you getting in their way. I don't know where you get these ideas. Last week, it was too much trouble to go into Meryton and now you want to travel all the way to London.' Mrs Bennet wagged a disapproving finger at Kitty as she spoke. 'Do continue, Jane.'

'Lizzy talks of new furnishings and making the house more her own,' said Jane, throwing a sympathetic glance at Kitty, 'but in truth I think it is all for show. Aunt Gardiner says she appears very content with things as they are.'

'Indeed, why would she not be?' returned Mrs Bennet. 'She is mistress of Pemberley, and Mr Darcy has ten thousand pounds a year!'

Her mother's abrupt shift to financial assessments brought the conversation to a momentary stop, a most welcome pause as it gave Jane the necessary space to remember the hour and the reason for her visit. She would come again soon, she promised, but now she and her sisters must hasten into Meryton to purchase the new ribbons, bows, and other accoutrements so necessary to young ladies, married or single, when engaged to a ball the following evening. Mary's avowal that she had no need of such fripperies and that she was only going to visit her friend Miss Gregory, was lost in the bustle of their departure.

CHAPTER 4

Longbourn
7 February

My dear Lydia,

I hope this letter finds you well. How I missed you at the Lucas's ball last night. What fun we would have had, just as before. Except now the militia is gone from Meryton and so there was not a red coat to be seen – and you of course have your Wickham, so perchance there would have been no entertainment for you.

Oh Lydia, all is so dull here now! I long to see you but I know not when that will be so you must write and tell me of your life at Newcastle. Are the Assembly Rooms very grand? Have you found milliners and dressmakers to your liking? With whom do you socialise?

Mary is as you remember her. She barely speaks to me, unless of course she has some advice that she feels will be of benefit for my immortal soul. Papa watches me as if I were about to elope with an officer – and how is that to happen now all the officers are gone away and I am hardly allowed out of Longbourn? Mama says she will speak to him about it but I think I will be shut up here for ever. And really, it is so unfair. I have done nothing wrong!

Should I say that? thought Kitty. Will she think I am saying she has done something wrong? She let it stand.

I wore my pale blue muslin to the ball, which I think suits me very well and Jane said so, too. I forgot to tell you, Jane and Bingley are back at Netherfield.

We made some new acquaintance at Sir William's. His brother John Lucas, the vice-admiral, is staying with them, and his two sons, Edward and George, were at the ball. I danced two dances with each, and I prefer George as he has more conversation and is by far the more handsome of the two. He is not following his brother into the navy and thinks of a life in the clergy. I must say he dances very well for someone who means to become a vicar! I would have found out more about him except that our conversation was interrupted by our beloved and loquacious cousin Mr Collins – yes, he was in attendance – who insisted on talking to him about his own living in Kent and simpering about that awful Lady Catherine. So strange, is it not, that Lizzy is related to her now, which means we are, too! And to think, Lizzy could have been Mrs Collins and we could have counted him brother. It is a wonder – and a blessing! – that he did not make his suit to Mary, for I believe she would have accepted him. They would be a perfect pair. Oh Lord, Lydia! Imagine that! Mr Collins at all our family gatherings. It was bad enough that he prevailed upon Mary and me for two dances. Of one thing you can be certain – I will never marry a vicar!

As for Mary, you will be amazed to learn that she danced two dances with the same partner last night. You will not be too surprised, however, when I tell you that it was only Marianne Gregory's brother, Timothy. He has been away at Oxford – I know not why – but is now returned to Meryton and is helping

Uncle Phillips. He is as serious as ever and scarce spoke two words to anyone save Mary and his sister. No doubt they have weighty matters to discuss, la la! She is welcome to his company, I should not know what to say to him.

Jane and Bingley are as happy as can be but now they are going away to London for several weeks. Everyone is leaving me! I am to lose my two most beloved sisters...

Kitty put down her pen. Was it true that Jane and Lydia were her two most beloved sisters? Jane, five years her senior, thought well of everyone and was not wont to chastise her or Lydia – unlike Lizzy, whose tongue was sharper and admonition more readily dispensed. Lydia, closest in age to Kitty, had always been her confidante and closest companion; they had been inseparable, sharing all their little triumphs and disappointments – until Lydia had deserted her for Brighton.

Yes, Kitty felt deserted, even a little betrayed, by Lydia. Despite what her family thought, she had not been privy to Lydia's plans to elope and had been as shocked and alarmed as everyone else at that part of her sister's reckless and damaging plan, the more so as she had imagined she was in her confidence. As for Lizzy, Kitty was surprised at how much she missed Lizzy, with her ready wit and perspicacity. She even missed her criticisms and attempts to tame her more flamboyant behaviours. It was odd, thought Kitty. As a small child she had adored Lizzy, trailing after her and seeking her attention, but her older sister had found her tiresome. At least that was how Kitty remembered it.

She read her letter through. Really Lydia did not deserve to be told her news when she barely wrote more than six lines in reply, usually at the bottom of a letter to their mother. 'My sisters may write to me,' Lydia had said airily on the day she and Wickham had departed for Newcastle. 'They will have nothing else to do.'

Now that she is Mrs Wickham, she does not share very much with me any more, thought Kitty. She has become so very important just because she is married. She will tell me how boring Longbourn is and pity me – while she talks about dances and officers and her wonderful Wickham!

Kitty frowned and was on the verge of crumpling up the letter. Instead, she put it to one side, took a fresh sheet of paper and wrote a briefer note to Lydia, omitting everything except details of the Lucas Lodge ball, what she wore and who danced with whom. She would not give Lydia the satisfaction of knowing she was unhappy. Besides, she had been more candid than was polite, and Kitty did not want her behaviour called into question. Things were quite bad enough already.

She looked around her room, a room she had once shared with Lydia. There was a desk where the other bed had once been, but otherwise everything was the same. Except that everything was so quiet now! There was no fun. No chatter. Kitty felt her eyes well up and pinched her nose to try to stop tears rolling down her cheeks. Stop it, she told herself. It will be even worse if you cry. You will look terrible as well as feel terrible.

Standing up, she took a deep breath, smoothed her dress and folded the letter she was going to send. The longer version she put in her desk drawer and then went downstairs. The library door was open but for once there was no sign of Mr Bennet. Feeling rather like a child who was not supposed to be there, Kitty entered the room and scanned the volumes around her. Theirs was a comprehensive library; Mr Bennet prided himself on keeping abreast of the newest works and keeping Jane and Lizzy up to date with the literature of the day. Her hand rested on a Radcliffe novel she had heard Jane speak of and she stood on tiptoe to pluck it from the shelf. As she did so she dislodged its neighbour, which fell noisily to the floor. In her confusion, Kitty picked up both books and fled. She was perfectly at liberty to read any of the books in the library but she could not bear to have her father find her there, to see his sardonic smile, his wonder that she, Kitty, should trouble herself with a book.

Chapter 5

True to his word, Mr Collins called on the Bennets a few days after the Lucas Lodge ball. His obsequious and unendearing manner was met with the required mix of resignation, respect and, from Mr Bennet at least, an expectation of amusement.

He was shadowed by a young man in travelling clothes. 'Mr dear cousins,' began Mr Collins, greeting each in turn. 'Such joy, such great joy to see you all. My dear Mrs Bennet, I trust you are well? My dear Miss Bennet, Miss Catherine.' Turning to his companion, he continued: 'Forgive me this liberty, but allow me to introduce Mr Robert Jones. He has today arrived from Warwickshire and my esteemed patroness Lady Catherine has given me specific charge of his journey to a living she has generously bestowed upon him.' Mr Collins paused, the better to allow his cousins to remember the munificence and largesse of her ladyship.

'You are to live in Kent, Mr Jones?' enquired Mr Bennet, as the party proceeded into the parlour.

Any reply was cut short by Mr Collins, who was keen to explain. 'Lady Catherine has seen fit to offer Mr Jones a living at a parish near Canterbury. Her ladyship feels this is both necessary and advantageous, and has been gracious enough to involve me in all her communications with Mr Jones.' Again, Mr Collins paused so that all might enjoy his success. 'He will accompany me and my dear Mrs Collins into Kent tomorrow.'

His protégé nodded, giving proof to the veracity of the speech.

'You must not think,' instructed Mr Collins, allowing himself a small laugh, 'that I should travel to Lucas Lodge for the mere frivolity of a ball. No, no! Although of course Lady Catherine would not forbid me such entertainment nor deprive my dear Charlotte of this opportunity to visit her relations.'

'How does Mrs Collins?' asked Mrs Bennet, tired of all reference to her ladyship and wishing to steer the conversation elsewhere. 'I am sorry to see that she is not with you this morning.'

Mr Collins clasped his hand to his chest and drew in his breath. A mixture of pride and confusion twisted his mouth into something between a smirk and a moue. Kitty watched in some small amazement as his face suffused with colour before he announced: 'Mrs Collins is, ahem, in a most delicate condition. She asked me to convey her good wishes to you, nothing else would have kept her away, I can assure you. My apologies if I am being indiscreet in front of the young ladies.' A small cough concluded his speech.

Kitty very much wanted to laugh, but kept her eyes down and contained herself. When she raised them, she saw her father looking in her direction. Once again, she assumed his displeasure, but Mr Bennet held her gaze and with the smallest raise of an eyebrow gave her to understand he shared her feelings. A small surge of happiness filled Kitty. Notice and approval did not go hand in hand in her world.

Having divested himself of this information, Mr Collins beamed at them all, ran his finger around the edge of his collar and, seemingly at a loss as to what to do or say next, took himself to the window where Mr Bennet was standing in silent contemplation of those assembled, and sought to engage him in his plans for improvement to his humble dwelling in Kent. Mr Bennet, whose interest in fireplaces, dado rails and appropriate colours for wall coverings was nothing if not scant, listened intently, amusing himself every now and then with an astonished 'Indeed?'

Mr Jones was entreated to join the ladies, who were seated around the fireplace. 'Do you know Kent well sir?' Mary asked him, when he was settled into his chair. Mr Jones was happy to respond and, within a few minutes, they had learned that he did not know that county at all but had every anticipation of finding the neighbourhood agreeable; that he had until recently been intended to go into the army and that events (he did not elaborate) had convinced him that a life in the clergy would suit him better; that a distant relation who had known Sir Lewis de Bourgh had been providential in procuring him the living; that he had a sister and a brother-in-law living in London, but that their timetable did not permit him anything other than a brief visit en route to Kent; and that he had heard that one of the Misses Bennet had recently visited Hunsford.

'My sister Elizabeth is a particular friend of Mrs Collins and spent some weeks at Hunsford last year,' Kitty informed him. 'I have not travelled outside of Meryton and its environs, though I should like the opportunity one day.'

Mrs Bennet made a small clucking noise.

'I hope one day to spend some time with my married sisters,' said Kitty, ignoring her mother, 'one of whom now lives in Derbyshire.'

'Ah, yes, so I have heard,' replied Mr Jones, his knowledge of the de Bourgh family having increased a thousand-fold since meeting Mr Collins, whose enthusiasm on the subject could not, he found, be quelled either by enquiry or silence. 'That would be Mrs Darcy of Pemberley,' continued the new recruit. 'Mr Darcy is related to Lady Catherine; she is his aunt, I think?' Kitty agreed that this was so, but here the conversation was interrupted. A discourse containing the words 'Darcy', 'Pemberley' and 'Lady Catherine' had alerted Mr Collins, who felt the need to be part of it. He hastened across and his officious interjections were such that all discussion ceased soon after save that of speculation on the state of the roads and whether rain was expected that evening or on the morrow.

Mr Collins, a man of little sense but great pomposity, was exercising unusual caution in his dutiful attendance upon the Bennets. Lady Catherine had, it was true, given her permission for him to visit, but this was partly in order for him to bring any news he could ascertain about her now estranged nephew and the impertinent woman who had become his wife. Thus far, Mr Collins had little to offer her ladyship in this matter and he did not think it would sit well with her if the only information he could take back concerned the new vicar's conversation with another of the Miss Bennets.

Mrs Bennet meanwhile, freed from Mr Collins's attentions, began to consider the eligibility of Mr Jones, and to speculate on the size of his living and what his income might be. Of course, she knew nothing of his family at this point, but such details could be gleaned. The dinner hour was approaching and she was toying with the idea of inviting the two visitors to dine. Accordingly, she quit the room in order to make enquiries of the housekeeper, Mrs Hill; it would not do to offer a meal that was not sufficiently impressive, even though, she assured herself, she had no desire whatsoever to impress Mr Collins. Her efforts were in vain, however. Upon returning to the parlour a few minutes later, it was to hear Mr Collins announce that, most regrettably, he and Mr Jones must depart. They were expected at Lucas Lodge within the hour.

Bows and curtsies were made and the pair took their leave.

'Well, Mary,' said her mother, as the door closed behind the visitors. 'What think you of Mr Jones? He seems a good sort of young gentleman. And with his own living. Canterbury is a fine place, by all accounts. I was glad to see you speaking with him. What did you speak of when I was gone? What is his income, do you know?'

'Mama!' said Kitty. 'You know Mary would not ask him such questions!'

'It is as well to know these things,' countered Mrs Bennet. 'Especially if he is looking for a wife.'

Kitty sighed, igniting her mother's ire.

'Do not get so high and mighty with me, Miss. What is to become of you if you do not get married? You two are not so pretty as your sisters; you cannot expect important matches.' She clasped her hands in her lap and looked from Kitty to Mary, her point made.

'That may be so, ma'am,' said Kitty, her voice rising. 'But we do not know that Mr Jones is looking for a wife; and if he were, let us not assume that that wife would be me or Mary! Must we always be looking for husbands?' It was an unexpected outburst, to all parties.

Mrs Bennet found herself momentarily taken aback. Mary took advantage of the silence to observe, 'Well, sister, if I am not mistaken, I rather thought that was your chief preoccupation. Certainly, it is the impression you give.' She bent her head back to her book.

Kitty glared at Mary and at Mrs Bennet, then excused herself to prepare for dinner, leaving her mother exasperated, her father mildly surprised and Mary somewhat smug.

In a small fury, she flounced to her room but stopped mid-stairs and wondered at herself. Mary's barb had found its mark. Dancing and conversing with red-coated officers and other dashing young men had long been her sole aim, and with Lydia by her side she had not thought to question it. Now the rules seemed to have changed. What was she supposed to do? What did she want to do? Why was it all her fault? She stamped her foot. Kitty didn't have answers to any of these questions, but she was beginning to comprehend that they needed to be asked.

CHAPTER 6

As could be surmised, Mrs Bennet's nerves, ever easily excited, were severely taxed by Kitty's unsatisfactory and ungrateful behaviour. She missed no opportunity to chastise her daughter for her irritating ways, lack of sense and general perversity. Mary also felt her disapprobation; she was castigated for her lack of sociability, her constant recourse to books and learning, and lack of enthusiasm for balls and dancing. Mr Bennet was called upon to speak to his disappointing daughters and impress upon them their mother's displeasure.

'What would you have me tell them,' he enquired mildly, when it was clear that some intervention on his part was the price to be paid for his peace and solitude.

'You must tell them I will not put up with this behaviour,' insisted Mrs Bennet, without specifying her daughters' misdemeanours. 'It is too vexing. They use me ill. It is not to be borne.' She shook her head at the unfairness of it all.

'Very well, my dear,' agreed Mr Bennet, and consequently took both girls to task for their unsatisfactory conduct, such as it was, and reminded them, quite unnecessarily, of their mother's nerves. Neither Kitty nor Mary could expect to benefit from such general instruction but Mrs Bennet was at last mollified.

Kitty, for her part, kept to her own company and her own room as much as was permitted, and considered the injustice of life. Neither parent particularly noted her absence. When such injustices became too much even for her, she sought respite in the novel she had found and its heroine's pursuit of love against all manner of adversities in sixteenth-century Italy. Were she or Mary to suddenly find themselves beset with proposals of marriage, Kitty supposed her mother's dissatisfaction with them both would evaporate, but she could do nothing to bring about such an immediate and happy solution. Mary and Kitty remained the unmarried Misses Bennet and as such the focus of her disapproval.

That her two eldest sisters had had more than their fair share of notice in the family was entirely due to their having been born before the others. Mr Bennet had been delighted to welcome his firstborn into the world, and had there been any disappointment in that child being a Jane rather than a James, would not have owned it to himself or any other. His indulgences towards Jane had been repeated when her sister Elizabeth arrived and he had, more than was fashionable or expected, taken great pride in being their father, guiding and playing and instructing them with a joy that was to surpass his being in company with his dear Mrs Bennet, whose own childlike ways were eclipsed by her daughters. In this way, both Jane and Elizabeth were secure in their place within their little commonwealth of Longbourn.

When the longed-for male heir failed to appear in the person of Mary, and then Catherine and Lydia, it may have been noted by a cynical observer that Mr Bennet's tolerance for daughters – and indeed fatherhood – began to diminish and while he would, if pressed, have professed love for all five there was no doubting that he lavished less attention on the youngest three than on the first two. Mrs Bennet's nerves, meanwhile, became more and more demanding as her brood increased and her husband's interest waned.

Mary, as she grew, sought her parents' attention by her accomplishments, treating each exercise in music or reading as proof of her ability and intelligence, earnestly exhorting them to hear her opinions, but instead of commanding respect and adulation she was, at best, merely tolerated. Lydia, in whom her mother saw her younger self – both in spirits and countenance – was a source of almost unwavering and narcissistic delight to Mrs Bennet. Consequently, she favoured her excessively, excused her constantly, and her husband made little attempt to interfere in his wife's treatment of their youngest child, unless it was for a little sport of his own.

Kitty, meanwhile, was just Kitty. A docile child, she had trailed after her adored elder sisters but they, like many older siblings, had not delighted in her presence and had sent her off to play with the younger ones. Only sickness and prolonged periods of enforced rest had brought Jane, and occasionally Elizabeth, to her bedside, and when she had fully recovered her health Lydia had so far inserted herself as her mother's favourite that it had seemed obvious that she should follow in her younger sister's wake and share all the delights and comforts bestowed upon her. Neither commanding nor being the centre of attention, Kitty had become more adept at observing than doing and, until the events of the previous year, had not questioned this order of things.

Over the course of the following few days, an uneasy truce settled into normal routine at Longbourn and the four remaining Bennets, each the centre of their own little universe, were content to be brought together by an invitation to Netherfield House. As Kitty had barely spoken to anyone for days, nor received a letter from Lydia with any interesting news, this was a welcome relief. She could be sure of a sympathetic ear in Jane and, besides, it would occasion a temporary escape from Longbourn.

As she came down into the hall to await the carriage, her mother examined her appearance. 'I thought you would wear the green sprigged muslin,' she criticised. 'It looks better on you but never mind, never mind. Too late now. Come along!'

Kitty who had, mistakenly as it turned out, thought she had acquitted herself rather well in the matter of her dress and hair, did not bother to respond; instead, she followed her mother into the carriage and took her place beside Mary. She could not arrive at Netherfield soon enough.

CHAPTER 7

As the Bingleys were shortly to return to London for the rest of the season, the dinner was the last they would host in the county for a while. Musical entertainment had been arranged for the small gathering, which comprised family and family friends. Although Kitty's intention was to seek out Jane or her friend Maria Lucas as soon as she arrived, her attention was caught by an elegant, silver-haired gentleman of around fifty years of age, who looked every inch the wealthy landowner. He was in the midst of a hearty conversation with Sir William Lucas and, as both gentlemen were blessed with sonorous tones, it was easy to understand that Sir William, who never missed a chance to converse with anyone upon whom he might impress his knowledge – slight though it was – of the Court of St James, was delighted to be in the company of another knight. Standing beside her father and doing her best to look interested in a conversation she had heard a hundred times before, Maria Lucas was delighted to catch sight of Mary and Kitty, and to deftly excuse herself in order to speak with the Misses Bennet.

'Who is that gentleman?' asked Kitty, once they had all greeted each other.

'His name is Sir Edward Quincy,' Maria informed them. 'We have only just made his acquaintance but I can tell you that he is an old family friend of the Bingleys and lives in Yorkshire, where his family have owned a large estate for some generations. Do you see that fair-haired lady over there?' She nodded towards a woman in pale rose silk who was chatting with Caroline Bingley. 'She is Sir Edward's daughter, now Mrs Stephen Bridgwater. She and Miss Bingley have known each other since their schooldays.'

Kitty glanced again at Mrs Bridgwater and back at Sir Edward, seeking a family resemblance but finding very little. Where the gentleman's features were strong and aquiline, adding to his somewhat noble mien, his daughter was round-cheeked and dimpled. 'She must resemble her mother,' observed Kitty, looking around to see if she could see Lady Quincy and prove her theory correct.

'That may be,' said Maria, who lowered her voice to explain, 'but Amelia, Mrs Bridgwater, was quite young when her mother died. Sir Edward was just saying to my father that his children often spent time with Charles, Louisa and Caroline Bingley when they were growing up.'

'You are well informed this evening!' exclaimed Kitty. 'How much you have learned in such a short time.'

'It was not difficult,' returned Maria, who was nonetheless rather pleased to have news to impart. 'Sir Edward is quite the conversationalist. I feared I would never get away and I could not think of anything sensible to say to him!'

'It is better to remain silent if one has nothing salient to contribute,' opined Mary, giving Maria pause for lip-biting contrition and her sister cause for mild exasperation.

As she looked around the drawing room at Netherfield, Kitty decided it had never looked more pleasing. The walls and some of the furnishings, the colour of pale peach in the daytime, appeared a darker golden colour in the candlelight and there were more paintings on the walls than she remembered from her last visit. The furniture was grouped in such a way as to encourage conversation and the general effect was one of warmth. This was Jane's influence, she knew. Peeping through into the dining room, the long mahogany table was sparkling with candelabra, crystal and silverware; Kitty thought how pretty it looked.

Jane's pleasure in entertaining her family was evident but she was not insensible to the personalities assembled. She had, therefore, given considerable thought to the seating arrangements for dinner and had decided the rules of etiquette could be bent a little in pursuit of harmony. Accordingly, Sir Edward was to her right but she had taken pains to seat her mother a little distance away, closer to Mr Bingley, who had command at the other end of the table, and Lady Lucas. Kitty and Miss Bingley she had placed next to Sir Edward and Sir William, and if strict accordance to rank had given way to a more pleasing distribution of individuals only those to whom convention was more important than pleasure were likely to complain, and then in private.

One person who may have taken umbrage at such arrangements, were she not seated next to Sir William, was Miss Bingley. A tall and handsome woman thwarted not so much in love as in an advantageous marriage, she was radiant in dark green silk, her fashion absolutely à la mode.

She bestowed her most charmingly artificial smile upon Sir Edward. 'How delightful it will be to return to London,' she began. 'I have so missed the company of our friends. I long to see them again and to visit the galleries and opera. What thought you of the latest exhibition at the Academy?'

'Good enough, my dear Miss Bingley,' returned the knight. 'But I prefer the theatre to the galleries, any day.'

'I quite agree with you, of course,' she replied. 'Mrs Siddons' Lady Macbeth is a masterpiece. Although, I must say I found that recent farce at Covent Garden quite lacking in humour. I found it wanting in every respect.'

'Did you, indeed. Interesting, interesting. Quite liked it myself. How did you enjoy the piece, Miss Catherine?'

'Oh,' trilled Miss Bingley, before Kitty could draw breath to speak. 'Miss Catherine does not like the theatre. She and her sisters prefer to stay in the country rather than visit London, is that not so, Miss Bennet? Although of course I will insist our dear Jane accompanies me when we are together in Brook Street.

There will be so much to do and see, but the theatre and opera must not be neglected.'

She smiled again, assured of her style, opinion and charm.

'You may be right, Miss Bingley. You may very well be right,' declared Sir Edward. 'Although country pursuits suit me very well, I must say. When I am not abroad, of course. Do you ride, Miss Catherine?'

Kitty did not ride, although at this moment she would have wished to say she did. Caroline Bingley spared her the trouble, 'You should learn,' she informed her, before acidly adding, 'but then I suppose your horses are usually needed elsewhere.' She turned back to Sir Edward, 'For myself, I cannot wait to return to our dear friend Mr Darcy's estate in Derbyshire; my sister Mrs Hurst and I so enjoy riding through the parklands there. You are still riding with the hounds in Yorkshire?'

In this way, Miss Bingley attempted to keep Sir Edward's focus upon herself but her plans were counteracted; family friend or no, the gentleman was equally determined to converse with the pretty young woman seated to his right.

'Miss Catherine,' he said, 'I fear we neglect your opinions. What amusements have you in Meryton?'

'Yes, Miss Catherine, do tell us,' entreated Caroline. 'Now that the militia has left Meryton, you must be at a loss for entertainment?'

Kitty was no stranger to Miss Bingley and her malice. Although not privy to Elizabeth and Jane's conversations about Mr Bingley's sister, she had overheard enough to know that Lizzy found Caroline arrogant and mean-spirited, and Lizzy's opinions were generally found to be solid. Moreover, her own experience of Miss Bingley had done nothing to challenge that view. Kitty maintained her composure and smiling demurely at Sir Edward, answered: 'It is true that the town is less colourful now that the militia has left but I can assure you that the Assemblies are as convivial as ever and that we do not want for company, no matter that our pleasures are less sophisticated than those of the city.'

It was, perhaps, one of the most considered replies Kitty had made in her short life. She heard herself speak and awaited a pointed response from Miss Bingley. The reply, though, came from Sir Edward. 'Well said, Miss Catherine. Give me the country over the city any day. Nothing like a day's hunting, eh? An afternoon with a good book?'

'As to hunting, I cannot say sir,' answered Kitty.

'And what of reading, Miss Catherine,' pounced Miss Bingley, feeling herself on sure ground. 'What has engaged your interest of late?'

Kitty had never felt more relieved. Her self-imposed isolation at Longbourn during the past few days had afforded her plenty of time. She had not only read the chosen novel but delved into the other book inadvertently taken from her father's library.

'Oh, I quite enjoyed Mrs Radcliffe's *A Sicilian Romance*,' she said of the first, affecting an airy nonchalance. Her words caught Jane's attention and the two sisters enjoyed a brief review of the book's merits. Sir Edward had read it, too, and offered his own reflections. For Kitty, this represented a minor triumph.

'I am sure you are a great reader, Miss Catherine,' said he. 'What other books engage you?'

'My father has a good library, sir,' she replied, thinking as she spoke. She had no wish to admit her recent reading was limited to one book. 'I am just beginning some of Mrs Wollstonecraft's essays,' she added, recalling the author of the second book that had literally fallen her way in the Longbourn library.

'My dear Miss Catherine! What a revelation you are. A revelation, indeed!' responded Sir Edward. 'She has some fascinating ideas. Although not favourably received by all, I must say. I look forward to your thoughts when you have finished it. I am sure there will be points on which we differ, although I am delighted to find a young lady so advanced in her reading matter. Delighted!'

Kitty thanked him, her heart pounding. She had little idea what his words meant nor, indeed, of the content of the book. She would have to make it her business to find out. She was grateful to Jane, who engaged her in less demanding subjects while Miss Bingley imposed her opinions on Sir William and Sir Edward. At the other end of the table, past the quieter conversation between the likes of her father and Mrs Bridgwater, Maria and Mary, her mother could be heard extolling the beauty of Jane. Mr Bingley smiled benignly on all.

Chapter 8

When the ladies withdrew after dinner Kitty felt that she had acquitted herself quite well and was feeling just a little proud of herself for not having done or said anything wrong or gauche. She risked a covert glance towards Sir Edward. How charming he was and so attentive! It was such a pleasant contrast to be in the company of someone who seemed to value her conversation; where Mrs Bennet lectured, Sir Edward listened. Kitty had not said a word to her mother or Mary since their arrival at Netherfield.

In the drawing room, she endeavoured to be of use to Jane by helping look after the guests. Miss Bingley and Mrs Bridgwater had removed to a sofa by one of the windows and were deep in private conversation, requiring it seemed nothing of anyone. She fetched tea and sat with Lady Lucas while Mrs Bennet fussed and fretted over Jane's domestic arrangements and felicity. Within a short while she had heard all that she could wish to know of Charlotte and Mr Collins and, when that topic had run its course, learned more than anyone could reasonably expect to know of the health and happiness of all the little Lucases, so Kitty was happy enough when Mrs Bennet arrived to reignite the conversation. Each lady would then happily attempt to outdo each other: Lady Lucas on the onerous requirements of Sir William's duties in London, the pleasure and responsibility of a home such as Lucas Lodge, the career prospects of her sons and her dear Charlotte's impending motherhood; Mrs Bennet on the beauty and accomplishments of her daughters – three married daughters, no less! – and, most specifically, her desire to see the magnificent estate of Pemberley and to meet all her new relations, not forgetting of course to mention Lady Catherine de Bourgh. It was a conversation – or more exactly two separate monologues – lacking any originality or exceptional insight but enjoyed by both ladies nonetheless, and Kitty's presence was entirely superfluous.

A painting, a landscape of a bucolic scene, hung over the mantel and Kitty went to study it. Jane joined her. 'It arrived yesterday, I think it very fine. Charles commissioned it. It is of a valley in Nottinghamshire, not far from Pemberley, which he has known since he was a boy. An uncle of his lived nearby and he is very fond of the place.

'He has been taking much more interest in the arts of late. He intends to visit all the galleries open to him when we are in London. I think he sees himself as quite the collector! He talks about whom he should commission to paint my portrait, if you please.'

'How soon you will be gone,' said Kitty, and unexpectedly her eyes welled with tears.

'Oh Kitty,' said Jane softly, sisterly affection engaged immediately. 'Do not be sad.'

'I cannot be otherwise,' returned Kitty. 'I am sad. I will miss you. I miss all of you.' She struggled, nearly sobbed, and with no little effort regained control of her emotions, conscious of the company and wishing to save herself further embarrassment.

Jane took her hand. 'Poor, sweet Kitty! I see that in my own happiness, I have quite forgotten you.' This sentence caused more tears to run quietly down Kitty's cheeks. Embracing her lightly and quickly, Jane bade her sister go and refresh herself before the gentlemen joined them, and promised she would speak with her privately very soon.

When she returned, the party was complete and there was talk of card tables. Sir Edward was at the pianoforte and urging his daughter to sing. With most efficient and ladylike modesty, she demurred, then, having been prevailed upon once more, accepted without hesitation. Mrs Bridgwater's voice was clear and light, and her performance rewarded with compliments and dainty applause. Caroline Bingley was next persuaded, and the two friends sang a pretty duet.

'Will you sing for us, Miss Catherine?' enquired Sir Edward, who stood by her side as they watched and listened. 'I am sure you sing very well.'

She thanked him but made her excuses; she had not the slightest intention of exposing herself to unnecessary censure from Caroline Bingley or anyone else in the room. Privately, she enjoyed singing but thought her voice inadequate. Aloud, she commended Mrs Bridgwater's performance to Sir Edward, who beamed with paternal pride. Mary Bennet then provided the company with an unremarkable and perfectly unimpassioned piano recital and the evening's musical interlude was about to close when Jane called upon her husband to sing for them.

Mr Bingley protested, genially of course, but Jane insisted and everyone delighted in this play of marital protest. Naturally, he could not disappoint Mrs Bingley but he did require her to accompany him, and so the pair took their places. It was thereafter unanimously agreed that Charles Bingley was a very fine tenor – something previously unknown to all but a handful of his closest friends – and that his command of voice and tone was as powerful as it was unexpected. Somewhat abashed at the genuine applause afforded him, Mr Bingley made light of any personal talent in himself and led his graceful lady away from the pianoforte before any encore could be demanded of them.

Mr Bennet was as impressed as any other present and said as much to Jane, and father and daughter conversed quietly together for quite some time. Meanwhile, the card tables were set up amid an atmosphere as lively and congenial as good music, good company and good food could provide. Kitty found herself once more placed by Sir Edward, together with Sir William and Lady

Lucas, Maria and Mary, and proved herself adept at vingt-et-un, leaving the table a few pennies richer than when she sat down. Even a small win is enough to lift a person's spirits and Kitty, though still sad to be losing Jane and Mr Bingley to London, was able to take some consolation in that they would not be gone from Netherfield for more than two months or so. That Sir Edward was impressed with her, or at least paid her many compliments, did no harm to her humour either, and she left for Longbourn buoyed and reasonably content.

CHAPTER 9

Longbourn
16 February

My dearest Lydia,

I have so much to tell you, but I am not sure where I should begin, and if I do, what to say or tell. Prudence should stay my hand, or should I say my pen? If only you were here with me! Well, I will begin! You are not afraid of what others will think, nor say. And it is such a fine jape. You will laugh, and think who would have thought this of Kitty.

I will stay your curiosity no longer; I will tell you what has occurred. Firstly, and I know not how, Jane has persuaded Papa that I may go to London with them! I am so happy! Before we went to Netherfield last night I would not have believed it possible myself. Jane is an angel, and clearly Papa thinks so too. I have promised to behave and do everything Jane and Bingley require of me, and of course I shall. When have I ever been less than truly dutiful?

They have a house for the rest of the season in Brook Street in Mayfair, not far from the Hursts' house in Grosvenor Street, where they went last year before Jane and Bingley were married.

Anyway, it is in a most fashionable part of London, though not too far from Aunt and Uncle Gardiner, so I will see them also.

The Hursts will be in London but they are expecting other friends at their house so the ever-charming Miss Bingley will be staying with us! I do hope she travels down with the Hursts, for I dread the long journey to London with Caroline for company. I could not say this to Jane, for she is her sister now, but she is a most horrid person and I know she thinks me her inferior. She may be handsome and have a greater fortune than all of us, but it would behove her to be more courteous in hiding her scorn. Ridiculous woman! I know you agree with me! Moreover, I cannot help but think the dress she wore last night would have looked better on me!

Bingley and Mr Hurst are travelling ahead of us and Jane intends to leave on Friday, which is but three days hence, so by the time you receive this letter I will already be in Brook Street, if all goes well and if the weather does not detain us. I do not think I have enough right gowns for London but Jane has promised to remedy this. I am so grateful to her for rescuing me from here.

Jane asked Mary to London as well, of course, but she said that she does not want to go! Can you believe it? I do not care of course and I certainly do not need Mary by my side, looking solemn and disagreeable all the time. I thought Mama would tell her she must go, talking all the time about fine young men and dances and how lucky she was to have a sister such as Jane, but Mary was as adamant in saying she would prefer to stay here. I know what it is to feel left behind – how I cried when you went to Brighton! – so I would not have minded too dreadfully if she was coming as well, but she is not – and there is an end to it!

Too excited at the prospect of London and all it promised, Kitty stood up and walked – or, more accurately, skipped – around the room, humming and hugging herself. How thin is the line between happiness and despair! Yesterday, all had been bleak and monotonous; today, every bright prospect was open to her. That morning, Mr Bennet had summoned her to the library and had been most serious in his expectation of her good conduct in London and she was left in no doubt that any breach of this faith would see her dispatched to Longbourn in an instant. Kitty was so deliriously happy she had forgotten to be peeved at the suggestion she would be anything other than the perfect example of maidenly decorum and had meekly nodded while her father, in a rare example of paternal concern and direction, delivered advice and instruction. When she was quite sure he had finished, she jumped up and hugged him, an act that took both of them by surprise.

'I think you are a good girl at heart, Kitty,' he had said, readjusting his spectacles. 'I expect to hear only good reports. Your mother expects you to find a suitable husband at your earliest convenience – two or three days should assuage her anxiety on that score – but you are at liberty to disregard that demand. Take some more books with you before you go; there is no need to wait until I am away from the library.'

Seeing Kitty's puzzled then alarmed face, Mr Bennet had merely raised an eyebrow and turned back to his letters, leaving his daughter to hurriedly pick out two volumes without much deliberation and quit the room with a last happy and heartfelt thank you.

That Lydia remained the conduit for Kitty's emotions was no wonder, there was no one else in whom she could confide. She sat down at her desk and took up her pen again:

The second thing I have to relate is this. I met the most charming man yesterday but it is not as you will think, dear sister. Although, I am not sure what I think, so I will just put my thoughts into sentences. When we were at Netherfield I made the acquaintance of a Sir Edward Quincy, quite an old gentleman to be sure — I suppose of forty-five years or more — whose children have been long-time friends of Bingley and his sisters, so the family has known him for ever! I was seated by him during the dinner and he was most gallant and attentive, which, given that my other neighbours were Sir William and Caroline Bingley, was no bad thing as you would well know. We talked a little of this and that, and I thought nothing much of it except that our conversation was clearly irksome to Miss Bingley, so I was amused about that, as you might imagine!

When the gentlemen joined us after dinner we sat down to cards and Sir Edward was at my table. I might say I think he contrived to be at the same table, but of course I cannot be sure. In any case, he was most courteous in his acceptance of a place by me. He is taller than Papa, and takes — I think I can be sure — a great deal of pride in his appearance. At any rate, he wears the latest clothes and his hair, though powdered, suits him well. He has a place in the country, he told me, but lives most of the year in London and he spoke so well of the galleries and theatre and amusements that I was quite in awe for a little while. Although, I hope I affected otherwise.

When the tables broke up, I thought to go and speak with Jane, but Sir Edward had me join him and his daughter, Amelia, and her husband Mr Bridgwater. They all live in Yorkshire but will be spending part of the season in London near us in Mayfair. Sir Edward said he hoped that we would be reacquainted there.

Why am I writing this? Kitty suddenly asked herself. I cannot send it. What if Lydia told Mama what I have said? She reread what she had written and wondered afresh. Was she so starved of company that any addition to her social circle was welcome? Was it because Sir Edward had made her feel a tiny bit important? Was she thinking of Sir Edward as a suitor? Good Lord, no, she assured herself immediately; he was almost as old as her father. Yes, Lydia would laugh! Kitty imagined Lydia reading her letter to Wickham and both of them laughing and laughing at her, saying how stupid she was!

She felt despondent again. There was nothing to be gained in writing to Lydia. She put the letter in a drawer with the other one that remained unsent, then went and lay down on her bed; it would be another hour before they sat down to dinner and if she went downstairs now her mother would tell her, yet again, what she should and should not pack for London, and in what order and so on and so on. Kitty stared up at the ceiling and counted the days until she could leave.

CHAPTER 10

Lond`on! Kitty felt she had stepped into another world, and given that her world thus far had been tightly bound by family and Hertfordshire society with smaller concerns and decidedly smaller outlooks, who can wonder at this transport? London's steeples and spires, its magnificent residences and grand churches, its parks and palaces, its shops and warehouses, the very scale of it all… all these were a source of wonder to Kitty, even before she had seen or explored any of them. To be in the same city as royalty and lords and ladies suited her romantic view of the universe very well. She had begged Jane to allow the carriage to detour so that she might glimpse Carlton House, the London home of the Regent, and, but for the late hour of their arrival, Jane might have agreed. Instead, she promised they would journey there soon, and after dusk, so that Kitty might see the new gas lamps illuminating Pall Mall – yet another source of wonder, and not just to Kitty, it should be said. Londoners still thought this new-fangled lighting a marvel to behold.

And there were so many Londoners! Wide-eyed and from the safety of her carriage, Kitty observed all manner of folk as they made their way into the capital. Although the carriage kept to the main thoroughfares, the variety of men and women she saw – their ages, their complexions, their attire – was more than enough to enthral, whether she was seeing clerks, merchants, servants, fish-sellers, beggars, gentlemen or their ladies. Noisy areas of bustle and business gave way to quieter streets of grace and elegance. It was all a delight to Kitty, who of course saw nothing of the city's innumerable and deep pockets of poverty and deprivation; all these were hidden from her privileged view.

Jane, to whom the sights of London were nothing new, enjoyed Kitty's enthusiasm, which for her at least alleviated some of the tedium and fatigue of their journey; Caroline Bingley managed to evince interest whenever Jane had something to say and exude a condescending air of ennui to all of Kitty's lively observations. Miss Bingley's maid, who travelled with them and had the care of several boxes on her lap, had taken refuge in sleep whenever possible.

At last, the horses and carriage clattered into Brook Street and stopped outside a lamp-lit, three-storey, brown brick terrace of substantial proportions. They had arrived. Mr Bingley bounded down the steps to welcome Jane; the ladies were escorted inside and up to the drawing room, where a fire blazed and a restorative glass of wine helped the travellers relax into their new surroundings.

Poor Kitty. Much as she wanted to admire the house and its furnishings, explore the rooms, converse with Charles and Jane and find out everything she could about London, her surroundings, the events of the forthcoming days, where they would shop, where they would visit and who and what would they see, she could take in no more... her head was awash with new sights and information and, after a little supper, she excused herself to her room – yet another source of delight – and was very soon abed and lost to her dreams.

At breakfast the next morning, some of those dreams were under discussion when Kitty arrived at the table.

'We are planning a small musical soirée here early in March,' explained Jane. 'Charles has already hired the musicians and the invitations will go out today.'

'A soirée!' How very grand that sounded. 'Will they be the same musicians who played at the Netherfield ball?' asked Kitty.

'Not this time,' replied Mr Bingley. 'A chap I know has recommended a string quartet he heard in London a few months ago, professionals all of them. Then we will have a harpsichordist and a couple of singers. Have the names somewhere, not sure where. Manning will know; everything is unpacked now.'

'Who will be invited?'

'Nearly everyone we know in London!' laughed Jane. 'Which is not to say we are expecting a very large group, although my acquaintance here is growing apace. It will be an excellent occasion to introduce you to our set, such as it is.'

This information was enough to send Kitty into a minor reverie: already she could envisage a sophisticated salon, alive with interesting young men and tolerably attractive young women among whom she could shine.

'There are a number of calls I really must return within a day or two,' Jane was saying, 'but as it is your first time here, I propose we take the carriage this morning and go around the better parts of the city.'

Kitty pulled herself back to the present. 'I should love that! That would be perfect! Will we all go?'

Mr Bingley demurred. Notwithstanding his having seen London's landmarks many times, he had some pressing business at his club, as gentlemen are wont to have and ladies are wont to ignore, at least those ladies whose minds do not run to suspicious behaviour. Miss Bingley – not yet arrived at breakfast and ignorant of the planned excursion – had yet to make any decision in the matter. Kitty fervently hoped she would decline. Whether the ever gentle and accommodating Jane wished the same cannot be known. Now that she was Mrs Bingley, unpleasant memories of her dear Caroline's previous machinations in trying to prevent her marriage to her brother seldom surfaced; Jane was, however, not entirely artless.

'We shall call in on Aunt and Uncle Gardiner,' she said to Kitty. 'They are close to the river and you will want to see that part of the city, also.'

Her sister gladly acquiesced. Not only was she happy with the thought of seeing her relations, she knew this would absolutely deny them the pleasure of Miss Bingley's company. That lady would have no desire whatsoever to venture into Gracechurch Street, where the Gardiners resided – good Lord! The area fairly reeked of trade and undesirables, and her dislike of such low-class activities was as intense as her memory was short. That the Bingleys owed their present wealth and standing to the business acumen of their ancestors in trade was a piece of family history that Caroline and her sister Louisa had managed to completely forget.

The other important business of the day was the imminent arrival of Jane's dressmaker, and to her great delight Kitty found that her presence was required. A dress (or two!) in the latest fashion, made by a London seamstress, with fabrics chosen by herself – with subtle advice from her sister – was more than enough to make Jane the best and most adored sister anyone could ever have in all the land. When Miss Bingley made her appearance for breakfast, she found Charles hidden behind the newspaper and Jane and Kitty deep in conversation about double-twilled muslins and brocades, satins and silks and Spanish net, the best colours for each and each other, and myriad smaller details concerning accessories and decorations. Kitty was in such fine humour that even Caroline's dictates – and the lady had many, being of the opinion that her own ideas of what was fashionable were unsurpassed and her taste flawless – were accepted with every appearance of gratitude and grace.

Chapter 11

Nearly two weeks had passed since Kitty's arrival and in that time she had learned much and learned also there was much more to learn. It was not just the scale and grandeur of London's architectural fabric that was opening her eyes to the world outside Longbourn. As she visited galleries and private houses with Jane and Charles, she became aware of a society more sophisticated than she had known existed. In manners and etiquette, there was much to be observed and although Kitty was absorbing the many little intricacies and emulating them, she was not confident. She felt her own lack of finesse and often found it easier to stay mute and watch the proceedings rather than fully participate.

Naïve as she still was, she was not ignorant to artifice, especially when observing Miss Bingley and Mrs Hurst, the two ladies she knew best outside of her family. She became fascinated watching Caroline manoeuvre her way around a salon, praising and disdaining to her best advantage, assessing the eligibility and suitability of the gentlemen in the company, smiling the while – a practised smile to be sure, but an effective one nonetheless. There was no doubt, thought Kitty, Caroline *could* be charming.

'How delightful to see you again,' she was saying to one of the ladies present. 'Your dear cousin Mr Marsh was just telling me you have delayed your return to Devon and so we can look forward to enjoying your society a little longer. Delightful! My brother so looks forward to seeing you all, and your cousin's advice is always so appreciated. Ah, there he is. Shall we join him?'

It was, as far as Kitty could tell, completely untrue. Mr Bingley found the unfortunate Mr Marsh a bit of a blunderbuss, or so she had heard him say to Jane; that he held any attraction for Miss Bingley was no doubt because of the friendship he enjoyed with an equally stuffy individual who had only wealth and a title to recommend him. That person now found himself the focus of Miss Bingley's complete attention and if he was unable to supply animated or even coherent conversation, she could provide sufficient for both.

Yesterday she had watched her talking to an older man of military bearing who had cornered her in conversation. 'He is another complete bore!' Caroline had whispered to Louisa Hurst only minutes beforehand, but this particular bore must have had some worth because Miss Bingley had been gazing into his face as if he alone could unlock the secrets of the universe, and nodding in apparently sincere agreement to everything he had said.

Kitty saw that Mrs Hurst sometimes played a part in these little charades, but also that her presence was not necessary. It caused her to reflect on her own relationship with her younger sister. Undoubtedly Lydia had been the queen and she the willing courtier, ready to aid and abet her royal highness wherever she were needed. That much she could readily accede, but contrasting Lydia and Caroline let in many more thoughts. Lydia was more honest and straightforward than Miss Bingley, she was more lively and boisterous and Kitty had been pleased to ride on her high spirits, which in turn lifted her own. Then again, that boisterousness had gone too far, and Kitty could see that now. She blushed as she thought of Lydia and herself shouting out to officers across the street in Meryton, at the pair's untamed behaviour at the local Assemblies, their lack of decorum in other public places.

The quiet conversation and subdued laughter of the elegant women peopling the salon in Audley Street in which she now found herself were the very antithesis of that behaviour. The reason, if one were needed, for such a gathering was the new portrait of the lady of the house, which now hung upon the wall for general approbation. Art and artists, exhibitions and galleries, these were the favoured topics for discussions. Did she prefer Gainsborough or Reynolds? Turner or Hogarth? Kitty dissembled and vowed privately to learn. She saw Jane gliding about as serenely as ever, listening with attention and speaking her opinions quietly but candidly. She watched Miss Bingley, always scrupulously polite when the social occasion demanded it, and heard her shrill little laugh as she apparently agreed with a witty remark.

Kitty had no desire to model herself on Miss Caroline Bingley or her ilk, but she did intend to become someone other than the Miss Catherine Bennet who was known to the good burghers of Meryton.

It was not just Jane and her friends who were exerting a subtle influence on Kitty. Charles was playing a role, albeit obliviously. It was part of Mr Bingley's routine to read the newspaper over breakfast in the morning and he invariably found something to exclaim over. Charles Bingley was no elder statesman – his interests lay more in the arts than in politics – but he was a man who took an interest in the world about him. His remarks over breakfast were obliquely intended for Jane from whom, even at this early stage of their marriage, a reply was rarely required.

'A bad business in the Indies! No good will come of this!' he would declare, or, 'What's Liverpool up to now?'

Kitty would listen, uncomprehending, but by quietly retrieving the paper after breakfast was finished and making her own researches, would discover what the new Prime Minister had been saying, what were the perceived problems facing owners of sugar plantations in the West Indies (and where in the world the West Indies were), Wellington's progress or otherwise.

It was, she had realised, as well to be informed – or if not entirely informed, at least aware, because Kitty certainly had no intention of holding forth on any such topical news. Not yet anyway. 'A man speaks of what he knows, a woman of what pleases her; the one requires knowledge, the other taste' – she had read that recently. She wasn't at all sure she agreed with it but ever since the dinner at Netherfield she had been dismayed at her own ignorance, so fortunately disguised during her conversation with Sir Edward. She required knowledge! She had been studying the volume that had almost dropped into her lap at Longbourn, Mary Wollstonecraft's *A Vindication of the Rights of Women*. Kitty could not identify with all the circumstances and posits put forward by the author, who had now fallen from grace, but she had never read such radical opinions before! That a woman's achievement of matrimony could be referred to as a 'paltry crown' was a blasphemous notion indeed in Kitty's world – Mrs Bennet would require smelling salts were she to hear it uttered! – and one she had never thought to question before. Were wives 'slaves or friends' of man? Kitty found herself excited by some of these disturbing ideas. What did Jane and Elizabeth think, she wondered? Had they read this particular book?

Of course she was not considering challenging the norms in her own life. However paltry the crown of matrimony might be to some, Kitty could not but hope to wear it one day, though, if she could possibly avoid it, she would prefer not to become anyone's 'spaniel-like' companion.

CHAPTER 12

The day of the musical soirée arrived and the house at Brook Street was a hive of activity. Although comparatively small – only around fifty guests had been invited – both Mr and Mrs Bingley (she especially) were keen to uphold the standards seen in houses elsewhere and so a string of servants, often vexed by auxiliaries who had been brought in solely for the purpose of helping, or hindering, those who knew better and best, processed up and down the stairs, into and out of the main rooms, carrying flowers and trays and candles and chairs and glassware and all manner of provisions necessary for an elegant evening in a fashionable part of London.

Jane, in command of this domestic battle station, maintained a slightly anxious calm, only occasionally called upon by the housekeeper to assuage affronted pride and assure that all would be well. In the middle of all this, the dressmaker arrived, providing a pleasant means of honourable retreat from responsibility and bustle, and the opportunity to pass opinion on the new gowns that had been ordered for herself and Kitty.

In Kitty's room, her dress for the evening was pronounced entirely suitable, and she and Jane happily fussed over it and what she might wear with it, and how best to arrange her hair and what ribbons she should choose, and would a shawl be necessary? 'Oh Jane,' said Kitty earnestly, after all had been deliberated and decided upon. 'I am so very happy. I am happier than I feel I ought to be! Go, go! You are the hostess. Look to yourself! You look tired, you should rest.'

'You are right. I do feel uncommonly tired,' admitted Jane, 'though I hope it will not be apparent to our guests.' She smiled and, with a quick embrace, was gone, leaving Kitty to attend to her own appearance. Later, when she went down to the drawing room she found Charles alone and only too pleased to find someone with whom to discuss the musical component of the evening.

'One of the violinists and the harpsichord player have just arrived,' said he, rubbing his hands together in anticipatory glee. 'Both will be playing at the Philharmonic Society's inaugural concert next week. They are setting up as we speak.'

Kitty comprehended at once that securing these two musicians was no mean feat. Mr Bingley's enthusiasm for them and the newly formed society was evident and infectious.

'You have not said what they will play, although I think there will be some Mozart?'

'Yes, indeed! You know my tastes there! Some Mozart, some Haydn and Boccherini — my particular favourites — but I have not prescribed every piece. I am happy to let the musicians choose the remainder of the repertoire as their talents and tastes dictate. Then I shall feel that I am part of the audience and not the organiser.' He nodded, confirming this idea to himself.

'Ah! I think I hear another hackney coach! That will be the rest of them arriving. We will wait a few minutes and then go up and see how they get on, if you would like?'

Kitty thought this an excellent idea and was struck by Mr Bingley's marvellous, boyish delight for this entertainment, which she now realised had been organised at his instigation and not her sister's.

'One of the violinists was recommended to me through Darcy,' he volunteered. 'He is Miss Darcy's music master when she is in London; he instructs her in the pianoforte. She is proficient in that, so let us hope he is as good on the violin! The 'cellist I know little of, except that he has a fine reputation.

'You are musical, Kitty? I cannot recall hearing you play.'

'I would like to be but I lack practice. And I suppose confidence. I am afraid of making mistakes. I used to play when I was a child.' How easy it is to say this to Charles, she thought.

'Well you must practise while you are here!' cried Mr Bingley. 'Jane plays well, as you know. You have no need of worrying about false notes in front of us! I play badly myself. We can play false notes together!' He laughed at his little jest, and Kitty smiled, too. It was a pleasant notion; perhaps she would practise more.

They waited a little longer and, as no one else had arrived in the drawing room, went up to the first floor to see how things were arranged. Kitty had not expected the musicians to be in such colourful costume, some wearing shades of crimson or forest green, and although at least half of them were quite young, all were wearing beribboned horsehair wigs lending them an almost regal air. She liked the theatricality of it; it added to the occasion. The room, which was usually divided in two by large folding doors, had been expanded into one grand area and the musicians were grouping themselves at one end. Only a few more candles remained to be lit, and the room was already bright and warm. The rows of chairs were in place and servants hovered alongside sideboards whereupon were wine and other refreshments.

'Excellent,' murmured Mr Bingley, looking about him and then, giving Kitty his arm, they went back down to the drawing room, where Jane and Caroline now sat awaiting the first guests.

Among the earliest were the Hursts, the Bridgwaters and Sir Edward. The usual pleasantries were exchanged, the chivalrous Sir Edward the most solicitous in his compliments to the lovely Mrs Bingley and the equally lovely Miss Bennet. Within half an hour, the company had swelled into a fashionable crush, with many spilling outside the drawing room in order to speak and be heard. Kitty found herself quite surrounded by new acquaintance and happily struggling to keep up with the introductions. All in all, though, she was quite relieved when they went upstairs and she took her seat in the front row next to Jane and Charles for the first of the recitals.

Sir Edward was seated to her left and drew her attention to the age and manufacture of the harpsichord. If he had hoped for more conversation from the fair lady, he would be disappointed however. From the moment the first violin began, Kitty was lost, completely transported to realms well beyond the confines of Mayfair. She thought the music sublime, reverential, as if it were reaching into her soul providing a balm, a release and something akin to joy. When the exquisite strings of the quartetto concluded, she had tears in her eyes. She turned to Mr Bingley, wanting to share her feelings but he was talking at once to Jane and the lady and gentleman sitting behind them. Applause and polite chatter had broken out all around her and she turned the other way to see Sir Edward regarding her, a benign, if bemused, expression on his face. 'I see you appreciate the music,' said he. Kitty, a little disconcerted by the intensity of his gaze, could only agree.

The recitals continued and if the pieces were all new to Kitty, and if the musicians were famed or otherwise, it mattered not a jot – she loved everything; she rejoiced in the power of the music and its execution and there was the beginning and the end of it all. One of the violinists was particularly good, she thought, or was it just the manner of his playing? He was in harmony with his companions, of course, but at the same time he seemed to be playing solely for himself. Perhaps it was because his wig had become a little askew that she noticed him in particular. Or perhaps it was because he was really rather a fine young gentleman, whose eyes, when not closed in concentration, were a very dark blue. She should not be thus distracted, Kitty thought, and gave back her attention to the ensemble as a whole.

When it was all over, she was loath to leave her seat, but Sir Edward escorted her into the supper room where she was happy to praise all that had been played. She heard her name spoken and turned to find Mr Bingley with a tall young man by his side, the very same violinist whose performance she had just been admiring and whose wig was now suitably adjusted.

'Allow me to introduce you to Mr Henry Adams,' he began. 'He is the gentleman I was speaking of earlier. An accomplished player, as you have just heard; and he is also Miss Darcy's music master. We have been speaking of the Philharmonic, and all that it promises.'

'Miss Bennet, a pleasure,' smiled Mr Adams.

Kitty was immediately struck by the rich, dark timbre to his voice. It suited him well, so she was not quite sure why she was surprised. She was also struck by his elegant figure, handsome features and wide smile.

'Mr Adams,' she replied, as these thoughts coalesced and she spoke his name. 'A wonderful concert, truly.'

'Quite agree with you in regard to the Philharmonic,' interposed Sir Edward. 'A very fine initiative, indeed. Very fine. And a capital performance tonight, young sir. You have been playing a long time?'

'For a number of years, sir,' said he. 'My father has always taught and composed music; he tells me I was five years of age when I first played the spinet. Badly, I am sure.'

'Mr Adams is overly modest,' declared Mr Bingley. 'Never mind the spinet anyway! We have heard you on the violin and I know full well you are proficient on the pianoforte. Furthermore, I am told you are one of the best music masters in all of London.' He clapped him on the shoulder as proof of his convictions. 'The violin solos were magnificent, I must say!'

The young man looked suitably pleased and embarrassed and made the requisite thanks and protestations.

'Have you been in London long, Miss Bennet?' he asked, deflecting attention from himself.

'Not yet a month.'

'And you are fond of music?'

'Very much, although better at listening than performing.'

'That is for others to decide,' said Mr Bingley. 'Now Miss Bennet is being modest.'

'I am not sure that is true,' protested Kitty. 'I do like to play, that is certain. And to sing. However, when I hear performances such as those we have just enjoyed, I feel it would be better to leave my deficiencies unexposed.'

'But you enjoy it, nonetheless?' enquired Mr Adams.

'I do. I cannot say why exactly, but I have always enjoyed music.'

'In my experience, that is the first advantage. Some of the young ladies I have the pleasure of instructing learn out of duty. They do not feel the music. They must play, so they do play, but I fear they derive little enjoyment from it. Not everyone has the gift of musical appreciation.' This was spoken lightly and addressed very much to Kitty.

'I had not thought of it as a gift,' she laughed. 'You may not think so either if you were to hear me play.'

'You should hear Miss Bennet play!' declared Mr Bingley, all bonhomie and good ideas. 'You said you would like to practise, Kitty, and we have here one of the best music masters in town. There seems little else for it but to enlist Mr Adams' help in that regard! What do you say to that? And you, sir, would your engagements permit it?'

'I should be delighted,' he replied, looking to Kitty, 'if Miss Bennet wishes it.'

Miss Bennet was momentarily confused. Of course she wished it! She felt quite ready to take instruction from the gentleman before her, whose appearance at least was so very attractive. On the other hand, perhaps he would be dismayed at her musical ability and she would be embarrassed beyond measure. She composed herself and a reply.

'I wish to improve,' she said, 'and I think that will not happen without some instruction.'

'Excellent,' declared Mr Bingley. 'Leave it to me. I will arrange it. Now, if you will excuse us, there is a gentleman over there with whom we must speak.' So saying, he led Mr Adams away, leaving Kitty to wonder at the speed with which musical instruction had been organised for her.

Sir Edward reclaimed her attention; could he find her a seat, fetch her some refreshment, a little soup, some tea? She thanked him and allowed him to do so. Jane, seeing Kitty alone, crossed the room to join her, bringing with her a couple of her friends, so that when Sir Edward returned it was to the company of his hostess as well as her sister, and the supper passed pleasantly enough.

A little afterwards, on her return to the other room, Kitty found herself once more face to face with Mr Adams, who was on the point of leaving. Both smiled and then both spoke at once; then stopping, each entreated the other to speak. The conversation stalled, then both spoke at once again. It was just the kind of gauche interaction often found when two strangers meet and find the other more than commonly attractive but their tongues inexplicably tied. When the conversation was finally allowed to flow, they managed to wish each other well and Kitty rejoined her sister and Mr Bingley, thrilled to be part of such an elegant evening and not a little delighted to have acquired a music master.

CHAPTER 13

Still in the habit of regarding Lydia as her chief confidante, Kitty continued to maintain the façade of writing to her. She therefore began yet another letter that would be consigned to her desk drawer rather than the post.

Brook St, 5 March
Dear Lydia,

Why, oh why, do I not sing and play? I should like to blame Mary, or Mama, but I cannot. It is entirely my own fault. I want to rectify this. The concert last night was sublime. We heard Mozart and Haydn and Boccherini and other beautiful pieces and the evening was just heavenly. Of course, I don't expect to play like the musicians that were engaged, but what joy it must be to express oneself through music, and give such delight to others.

Charles, it turns out, is a great enthusiast for all things musical. We are, I think, to attend more concerts shortly. Jane is very happy today, although a little tired, and, all in all, the evening was deemed a great success. So many fashionable young men and women, and some of them are such gossips but in a quiet and rather refined way. I learned rather more than is decent about a certain young lady, recently married, whose behaviour is raising eyebrows. The person who expounded the tale expects to see some allusion to it in the papers. Imagine! Mrs Hurst was part of the conversation but seemed to find nothing out of the ordinary in it. Perhaps I am just ignorant of the ways of this set! Miss Bingley would no doubt say so, but I have been rather clever in avoiding her lately. She has been devoting most of her attention to a certain gentleman, a friend of a friend of Bingley, who owns land in Gloucestershire. Poor fellow! She may get him, and then I shall feel sorry for him, although I know him not at all and he is not at all handsome. Here is how some of it goes:

'Oh, Mr Phillips,' says Miss Bingley, all elegance and charm. 'It is a pleasure to see you here. You will be staying for the rest of the season?'

'For part of it,' returns he, but 'My duties at home may call me away sooner than I would like and, sadly, deprive me of your excellent company. A lady such as yourself could feel no comparable delight outside London, I fear.'

'Oh Mr Phillips, how can you think so? I am uncommonly fond of country life,' declares the indefatigable Miss B. 'Whenever I am in London, I believe myself the happiest person alive; but then when I am in the country, I believe myself the happiest. It is a mystery, is it not? In the country, though, one feels the beauty of nature so much more, do you not agree?'

Of course Mr P thinks this, and Caroline knows he thinks this, and so the little inquisition continues, although he of course thinks she is merely being sweetly curious. 'Do tell me more about Longmeadow House, I believe you have made many improvements of late?'

He has; he rattles on rather and she looks all amazement that such a man can organise so many things. At one point, our lovely Miss B almost loses concentration but covers it delightfully with: 'Oh do forgive me. I was quite lost in imagining the house, and the aspect it affords over the park. How clever of you to engage such an excellent architect.'

And Mr P beams with pride at his perceived ingenuity, when really all was recommended to him, and money is what has brought him his flair. And Caroline, in this instance! How high – or how low – is her price?

Kitty laughed, sat back. She was very much enjoying herself. It is quite remarkable how siblings can be so different, she thought. Charles is the opposite of Caroline in nearly every way. Then again, she questioned, why should it be remarkable? Her four sisters were quite different to her and each other. Nonetheless, it was interesting that the Bingley women were so full of spite when their brother was not. He, of course, had all the advantages of a first and only son, but Miss Bingley and Mrs Hurst were not without fortunes. She wondered about their parents and how their lives had been as children; how different would it have been to her own? What had been their petty rivalries and shared interests, who had been the favoured child? People really were quite fascinating.

Her thoughts went to Henry Adams. She was glad her mother had not been present to interfere and cajole, or dismiss as inferior a man whose wealth and prospects had not been established. Mrs Bennet, had she observed Sir Edward's attentions to her daughter, would be much more interested in him, and Kitty was also ready to own that he was charming, as well as well travelled and interesting, full of facts about places she would love to visit one day. Henry Adams, on the other hand, was – by all accounts – a musical genius, perhaps even skilled enough to teach her how to play in public.

She must, she resolved, as she put her letter into the drawer with the others, start keeping a journal. It was hardly a revolutionary thought but one that was new to her. So much was happening, it would be an excellent record of what was becoming a much more interesting life. She liked London, she liked Brook Street; at this very moment, she quite liked herself.

Humming, Kitty went downstairs to find Jane and talk once more about everything that had happened the night before, and to find out what was going to happen next.

Chapter 14

After the excitement – and avowed success – of the Bingleys' soirée, life at Brook Street returned to its usual calm. There had been a flurry of morning visits, of course, from those eager to thank Jane for her gracious hospitality and pick over essential details of who had spoken to whom, and about what; whose appearance delighted and whose was less than sparkling; and even, on some occasions, discussion on the music.

Concerning the latter, Kitty was expecting her first tuition from Mr Adams the next day. Charles had been most efficient in that regard. As a result, she was apprehensive although she could not decide what worried her most – her musical abilities or the presence of the gentleman himself. Jane, divining both concerns, concentrated on the first and spent some time with her sister at the pianoforte, revising with her and reliving tunes and airs that had been part of their childhood at Longbourn.

Their comfortable reverie was interrupted when Kitty suddenly asked: 'Shall we ever see Lydia again? Mama, of course, expects her to visit by the next carriage but I am not such a simpleton to believe that. Father will not hear her name spoken. Lydia's marriage was hasty and the circumstances ill-advised but there is more, I am sure there is, and no one will tell me…' She stopped, waited.

Jane was ill-prepared for the question and struggled for a suitable response. Dissembling was not in her nature and a momentary struggle between truth and obfuscation ensued, but the appeal in Kitty's eyes decided her upon a candid answer.

'Of course I believe we shall see her again,' she began.

'But when?' persisted Kitty, seizing the moment. 'And why must we not speak of Lydia and Captain Wickham?'

Jane, who strove to think the best of everyone, could not – or would no longer – paint Wickham in a wholly favourable light. Even so, it took some effort for her to speak ill of him.

'What I shall tell you is in confidence,' she continued. 'We must be discreet.' Having received Kitty's tacit assurance, Jane then did her best to explain Wickham's actions, defend both him and Lydia and give quarter to all parties. Eventually though, the truth filtered through and Kitty, at last, had a fuller account of what had happened: how Wickham had left Brighton in order to escape his debts (Jane did not dwell on Lydia's enthusiasm for the elopement or Wickham's knavish behaviour in seducing her); that her father and Uncle Gardiner had been unable to find the pair in London; that Lydia's actions were poised to bring scandal on all members of the Bennet family; and that it was only through Mr Darcy that the miscreants were finally found, and that he had been the person responsible for coercing Wickham into marrying Lydia.

'Mr Darcy!' exclaimed Kitty. 'Indeed,' concurred Jane, and paused to allow Kitty to wonder at the reason for his intervention and how the marriages of both herself and Elizabeth would not have taken place had he not been so noble. As can be surmised, these revelations took some time to settle and Kitty, like others before her, found herself revising her opinions of the taciturn and stern Mr Darcy. Lydia and Wickham were likewise contemplated. She had not known that Wickham had been so gravely in debt, nor that he had been forced to marry her sister; Lydia's comments in her letters had implied mutual adoration. And Mr Darcy had been her saviour! It really was both wonderful and unbelievable.

'Mr Darcy!' repeated Kitty. 'But why would he do such a thing? All for Lizzy?'

'I think we can believe just that,' said Jane, who felt obliged to keep silent on part of the story: the part that concerned

Wickham's earlier and very nearly successful attempt to elope with none other than Mr Darcy's sister, a girl even younger than Lydia. Mr Darcy had foiled that plan and in order to guard his sister's reputation had not made Wickham's character known, a fact he reproached himself for when Wickham repeated his behaviour with Lydia.

'Now Kitty,' reminded Jane, 'this is in the past and it must remain so. Time will heal and our father, I am sure, will consent to seeing Lydia again one day. Charles and I will certainly receive her but I am not sure when that occasion will be. As for Wickham and Mr Darcy, I cannot say. Wickham has behaved intolerably to Mr Darcy; there is more there than even I know, but Lizzy can be believed when she says that her husband has done everything he could rightly be expected to do in furthering Wickham's circumstances but that his actions have been met with ingratitude and scandalous behaviour. Lizzy would not speak so were it not true.

'For Lydia's sake,' she continued, 'we must hope that the married state will persuade Wickham to live a better life.'

Kitty nodded, still a little dazed by what she had learned. 'Does Mama know? Mary?' They did not. Not even Mr Bingley was aware of all the details, added Jane, and Kitty, rather than feeling put out that she had not been told the tawdry story before, was pleased and proud to know that Jane had deemed her worthy of tact and discretion.

Any chance of further discussion was ended with the arrival of Mr Bingley, who stopped in the room only long enough to apologise for his intrusion into the ladies' music practice, smile fondly at his wife and deliver to her two letters that had just arrived: one from Longbourn; the other from Elizabeth in Pemberley.

'Oh! Which shall I open first?' wondered Jane, before fixing on the missive from Longbourn.

'It is from Papa,' she informed Kitty. 'He writes, *"all is well though the house is very quiet now that they are but three..."* that he particularly misses the noise of slamming doors and arguments between Kitty and Mary... Don't look so offended, Kitty! He is only teasing; you know his way. What else? *"Your dear mother is quite well, as are her nerves which, of course, rarely give her a moment's peace..."* Mary sends her regards to me and Mr Bingley and, of course, to Kitty... that Mama *"received a letter from Lydia, though to call it a letter is an exaggeration for it was little more than a note and contained nothing of any substance. If you are interested in regimental dress and what the ladies are wearing at the Assemblies in Newcastle, may I suggest you apply to your dear mother for the detail. She will be most pleased to elaborate. In short, Lydia and Mr Wickham are in good health, it seems, and no doubt enjoying themselves beyond their means..."*

'I am glad they are settled,' said Jane, before continuing. 'He says that *"a letter from Lizzy arrived last week. It would seem that the mistress of Pemberley has been making many new acquaintances; she had not anticipated the interest that a new Mrs Darcy would excite in the neighbourhood. (We are not all surprised, I am sure!) She has been scampering about the many woods and glades in her great park but rain and storms have hampered her a little in that pursuit. Poor Lizzy! She has had to stay indoors more than she would have liked – and in such a tiny house as I believe Pemberley to be! There are many references to 'her dear Darcy', and I should be alarmed if this were not so, but I dare hope she is not sparing him her wit and perspicacity! I would not have my Lizzy subdued by greatness..."*

'Poor Papa, he does miss us all but especially Lizzy, I think.' Jane turned back to her letter. 'Ah, now he asks, *"How does my dear Kitty? I have seen her letter to her mother and am not at all surprised to hear she approves of London very much. I am glad of it. Tell her I enquire after her. I do not expect correspondence but am happy to receive same – as long as the news is good. Pray spare me reports of the attentions and affections of feckless young men."*

Kitty stiffened at this, feeling it as yet another rebuke. 'It is just his way,' reiterated Jane, reaching for her sister's hand. 'Do not doubt our father's affection. He says less than he feels.' She read aloud the letter's closing statements and Kitty made her own interpretations of the remarks pertinent to her. Jane meanwhile, impatient for Elizabeth's news, turned to the other letter, which read:

Pemberley
5 March

My dearest Jane,

I write in haste but with happy news. As I told you in my last letter, we had no immediate plans to be in London but it now transpires some urgent business calls my dear Darcy to town. I cannot spare him — of course! — and, that being so, we are all decided that we three shall travel to London together and arrangements are being made for our departure as I write this.

I need not say how very much I look forward to seeing you. We all do. Now, dearest sister, please contrive to limit your engagements in such a way that will permit of receiving me and mine. I fully intend to take up as much of your time as you can spare.

We, and Georgiana is included in this we, expect to be in Berkeley Square a fortnight from today, and you may depend on me sending word as soon as we have arrived.

Until then, I send my fondest to you and Charles, and Kitty.

Your affectionate sister,

Lizzy

'Oh, that is but ten days!' cried Jane, clapping her hands in delight. 'I must write back immediately.' Kitty, equally excited, jumped up and pulled Jane to her feet. 'What fun we shall have!' she laughed and, linking arms, the pair half danced, half walked out of the room to find Bingley and share the news.

CHAPTER 15

Kitty was already seated at the pianoforte when Henry Adams's arrival was announced. She had thought about taking the air that morning, in order to calm her nerves, but it was raining heavily outside and showed no sign of abating, so a few brief turns about the room had been her exercise. Then she had thought she would practise some of the pieces she and Jane had played the day before. Then she wondered what Mr Adams would look like without the horsehair wig – she hoped there was hair underneath that wig! – and whether he would be caught in the storms outside.

All this conjecture was ended when he was shown into the room. He was soberly dressed in grey and black, and his hair was almost black, too, his dark curls just a little unruly but in a perfectly fashionable way. She greeted him most politely and waited for him to begin. She had decided that, as he was to be her tutor, efficiency and proper attention was required of her; besides, she was fully committed to the serious business of understanding and playing music. Accordingly, nearly an hour passed before any conversation took place that was not related to scales, tone or composition. Indeed, it was only Kitty's increasing frustration at her inability to master a sequence of notes that prompted Mr Adams to suggest she stop for a few minutes and rest.

'That piece causes trouble for quite a few players, you know, but I wanted to hear you play it for it helps me understand your competence and what you have learned thus far.'

Kitty sighed.

'Do not be so critical of yourself, Miss Bennet! Not at this stage, please. There will be time for that later on, when we advance.' He laughed, hoping to elevate Kitty's mood. 'Do not underestimate your skills. We have only just begun but with practice you will make progress. It seems to me you have an innate understanding of the way the music should be played, an appreciation of what the composer wanted – and this is very important. It is something I cannot teach, but only you can feel. Do you see?'

Kitty saw this as a compliment and her confidence rose a little.

'I should like to hear you sing,' he continued and, without giving Kitty time to protest or demur, he moved behind the pianoforte and led her in front of it.

'Anything you like, Miss Bennet. A song you learned as a child; something you are fond of; something you have heard lately?'

Kitty was mortified. She felt her colour rise but, with it, a determination not to appear young and foolish in front of Mr Adams. Even so, she hesitated; yes, she could sing – everyone could sing – but did she sing well? She thought not.

'Anything that comes to mind,' he reiterated. 'When you are ready, breathe deeply and begin.'

Kitty took a deep breath as instructed, looked at the ceiling, opened her mouth. And stopped. She looked at the ground, fighting with herself to continue.

'I have a better idea,' said Mr Adams, unperturbed and rifling through his sheet music. 'We will sing together. Do you know this one?' Kitty looked and nodded. 'Very well, then. With me, on the count of three.'

They began. Henry Adams' pleasing tenor filled the room and Kitty could hear her clearer, lighter voice as she accompanied him, wavering slightly at first and then rising in strength and volume as she began to realise that they were in harmony. After two verses, Mr Adams stopped singing but gestured to Kitty to continue, and she found that not only could she continue, but that she was quite carried along by the melody. Her whole being was given over to achieving the notes and taking pleasure in the sound and song she was making. As the last note trembled and died, Kitty felt a mix of triumph and fear, hardly daring to look at Mr Adams for his reaction.

The music master remained silent for a moment, an agonisingly long time when one is hoping for praise and encouragement but fearing none will be forthcoming, and eventually said: 'That was well done. Not perfect, as I am sure you are aware, but there is a crystal quality to your voice that is not often heard. With practice, believe me, it can be made even clearer. A fine soprano, indeed. If you are prepared to work.'

'Oh, I am! I am!' Kitty assured him, laughing in relief. 'If you really think that I can improve?'

'Certainly, I do. It will take some practice and application, but I venture that you will be surprised at your own capabilities. However, I think we have done enough for today. Do you agree?'

Kitty did most certainly agree and, having determined on further practice two days' hence, the conversation turned to the newly formed Philharmonic Society, whose inaugural concert was taking place that evening, and then to Georgiana Darcy who, Kitty informed Mr Adams, was expected in London within a week.

'I understand Miss Darcy is proficient in the pianoforte,' said she.

'That is so. She has been playing for many years now. She now has a fine Broadwood grand in the Berkeley Square house. No doubt you will see for yourself once the party has arrived.'

'I am sure I shall, although I would not presume to play it. I do not wish to expose myself to ridicule.'

'I think that unlikely. Your playing is entirely competent; you merely lack practice and some easily learned skills. You will be surprised at your abilities. Unlike many young ladies, it seems to me you enjoy playing and if that is the case an audience is quite unnecessary.'

Kitty had to admit that she did enjoy playing, something she had repressed for many years in the belief that she had no talent. Her sister Mary, who had studied music assiduously and could no doubt match Mr Adams on theory and historical detail, was a mechanical and plodding player whose performances could render an audience silent for entirely the wrong reasons. Mary had never let critical self-assessment stand in the way of recitals. The last time her sister had taken possession of a pianoforte outside Longbourn was at a ball at Netherfield and it was not a happy memory, although the only person unaware of that had been Mary herself. Kitty had no wish to make a similar discordant mark but perhaps, if her teacher were to be believed, she might not.

'What of you, Mr Adams. How do you come to play and sing so well?'

'I really cannot take too much praise for the gifts nature has afforded me but I must credit my father for teaching me most of what I know. He is a fine musician himself. He has been the organist at the French Embassy Chapel for many years as well as at the Oxford Chapel in Marylebone. He tells me that as a very young child I would make noise with whatever "instruments" came to hand – anything from a kitchen pot to a whistle, I understand – so he was forced to give me a recorder and when that became too much he taught me to play the spinet. So you can see that I ought to have improved considerably with so much practice and attention. I have been fortunate, too, in being afforded opportunity to keep playing through teaching and at the church.'

'I should like to have heard you play the kitchen pots,' said Kitty, smiling.

'I am not sure you would,' returned he. 'My mother was quick to remove them from me. Said I hurt her ears. *J'ai mal aux oreilles!* I do not speak French, but I know that phrase very well!'

'Your mother is French?' Kitty was not sure she had met anyone of French extraction before; this made Henry Adams even more interesting.

'Yes, from Normandy. My father met and married her there, and they came to live in London a year later. She is a fine singer herself.'

'My mother does not sing, but she would have confiscated any pots or pans my sisters and I were playing, I am quite sure. She has very delicate nerves and does not tolerate noise well, unless it is of her own making.'

'But you had a pianoforte in your home?'

'Indeed yes, we still do. My eldest sisters are quite proficient and used to teach me a little when I was young but – I am not sure why really – I stopped playing for quite a while.' It was when she was recovering from her illness, Kitty remembered, and Elizabeth and Mary would jostle for whose turn it was to play and, as she feared she could not compete well, it had been easier to let them be and just listen. Why was I such a passive creature? Kitty wondered.

'It is getting late. I will take my leave of you now,' said Mr Adams, breaking into her thoughts. 'I look forward to our next meeting the day after tomorrow.'

'Yes. Forgive me,' said Kitty. 'I was quite lost in memory for a moment.' She bade him farewell and he was gone. She thought back to the evening she had first heard him play, and smiled. Yes, she very much wanted to improve her musical skills and if the audience consisted solely of Henry Adams, well let it be so.

CHAPTER 16

A few days later, Charles came to the breakfast table looking most pleased with himself. He had secured tickets to the Philharmonic Society's second concert at the Argyll Rooms in Westminster. 'I tried dashed hard to get some for the inaugural performance last week but the subscription was sold too quick,' he told Jane. 'By chance I met Sir Edward at the club and – I don't know how – but the fellow said he could offer me four places – something about friends of his having to return to the country earlier than they had expected, family fracas of some kind. I wish them well of course, but fine luck for us, I say. Of course, I took them straightaway. We are not engaged elsewhere on Monday, my dear? I am sure we are not.'

'No, indeed,' answered Jane mildly. 'What an amiable gentleman Sir Edward is. It is most kind of him. His daughter and her husband are still in town?'

'Indeed, they are, and will be attending the concert with him. Has Mrs Bridgwater mentioned it to you, Caroline? You will come with us, I trust? And you, Kitty, I have included you in our party of course. There will be three Mozart pieces, some Haydn and Bach. I have details of the programme somewhere, I will find them for you this morning.'

Kitty's enthusiasm for the entertainment more than compensated for Miss Bingley's world-weary acquiescence. To visit the Argyll Rooms and hear a concert there was yet another delight for Kitty, another piece of London and its culture that she anticipated with pleasure. She had read the reviews of the inaugural concert, which had featured Beethoven and Boccherini, as well as Mozart and Haydn 'whose sinfonias blazed like a comet in our musical atmosphere', and was exceedingly pleased to be going to something so new and exciting. She would discuss it with Henry Adams when she saw him next; she was sure he was acquainted with some members of the society, perhaps the musicians themselves.

She found herself very much looking forward to her lessons with Mr Adams – she had seen him twice now and he would be at Brook Street again that day – and her appreciation of music, of scales and tones, was increasing rapidly. As was her appreciation of Mr Adams himself, whose hair had a most becoming habit of falling on to his forehead when his playing became animated. Such personal attributes may have caused her momentary distraction from her playing, it is true, but her wish to impress and please him with her musical progress spurred her on more than any other maestro might have done. Altogether, it was a happy mix of natural talent, youthful enthusiasm and the frisson of mutual regard. Kitty dared to believe that Henry Adams rather enjoyed her company, too, and not only as a music master.

Alas, he was not a man of fortune, not even a small fortune, and Kitty was no heiress who could rescue him from impecunity. Had Mrs Bennet the ability to read her daughter's thoughts, it is hard to know whether she would be alarmed or enraptured at Kitty's practical view of his prospects and her increasing acceptance for the need, if not the desirability, of an advantageous match. With two of her sisters so very well married, it was perhaps entirely understandable that Miss Catherine Bennet would be looking beyond the previous, purely superficial, attractions of an officer in a red coat. Still thinking about the agreeable albeit poor Mr Adams, and the Philharmonic Society's concert, Kitty wandered over to the pianoforte and gave herself up to practising.

As it turned out, her next lesson was either too demanding or Kitty's patience was too short. In any event, she was hard put to restrain her annoyance over her own shortcomings. Luckily for both parties, Mr Adams had more experience in teaching young ladies how to overcome their frustrations with musical instruments than Kitty had in exercising forbearance. He had heard outbursts of despair before – much worse than Kitty's disheartened remonstrances to herself – and was able to weather such storms and calm the waters. In Kitty's case, the solution was really quite simple: he bade her sing the lively Scottish air she had learned a couple of days before, which proved not only an excellent way for her to vent her spleen but a chance to give her voice its range. The lesson ended to the satisfaction of both, even if Kitty was a little exhausted and in need of an hour's respite before she could attend to her appearance for dinner.

***

The following Monday, the Bingley party arrived at the Argyll Rooms at a fashionable hour and were quickly espied by Sir Edward. Bingley and he greeted each other warmly, indeed Sir Edward was openly pleased to see all four of them. His enthusiasm was always evident; Kitty liked this trait in him. He begged leave to present the two gentlemen by his side. 'My nephews, Mr Frederick Fanshawe and Mr William Fanshawe,' he declared them to be. 'Known this pair since they were boys. Rascals when they were younger. Rascals! Isn't that so?'

The Fanshawes made no comment to this jovial introduction and simply bowed. Kitty saw two gentlemen, of between twenty-five and twenty-eight years, each with fair complexions and fair hair, who dressed and carried themselves in a way that bespoke wealth and privilege. There the similarities between the brothers ended: the elder, Frederick Fanshawe, was very tall, sturdily built and – if this can be possible – almost too handsome, his nose aquiline like his uncle's and his hair worn just so. There was in his expression a slight hauteur and the knowledge that his looks commanded female attention. William, the younger brother, whose height and frame were not in any way lacking, *appeared* small in comparison with his sibling, and his features, though quite regular and pleasing, were not so haughty; he had an altogether more gentle mien. At any rate, the younger brother smiled a welcome; the elder merely nodded.

'Thought I'd get these two to the concert. This one,' Sir Edward indicated William Fanshawe as he spoke, 'does not need any persuading to hear music well performed but as for his brother! Eh, Freddie?'

'My uncle does me a disservice,' countered the elder Mr Fanshawe, with a slight smile to the Bingleys and Kitty. 'I am very happy to be here tonight.'

'As are we, as are we,' returned his uncle.

Miss Bingley began commenting on the evening's programme to the Fanshawe brothers and Sir Edward turned to Kitty.

'Very glad I am to see you again, Miss Bennet. You are well? Come along now, tell me what you have seen since you arrived in this wonderful capital of ours.'

'I hardly know where to begin!' said Kitty, but she found a place to start. 'We have been to the theatre, the one in Covent Garden; my brother Mr Bingley arranged a viewing of art – he is particularly fond of landscapes – at one of the private galleries near Pall Mall, and there is to be an exhibition of Joshua Reynolds' work soon! No doubt you know that?'

Sir Edward nodded, and Kitty rattled on. 'Just seeing all the places I had only heard of before, such as the Tower and Buckingham House. I have seen the Horse Guards parade, such a spectacle! There have been parties and concerts, and now this one!'

He smiled at her enthusiasm. 'Where else to be in the season but London, eh? It's noisy, can't be denied, and the air's a bit smoky, to be sure, but where else to be! I know some people prefer Bath. Those two nephews of mine,' he said, nodding towards the Fanshawes, now conversing with Bingley and Jane, 'they like a few weeks in Bath.'

'Indeed,' said Kitty, who knew nothing of Bath except its location. 'Where do they reside when they come to rest?'

'Up in Yorkshire, estate near Doncaster. Suits them very well, not too far from the races, you know.'

Kitty did not know but allowed herself to be told. Frederick, William and their sister Felicia were the children of Sir Edward's sister Alice and her husband, Sir Frederick Fanshawe. From the manner of his telling, Kitty observed that Sir Edward was fond of his sister and her offspring and made it his business to visit whenever possible – which, given the demands on his time did not seem at all onerous, was quite frequently, though he said he preferred to travel only in the summer months. He gave Kitty a fuller description of the house and the grounds than she thought to receive, but she listened and smiled attentively. She wanted him to talk more of the two Mr Fanshawes, but could not think of a subtle way to turn the conversation to them.

'We should go in, don't you think?' said Sir Edward, interrupting his own monologue. Kitty looked and saw there was a gentle movement towards the concert room itself; the ladies in their pastel silks and vibrant satins had, almost as if some silent signal had been given, begun to attach themselves to the arms of their menfolk and rustle en masse to their seats.

Mrs Bridgwater was coming towards them to claim her father's attention, bringing with her Jane and Bingley. Kitty noticed Miss Bingley was devoting her conversation to Frederick Fanshawe. He must have more than looks to recommend him then, she thought; Caroline was not one to waste her charms on paupers.

Mr Bingley handed Kitty a programme and a few moments later the audience was entranced by the overture from Mozart's *The Magic Flute*. Kitty didn't profess to understand the technicalities of the score, she just enjoyed the music, and although this took nearly all her attention, she could hardly be blamed for a covert glance around, just once or twice. A sideways look at Mr Bingley proved him to be content, quite engrossed; most of the patrons, she noted, were similarly absorbed. Nearly all! A glimpse at Frederick Fanshawe showed him to be more preoccupied with his coat buttons than with the music. She was wondering at this – and him – when he suddenly turned his head to find her observing him. Embarrassed, Kitty averted her gaze and paid proper respect to Mozart.

The audience, who had been largely and unusually silent during the performances, gave vent to their appreciation as the first part concluded. Many were very proud of themselves for simply being there; others were applauding the initiative as much as the music.

'I am surprised,' Kitty remarked to Jane, 'that a city such as London has had no proper symphony orchestra before this. We have talented musicians enough.'

'I agree with you entirely there, Miss Bennet,' said William Fanshawe, who had appeared at her side. 'And we have the cream of the crop here, I think? I was quite entranced throughout. Do you feel the same?'

'I do, sir,' said Kitty, pleased at his attentions and company. 'Which was your favourite piece? The overture? Perhaps the notturno?'

'I think the overture. Do you agree?'

'I do. It was remarkable. And do you like opera, sir?'

'Ah, you may have caught me there,' responded Mr Fanshawe, with an apologetic smile. 'I shall answer yes and no, if that is not too perverse. I appreciate the skill and presentation but I am not sure that I appreciate everything I should.'

'And I appreciate your frankness,' returned Kitty. 'For myself, I am no connoisseur. I have seen but one opera, though I would certainly like to see another.'

'I appreciate your candour. I shall await your opinion on the *Don Giovanni*. Ah, here comes my brother to give us his opinions.'

Frederick Fanshawe protested he had not come this way to inflict his opinions on anyone, but to glean those of others. 'Not so much *your* thoughts, sir,' he told his brother, affecting disdain.

'You will tell me more – or perhaps less – than I need to know. I would prefer to ask Miss Bennet for her views.'

'I think my view is representative of the audience in general,' said Kitty, 'which is that we are all delighted with what we have heard so far. What do you think, Mr Bingley? You are better able to appraise the performance than I.'

He, of course, was pleased with every aspect of the evening so far and happy to say so, leaving Kitty to silently assess and admire the two Fanshawes until it was time for the musicians to resume.

The second part of the concert held the audience rapt, just as the first had done, and it would have been strange indeed had no grateful applause been heard at its close. It was, thought Kitty, quite surprising how much noise three hundred people could make and interesting, too, that the concertgoers were not drawn from one strata of society. Certainly, she could see members of the aristocracy present, but they did not dominate; the audience was drawn by a love of music and art, indiscriminate of rank and position. It was refreshing.

As the crowd made its departure, Sir Edward emerged from the crush, the Fanshawes in tow. 'Excellent, was it not, Miss Bennet? Excellent! The society says its mission is to perform the best and display the genius of the masters. Can't argue with that, no?'

'I thought it superb, Sir Edward. We are indebted to you for obtaining our seats.'

'Not a bit of it, glad to have been of service. Capital, capital! Well, please excuse us,' he said, speaking for himself and his nephews. 'We are expected elsewhere. Good evening to you all.' Thus, the three gentlemen departed, leaving the Bingley party to assemble themselves and find a carriage to take them to Brook Street and Kitty to wonder if she might see the Fanshawe brothers again. Her mother would no doubt approve of them.

Chapter 17

Elizabeth was expected within the hour and Kitty found herself quite agitated. It was but four months since she had seen her but it seemed longer, and so much had happened in that time. She was nervous about meeting the Darcys and could not but suppose that Georgiana would be proud and aloof, a feminine and sharply fashionable version of her elder brother. Miss Bingley was forever lauding praise upon her and in Kitty's imagination she had become quite as cool and overbearing as both Caroline and her sister Louisa. Moreover, Miss Darcy had her own establishment in London, a fortune of thirty thousand pounds and was deemed beautiful; all in all, she was a terrifying prospect. Still, Kitty reasoned, Lizzy would be there; she could be relied upon to smooth awkward moments. She had checked her appearance, fiddled with her curls, adjusted her neckline and was now pacing the room, unable to stand still. Kitty took another deep breath, picked up her book – she and Jane had visited the lending library together only yesterday and found it well stocked – and went slowly downstairs.

In the drawing room, she found the usual arrangement: Jane and Bingley together on the sofa near the fire; Mr Hurst semi-somnambulant on a chaise; Caroline and Louisa deeply absorbed in each other's company and taking a turn around the room, the better to preserve and flaunt the new gowns both were wearing. Nonetheless, the atmosphere was relaxed and Kitty was welcomed, and bade sit by her sister. Both were alert to the sounds of passing carriages and when one finally clattered to a halt outside the house, all formalities were dispensed with and Jane and Kitty were at the door to greet the visitors before they had had a chance to alight.

'Lizzy! You look so very fine!' was Kitty's initial observation as Elizabeth was handed down from what was undoubtedly one of the newest and most elegant liveried carriages seen in a city that excelled in displays of wealth. Lizzy might have hushed her but too soon she was in Jane's embrace, followed by Kitty's, and then the three stood aside to allow the other passengers to alight.

With his customary polished reserve, Mr Darcy began the introductions: 'Mrs Bingley, Miss Bennet, I trust you are well. Allow me to present my sister, Miss Darcy.' The ladies curtsied, exchanged looks. Georgiana Darcy was as elegant and finely turned out as her status befitted, but the arrogance Kitty had been expecting was not apparent. She was tall, like her brother, and carried herself very erect, but her eyes, rather than scanning distant horizons in search of some misdemeanour or fault, were modestly downcast.

'I think,' laughed Lizzy, pulling her cloak closer and looking up at a leaden March sky, 'it would be a great deal better if our acquaintance was furthered inside. We have all been longing to see you, have we not Georgiana?'

Miss Darcy smiled her assent and allowed Jane to lead her into the house. As she followed, Kitty observed that her manner towards Jane was all warm politesse; there was, thus far, nothing in Georgiana's behaviour from carriage to drawing room to cause Kitty alarm.

Caroline Bingley, meanwhile, was having no trouble containing her unabated joy at the sight of Mrs Darcy, but the veneer of civility – indeed, friendly accord – that was now required of her if she wished to continue to court the society of Mr and Miss Darcy was a more difficult task. Having acquired Jane Bennet as a sister was bad enough, but she had the dark consolation that she had done all she could to prevent the match and, in charitable moments – were she to allow herself any – might have seen that her brother had made a worthy choice. Slowly and painfully, she had had to accept that particular mésalliance. The pretensions of Miss Elizabeth Bennet in getting and marrying Fitzwilliam Darcy were, however, hardly to be borne. To witness equal, or any felicity, in that union would be a trial, both of and for personality. Now that her own, completely fanciful, notion of becoming Mrs Darcy had been extinguished by a country nobody she fervently hoped that Darcy regretted his choice of bride. She was, of course, delighted to see Elizabeth.

'My dear Mrs Darcy, how charming you look!' she exclaimed, crossing the room to welcome her. 'And Mr Darcy, Miss Darcy, you are looking exceedingly well.'

'I thank you, madam,' replied Mr Darcy, answering for himself and his sister. 'And yourself? I hope we find you well?' Further civilities were stopped by Mr Bingley's jovial and heartfelt pleasure at seeing his old friend and his new wife. 'Darcy, it has been too long,' he declared, clapping a hand on his back. 'Mrs Darcy, you look enchanting as ever.' He kissed her hand, looking all mock permission to her husband, and drew the pair over to Jane. Kitty followed.

'It seems an age since we last met,' continued Miss Bingley to Georgiana, loath to allow her to escape. 'Mrs Hurst and I were saying only last week how we longed to see you, and now you are here! Mr Darcy is very wrong to confine you to Pemberley when there is so much to enjoy here in London.'

'I am sure you are right,' replied Georgiana. 'I must learn to love London society more.'

'Indeed you must, my dear Miss Darcy. We will go visiting together, if your diary permits. I should be most happy for your company.'

'You are too kind, Miss Bingley. My dear sister Elizabeth and I have been discussing concerts and other engagements. No doubt some of our interests will intersect. Elizabeth will know. She is become invaluable to me, I will ask her directly,' said Miss Darcy, looking around the room for her sister-in-law and quite unaware of the arrow she had just delivered to Caroline's heart. Elizabeth, in conversation with Kitty by the window, caught Georgiana's faintly imploring glance and supposed she really must avail herself of Miss Bingley's company. She took Kitty with her; it would be unfair to deprive her of Caroline's condescending eloquence.

'How do you like Pemberley, Mrs Darcy?' she began. 'Such a different house from your home. So much larger than Longbourn; you must find the change quite challenging.'

'Not at all, Miss Bingley. How kind of you to concern yourself on my account but please set yourself at ease. Pemberley is my home now, and I love it quite as much as Darcy and Georgiana. The more so because they are part of it.' Elizabeth directed her gaze squarely at Caroline, her gracious smile and open countenance masking any irritation – or even, just possibly, triumph – she may have felt towards her interrogator.

Kitty watched, inwardly proud and delighted. How in control Lizzy was!

'The grounds and the park are so exquisite,' continued Miss Bingley. 'Mrs Hurst and I have often ridden across them. Such delightful sojourns we have had at Pemberley. What a shame you do not like to ride, Mrs Darcy.'

'Oh, but Elizabeth does ride,' countered Georgiana, without thinking. 'She has had just a few lessons recently and my brother says he saw none who had learned so quickly. They often ride out together. I think they must have covered nearly every inch of the estate by now.' She turned to Mrs Darcy for confirmation of such a long speech.

'Not quite,' said she, 'but it is my intention to explore all of it. I do like to get out in the fresh air, Miss Bingley, as you will remember. And Georgiana is becoming quite my partner in crime in my outdoor pursuits.'

Caroline managed a tight smile. She did remember Elizabeth's predilection for brisk walks and fresh air, and how, quite unfathomably, Mr Darcy found this attractive in a woman rather than intolerably unrefined. 'And have your relations visited you in Derbyshire yet, Mrs Darcy?' she enquired sweetly, hoping to disarm Elizabeth. The former Miss Bennet may have elevated herself by marriage but her mother was an embarrassment and, so too, her younger sisters, especially the disgraced Lydia.

'As yet, only my aunt and uncle, Mr and Mrs Gardiner,' answered Elizabeth, unperturbed. 'Of course, Jane and your dear brother will visit in due course. And Mary and Kitty, too, no doubt.'

Kitty, hitherto content to be a silent witness to this tender exchange, nearly cried out in delighted surprise at the promise of an invitation. Instead, she took her cue from Elizabeth and merely smiled at Caroline and Georgiana, whilst wondering when, and for how long, she might go to Pemberley. She was saved deeper speculation on the subject, and Caroline prevented from further jealous inquiry of Elizabeth, by Mr Darcy's joining them. The change in Miss Bingley's demeanour – from sugar-coated animosity to a kind of cloying courtesy – was immediately apparent. Kitty watched with pleasure Mr Darcy's attentions to her sister and his quiet pride in her. As the conversation continued, she became aware that Miss Bingley would not dare risk any slight of her in his presence. She also saw a deeply disappointed woman; Lizzy seemed impervious to her cloaked hostility but Caroline Bingley made Kitty nervous, although she could not say precisely why. Georgiana Darcy, she noted, seemed content to let the discourse flow around her and was much less intimidating in real life than Kitty's imagination had conjured. Indeed, she was almost on the point of asking Miss Darcy her views of London when dinner was announced and Jane led the way into the dining room.

CHAPTER 18

The excitement – on the whole, benevolent – occasioned by Mrs Fitzwilliam Darcy's arrival at a drawing room in Brook Street was as naught compared to her entrance into the salons of London's elite. Long regarded as one of the most eligible bachelors in England, many a mother had urged her daughter to try to get Mr Darcy for herself, and those same mothers, along with their disappointed daughters, curious matrons and ever-inquisitive aunts, were eager to view this young woman of insignificant means and family who had ensnared his heart, and more importantly his fortune.

The new Mrs Darcy felt sufficiently equipped to deal with the anticipated coolness of London's high society, but she was under no illusion as to her novelty to that company. Darcy had remarked more than once that should anyone cut Elizabeth they would henceforth be cut by him and become persons of absolutely no importance to either of them. She, in turn, had assured him of her complete disinterest in making a mark in fashionable society. On his first morning in town, he had sat in his carriage as his footman presented the cards that announced the presence in London of Mr and Mrs Fitzwilliam Darcy to various friends and acquaintances. He had been gratified by the number of cards that had been returned the next day, presaging the customary 'wedding visit' at the Berkeley Square address.

In a very short space of time, Mrs Darcy had had the pleasure of meeting some of the finest and most fastidiously fashionable ladies that London could offer, and had borne their scrutiny with bemused tolerance, properly disguised as elegant attention.

Jane, when she visited shortly afterwards, was both pleased and amazed at the row of gilt-edged cards propped up along the mantelpiece in Elizabeth's drawing room. It was impossible and tiresome, Lizzy remarked, to remember the names and titles of all the ladies who had called during the past few days, effusive in their delight to count her among their set and invite Mr and Mrs Darcy to dinners and balls.

Darcy had maintained a straight countenance when Elizabeth had regaled him with her accounts of exacting courtesies and occasional foibles.

'I trust,' he said at last, 'there were one or two ladies whom you deem worthy of your notice. Do not forget, Eliza dearest, that I have known some of these families most of my life.'

'My love,' said she, taking his hand and smiling up at him. 'I am only teasing. Everyone has been most polite and courteous and it is all so very charming, as well as just a little amusing. Mrs Darcy will be delighted to accept the invitations of all who have been kind enough to proffer them, and if I were to enjoy some company more than others, would that be so very wrong?'

'You know I would not contradict you on that score,' her husband replied gravely, wondering where this would lead. 'Who has particularly gained your approval thus far, may I ask?'

'Why only the ladies of earls and baronets, my love,' said she archly and before he could protest pulled him down onto the sofa to discuss the invitations so far addressed to Mr and Mrs Fitzwilliam Darcy.

In consequence of this flurry of social interest, Elizabeth and Darcy were invited to the home of Lord and Lady Milton for dinner. Her ladyship was generally regarded as one of the most important hostesses in London, and inevitably Mrs Darcy would be under a much more comprehensive and concentrated scrutiny. First impressions, as Lizzy very well knew, were persuasive and on the day of that dinner she found herself thinking about what to wear and taking more care with her appearance than was her wont. Kitty, who had called in to visit (without first presenting a card), was keen to help and give advice, however superfluous that might be given Elizabeth's own fairly constant opinion of what was right or not in the matter of dress. They had debated the merits of a new primrose-yellow silk gown against an equally new and fashionable rose damask and the former had won the day, a decision helped considerably by Mr Darcy, who had returned from his London bank with a cache of his late mother's jewellery that he presented to his wife as her own. Among the treasures were some fine emeralds, set into a necklace and matching earrings. Kitty was in raptures.

'Lizzy! You must wear these!' she exclaimed, holding the earrings up to her ears and looking at herself from various angles in the glass. 'I never saw such splendid stones, look how they sparkle! They are perfect for your dark hair and that yellow silk. Try them now, I cannot wait.'

Elizabeth obliged and had to admit that large and glittering emeralds really should be a part of every woman's wardrobe; she did not understand how she had not known this before. Her thoughts went to the portrait of Lady Anne Darcy, her husband's mother, which was hanging in the gallery at Pemberley. She had worn these emeralds for that painting. 'And these,' demanded Kitty, putting into Lizzy's hair two small ivory combs, embedded with smaller emeralds and diamonds, and standing back to admire the effect. 'You will be Cinderella to Prince Charming. All eyes will be upon you,' said she, admiringly.

'Well I have no intention of turning into a shoeless beggar at midnight,' retorted Elizabeth, 'but you are playing a very good Fairy Godmother. Now help me rearrange these combs, I think they could be better positioned.'

'Oh, Lizzy! You have such beautiful jewels. I would die for one bracelet or one necklace such as these.' Kitty placed a ruby pendant around her neck and matching bracelets on her arm, and skipped around the room presenting her hand to imaginary suitors. 'Oh, my dear Lord Whoever-You-Are. I am much obliged to you but I cannot dance the next two with you, my card is quite full! Oh Sir Somebody, my deepest regrets.'

'I think you would enjoy this evening more than I,' said Elizabeth, smiling at Kitty's charades. 'I suppose there may be plenty who would like to see me fall, although I shall not give them that pleasure. Indeed, why should I?'

'Lizzy, they will have to be pleasant to you! You look beautiful, you have always been a ready wit, and you are sparkling within and without...'

'You sound just like Mr Darcy!' interrupted Elizabeth.

'... and you have a handsome and rich husband, who adores you! Don't think I haven't noticed. Really, Lizzy, you will be the belle of the ball. I insist!'

'Well this is a reversal, is it not?' said her sister, laughing. 'You giving me advice! There is hope for us all!' She was looking at Kitty's reflection in the mirror as she said it, and realised, for the first time, that her sister was becoming different – and much improved – now that she was deprived of Lydia's company and influence.

'But thank you, dear Kitty,' she continued, in a softer tone. 'I will endeavour to look and do exactly as you say. Now, give me back those bracelets and the necklace so I can stow them safely. I had best not lose them within an hour of receiving them!'

With a show of distress, Kitty handed them back. 'I must return to Brook Street. I will tell Jane how fine you look and we shall both expect you at the house in the morning so that you can tell us how great and grand your husband's circle is, and how well received you were.'

***

On her way back to the Bingleys' house, Kitty thought back on the afternoon and her time with Elizabeth and was buoyed by it. It was unusual to get Lizzy to herself, still less taken into her confidence about anything even slightly troubling. She had even seemed pleased with her advice! It brought back childhood memories of trying, usually unsuccessfully, to get her sister's attention and approval. She had not advertised to Elizabeth that her reason for leaving was another music lesson with Mr Adams. Surely she need not fear ridicule from her now? Kitty hoped not, but she was not entirely certain.

Walking into the drawing room at Brook Street, she was mildly surprised to encounter Miss Bingley and Miss Darcy, evidently just returned from a shopping expedition. A selection of scent bottles and combs were arrayed on a side table and Caroline, having but curtly acknowledged Kitty's presence, left Georgiana to elucidate. 'We have been to Floris in Jermyn Street. It is quite delightful.' She proffered a small phial to Kitty, declaring it to be her favourite.

Kitty, who had thus far merely passed by Floris but knew of its popularity, inhaled a light, citrusy cologne and passed it back to Georgiana with an approving nod. 'I should like to visit that shop,' said she. 'Have you also been to that other perfumers, Atkinsons? I hear he keeps a bear in his shop! Can you believe it? I am not sure I should like that at all, but I am curious!'

Georgiana had heard the same. 'Perhaps we should visit. I will try to persuade my brother to accompany us and save us from any wild animals.'

Feeling flattered at this lighthearted exchange, Kitty was about to sit down but remembered her appointment. 'We have a mutual acquaintance, Miss Darcy, in your former music master Mr Henry Adams. I am expecting him here at any moment.'

'I did not know you were fond of music, Miss Bennet. How lovely. Nor that you knew Mr Adams. I have been meaning to write to him to let him know I am in London. This is most fortuitous. Perhaps I could take up a few minutes of his time to enquire after him and his family. His sister Rose was married recently, I think. If you don't mind, of course.'

'My dear Georgiana, why should Miss Bennet mind? She will be only too pleased to accommodate you. She could learn much from you,' Miss Bingley informed them both.

Georgiana and Kitty looked at each other, both a little uncertain as to how to interpret and act upon this instruction. Georgiana was acutely aware of Caroline's abrupt manner and wondering how best to alleviate any distress, when Kitty spoke. 'Of course not, Miss Darcy. Pray let us go right away to the pianoforte. Miss Bingley, do excuse us.' So saying, she went to Georgiana and offered her arm, whereupon the pair quit the room.

It was done very swiftly and Miss Bingley was quite taken aback; this was not the result she had intended. How awfully tiresome this plague of Bennet sisters was.

CHAPTER 19

Brook Street, March 1813
An Observation of Modern Manners
by C. Bennet

'Mr and Mrs Byron Merriwether.'

A murmur of interest rippled through the assembled throng, representative of London's elite, as Isabella and Byron Merriwether descended the wide staircase. None could fault Mrs Merriwether's appearance (though there were some who tried). Her dress of yellow silk offset with silver grey was both fashionable and worn with aplomb. It showed her elegant form admirably.

'And those emeralds, did you see them?' asked a plump matron, rather too loudly, of her husband. 'She has only lately come by those, you can be quite certain.'

'Did you know Lady Anne, Mr Merriwether's dear mother? I could count her among my closest friends,' said another, whose acquaintance with that lady had stretched no further than a curtsy. 'I am sure she would have wished, nay demanded, a more appropriate match.'

The gentlemen, it has to be said, were rather more willing to approve of Mrs Merriwether than their womenfolk. They saw a vivacious and attractive young woman with shining dark hair and a fair countenance, who seemed to be enjoying her husband's company. Something which to many of the gentlemen present had become a distant memory!

'She looks an ordinary sort of girl... nothing exceptional,' opined another matron, fanning herself vigorously as if also to fan Mrs Merriwether back into obscurity. 'Quite plain, too. I hope Merriwether does not live to regret his decisions.'

'Oh, he probably will,' rejoined her companion. 'Her family is nothing, you know. You have heard about the youngest sister? Quite the trollop, I understand...'

Kitty stopped and crossed out the last sentence, shocked at herself. It wasn't right or fair of her to malign Lydia. London snobs, not her family, were fair game for her pen.

'Oh, look. There's Lord Weston. This will be interesting. What will Merriwether do if he cuts her. Oh, my dear, he has! He has!'

Byron Merriwether, who had neither the patience nor the inclination to suffer fools, had indeed noticed Lord Weston's insult to his wife, but rather than challenge him to a duel on the spot, favoured the gentler sport of dancing and so led his wife into the ballroom. She maintained an air of insouciance throughout.

Difficult, thought Kitty. What had Lizzy really felt when Lord Westhope/Weston had ignored her so rudely? Should Darcy fight a duel? No, Darcy/Merriwether would not do that, would he? Duelling was illegal, but it didn't stop them happening. Her imagination took her to a cold, misty morning, perhaps on Hampstead Heath. She had heard that was a scenic and romantic spot. Deserted at dawn, except for wronged gentlemen, their antagonists and their seconds. Her mother had quite convinced herself that Mr Bennet would fight a duel with Wickham after the infamous elopement from Brighton. Kitty could not imagine her father fighting anyone, let alone at some deserted spot at dawn! Anyway, if Merriwether was to fight a duel and kill the dastardly Lord Weston, he would have to flee overseas and where would that leave the fair Isabella?

'I will not live in England without you, sir. Wheresoever you go, I shall be with you.' Merriwether looked into his wife's dark eyes and knew he could never leave her.

No good, thought Kitty. I don't know enough about the continent to write their future there. She turned her thoughts back to her sister. Apart from the odious Lord Westhope, Mrs Darcy had been well received by many other guests, including of course the host and hostess. Lizzy had been introduced to a Lady Albany – by all accounts, quite the person whose acceptance was required if one was to breach the self-important, self-imposed defences of London's ton – and by refusing to act in the usual deferential manner had quite piqued her ladyship's interest, the result being an invitation to the famed Almack's Rooms the following week. Elizabeth had professed herself quite unmoved by this munificence, but Kitty thought she had detected a victorious gleam in her eyes and even Mr Darcy had acknowledged she had made a conquest of the dowager. Not even the aristocracy was assured admittance to Almack's, so great was the adjudicating power of its society patronesses.

As for Isabella and Byron, well they would have to wait and see what happened to them, Kitty decided, gathering her papers and pen together. She put her 'musings' as she now called them into her work bag with her sewing things, where they would be free from detection, and hurried downstairs in search of Jane, and breakfast.

'The rain has stopped at last,' her sister remarked to Kitty by way of greeting. 'I think we can expect Lizzy and Georgiana this morning.'

Kitty looked out of the window. Three days of rain had prevented all but the most necessary activities and she was keen to leave the house as well as looking forward to seeing Georgiana. Mr Darcy had been prevailed upon to escort them to Atkinsons, so there was the exotic promise of seeing a real bear, plus the novelty of London's smart shops, which, with their linens and laces, ribbons and bonnets, were a constant source of joy to Kitty. I feel like a caged bear myself, she thought, surveying the sky. If the weather held, though, they might even find themselves promenading in Hyde Park that afternoon.

As it turned out, some matter of business prevented Darcy from the delights of shopping, but the ladies found themselves quite brave enough to visit the various establishments, even those with wild animals, without his protection and more at liberty to indulge themselves in protracted discussions over their purchases. When they had exhausted themselves in and around Mayfair, Elizabeth proposed they travel on to Gracechurch Street.

'I want to choose new fabrics and papers for Pemberley and Aunt and Uncle Gardiner will know which are the best drapers and warehouses.' No one had any objection, so the journey was begun, with Kitty leading the questioning as to what Lizzy proposed and revealing a surprising depth of knowledge as to the latest furnishings, chinoiserie and Egyptian-influenced styles.

'Where do you come by this information?' Elizabeth asked her in astonishment.

'From *Ackermann's* magazine,' replied Kitty, feeling defensive yet at the same time sure of her ground. 'Mr Bingley always takes it.'

'I think it is as well we have Kitty with us. I am glad someone reads it,' said Jane, leaning back in her seat. 'I confess I have read nothing lately, not like this voracious bookworm.'

'You're reading again, Kitty? You liked to read as a child. This is excellent news. As to styles,' resumed Lizzy, 'I think I favour chinoiserie, at least for some of the bedrooms that have not been used for many years. I have no wish to change everything, but I can see that some parts of the house are in need of refurbishment and I have been charged with this task. Georgiana, you must guide me in this as well. We cannot have the new mistress of Pemberley seen to be lacking in taste and finesse.'

'That is not likely, Elizabeth,' murmured Georgiana, 'though I am happy to be of assistance if I can.'

'And when we have made every room in the house new again, I can turn my attention to the grounds. Perhaps Humphry Repton should be our man, there. What do you think?'

Georgiana, to whom this remark was addressed, was too surprised to reply. 'I do but jest,' Lizzy laughed. 'Mr Repton may be the most lauded landscape architect in England but we have no need of him. I would not change one single thing about the park and grounds. I have called Pemberley my home but a few months and already I long to be back there, especially now that spring is almost here. It was not our intention to be in London for the season, we are only here because some business of Fitzwilliam's called him here.'

'But you will stay till the end of the season?' asked Kitty.

'I think not. If this weather holds and all other things have been satisfactorily concluded, we will return in a fortnight. I would rather see the trees in blossom in Derbyshire than hear of the exploits of the ton, fascinating as those are to me.'

'Oh! Lizzy!' cried Jane. 'We live too far apart! But of course, I understand.'

Kitty, at a loss as to how anyone could prefer rural life to the pleasures of town, did not have the chance to air that opinion. They had arrived at the Gardiners.

Chapter 20

Despite Elizabeth's assertion that she was ready to forgo all London's attractions, there was no doubt that the presence of Mrs Darcy was welcome at a great many fashionable addresses. Honour had been served; Mr Darcy's choice had been vindicated; no duelling would be necessary. The couple's appearance at Almack's had firmly placed them among the elite, though they were possibly the two most ungrateful elites in all of London. Kitty thought it wonderful and took vicarious delight in all Lizzy's engagements.

It was a mild day for late March and, having spent an hour or two shopping near Piccadilly, Jane and Kitty had decided upon a stroll in Green Park to take advantage of the intermittent sunshine. They had walked as far as the reservoir, found an empty bench and were now watching a family of ducks on the water.

'Well, Kitty,' said Jane. 'We have been in London five weeks now. Has it been everything you thought it would be?'

'It has been the best adventure,' replied her sister. 'Of course, I did not know how it would be, but I find it so exciting to be in town, so close to the centre of everything. And it is such a surprise to find so many parks. I love this one and Kensington Gardens best – I cannot decide which is my favourite. And I love the concerts and the theatre and visiting the salons with you, Lizzy and Georgiana. I do not miss Longbourn at all!

'Although of course I miss Mama and Papa,' she added quickly.

'You are quite the *mondaine*!' laughed Jane. 'For myself, I find I grow a little weary of so many engagements. I think I am happier in the country. Do not be too disappointed in me!'

'Never!' cried Kitty, although feeling a little alarmed that this conversation may presage a return to Netherfield and an end to her present pleasures. 'I have learned so much since I was here; of manners and etiquette, and so much more. I have become better acquainted with my new brothers-in-law, as well! Although I think I know Mr Darcy no better now than I did when first we met.'

'He does present a rather taciturn and stern demeanour, I cannot deny it, but Darcy is a fine gentleman and he adores Lizzy. That much is plain. You will like him more when you know him better.'

'I do not know when that will be. I think he disapproves of me.'

Kitty fell silent for a few moments. 'I can see you and Lizzy have chosen well and that you are happy,' she said, eventually. 'However, I am at a loss to know how one decides on a husband. When I think of Wickham; how we were all so misled. How does one know? Yet Lydia seems happy. At least, she seems so when she writes.'

'I do not know how to answer that question, Kitty, except to say there has to be a little prudence mixed in the passion. Lydia let her desires override her sense and we can only hope that the passion remains to keep her happy in her married state. I would not advocate marrying without love – never! – but at the same time it is necessary to look to the future and to the character of the man with whom one pledges to remain for life. A sense of honour and what is right is very important, as well as a caring disposition – these are all essential. I feel exceedingly fortunate to be Mrs Bingley. I am sure in time you will find someone who can both make you happy and provide for you.'

'I wish that, too, of course, but I hope I will not become like Charlotte Lucas and have to marry out of desperation. No, do not deny it, Jane! That is what she did. Lizzy would not have Mr Collins, and for good reason! For as long as I can remember, it has always been known that you would marry well because you are beautiful and good – no, you cannot contradict me there, either! – everyone in our family and beyond would say so. Lizzy has married well also, but do you not think perhaps she has been lucky?'

'Lucky? In what way?'

'I only mean that Lizzy is always so sure about everything. She does not worry about others' opinions and yet everything still turns out all right. She would not have Mr Collins! – and of course she should not have had him – but she didn't hesitate. And now she is Mrs Darcy! There are plenty who would say that is lucky. But what I mean is that Lizzy is so confident – I wish I could be more like her – and because she is so assured, she is completely herself and people still admire her. She seems fearless. She has always seemed so. I should not say it is luck, it is her wit, and charm. It is her character.'

'Do you fear people do not like you, Kitty?' asked Jane, quietly.

'I am sure of it! For years I have been told I am one of the silliest girls imaginable by our own dear Papa. Vain, ignorant and idle. I am not as lovely as you, not as clever as Lizzy, not as lively as Lydia. Not as condescending as Mary' – Kitty allowed herself a smile – 'that is something, I suppose. But I do not want to be dismissed as ignorant and idle. And I do not think I am vain, really I do not!'

'No more do I, Kitty; be assured of that. Do not take so bleak a view about yourself. As I recall, our father thinks all the members of our sex ignorant and foolish. He speaks in jest, but his humour can wound. If you have a disposition such as Lizzy's, you take the barb, laugh and throw another back. You are right in thinking Lizzy lucky, but perhaps not in the way you are imagining. I think her lucky because she does not doubt her worth and that is, I think, what makes her appear fearless. She arms herself by observations of other people's foibles and in resolving not to be like them gains her own peculiar strength.'

'Lizzy *is* lucky,' insisted Kitty, 'in that she has found a man who loves her, is wealthy enough, and to whom she can give love in return.'

'In that, I too am lucky,' reminded Jane. 'Like me, Lizzy would have found it impossible to give herself to someone whom she could not love and respect. You must exercise patience. We five have little in the way of fortune so must rely on our good characters and sense, and you have as much sense – whatever Papa may say – as anyone, if you choose to use it. We do not cease to love Lydia because she has made what could be – what many will say is – a grievous error, but neither can we forget that her behaviour so nearly dragged all of us into her disgrace.

'Never since you have been with us in London have I had cause to worry for your manners. Your former wild exuberance seems to have been forgot, and I am glad of it.'

Kitty looked grateful and smiled at her sister. 'I must own my mistakes and be thankful that I have not transgressed too far. Truly, though, I do not know what to wish for, apart from a good marriage. I do not think I would be a good governess or a teacher, and as Mama is always at pains to point out, Longbourn cannot be my home for ever.'

Chapter 21

Her vocal range was increasing – Mr Adams had told her as much – and she knew it herself, just as she knew her fingers were becoming more dextrous in mastering more complicated pieces on the pianoforte. She could hardly believe her own progress. She had practised daily when she was quite young but that had stopped abruptly when she was seven or eight, when she had been ill. Perhaps, she thought, all that early work had stood her in good stead after all.

The house was quiet on this particular morning and as she practised the pieces Mr Adams had suggested, Kitty contemplated her future. Would she be like Caroline Bingley, living her life in the household of one of her siblings?

Kitty could not easily envisage Caroline Bingley married. Petty and cold-hearted before she lost the Mr Darcy she never had, Miss Bingley's present disappointment in that regard had only honed her malicious tendencies, and because Elizabeth Darcy was impervious to her – and Caroline was very well aware that casting any aspersions, however slight, about Mr Darcy's choice of wife would not be wise – Kitty had become a convenient target for her sustained antipathy. This was irksome rather than worrying, and Kitty had resolved that Miss Bingley's thinly veiled insults would not unsettle her; in fact, it had become a matter of personal pride that she would not stoop to her level nor be affected by her asides. Instead, she concentrated on her vision of the Miss Bingley of the future, still unmarried, still disappointed and still stewing in spite and unhappiness. This, Kitty reflected, might be something of a trial for Jane, if Miss Bingley was living at Netherfield. Horrid thought! Playing the wrong notes on the pianoforte jarred her out of that particular reverie, and she turned back the pages in order to start again.

I am not yet twenty, thought Kitty. My situation is far from desperate – but it will be but two or, at the most, four years before I will be regarded as leftover Christmas cake. I have no fortune but, thanks to Jane's and Lizzy's marriages, I have some connections now and London does offer promise. She thought about the two Mr Fanshawes. They had been attentive to her and she was sure they were of good character and eligible, but she had not spoken above a dozen sentences to either. Hardly enough to form a proper opinion. She had seen Sir Edward since the concert at a dinner given by the Hursts, but his nephews had not been there. She thought that William Fanshawe was preferable to his brother, but this was an impression rather than a considered judgement. Furthermore, who knew what attachments the brothers may already have?

There was Henry Adams, of course, but it would not do to think of him, much as she liked to. She suspected that he was looking for a rich young lady, and he would probably find one for he was handsome enough and intelligent.

As to Sir Edward, Kitty owned that she was really very fond of him. Chivalrous and somewhat old-fashioned, he treated her like a lady, and she never felt belittled by him. On the contrary, he deferred to her opinions, was interested in what she had to say and engaged her in discussions that she found fascinating. He was well travelled and she loved to hear of his adventures on his Grand Tour and descriptions of places in Italy and France (it had been some time since he had undertaken that tour but he spoke of it as if it were yesterday). These chimed with descriptions of the romantic (and sometimes forbidding) places she had read about in novels. In literature too he was a fine conversationalist; he appeared to have read everything she had or wanted to read, and he had introduced her to new works and parodies, which she was finding interesting and amusing by turn. Flattered as she was by his attentions, Kitty did not want to question Sir Edward's particularity to her. He was of the same age as her father and she chose to think of him paternalistically. Nothing in his manner or words had ever suggested théirs was anything but a social friendship, but Kitty had seen that they had been observed with more than passing interest and it made her uneasy. Why did he seek out her company? Surely he could not be viewing her as a wife?

She stopped playing. Lady Catherine Quincy! How very grand that sounded. That would make people see her differently. Mama would certainly approve. Miss Bingley would be mortified, which would be a fine thing. Papa, Jane and Lizzy would be amazed? Or appalled? And Sir Edward's daughter, Amelia…? Lord, was she the same age as Jane? Kitty checked her imagination… this was ridiculous, she really should not be entertaining such wild thoughts, thoughts that would be better used for characters in a novel, a comedic one at that. After all, what would Sir Edward want with a poor creature like herself? She did like him though; was that enough? Charlotte Lucas had less to like about Mr Collins and she had accepted his proposal. Enough! Charlotte was twenty-seven and, Kitty told herself sternly, there has been no hint of intimacy, no declaration, still less a proposal – and if there were, she would be horrified! Really, Kitty! she chastised herself. How foolish you are to be even thinking such things. You are becoming like Lydia again.

She resumed playing and made herself concentrate on the notes and the pace. Georgiana was expected at any moment and they had agreed to practise a duet together.

CHAPTER 22

The infectiously happy sounds of laughter reached Jane before she reached the drawing room door and she was smiling – although she did not know the reason – before she opened it and found Georgiana and Kitty beside themselves with mirth, barely able to stand.

'Whatever is going on? What are you two doing?' she enquired, watching their faces as she crossed the room to claim her usual place near the fire.

'It's nothing,' said Kitty, and collapsed again into helpless giggles.

'Georgiana?'

'Really, Jane, it is nothing,' began Georgiana, before she too was rendered speechless, falling onto Kitty's shoulder and making every effort – with no success – to suppress her own laughter.

'What is it?' Jane repeated, her expression amused as she waited for the pair to regain their composure. 'Clearly something most entertaining.'

Her remarks merely set Kitty and Georgiana into fresh spasms of laughter and it was a few minutes before they were calm enough to speak.

'We were just remembering something that happened at the dance last night,' said Kitty, wiping her eyes with a fragment of lace. 'It really isn't that funny…'

'So I perceive,' observed Jane, much bemused. 'Is there more to this tale?'

'No, not really. It's just that people can be so very ridiculous…'

'And Kitty is so fine at impersonating their droll ways,' added Georgiana. 'We were playing at charades. In truth, she is too clever.'

'Why, thank you my dear, dear Miss Darcy,' said Kitty, in a very deep voice, affecting a haughty expression and closing one eye. 'What a remarkably fine lady you have become.'

At this, both young women teetered on the point of collapse once more, and with something of a supreme effort, collected themselves and sat on the sofa opposite Jane, who found the situation almost as funny as they did.

'Kitty, I have not laughed so much for such a long time,' declared Georgiana. 'Indeed, I do not know when I have laughed so much. I cannot really say what is so very amusing, but my sides ache and it is all very fine!'

Kitty fanned herself by way of reply, and a short silence ensued. Jane announced she would ring for tea, over which she would very much like an account of the evening that had caused so much mirth.

That Catherine Bennet and Georgiana Darcy might, in the space of a very short time, become firm friends and confidantes had not been foreseen by either of their families, an appalling lack of foresight really, given their age, general diffidence and the fact that each had grown up in the shadow of a more forceful sibling, or two.

Georgiana, who had had little female company of her own age – the friendships she had formed while at school had been mainly shallow affairs, hampered by her shyness, usually mistaken for arrogance – was more than ready to like Elizabeth's sisters. Kitty likewise had been lonely and was delighted to find a friend to fill the empty space created by Lydia's physical and emotional removal. Miss Bennet had soon become Catherine, then Kitty; Miss Darcy had become Georgiana; and, until very recently, no one had really noticed what should have been an expectation.

Jane saw and felt the happiness of their bond. The three of them had settled into a more restrained discussion of the day's events – and the unintended absurdities of social interaction – when Mr Bingley and Mr Darcy entered the drawing room, and the conversation took a different turn.

Only that morning Darcy had been told of a property in Nottinghamshire, a substantial house with ample grounds, much prized by its original owner who had bequeathed it to an ungrateful relation, so ungrateful indeed that he now wished it sold. Although there were no immediate plans to vacate Netherfield, Bingley had every intention of fulfilling his late father's wish for him to acquire an estate of his own one day. Where or what or when that should be had caused him little concern hitherto, much to the chagrin of his youngest sister, but his responsibilities as a married man had sharpened his focus of late. Whether it would have been thus honed without the aid and advice of his friend Darcy is a matter of speculation, but it would not be the first nor the last time Charles Bingley deferred to the former's opinions.

'It is called Dapplewick Hall, my dear,' he informed Jane. 'Quite a new place, not twenty-five years old, and classically proportioned. There is a cantilevered staircase and the drawing room ceiling is in the Adam style, according to Darcy here. The grounds are quite extensive and should offer good shooting. I think I must have passed close by the nearest village when I was in Nottinghamshire as a boy, though I cannot recollect ever seeing it. Darcy says it is only thirty miles, perhaps less, from Pemberley, which I am sure would speak in its favour?'

'Indeed, you are quite right, Mr Bingley. That would suit me very well,' said Jane, then teased, 'but what of your plans to replicate Pemberley?'

'Oh, you know I just said that to please Caroline and ruffle Darcy,' returned he. 'Besides there can be only one Pemberley and only one master of it! Is that not so, Darcy?'

The master of Pemberley raised an eyebrow in acknowledgement.

'How came you to know of the house, Fitzwilliam?' asked Jane.

'My steward is in town. He told me that he had heard the new owner wishes to dispose of it. I have long thought it a most well-positioned house, close to a very old church and not far from a pretty little village. I believe the present house stands on the site of a much older one, perhaps an old castle, but my information is uncertain on the latter point.'

'Well, if you approve, I shall make further enquiries,' said Mr Bingley addressing his wife, who was inclined to approve in principle. She resolved to speak privately about it with Elizabeth, who may have further intelligence. It would be a very pleasant thing to live within such close proximity to the Darcys.

Kitty, meanwhile, was quietly alarmed. She hoped that this Dapplewick Hall, with all its apparent attractions, would be found entirely unsuitable. She preferred to think of the Bingleys remaining at Netherfield.

CHAPTER 23

'Is Jane not coming down to breakfast?' Kitty asked Mr Bingley the next day.

'No, not this morning,' said he, from behind his newspaper. 'Something has been sent up to her.'

'Is she unwell? Should I go and see her?'

'She says she is just tired. There is no need for concern.'

Jane had been tired a lot of late, and Kitty believed she knew the reason why. She kept her thoughts to herself during breakfast, not wishing to air them in front of Caroline, but as soon as the opportunity presented itself she found Jane.

'You are tired?' she said, looking at her intently.

'Yes,' agreed Jane, unable to stop smiling. 'I may be yet more tired in the months to come. But I am very pleased to be so very tired. You have guessed why, I think?'

Kitty's response was a cry of delight. She threw her arms around Jane and declared she was overjoyed at the prospect of becoming an aunt.

'Who knows? Apart from you and Mr Bingley, of course!'

'Just you and Lizzy at present. I must write to Mama and of course we shall have to tell Caroline.'

'I am so very happy!' added Jane, somewhat superfluously.

The news of her impending motherhood was soon shared farther. Miss Bingley also declared her delight, although her effusions were a less reliable indicator of her joy. It had occurred to Kitty that Jane's condition would prevent any move to

Nottinghamshire in the near future and this only added to her happiness. Mr Bingley was all admiring concern for his wife and took every opportunity to see to her comfort, treating her as though she had suddenly become glass. It was through him that Kitty discovered that he and Jane were planning their return to Hertfordshire.

'I shall miss the theatres and the concerts of course, but although the weather here has improved, the clean air of Netherfield will suit Jane much better,' he declared at dinner. 'We think to return within the week after next.'

It was not at all what Kitty wanted to hear. She did not miss Longbourn, she felt quite at home in London. She had become accustomed to seeing Georgiana every day, Lizzy and Mr Darcy almost as often. To be returned to Longbourn, the pleasure of her parents' and sister's company and the monotony of country life in exchange for the society and interest of London was sobering.

'I am sorry we shall have to cut short our stay,' said Jane, reading Kitty's thoughts. 'I hope you are not so very disappointed. Let us think, shall we, about what we will do here in the days remaining?'

Kitty gathered her resources and managed a convincing smile. 'I cannot think of a better reason for your leaving, Jane. I would not want you detained in London on my account, not now. Besides, I shall make a complete nuisance of myself at Netherfield, fussing about you as much as I can.'

'Ha! I think you will have sturdy competition on that count from our Mama once she hears the happy news but I will be glad of your company. In fact, I shall rely upon it.'

Jane turned to Miss Bingley. 'Will you return with us, Caroline?'

'Sadly, I cannot,' said she, bestowing a most sorrowful smile upon her dear sister. 'I have engagements I must keep with Mr and Mrs Hurst and others of their set, although I should so much like to be of assistance to you.' She shared her pained countenance with her brother and Kitty, before adding: 'I shall call on Louisa this morning and make arrangements to stay with them. May I tell them the reason for my move?'

'Please do,' said a proud Mr Bingley, 'and say we shall all dine together before we go.'

Had she had time before preparing for that evening's theatre engagement with Georgiana and the Darcys, Kitty would have tried to make sense of her thoughts by writing them down. As it was, they tumbled around in her head and she wondered as she waited for the carriage at how quickly circumstances changed. Elizabeth had spoken of returning to Derbyshire within a week or so, but Kitty had not imagined the Bingleys and she would be leaving London before them.

As soon as she could speak privately with Georgiana, she informed her of the day's events. As she had anticipated, her friend was equally loath to be separated so soon.

'It is nearing the end of the season, though,' Georgiana ventured, by way of compensation.

'It is, but I wish we could stay longer nonetheless.'

'And I too. You must promise to write. I trust you are a good correspondent?'

'When I wish to be,' replied Kitty, remembering letters unwritten. 'To you, yes!'

'That much is settled, then. And you will be an aunt!'

'Yes, I shall, and I am happy at that thought at least. It will be something to divert me. I fear there will be little to write about otherwise.'

'Well, we can tell each other all our little nothings,' replied Georgiana, 'and make plans for your coming to Derbyshire in the summer.'

'Really!' cried Kitty. 'In the summer?'

'Of course,' replied Georgiana, to whom it seemed the most obvious invitation in the world. 'Look, my brother and Elizabeth are waving at us. It must be time to take our seats.'

They followed the movement of people up the stairs and found their box.

'At least we are seeing a comedy,' said Georgiana. 'A tragedy would be too hard to bear in these circumstances.'

Kitty agreed, but the invitation to Pemberley had brought her up from the brink of despair; it quite influenced her enjoyment of the play.

When the performance had finished Mr and Mrs Darcy exchanged pleasantries with a few of the other theatregoers, satisfying the needs of convention, but no one was anxious for company outside their own party. At supper afterwards, Georgiana and Kitty spent some time devising plans for their remaining week together. High on their list of priorities were various fashionable shops and establishments in Mayfair and Oxford Street, purveyors of goods and haberdashery best purchased in the capital for display in the country; a long-anticipated visit to the Royal Academy; correspondence to such acquaintance as deserved same, though Kitty could think of no one who need be informed – she would see Henry Adams at Brook Street within a couple of days, the rest would be taken care of in morning calls.

'Let us all go to the Academy together?' said Elizabeth. 'We have been meaning to visit since we first arrived. What think you, Fitzwilliam my dear?'

'In that plan, I am most happy to comply. I hear it is a fine exhibition.'

The hour being late and there being little else to discuss, the carriage was summoned and Kitty soon found herself ushered into Brook Street, with promises made by her sister and Georgiana that they would meet on the morrow. As she prepared for sleep, fragments of the day flitted across her mind. Now that the initial shock about leaving London had subsided, her thoughts had become more rational, more mature: Jane was to have a child; she was to return to Longbourn; the Darcys were returning to Derbyshire; she was invited to Pemberley in the summer. Yes, it would be hard to leave London but she was very happy for Jane and she knew she would see Georgiana and Lizzy again, and quite soon. This is the end of my music lessons, she thought, at the same time resolving to continue playing when she returned home. She felt confident enough now to withstand sarcasm and denigration from the rest of her family upon that score. She knew she had changed, become more resilient and confident. Her father may still think her silly but she would make him see that he was wrong. She had learned that other people valued her company.

Her thoughts turned to Henry Adams; she could not imagine when or if she might see him once she had left for Longbourn, and that gave her pause but, with a little toss of her head, she attempted to dismiss his image from her mind. She found him most agreeable company but he had not shown her any particular regard, so there was little point in considering him as anything other than a friend. Rather like Sir Edward, she thought. There were the Fanshawes, too. She would not see them again either, which might be more of a loss. Her mother would be most dissatisfied to discover that she had made no conquests in London. She blew out the candle, lay down and gave in to sleep.

Chapter 24

When Kitty awoke it was to the sound of rain pattering steadily against the window and she pulled aside the heavy brocade curtain to see a sky that was grey and threatening. The first day of April and a day to match my mood, she thought, her head full of what had happened yesterday. Pulling a shawl tight around her, she sat down at the little table in her room. There was light enough to enable her to write and Kitty wanted to record her memories before she left London. It was as if leaving without tangible evidence of her stay would render the whole experience a dream; she would be back at Longbourn unable to believe it had happened at all – and such a lot had happened.

I am enchanted with London and all that I have seen here. I have felt at times an outsider, an invisible person in the salons and theatres and concert halls, just observing such fashionable ladies, such sateens and colours, such feathers and headdresses. And the proud gentlemen – of all shapes and sizes, and not always so fashionable – especially the rotund Sir Merrick at Lady Bracken's, such a very short man in stature but so very stout, his breeches so tight and buttons almost popping.

Such a difference from our Meryton Assemblies; London manners, too, so very different from ours in the country. Would I want to live here for ever? I think only if Jane or Lizzy were here; it would be so daunting to make one's own way in this society. So many new rules of etiquette to learn! Who knows whom, and who likes and does not like whom, who hates whom!

Jane and Charles have been so welcoming; I shall never forget their kindness and for showing me so much that is new and exciting. I love Jane more than ever; she is so sweet and loving. She will be a wonderful mother. They are so suited, both so gentle. Charles has been excessively kind to me as well. Who would have known he was so passionate about music? He has been so encouraging; even playing a duet with me! At least they will be close by at Netherfield. Already I long for concerts, and theatres too!

So many pleasure gardens in London, but Kensington Gardens is my favourite, for the Serpentine. And Hyde Park – what a spectacle that is with everyone parading and preening in their finest attire. Mama will be so pleased to hear of the people, the lords and the ladies I have seen. I have never asked her whether she likes London or not.

And I have seen a bear! A poor forlorn creature tethered in Atkinsons, not so fearsome as I had anticipated although I did not want to go close, and I have no desire at all now to see the Royal Menagerie, but I am glad to have seen the Tower and St Paul's and Westminster Hall and the Queen's Palace, so many places. Lord, how small home will seem, but I must be resolute and know that I will escape in the summer.

How happy Lizzy is with Mr Darcy; she is Lizzy still but even brighter and sharper. I shall be sad to see her go back to Pemberley as well. How fortunate for me that her visit was made early or we might have missed each other and I would never have met Georgiana. I hardly know Mr Darcy any better though; I am sure he disapproves of me although Georgiana says this is all my imagination. Dearest Georgiana. I am not sure which or whom I shall miss the most: London or Georgiana. To think: I thought she would be fearfully proud but she is become my best friend, she is like a sister to me. I should not think it, I know, but I feel closer to Georgiana than to Lydia now that she is gone away. I do not think Lydia thinks of me any more, which was hard at first but now I think I can understand. She is too busy in her new married life and will be surrounded by officers, all of whom she will want to impress.

I think Georgiana and I comprehend each other well. How strange that she and Lydia are of the same age but how different have been their lives and how different their characters; she would do nothing to presage a scandal, of that I am sure.

I should write to Lydia. There is much I can tell her now. I wonder what news she will have for me. Perhaps she will soon be in the same condition as Jane? Lydia as a mother, though, that I cannot imagine – it is indeed a wondrous thought.

Kitty stopped writing. She could hear sounds that meant breakfast would soon be on the table and she was not yet dressed. She put away her papers and made herself ready.

Breakfast at Brook Street was always a relaxed affair and was today even more so – given the wind and the rain outside, neither Bingley nor Jane was in a hurry to go anywhere. Kitty gave them a fine account of the play the previous evening, and also raised the subject of seeing the exhibition at the Royal Academy with the Darcys (a plan that was readily agreed to), but forbore to mention the tentative invitation to Pemberley in Miss Bingley's presence. Fortunately, that lady wasted no time in commandeering the carriage in order to call on the Hursts, and took her brother with her, leaving Jane and Kitty at leisure.

'That will be another adventure for you,' said Jane, pleased. 'I had thought I would see Pemberley this summer but now you will see it before me. I really must write to Mama this morning to tell her we will be at Netherfield soon. What trouble I shall be in if Aunt Phillips sees the servants arriving in advance of us! I have not mentioned my condition yet; she would be chiding me for being in London if she knew.'

'Or calling for Papa to come here directly and bring you home! You will be responsible for quieting her nerves! Well, at least I hope so. What is it Papa says? A "return to querulous calm"? Well, I shall write to Lydia then, and perhaps she will return the favour.'

Both settled into the drawing room and began their correspondence, straightforward for Jane and a little more complicated for Kitty, who was determined not to write too long a letter and was therefore deliberating on what to leave out and what would impress most. It was odd to be writing to Lydia more out of duty when once they had chatted about everything and everybody without giving it a second thought. There was no doubt her perspective on Lydia had shifted. Jane's revelation about the circumstances of her wedding almost made her feel sorry for her, but it was difficult to feel too sorry for Lydia, especially as she seemed perfectly happy being Mrs Wickham. I am the one who has changed, thought Kitty. I am the one who now sees more and wants more than to be married to just anyone! Is this a good or a bad thing though? There are things I cannot change! They were hard questions to answer, so she satisfied herself with giving her sister, among other things, a brief account of the play and of her invitation to Pemberley that summer.

She had just finished the letter and sealed it when the sounds of a carriage coming to a stop outside brought her to the window and, peering discreetly, she ascertained it to be carrying the Darcy livery. Moments later Georgiana was shown into the room looking almost agitated. She allowed herself to be greeted affectionately by Jane and Kitty, both of whom were about to enquire whether something was wrong when Georgiana spoke: 'Forgive me for arriving at this hour but I could not wait a moment longer. Kitty,

I have spoken with my brother and Lizzy and we would all be most obliged if you would do us the honour of accompanying us to Derbyshire next week.'

Her request made, she stopped and caught her breath, looking at Kitty as if there might possibly be a negative response. She was sorry, she said, that the journey would be direct, that they would not be making diversions to Oxford or other places of interest. Kitty was all astonishment, but of the happiest kind, and she found she had to sit down. What cared she for Oxford or anywhere else? The matter was settled within an instant: with her father's approval – and she doubted not that it would be forthcoming. She would write immediately! – Kitty would be travelling north in just a few days and all her anxieties about leaving London, until that moment the most alluring place on earth, simply disappeared.

CHAPTER 25

Happily ensconced in the Royal Academy Exhibition Room, Kitty was studying one of Thomas Lawrence's portraits so intently that she did not at first hear the voice at her elbow. Eventually she turned to find herself looking at a familiar face. 'Sir Edward,' she smiled. 'How very pleasant to find you here. Oh, and Mr Fanshawe, as well.' Taken by surprise by the sight of both Sir Edward and his nephew Frederick, Kitty was momentarily disconcerted. She had not expected to meet either again so soon. 'How do you do?' she said, collecting herself. 'Please allow me to introduce Miss Darcy.'

The two gentlemen bowed. 'A pleasure indeed, Miss Darcy,' said Sir Edward. 'There are a great many people here today, are there not? Driven inside by the weather no doubt, what?'

'Or perhaps to see these wonderful portraits, sir,' said Kitty. 'The colours are so rich and the faces positively vibrant. Miss Darcy and I have been trying to decide which we prefer but have not reached a conclusion as yet.'

'You are here with Mr and Mrs Bingley?'

'Indeed we are. I believe you will find them in the next room.'

'Capital, capital,' declared Sir Edward. 'Must find him, splendid fellow, but first, Miss Bennet, I should be pleased to know how you liked the Maria Edgeworth novel?'

'I liked it very well indeed, I was quite taken with the plot and the characters. You were right to recommend her. I thank you. I have been remiss in returning it to you but I shall remedy that at once. Miss Darcy and I will be leaving London tomorrow for Derbyshire.' Kitty felt a surge of happiness in speaking those words.

'That is grave news indeed, Miss Bennet,' returned the ever-gallant gentleman. 'The book I can do without but it is very remiss of you to deprive us of your company.' He turned to Frederick Fanshawe for affirmation.

'I agree, it is most disappointing news! Especially as we have only recently become acquainted. We shall have to make the most of your company today. What think you of the exhibition, Miss Darcy? My uncle and I have only just arrived. Perhaps you and Miss Bennet can direct us to the paintings we should see first?'

Slightly flustered by this appeal, Georgiana nevertheless managed to acquiesce and she and Kitty retraced their steps to show their companions the portraits they favoured.

'Your home is in Derbyshire?' enquired Mr Fanshawe of Georgiana as they stopped to consider a very large portrait of an aristocratic lady.

'That is so. I am in London with my brother and his wife.' She paused, hoping Kitty might further the conversation, but she and Sir Edward had stopped to consider another artwork. 'And you, Mr Fanshawe?' she continued. 'You are here for the season?'

'We were here earlier in the year, but for the past few weeks my brother and I have been visiting relations in Bath. We decided it would be entertaining to stay awhile in London on our journey home to Yorkshire but I am not sure when we will start that journey. There is always some good reason to postpone it! I wonder we have not seen you about town. We had the pleasure of meeting Miss Bennet and Mr and Mrs Bingley at the Philharmonic last month.'

'It preceded our arrival,' said Georgiana, as they moved along the gallery. 'I believe it was an excellent concert.'

'It was very good. No doubt you play and sing yourself? I am sure you do!'

Miss Darcy was forced to admit she liked to play the pianoforte and the harp. Kitty, still engaged by Sir Edward and following a short distance behind, could see that Georgiana was flattered by Frederick Fanshawe's attentions and making an effort to overcome her shyness. *She likes him*, Kitty thought, and why not? He did cut a fine and imposing figure. Across the room, she caught sight of Mr Darcy who, with Elizabeth, was contained in a knot of people who looked to be discussing the merits of one of the paintings. His attention to the group was not complete, however; his expression stern, he was keeping a close eye on the gentleman talking to his sister. Kitty thought this quite endearing – if only he didn't look so severe! – but her own attention was distracted by William Fanshawe, who had arrived to join Sir Edward and herself.

'I think you will find me a better critic of art than of music,' he said to Kitty, after he had expressed his pleasure at seeing her again. 'I have been looking at the portraits in the other room. Some very fine ones. I wish I could paint half so well.' Then, noticing his brother, he asked, 'Who is that lady with whom Frederick is speaking?'

'My friend and sister, Miss Georgiana Darcy,' said Kitty, quietly proud. 'Shall we join them?' It was but moments later, when the little group of five was studying a portrait of Queen Charlotte, that Darcy strolled over and more introductions were made. He is not come for conversation, thought Kitty; he is here to chaperone Georgiana. She was right, of course, but it was lightly done and soon the Bingleys and Elizabeth arrived to swell the party.

Sir Edward had quickly made the connection between the name of Darcy and the estate at Pemberley, which provided him with much conjecture as to which acquaintances they might have in common in that part of the world. It was an avenue Mr Darcy seemed loath to pursue – he was not a man to make his private life public – and the more Sir Edward talked the more Mr Darcy withdrew until the only comments that came freely from him concerned the artworks.

Under the watchful eye of her brother, Georgiana had a pleasant afternoon in the company of the elder Mr Fanshawe, and Kitty similarly enjoyed the conversation of his brother, William. When they left the Academy, Miss Bennet's and Miss Darcy's imminent departures were lamented by the gentlemen, and all looked forward to meeting again, whenever or wherever that might be.

Intrigued by Sir Edward's attentions to Kitty, Elizabeth detached her sister from the others in order to speak to her privately.

'Sir Edward takes quite an interest in you,' she remarked.

'I suppose he does,' said Kitty. 'He is interested in everything and everyone, I think.'

'What do you know of him?'

'Sir Edward? He is the father of an old school friend of Miss Bingley, whose name is now Mrs Bridgwater, and he has been a friend of the family for some time, I believe.'

'I hear he has a property in Yorkshire. There are a number of grand old families in Yorkshire but I have not heard the name Quincy.'

'Nor I,' said Kitty. 'He did tell me once that his sister lives near Doncaster, but as to his own estate I have no knowledge of that. I don't think he spends much time there, wherever it is.'

'I wonder he did not marry again,' Elizabeth observed, blandly.

Kitty knew she was being interrogated, but for once she was not concerned. She was quite happy to assuage Elizabeth's curiosity about Sir Edward. As far as she was concerned he was a perfectly pleasant, if rather old, gentleman.

'I have never thought about why that might be,' she said. 'It is not a topic that has ever been discussed! Although I do think he is lonely and London life diverts him. He had two sons, you know, and both died within a year. The eldest was in the Navy and perished in the West Indies, I do not know the particulars; the younger died soon after in a riding accident.

Amelia is his only surviving child. He is inordinately fond of his nephews.'

'They *appear* to be fine young gentlemen.'

'Yes, they do indeed, but I hardly know them. It is only the second time we have met. Neither can I tell you,' she added, *sotto voce*, 'their incomes or prospects!'

'I am sorry,' laughed Elizabeth. 'I have no wish to sound like Mama! I am interested, that is all.'

'Miss Bingley may know the family better. You could ask her,' suggested Kitty sweetly.

'I am not *that* interested,' retorted Elizabeth and, having caught up with the rest of their party, she was obliged to drop the conversation.

Chapter 26

Kitty was not quite ready when Henry Adams's arrival was announced for what would be their last meeting at Brook Street. Although neither had acknowledged anything other than a mutual interest in music, Kitty always took singular care about her appearance whenever she was to see him. Dissatisfaction with her hair was the cause of her trouble on this particular morning and she hurriedly adjusted it as she went downstairs. She had tried dismissing her attraction as a silly little infatuation and intended to forget all about him as soon as she had quit London.

He greeted her in his habitual warm and polite manner and Kitty took her place at the pianoforte.

'I trust, Miss Bennet, you have been practising as instructed,' he said with mock severity.

'Indeed sir, I would not dare do otherwise,' returned she, coquettishly.

'Very well. I am pleased to hear it. Shall we proceed?'

Proceed she did, and whether it was the desire to impress or the result of application – who could say? – Kitty's fingers fairly flew over the pianoforte and she forgot about everything except the sound of the sonata as it filled the room.

'Bravo!' cried Mr Adams when the last notes had reverberated into silence. 'Miss Bennet, you are without doubt one of my best pupils, and I have been teaching some for a much longer time. Your progress has been quite remarkable.'

Kitty felt herself blush at the compliment and hid her face behind the music sheets as she murmured her thanks. She was of course thrilled at the praise.

'I have been thinking what would be best for you to try next,' said Mr Adams, looking at his protegée, 'and I will have new scores within a few days. I think you are quite ready to move on to more complex pieces. I trust you agree?'

Kitty took a deep breath. 'With regret, I must tell you that I shall be leaving London in two days. I am to travel with the Darcys to Pemberley and spend some time there.'

Her instructor was quite shocked at this announcement – some may have described his countenance as crestfallen – but it was only for the briefest moment; he recovered himself very well.

'It was all arranged very quickly,' said Kitty by way of apology, but she had noticed his reaction and was wondering what it betokened. 'I confess that while I want very much to see Derbyshire, I am sad to be leaving London. There have been so many wonderful experiences here and I can assure you that your tuition has been very enlightening (Enlightening? she thought, what I am talking about? That is completely the wrong word. I am stupid)… and I am so pleased to have made your acquaintance.'

'And I, yours,' returned he. 'I had not thought of you leaving so soon. To Pemberley, you say?'

'Yes,' agreed Kitty. A heavy pause ensued as each wondered what to say next.

'I hear it is a grand estate.'

'I believe so.'

'You leave the day after tomorrow?'

'We do, yes.'

'Miss Bennet, please forgive the presumption,' began Mr Adams, looking earnest, 'but I…'

Kitty waited, a questioning expression on her face while the young man seemingly struggled for the right words to express himself.

'That is to say…' he resumed, and stopped again. 'I mean, that is to say, may I wish you a safe journey and I look forward to seeing you the next time you are in London.'

'I thank you,' said Kitty, wondering what else she could say. 'I have so enjoyed our lessons,' she ventured. 'You have been very patient and kind with me.'

'Not at all, not at all. I assure you it has been my pleasure.' He paused. 'You must continue playing. I would like to think you will.'

'I will; this I can promise.'

'Well, I wish you a safe journey,' Mr Adams reiterated, beginning to gather his portfolio and music sheets. 'Please pass on my good wishes to Mr and Mrs Darcy and Miss Darcy. I wish you a safe journey.'

'Thank you,' said Kitty as he left the room. She went to the window and waited for his appearance on the steps, then watched him as he walked down the street.

In need of conversation to distract her, Kitty went in search of Jane but when she found her she was asleep on the sofa, a hand laid protectively across her stomach. She crept out of the room as quietly as possible and went upstairs; she was only halfway through packing her trunks, ready for their removal to Berkeley Square that evening. The journey northwards would begin early in the morning. Elizabeth said it would be three days before they arrived at Pemberley as they intended to break the journey near Northampton on some business of Darcy's.

They would travel via Longbourn, of course, and Kitty wondered how her mother would behave towards Miss Darcy. She could tell that Elizabeth was torn between seeing their parents, or more specifically their father, and anticipating the embarrassment that Mrs Bennet would inevitably cause. To his credit (or perhaps because he was simply hoping for a decision that would not involve him), Darcy had remained largely silent when these plans were aired, although Kitty sensed he was bracing himself for the onslaught of Mrs Bennet's attention and – as far as that lady would feel able – affections. Kitty, uncharitable as it may be deemed, had no wish to stop at Longbourn; she feared her mother would find some excuse to prevent her from travelling to Derbyshire and on that her heart was set.

She set about packing the rest of her belongings, leaving only what would be needed for the journey and the morrow. Her journal and pens were among the things left out. She was now in the habit of writing in her journal each night before she went to bed.

CHAPTER 27

Jane had planned a quiet family dinner on the eve of their joint departures, the Bingleys to Netherfield, the Darcy party to Pemberley, and Miss Bingley to the Hursts, but Elizabeth arrived at Brook Street that morning with news that threatened such an arrangement.

An express had arrived for Darcy with alarming news. His steward had written to say that there had been a fire that had destroyed two of the tenants' cottages at Pemberley and damaged others. No one was hurt but there had been property losses and much consternation; foul play was suspected. Fortunately, there had been no threat to the main house, and the outhouses and the stables were all intact, but Darcy's presence would be necessary at his earliest convenience; the magistrate had been summoned and letters were being sent to London and to Derbyshire.

'But this is dreadful,' cried Jane. 'And the fire was thought to be deliberate? Why would anyone do such a thing?'

'I have no answers to that,' replied Elizabeth. 'Darcy is most concerned, of course, and not a little angry and wishes to be at Pemberley as soon as possible in order to put things right. His consolation is that no lives have been lost. He assures me that nothing of this nature has happened before, and he is at a loss to understand it.'

Kitty was as shocked as her sisters but also concerned this would necessitate a change of plan, one that would mean leaving her behind. She could not bring herself to ask the question. Jane spoke instead:

'But will you go straightaway, Lizzy? Must you depart this instant?'

'No, we will leave tomorrow morning, early as planned. I thought our departure would need to be brought forward but Darcy has sent word on ahead, and is gone to the city to see his solicitor. He will return this afternoon. But unfortunately, Kitty,' – Elizabeth turned to her younger sister, who in that instant anticipated her dreams crashing to the ground and was steeling herself – 'we will not stop in Hertfordshire to see Mama and Papa. It was to have been a brief visit, and I fear we will disappoint but hope we shall be forgiven. I have already written to Longbourn to explain.'

Kitty's face registered shock and confusion. 'It cannot be helped,' said Lizzy. 'If you would rather delay your visit, and return with Jane, then…'

'No, no. I am just upset by all these events,' replied Kitty, quickly regaining her composure. 'My trunk is nearly packed. It can be sent to Berkeley Square as soon as you like so that all is ready at first light. I can finish it now, if that suits you better?'

'There is time yet,' Elizabeth assured her, and turning to Jane: 'Our dinner can go ahead as planned. Darcy sends his apologies in case he is delayed, but there is no need to change our arrangements.'

In the event, Mr Darcy was returned in time for dinner, and did his best to hide his preoccupation with events at Pemberley, reasoning that all that could be done thus far had been done. The assembled party asked their questions, and assurances were given to the best of his ability. Darcy seemed determined not to let the matter monopolise the conversation and, despite the underlying distress, a convivial atmosphere enveloped those seated around the table. In addition to Mr and Mrs Bingley, his two sisters and brother-in-law, Mr and Mrs Darcy, Kitty and Georgiana, were Mr and Mrs Gardiner – whose company Miss Bingley and Mrs Hurst were obliged to bear as best they could. As the Gardiners' manners far exceeded their own, the Bingley sisters were the only ones to feel the degradation of their situation. Moreover, Miss Bingley had the pain of seeing Mr Darcy behaving to Mr Gardiner as if he were his equal. It was quite taxing for her. Kitty watched it all with concealed amusement.

After dinner, the ladies withdrew and the tea things had only just been brought in when the footman followed, bringing with him two letters just then delivered.

'They are from Longbourn,' announced Jane.

'Two letters from home?' said Kitty. 'They cannot be in response to Lizzy's letter so soon. I hope all is well.'

'I should open them now,' said Jane, curious but not wishing to seem discourteous to her guests, none of whom showed any objection. Elizabeth stood behind her, the better to see what news there was and her sisters' expressions were such that Kitty cried out, 'What is it? What is the matter?'

The alarm in Kitty's voice drew the attention of Mrs Gardiner and Georgiana, who were chatting on the far side of the room.

Jane, quick to assure them that nothing was wrong, did not elucidate but instead quickly opened and perused the contents of the second letter, then turned to Lizzy, whose astonishment and surprise mirrored her own.

'What is it?' repeated Kitty. 'What do the letters say?'

'I will let them speak for themselves,' said Jane. 'My summation could not do them justice.' She handed them both to Kitty. The first, from Mrs Bennet, was as follows:

Longbourn 5 April

My dear girls,

We are all in confusion here! Mary is to be married! And he will take her off to India and we will never see her again! Oh, I do not know what to think. For Mary is happy, you see, and thinks naught of going away from Longbourn, and on a ship! Mr Bennet has given his permission and says there is nothing he can do.

But Jane, my dear, I cannot think straight on it. You cannot have known, of course. None of us did. Who would have thought it? Mary married! What think you about it? I am quite exhausted and the young man only came to the house yesterday. Mary had said nothing until then! Aunt Phillips tries to help but I do not know, really I do not. My poor nerves! It is wreaking havoc on my poor nerves.

The banns will be read on Sunday, and then it will all be done. And none of you here! It really is too bad. Mary says it would be appropriate for Mr Collins to marry them. Mr Collins, if you please! If he were not our cousin, I would have more to say on that matter!

Of course the Gregorys are a good family, and Timothy Gregory seems a pleasant enough young man – I say seems for I do not know him well – and his father will help him, he says, with a cottage near Meryton but what good is that if Mary is to be taken to India?

I must write now to Lizzy and Lydia. My dear Jane, when do you return to Netherfield?

Your loving mother

'Timothy Gregory!' was all Kitty could say. Like her sisters, she was almost speechless. She handed the letter to her aunt and turned to the other, which was from her father and dated the same day:

Longbourn 5 April

My dearest Jane and Kitty,

Life, as you see, continues outside the bustle of London where things of great import happen all the time, but I confess Mary's news has taken us all by surprise. Please do not allow yourselves to be too alarmed by your dear mother's letter, although what she writes is true.

Your sister is indeed engaged to be married – to Mr Timothy Gregory, brother of her friend Marianne – and seems perfectly content to be so. It is not often that one can remark that Mary appears happy, but I venture to say that she is and in this we can rejoice. Your mother informs me that Mary has been much in the company of Marianne Gregory of late, a situation that portended nothing strange as she has been without the company of her sisters, and it would appear that even Mrs Bennet had no thoughts of a possible romance.

The gentleman came to me yesterday to ask for my consent to part with her. He looks to be a fine, upright sort of fellow, although a little earnest, a quality which no doubt endears him to your sister, and was most assiduous in assuring me that he is in a position to offer Mary a comfortable home. Although not in possession of a grand fortune, he has sufficient means and expects, he says, to inherit a small sum on the demise of an elderly relation in due course.

Meryton, alas, may not hold him for long for Mr Gregory has a missionary bent and is much taken with the idea of spreading the word and saving the less fortunate in parts foreign – 'the heathen lands', as he fondly describes them. Some of his acquaintance at Oxford are already advanced in plans to travel to India or the South Seas, and have become ordained for this purpose. Our Mr Gregory has not yet taken orders but considers it likely he shall. Mary has taken up his calling as if it were her own and imagines for herself a life of good works on darker continents. Her zeal does not admit difficulties as to travel or health or heat, indeed any hardships whatsoever that may be encountered in pursuing a missionary life, and so it is left to your dear mother to worry herself about all such eventualities.

The banns will be read on Sunday, so Meryton and the congregation will have much to discuss, and I am confident your sister will be married within a month. As far as one can ever predict happiness in the married state, this match seems as likely to succeed as any other.

What interesting times we live in, my dears. You must acquaint me with your news from London for I own I have no more to add at this moment. I pray you share this letter with Lizzy if it arrives before her departure north.

Your affectionate father

The effect of such correspondence on the party can be imagined. The Bingley sisters and Georgiana, none of whom were well acquainted with Mary, received the news with equanimity tempered with mild surprise. Among the others, disbelief was the first reaction, followed by incredulity and then, in the case of Jane and Mrs Gardiner, congratulations and pleasure for Mary. Kitty was applied to for her knowledge of Timothy Gregory, and she told what she knew of him, which was really very little. Elizabeth shook her head and wondered how the match had come about. Kitty though, felt almost faint. Having barely recovered from the threat of losing her trip to Pemberley, this was another blow. I am the only unmarried daughter now, the only remaining Miss Bennet, she thought. India? Timothy Gregory! Really! What a sly thing Mary turned out to be!

CHAPTER 28

The news of Mary's betrothal did not alter the Darcys' travel plans and the journey to Pemberley was as swift as reasonable comfort would allow. Elizabeth had wondered if Darcy might ride on ahead, but he would not hear of it. Ever the gentleman, manners and caution forbade any idea of his wife and sister (and his sister-in-law) travelling unaccompanied. Therefore, the party set off at first light as arranged, and the early hour was not conducive to conversation. At each stage of the journey, Darcy sent a rider on ahead to the coaching inns to alert them of a need for fresh horses and, with necessary stops for refreshment, they were able to cover nearly sixty miles on the first day.

On that first stage of the journey, the countryside held few surprises for Kitty and it was with but the mildest pang she realised that they had passed within ten miles of Longbourn. Unsurprisingly, her thoughts returned again and again to Mary and her pending nuptials. She had, she now understood, assumed that Mary would never marry; that she would become a governess perhaps, or remain a companion to their parents in their dotage. Mary, with her self-righteous ways and strict mores, had never shared her feelings, so it had been easy to assume she had none. All my sisters, she thought, have secured futures for themselves and I am left behind. Mama will be concentrating all her efforts upon me now. Given her apprehensions on the subject, it was no small relief to Kitty to be in a coach travelling as far from home as she had ever been.

The weather was clement, which helped their progress, and towards the end of the second day, as they journeyed through the Midlands, Kitty noticed cotton mills and factories in the middle distance. None of her companions acknowledged this change in the rural landscape so she kept quiet, resolving to ask Lizzy or Georgiana about it in private. Elizabeth and Darcy spent most of the journey in companionable silence and Kitty was glad of Georgiana's conversation about music and books and places that they passed on the road and, of course, her plans for the time they would spend together at Pemberley.

She listened and contributed little, acutely aware of saying the wrong thing in front of her stony-faced brother-in-law. Mr Darcy, for his part, did not mean to be forbidding but his face, in repose, had a serious aspect and his concern for his tenants and property had lent his mien a sterner aspect than usual. Only when the party stopped at the inn for the night did Kitty begin to relax and feel excited at the prospect of seeing Pemberley on the morrow.

Rolling hills and uplands became the norm as they continued into Derbyshire, the scenery becoming more rugged and imposing as they journeyed closer to the Peak District. Kitty took it all in, tired but excited to see their final destination. Her worries about being the only remaining Miss Bennet were dissipating in anticipation of a fresh adventure and new places to explore. What she would find she didn't know, but she and Georgiana had chatted quite late into the evening the previous day and Kitty's optimism was fully restored. To match her mood, the sun had obligingly appeared in a light blue sky and a few scudding clouds were being sent on their way by a crisp April breeze. That there were lambs in the fields, and that those fields were fresh and green, only added to the picture of bucolic bliss.

Their last change of horses that afternoon was at Matlock, and Mr Darcy felt able to consign his precious cargo to the two Pemberley servants who awaited them there and to travel on ahead. Kitty watched as he gave precise instructions to the coach driver and riders, all of whom were well acquainted with their surroundings, and then bade a solicitous and fond farewell to Lizzy. She laughed and told him she would see him very soon, but reached out and took his hand, holding his gaze. Kitty saw Mr Darcy's features soften in that instant; of course, she had seen this happen before when he was with Lizzy, but in the intimacy of the coach and after such a long journey, she was touched at the depth of their affection.

Kitty was now experiencing a journey that Elizabeth had made for the first time but six months earlier, although without the trepidation that the latter had felt in trespassing onto the Darcy estate. They approached the Pemberley Woods and turned in at the lodge and Kitty saw a very large park and a great variety of ground. She looked at Elizabeth, who smiled and said to wait, for there was a way to go yet.

'But Lizzy, there are deer!' Kitty exclaimed.

'There are indeed,' concurred Lizzy, taking delight in her sister's enthusiasm. 'There are more creatures than I know in this park. Georgiana, how many deer are there?'

Georgiana couldn't say; she wished she knew. Kitty didn't care and she watched entranced until the animals were lost to view as the road curved, and they ascended through the trees for half a mile or so until they reached a summit. Then she saw Pemberley House, a magnificent pale stone edifice situated across a valley, backed by a ridge of woody hills and foregrounded by a large lake that reflected the building, adding to its grandeur.

'Lizzy!' cried Kitty. 'Is this Pemberley? This is where you live! It is magnificent.' She looked at her sister in awe.

'I am glad you approve,' smiled Lizzy. 'We like it, do we not, Georgiana?'

'Lizzy! You are impossible!' said Kitty. 'It is a castle. You are a princess. We are all in a fairy tale. Am I awake?'

'You are awake Kitty,' laughed Georgiana. 'We shall have to show her the dungeons, shall we not, Elizabeth? Do we have any ogres?'

Kitty looked from one to the other, and back to Pemberley House. They may not know it, she thought, but this is a fairy tale to me.

CHAPTER 29

Kitty's first impressions of a very great house were only reinforced as she stepped out of the carriage and past the row of servants waiting to welcome their mistress home. In the entrance hall, she took in the grand proportions of a fine staircase and was aware of portraits lining the walls and an enormous candelabrum suspended from a very high ceiling; the afternoon sun cast shafts of light across the space, giving everything a warm and golden glow. It seemed at once grand and comfortable. This is Lizzy's home, she thought again, before her attention was taken by the lady of the house herself, who together with Georgiana was keen to settle Kitty into her room.

'There will be time after dinner to show you around,' promised Elizabeth, 'but you will want to retire for a while before then. Georgiana has chosen the Rose Room for you, principally I think because it is close to her own.'

'You are quite right,' declared Georgiana, taking Kitty's arm. 'But also because it is a beautifully light room, with a fine aspect towards the lake. You will like it. It used to be my room when I was younger, and sometimes I wonder that I ever allowed myself to change it. Don't worry, Mrs Reynolds,' she continued, turning to the housekeeper, 'I will show Miss Bennet the way.'

Mrs Reynolds, who had noted Miss Darcy's easy familiarity with Miss Bennet, nodded and said a maid would be sent directly to help the young lady unpack her things. The pair left her and

Elizabeth discussing household minutiae, and Kitty was led into the stately confines of Pemberley House.

She was delighted with everything she saw. She followed Georgiana down wide passages whose dove grey and pale blue walls were ornamented with mirrors, landscapes and portraits. Through an open doorway she saw what she took to be a small sitting room; there were other doors, closed to her for now but with the promise of discovery in the days to come, and then they stopped at another open door and she saw a large, airy room, with tall windows admitting light enough to illuminate a huge bed covered in the palest pink damask, and on the dressing table a glass vase filled with darker pink and cream carnations.

'Too early for roses,' said Georgiana, bending to smell the flowers. 'I hope you like this room?'

'I think it is wonderful,' said Kitty, taking in the large mirror over the mantel, the little rosewood table beside the bed, the velvet upholstered chair and the writing desk placed between the windows.

'And I am so happy you are here!' said Georgiana. 'Annie will be here at any moment to help you when your things are brought up. I shall be in my room – it is just down the hall, I will show you before dinner – and return in an hour or so and we can go down together.' She smiled a goodbye and Kitty was left alone. She sat down on the edge of the bed and looked about her. It was the biggest room she had ever called her own, and so very well appointed. She lay back on the bed for a moment, looked at the ceiling, closed her eyes, then got up and moved to the window. She could see a little stone bridge over the stream that ran into the lake, stands of trees in the distance and great expanses of green.

Who would have thought that I would be standing here now, she mused. If Bingley had not taken Netherfield, he would not have met Jane and none of this would have happened, I would still be at Longbourn, someone to be tolerated and ignored – rather like Mary was, until just now. I have been given an opportunity, she realised in a moment of pure clarity, to be someone else. Not someone famous or grand, she reasoned, but someone who is capable and good, someone who is thought to be accomplished and worthy of attention, someone who can venture an opinion without fear of censure, someone of substance, like Jane, and Lizzy. I am, she told herself, Catherine Louise Bennet, daughter of a gentleman, well bred and, now, well connected, and from this day my demeanour shall never let me down. It is a new beginning, she declared to no one, and it all seemed perfectly right.

***

In due course, the new Miss Bennet took her place at the dining table at Pemberley, in the company of her nearest and dearest, none of whom knew that a changed person was in their midst. Naturally, the main topic of conversation was the fire and its consequences but Darcy was at pains to subdue speculation and outrage. The root of the matter, he said, was poaching. A couple of weeks before one of the tenant farmers had apprehended a poacher, a man known to his steward Mr Field, on account of previous offences on neighbouring estates, and the villain had, not for the first time, been treated leniently and warned off. The farmer, who felt the matter had not been taken seriously, had subsequently called out the miscreant in the village, and the ensuing brawl had left the poacher, a man by the name of Walden, rather the worse for the encounter. The speculation was, said Darcy, that one of Walden's brothers, a man of limited intellect, had decided to retaliate for perceived wrongs and the situation had escalated. Now the matter was before the magistrate and the consequences for the poacher, a man with a large family to feed, and his brother looked dire.

'It is,' he said, 'now beyond my control. Field has already begun to make the necessary arrangements to restore the cottages. I shall call upon Fothergill tomorrow to ascertain his views.'

'Lord Fothergill's property borders Pemberley,' Elizabeth informed Kitty. 'I will visit Mrs Moore and her children tomorrow,' she continued, referring to the family whose home had been destroyed by the fire. 'You said they are lodging with their cousins?'

Darcy affirmed it was so.

'I could come with you?' offered Kitty, wondering if this offer of assistance would be dismissed outright.

'Why not,' responded Elizabeth. 'I will speak with Mrs Reynolds in the morning and we will take some provisions with us. Although it is not quite the introductory tour of Pemberley I had envisaged for you!'

'I should like to accompany you,' reiterated Kitty and the conversation shifted to less sensational local and domestic matters.

Their journey, and the reasons that had accelerated it, meant that none of the party were at their sparkling best and no objection was made to retiring early. Georgiana and Kitty went up together. 'I shall not go with you to the cottages tomorrow,' said Georgiana, stifling a yawn, 'but we can spend the afternoon together. I shall be entirely at your disposal then.' And so they parted. As she settled into her spacious bed in her new room, where the embers of the fire still glowed, Kitty's last thoughts before sleep overtook her were of new beginnings, new possibilities.

CHAPTER 30

Their visit to the Moore household the following day, the sort of April day described as fresh, gave Kitty a greater overview of the grounds and the workings of Pemberley. She had gone with Elizabeth to the herb garden to collect some rosemary and basil to add to the basket of goods the cook had prepared for them to take and she was taken aback at the size of the gardens and glasshouses that stretched across that part of the estate. They grew their own produce at Longbourn of course, so that the land at Pemberley was cultivated should not in itself have surprised her, but the scale of the operation was new.

Her wonder only increased as they rode away from the house through woody glades and on to a smaller, winding road that led to a cluster of cottages and outhouses. The grounds seemed to go on for ever. Elizabeth bade their driver go close to the properties damaged by the fire so that they could see for themselves what had happened. Already, labourers were beginning the work of clearing and rebuilding, but the two dwellings were a sorry sight; one almost razed and the other in need of much restoration. Noticing Mrs Darcy, the men touched their caps in salute and Elizabeth called out a cheery good morning – Kitty felt obliged to follow suit – and then they turned and made their way back to the cottage that now housed the Moores.

On arrival they found the local vicar, Mr Marsden, in attendance and Mrs Moore, already flustered by her first important visitor, now set about finding places for Mrs Darcy and Miss Bennet to sit while shooing away two small children, who were evidently in awe of all the strangers in their midst. Elizabeth made the introductions, insisted they would not stay long and wanted only to assure Mrs Moore that she felt for the family in their plight and would offer assistance in whatever way was necessary until they were rehoused.

Mrs Moore bobbed her thanks while trying to rescue Mr Marsden from one of her offspring who had attached herself to his boot. The vicar merely laughed and scooped up the troublemaker, a girl of about three years, who turned her attention to the leather satchel he wore over his shoulder. Here was a different kettle of fish to Mr Collins, thought Kitty. She saw before her a portly and affable man with easy manners, whose concern was clearly for others and not for himself; someone who went about his business quietly and without fuss. She noticed another parcel of provisions on the scrubbed wooden table and guessed that these had been given by Mr Marsden and his wife. After a few more minutes, Elizabeth, making her farewells, said they would no doubt meet again on Sunday and motioned to Kitty that they should leave.

Back in the sunlight, Kitty shaded her eyes as she took her place in the carriage beside her sister. 'Are such visits expected of you,' she asked quietly, 'now that you are the lady of such a grand estate?'

'In truth, I don't know,' responded Lizzy, equally softly in order not to be overheard. 'It has been a long time since there was a Mrs Darcy in residence at Pemberley and I have no idea what Lady Anne might have done. I am learning every day. I have a certain responsibility to the tenants, I think, but if there is a handbook for prescribed behaviours, I have yet to find it. I felt it necessary to visit and let them know they are not forgotten.'

'It seems to me that you are doing admirably, Lizzy. You do everything with such aplomb. Did you realise what an undertaking such a large estate would be?'

'Before I agreed to marry Darcy, you mean! No, I did not. I did not give it a moment's thought. I saw only the man – and

Pemberley, of course! Lucky, is it not, that I am not a complete stranger to the workings of a household? Do not look so concerned!' she laughed. 'I would not change a single thing!'

They rode back to the house by a different route so that Kitty could see more of the grounds. They followed close to the stream for a distance, and sheep and cattle could be espied in the neighbouring fields. Nearer the house was a pretty flower garden with a white folly, which Elizabeth promised was a fine spot for summer picnics, and then they made a detour so that she could point out the stables and coach house.

'Do you really ride now?' asked Kitty. 'I thought you hated it. You always insisted you never wanted to learn.'

'Ah, this is yet another of my newfound marital responsibilities!' owned Lizzy, making a rueful face. 'Fitzwilliam loves to ride and was quite surprised that I did not. I could not let him think I was too afraid! Besides, I found I wanted to accompany him when he went out riding. It is so very beautiful hereabouts.'

'But were you afraid?'

'Indeed I was. I was extremely nervous, but of course I did my best to hide it. If my dear husband noticed, he was too chivalrous to comment. I am still a little wary on horseback, you will not see me galloping across the fields! You are too young to remember but I had a nasty fall from Honey, our old pony, when I was about five and I steadfastly refused to countenance riding after that. Even Jane could not convince me otherwise.'

'So love really does conquer all then,' observed Kitty with a wry smile. 'And I thought you were fearless!'

'No, did you really? That would make no sense. A little fear, now and again, sharpens our senses, don't you think? As long as it is nothing too grave, of course. Do you want to learn to ride while you are here? The mare Mr Darcy has given me is both placid and intelligent; I will share her with you if you would like, but I would not presume to teach you. You will need guidance from a better rider than me.'

'Thank you, but no,' said Kitty, quickly. 'I am content to watch your progress. I prefer more sedentary pursuits, I am not so strong as you!' She was, however, quietly astounded that Lizzy, who always seemed so very confident, had her own frailties – frailties she determined to overcome, Kitty reminded herself, and that was something to emulate. She cast a sideways glance at her sister, who had her head back and eyes closed in a brief homage to the sun. How does she manage everything so well, she wondered, not for the first time.

CHAPTER 31

No one, not even Elizabeth, could take greater delight in exploring Pemberley and its surrounds than Kitty. Georgiana had shown her all the principal rooms the day after she had arrived. She had marvelled at Darcys, past and present, in the portrait gallery and great hall (she supposed there would be one of Mrs Elizabeth Darcy up there soon); had looked through the various chambers, including those Lizzy had a mind to refurbish with or without chinoiserie; admired the music room, with its excellent and very new pianoforte and, of course, Georgiana's harp; skipped around the ballroom (a ballroom! She was enchanted!); and repeated again and again how beautiful everything was. The two young women had then ventured outside so Kitty could examine the kitchen garden and listen to the gardener's complaints about blight; see the greenhouses and wonder about pineapples and peaches; cluck at the chickens; admire the topiary; and check the progress of the spring daffodils in the garden.

When her curiosity was suitably sated, Kitty allowed herself to be led inside and, after a little discussion, the pair decided the music room should be their next venue and that they could bear to play a little piano together. It was a perfect introduction to Pemberley and Kitty was in heaven.

***

A few days after Easter, a letter arrived from Jane, confirming their safe arrival at Netherfield, and in early May – by which time Kitty was very well settled into the Darcys' fine estate; she found, as others before have discovered, that adapting to improved circumstances requires no great effort – another letter from her arrived, this one containing an account of Mary's wedding.

It was a happy but quite solemn affair. Mary insisted that she wanted little in the way of fuss and, despite our mother's best efforts to persuade her otherwise, she had her own way. Charles and I went early in the morning to Longbourn, where we had a slight breakfast together. Mary had allowed herself a new dress, of pale green muslin spotted with white, which became her well and in that, at least, Mama was satisfied. A little before eleven, the bride and our mother and father left in the carriage, and we followed in ours, hoping that the grey clouds would not turn to rain before we arrived at the church.

The day had an altogether different air to our festive services last autumn, dear Lizzy. There were but a few flowers by way of decoration and very few people in the congregation. Mr and Mrs Gregory were there of course, along with Marianne and the bridegroom, and all looking very content – although he was, as you might expect, just a little nervous. Aunt and Uncle Phillips were invited but Mary wanted no other friends; I hope the Lucases and others of our acquaintance were not offended.

Mr Collins was not in attendance; I do not know what came of that suggestion and thought it best not to make enquiries. In the event, the service was read by our own vicar and Papa gave Mary away. It all seemed rather serious and businesslike, although the happy couple were – and I hope will always be – happy in their own way. Mama shed a few tears, of course. Our father said very little to anyone, although I am sure he likes Mr Gregory well enough.

Afterwards, we all went back to Longbourn, where we sat down to a very fine breakfast, with an excellent wedding cake the centrepiece of the table, and Mary and her husband were at last able to smile and receive our congratulations, and Mama was able to fret to her heart's content and worry about their future and where they will be. Mr Gregory senior is an amiable gentleman, seemingly very pleased with both his son and his new daughter and I think Mary will be happy.

The bride and bridegroom left mid-afternoon to their new lodgings, a cottage not far from Meryton on the road south, and the party broke up shortly afterwards. You will ask what are their plans but I have no definite news to tell you, except that they are determined to travel to India and do good works, whatever that means. Charles ascertained as much from his conversation with Mr Gregory, who told him that he has been making enquiries as to sailings and so forth, and spoke of his friends who had already embarked. Mama is still most upset at the thought of Mary's undertaking a missionary life, so there was a small conspiracy not to mention such possibilities at the wedding breakfast for fear of spoiling the day. I confess I find it hard to believe that Mary will soon be so far away, but if it is her wish – already she talks of a calling – then we must respect her faith and hope for her health and safety.

I will write soon when I have more to tell.

Kitty and Elizabeth read thus far in near silence. 'There is more,' announced Lizzy. 'She has added to the letter.'

I had not time to send the above before dear Mama called. She is well and asks after you both. She says she will write directly. Mama is a little bereft; I am concerned for her, I confess. Although she can now tell all of Meryton that she has four daughters well married, she feels the loss of our company dearly. She complains that Lydia does not write as often as she should – but that is just her way. It is well that we are close by and she is delighted to hear my own happy news. Quite a distraction for her poor nerves!

I am glad to be out of London and here at Netherfield although I could wish you were not so far.

Yours, affectionately

'Mama will be a daily visitor to Netherfield,' said Elizabeth, as she looked up from Jane's letter. 'I only hope Jane's nerves can withstand her attentions. Mrs Mary Gregory! It sounds well, I suppose.'

'I should not say so but it seems strange to think of Mary married,' said Kitty. 'It is so unexpected! But then I did not expect you to be married to Mr Darcy, so I am no seer of such events. Even so…'

'I know,' agreed Elizabeth. 'Who would have thought a year ago that four of us would have changed our names. Mama will not know where to direct her attentions, or rather she will! It is as well that you are not at Longbourn. She will be impatient to find a suitor for you now!'

Kitty knew the truth of that statement. 'I know nothing of India and the work of missionaries. Do you? Will Mary go, do you think?'

'I think she will. Mary is nothing if not determined once she gets an idea in her head. We will find out soon enough I have no doubt. Let's go and find Georgiana. I think we would all benefit from a walk.'

CHAPTER 32

Although acutely aware that she was the only remaining Miss Bennet, Pemberley offered plenty of distractions. Within a few weeks, Kitty's awe at its majestic proportions had given way to familiarity, and her room, her run of the house and grounds became the norm. Not that she was ungrateful; she was happier than she had ever been and her fervent wish was that nothing should change to remove her from her present idyll.

Georgiana and she spent most of their days together, either in the music room, walking the woods or reading companionably yet separately in the library. Kitty refused all attempts to learn to ride but was persuaded to venture on sketching expeditions with Georgiana, often as not with Lizzy, when the sisters would take it in turns to read aloud while the artist was absorbed with her landscapes.

Kitty's introduction to archery, at which Georgiana was quite the Diana, was a day of much hilarity. Elizabeth's prowess with a bow was no greater than Kitty's, and Mr Darcy, watching, clearly found the experience highly entertaining – so much so that he laughed heartily. Kitty had never heard him laugh outright before and the day did much to break down barriers and establish an easier communication between them. She no longer feared to address him, as once she had, and he, who had not known he was such a forbidding figure, felt only benevolence towards this young woman who was at once his wife's sister and his sister's beloved friend. He seemed to have quite forgotten the wild child who, with Lydia, had so repulsed him at balls in Meryton. In short, a respectful and fraternal relationship now existed between Kitty and Mr Darcy – she could not imagine herself ever calling him Fitzwilliam, of course, which Elizabeth found amusing.

Occasionally, a letter arrived from Lydia to which Kitty responded, tailoring her news as if to guard Pemberley and its inhabitants from her sister's curiosity. Knowing what she now did about Wickham, coupled with her greater appreciation of Darcy's role in rescuing Lydia from ignominy, stretched her loyalties to both parties. Distance, too, had given Kitty perspective in which to reflect on her reliance on and emulation of Lydia and often, when reading her sister's invariably short and untidy missives, she was shocked by a turn of phrase or an observation she felt a little crude. Her sister's reaction to Mary's wedding had given Kitty pause. She had started to read the latest letter in the drawing room, where she had been sitting working with Georgiana and Lizzy, but the initial lines had been so unfeeling that Kitty had pocketed it and taken it upstairs to her bedroom for private perusal. As with so many things, Lydia thought the marriage a huge joke.

> *How I laughed at the thought of Mary, a book of sermons under her arm, preaching and prating to poor unfortunates. She would bore them to death! Of course the real wonder is that she is married at all! Her Mr Gregory must be a humdrum fellow! I can scarce remember what he looks like, but I would know him if he were handsome. And they are off to India, perhaps that is for the best...*

The remainder of the letter continued in the same mocking vein, unless it was something that pertained to Lydia or her dear Wickham, and quite disgusted her sister. Whatever Kitty felt about Mary's decision, she respected it and was slightly in awe of the new Mrs Gregory's dedication to helping the less fortunate. It was wrong of Lydia to belittle her for it, especially when her own conduct left so much to be desired. Her letters mentioned dances and card parties and accounts of insalubrious japes among the officers, always referred to as the best of fun. She would laugh at me, were she here, thought Kitty; and mock me for having no suitor and no assemblies to attend to find one. 'Well,' she said to her reflection in the mirror, 'I am perfectly content here. What need have I of that sort of fun?'

The social activities outside Pemberley into which Kitty was now drawn revolved around several families who lived in the vicinity. In general, the Darcys' neighbours were interested and interesting people, whose hospitality was both refined and relaxed and, more often than not, they hosted dinners that progressed into impromptu musical evenings, often with dancing. It was on one such occasion that Kitty, before she had time to resist, found herself seated at the pianoforte with Georgiana playing one of the many pieces they had practised together. It was a pretty performance and well received in general, but what made it memorable for Kitty was Elizabeth's commendation. 'I had no idea your playing was so improved. That was very well done,' she had said, and Kitty's heart had swelled with pride.

Not everything was entirely perfect, though. A consequence of Darcy visiting Lord Fothergill was an invitation for him and his family to dine at Pemberley, and so it was that Kitty found herself seated at the same table as an earl and his lady, an event that would once have caused her much nervous anxiety. There had been Fothergills at Fothergill Abbey for generations, she learned, and given that Lady Margaret had borne four children to her husband, three of whom were sons, the family line was in no danger of imminent collapse. Her ladyship had little conversation; her chief interest in life appeared to be her children and agreeing with everything her husband said, and what he said meant little to Kitty as he referred to people and places she knew naught of. Only two of the lesser Fothergills, as Kitty dubbed them, were at the dinner: Rose, a pretty but otherwise unremarkable young woman, and her younger brother Marcus, a resolutely silent youth. Despite the best efforts of the hosts, the conversation at that dinner table had not been stimulating. Kitty had watched Elizabeth feigning interest as Lord Fothergill gave forth on his ideas about agriculture, drainage and the need for a stern hand with poachers, while Darcy, not a man given to excessive speech, had bordered on the loquacious in his attempts to engage Lady Fothergill.

'Good Lord, Mr Darcy!' Lizzy had exclaimed, as soon as the doors were closed on their visitors. 'Next time you are of a mind to invite that family, let us be sure that others are also at the table. Or was that a test of my endurance?'

'Not intentionally, my dear,' he had responded, looking a little pained.

In the event, soon after that occasion, their family circle was expanded by the arrival of Colonel Fitzwilliam, Mr Darcy's cousin on his mother's side (and so, Kitty knew, the younger son of an earl), who habitually spent the summer months at Pemberley whenever his duties allowed. Kitty had heard much about the colonel: from Georgiana, who revered him almost as much as she revered her brother; and from Elizabeth, who had first made his acquaintance a year previously when he and Darcy had been staying with their aunt, the formidable Lady Catherine de Bourgh, at her country seat of Rosings in Kent, and she had been visiting Charlotte Collins, whose parsonage adjoined her ladyship's property.

With such positive endorsement from both sides, Kitty was predisposed to very much approve of Colonel Fitzwilliam and she was not disappointed. He in turn expected to delight in a young woman who was at once the sister of Elizabeth, whose personality had charmed him from their first meeting, and the trusted confidante of Georgiana (who was also his ward, a responsibility he shared with Mr Darcy). All in all, one might have expected romance to bloom immediately between the good colonel and the newly demure damsel but life does not always present such easy enchantment. Colonel Fitzwilliam was handsome enough in his way, a couple of years older than Mr Darcy and steady in character. However, it should be remembered that he was only the second son of a lord, a gentleman to the core but a gentleman not about to inherit – hence his military career – and, as he had remarked to Elizabeth, somewhat candidly, the summer before, for this reason he was not at liberty to marry where he chose. Kitty, for her part, liked Colonel Fitzwilliam well enough, but he did not set her heart aflutter. She wondered about him in private, for he was a very eligible man and well qualified to win her heart but, she owned, in this regard he did not compare favourably to Henry Adams, whom she found herself thinking about rather too often and, as she constantly reminded herself, to no good purpose.

CHAPTER 33

June brought sunny weather that was warm enough for picnics in the park and painting en plein air. On one such day, the Pemberley party arranged to meet at the folly, an amusing if not particularly authentic rendition of a small Greek temple that a previous Darcy had been inspired to build after his Grand Tour and which now served very little purpose other than providing an attractive subject for painting and a little shelter from the elements. The ladies set off together on foot, having waved goodbye to Mr Darcy and Colonel Fitzwilliam, who had ridden off on horseback to make a circuit of the estate.

'I have been informed,' announced Elizabeth as they strolled beside the stream, 'that it is incumbent on the mistress of Pemberley to host a summer ball. Mr Darcy has kept this obligation from me until now.'

Georgiana looked at Lizzy, alarmed by her resigned tone, but Kitty knew her sister better.

'Well,' said she, 'you had better make sure it is a good one. Your reputation is at stake here.'

'Indeed, it is. I understand Lady Anne was renowned for Pemberley's summer balls.'

'You'll manage, and manage very well,' returned Kitty. 'You know you will.'

'Thankfully, I have Mrs Reynolds to help me. And you too, Georgiana. You shall not escape responsibilities here. You have the advantage of knowing how these balls go.'

'I am afraid I cannot help you, dearest Lizzy. I have small recollections of rooms filled with flowers, and lots of candlelight reflecting on glasses, but I was too young to be allowed to stay up. I remember my mother looking quite beautiful in a green silk dress and I think that must have been for the ball, but I was but four years old, and it may not be a true memory.'

'Forgive me,' said Elizabeth. 'You lost your dear mother at such an early age. She would be proud to see you grown into such a lovely young woman.'

Kitty looked over to Georgiana. She could discern a faint blush at the compliment.

'Perhaps,' continued Elizabeth, 'this ball could mark your coming out? It would be a fine thing to re-establish a tradition with such an event. But only if that is something that would please you.'

'I had not thought of it,' said Georgiana, her colour rising. 'I mean, I would like to ask my brother. A summer ball would be enchanting but...'

Kitty came to her rescue. 'I think it all sounds perfectly divine, with or without your coming out. I am "out", am I not, Lizzy? And it was quite painless. Although I was never in any danger of being presented at court. Just think, though, a ball in your honour among your friends in Derbyshire... so much easier than an equivalent affair in London.' She was still surprised at Georgiana's modesty and shyness.

'You are right,' said the latter, looking from Kitty to Elizabeth. 'I suppose I must think of these things.'

'Let us wait and discuss it with your brother,' said Elizabeth, resolving not to pursue the idea. 'You may decide that London is a better choice.'

'When do you propose to hold the ball?' asked Kitty, manoeuvring the attention away from Georgiana. 'And perhaps it ought to be Mrs Elizabeth Darcy's ball, first and foremost?'

'In answer to the first, tradition has it that the ball is held in August. The full moon is in the middle of the month this year.

As to the second, perhaps you are right. Do not look so worried,' she said to Georgiana. 'At present, it is just a summer ball and, as it must proceed – or so I am told – then we had better enjoy it, do you not think?'

'Will Jane travel to Derbyshire?' wondered Kitty.

'I do not know,' said Elizabeth. 'I fear she will not, although I would dearly love to see her. She does not complain – when did Jane ever complain? – but Mama wrote and made mention of Jane being told to rest and I hope that means Mr Bingley will insist that she does. I do miss her so. I shall insist she comes to Pemberley for Christmas. We shall have three Bingleys to welcome by then.'

'Ah, but there are already three Bingleys,' said Kitty, looking arch. 'You have not forgotten Caroline?'

'Miss Bingley and Mr and Mrs Hurst usually spend some weeks with us during summer,' said Georgiana before Elizabeth could respond. 'Mr Bingley too, of course, as he and my brother are such great friends. It will be strange not to see him here this year but I suppose his sisters will come without him.'

'I daresay they will,' said Lizzy, resolving to speak with Darcy on the subject at the first opportunity. She had quite forgotten about Miss Bingley and receiving her as a house guest was a prospect as welcome as snow in July. Snow would be warmer, she thought.

Kitty's thoughts were running in tandem. The Bingley sisters would not want to miss Elizabeth's first summer ball and they would be at Pemberley without their brother's genial presence to check them. Aloud, said she: 'Will you invite Mama and Papa?'

'Of course, and I would be delighted if they accept. I am not convinced, however, that they will come.

'Mama is not one for travelling,' she explained to Georgiana, 'although she will very much want to see where I am living and meet you. To Papa, the journey would present no problem but he only goes to balls under protest. If he comes, I would not be surprised if he contrives to have himself locked in the library for the duration and not discovered until the following day.'

'Mama may not want to leave Jane, either?' suggested Kitty.

'You are right, I am sure. I will let them know when the ball will be and we will see. It may be that everyone prefers to come here at Christmas. Aunt and Uncle Gardiner as well.'

'Last Christmas was so joyful,' said Georgiana, smiling at the memory. 'I cannot recollect one better. I enjoyed it so much more than being in London. You will see, Kitty.'

Kitty hoped she would. There had been no discussion as to quite how long she would stay at Pemberley and she felt a little nervous every time an opportunity arose that might indicate a return to Longbourn.

They reached the folly, where Georgiana's easel was already set up, and made themselves comfortable. The painting, half completed, showed promise. 'I wish I were so talented,' said Kitty. 'I cannot paint and can only draw a little. You do everything so well.'

'Nonsense,' said her friend. 'I do some things reasonably well and then only because I am determined that I shall achieve a satisfactory result. You have not seen me in despair because I had got an angle quite wrong, or because I had spent days, wasted days, trying to achieve an effect of light.'

'Very well,' laughed Kitty. 'I am scolded, but I think you have a talent for painting that I do not possess. Moreover, I think you enjoy it, and perhaps that is the difference.'

'I do enjoy it, that is true. Just as it is true of playing the pianoforte and harp, where again it is necessary to practise to improve. You would agree with that, would you not?'

'I do,' said Kitty, 'and I am happy to practise at the pianoforte, as you well know.'

'You are a better player than me now,' said Elizabeth. 'Father would be astonished at your proficiency.'

Kitty was happy to accept such a compliment.

'Besides,' continued Georgiana, stepping back to survey her work, 'each of us has our own talents. I prefer to paint and play and sing, it leaves less time for netting and petit point, which I do not like at all.'

'No more do I,' said Lizzy and Kitty simultaneously and in exactly the same tone.

Georgiana laughed with them. 'I could wish,' said she, 'to be more like both of you. You are each so witty and at ease in company, and you are both such avid readers. You quite put me to shame.'

'I am not witty,' protested Kitty.

'But you are,' insisted Georgiana, loyally. 'You have such a flair for observing others' foibles and imitating them. You know you do. And what of the song you wrote? I have never composed a song.'

Elizabeth looked askance at Kitty.

'It was more of a little poem, really,' said she, embarrassed. 'Nothing to be commended.'

'I should like to hear it sometime,' said her sister, opening one of the books she had brought with her.

Kitty held her breath, hoping Georgiana would remember to say nothing of the short story she had written, which she had shared with her under pledge of secrecy. It had come about after the dinner with the dreary Fothergills and Kitty had amused herself by putting some adventure into that family's lives. She had enjoyed writing it – and was quite pleased with the finished tale – but although Georgiana had laughed and found it all most diverting, Kitty feared Elizabeth would disapprove of such a mordant rendition of their neighbours.

No more was said, however. Georgiana was concentrating on her painting, leaving Kitty relieved and in peace to think about how much she did enjoy writing, if that was what she could deem her little musings. And Georgiana had said that she observed other people and their foibles. Was not that exactly what Jane had said about Elizabeth!

Elizabeth was reading *The Sorrows of Yamba*, a paean against slavery authored by 'A Lady'. She had picked it up, she said, thinking of Mary, though it pertained to Africa more than India. Kitty picked up the other book, which turned out to be Fielding's

Tom Jones, and silence ensued, broken only by the rustling sounds of summer in parkland, the turning of pages and Georgiana's paintbrush swishing about in the water jar.

The gentlemen arrived, full of energy from their exertions and extolling the virtues of the day and the weather. 'What say you to an outing one day?' said Colonel Fitzwilliam to no one in particular, as he lay down and stretched out on the grass. 'Perhaps to Stanton Tor or the Black Rocks? Have you been there yet, Miss Bennet?'

She had not and Colonel Fitzwilliam sat back up and feigned outrage on her behalf. How could Darcy have so neglected his charming guest, it must be set to rights immediately. She had not visited Matlock Bath or Buxton? He was appalled. Mr Darcy allowed himself to be castigated by his friend, Elizabeth made a show of defending him, Kitty protested she had no need to put anyone to any trouble and within no time at all, adding to the pleasures of the day, the five were planning day trips to see the sights nearby.

CHAPTER 34

The date of the summer ball – set as 12 August and a good seven weeks away – was close enough to anticipate but not so close as to cause anxiety or involve Elizabeth or the household in flurries of preparation. It was too early to send out invitations but she had notified Jane of the event, acknowledging the likelihood that her sister would be unable to travel and reiterating the wish to see her – and her family! – at Pemberley at Christmas. Jane's letter in response affirmed her health was good but that she had been advised against long journeys, that their mother was a frequent visitor, their father well and that she and Mr Bingley were serious in their contemplation of Dapplewick Hall as a future residence. There had been correspondence with its owners and as a consequence Mr Bingley would visit the house soon, and given its proximity to Pemberley – and Jane had added an exclamation mark here – he hoped very much to be in their company within a week or so. She thought Mr Darcy might have more precise information.

Elizabeth applied to her husband immediately and found he had been in touch with Mr Bingley on that very subject, having heard that other parties were also interested in purchasing Dapplewick. 'I have advised Bingley to inspect the property as soon as he can,' he told her.

A letter from Mr Bingley arrived the following day, confirming his intentions to travel north. He would be accompanied by his friend Mr Bridgwater, whose wife was presently staying at

Netherfield with Jane, and they expected to arrive at Pemberley the following Tuesday. He had, he wrote, made arrangements to view Dapplewick Hall and also planned to visit another property, Hazelton Place in southern Yorkshire, that Bridgwater knew of through his father-in-law, Sir Edward. He trusted Darcy would be available to accompany him and dared hope that Mrs Darcy would be amenable to joining them likewise.

Elizabeth had no objection and daily expected a letter from Jane, requesting the same. To have the Bingleys settled close to her in Derbyshire would be such a happiness she hardly dared to speak the wish aloud. Kitty, when told, was considerably less elated and could only express a desire to be part of the viewing party and then Georgiana wanted to go also, so that the potential purchase of a Bingley estate acquired its own commission and became a small tour of the neighbourhood.

Kitty was delighted to see Mr Bingley again, even if she did not care much for the reason for his visit. She was completely at ease in his company and could happily converse with him on a variety of subjects without feeling ill-informed or silly; he had, quite unwittingly, fallen into the role of her mentor. He, in turn, was as happy to see Kitty as he was others of the Darcy household and only sorry that his dearest Jane was unable to be with him to enjoy such convivial company.

During dinner that evening, Mr Bingley dispensed details of the daily routines of Netherfield House, Meryton and its environs, interspersed with what news there was to offer, which in brief was that one of his favourite horses was lame; that Sir William Lucas was suffering from gout and thought to go to Bath; and that there was a new proprietor of the inn in the village, but he could not remember his name. From Mr Bridgwater, they gleaned details of Hazelton Place, constructed some sixty years ago on the site of what had once been a sixteenth-century palace.

'A palace!' cried Kitty. 'How romantic.'

'Romantic, possibly,' said Elizabeth, 'but I think a sixteenth-century palace would not be very comfortable now.'

'Sir Edward says the new wings are modern, with quite a number of guestrooms,' said Mr Bridgwater, returning to his theme. 'He attended a house party there a few years ago. We will have to discover the rest when we get there, but I do know the village is very picturesque and that some of the families nearby have been there for generations.'

'How is Sir Edward?' enquired Kitty.

'Quite well, I thank you. He is staying with his sister Lady Fanshawe presently, so we shall see him at Doncaster. On Lady Fanshawe's behalf, as I have told Darcy, he has invited us all to dine at Danson Park and will not hear of our returning to Pemberley until the following day.'

Kitty merely nodded, although she was wondering whether Frederick and William Fanshawe would also be in residence. She had not thought to see the brothers outside of London and was a little surprised at the feelings this news excited. She risked a glance at Georgiana, who gave her to understand by the smallest flicker of her eyebrows that the information had indeed registered.

The conversation reverted to the merits, as so far known, of Dapplewick Hall, about which Mr Bingley was pleased to discourse, with reference of course to the superior knowledge of his friend, Mr Darcy.

'I hope to make a decision before I return to Netherfield,' he informed all those at the table, 'and I have a request to make of you, my dear Elizabeth, that comes directly from your sister. She says that you are to be her eyes in this matter and that she is sure that if you approve of Dapplewick or Hazelton then she is sure to approve also.'

'Dear Jane,' responded Lizzy. 'You know I will give my opinions only too readily. I hope you will have some choice in the matter as well!'

The business of choosing began the next day and Dapplewick was under appraisal three hours after the party had set out from Pemberley. Built of grey stone, the house itself was quite modest in appearance but it was charmingly situated among meadows and grasslands, with some fine copper beech and oak trees adding to the picturesque scene. Despite the fact she wanted Jane and Bingley to remain in Hertfordshire, Kitty could see that the house and its surrounds were quite delightful. Perhaps it will be too small, she said to herself, but then remembered that most country houses were going to appear small in comparison with Pemberley.

They wandered around the apartments, which they found to be large, lofty and well arranged, and no fault could be found with the proportions of the drawing room, nor the dining room. The wall and ceiling decorations were approved, as were the mahogany doors and the large windows, and the building itself was in good repair, it being less than thirty years old. Kitty imagined herself living in it, placing furniture in various alcoves, ordering fabrics for curtains. Would she have her portrait painted? She couldn't quite decide.

'What do you think?' appealed Bingley to Elizabeth, after they had strolled outside again, and were in sight of the stables.

'It is charming,' she replied, 'and the pastures and woods around about have much to recommend them, too.'

'But will your sister like it, do you suppose?' He spoke to Elizabeth and Kitty, but she knew that it was Lizzy's opinion that mattered.

Elizabeth considered. 'On the whole, I think so. The house is compact but there is land enough to build on should you want to add a wing, and the aspect is superb.' She thought Jane would be happy to be mistress of such an estate, especially given its proximity to Pemberley, but she was loath to make a decision on Mr Bingley's behalf. She took his arm and they returned inside; Elizabeth wanted to assess once more the views from the principal rooms. Kitty and Georgiana followed.

'It does have good acreage,' said Mr Bingley, as he gazed out at the surrounding countryside. 'I declare I like it better than Netherfield already. What say you, Kitty? Georgiana?'

'It is a fine house,' Kitty heard herself saying. 'I can picture you and Jane living here.'

Mr Bingley beamed. Kitty smiled back. As fond as she was of Charles Bingley, she knew, as anyone who knew him well knew, that he liked to canvass opinion rather than make his own. At least his sister isn't with him to dampen his enthusiasm and find fault with everything, she thought.

The gentlemen were now conferring with the owner's steward but no decision would be made today. They would be setting off for Yorkshire and Hazelton Place on the morrow.

The business concluded, the party split up: Bingley, Bridgwater, Darcy and Elizabeth returned to Pemberley directly; Colonel Fitzwilliam, happy to accompany the two young ladies, made good on his promises to show Kitty new places and landmarks thereabouts, and declared they would take the more circuitous route via Matlock Bath.

CHAPTER 35

The following morning Kitty woke early, full of conjecture about the day ahead. She hardly knew which to anticipate most: the journey itself, through parts of the country she had yet to see; the anticipated meeting with the Mr Fanshawes (she had discussed the possibility of their being there with Georgiana and both agreed, largely because this was what they both wanted and no other conjecture was pleasurable, that their presence at the family home was probable); or the opportunity to view another grand country house, of which her sister might soon be mistress.

Opening the window, she found the day was already warm. It hadn't rained for weeks but the lawns she could see were quite green and the borders full of summer flowers. In the middle distance, she caught sight of Colonel Fitzwilliam coming back from his early morning ride but he soon disappeared from view, no doubt making his way towards the stables. How charming he had been yesterday, she reflected, so concerned for her comfort, and of course of Georgiana's. Nothing in his demeanour or looks had hinted at any romantic interest though, and Kitty was not sorry about that. She would be pleased to count the colonel as a friend.

The house and grounds were still quiet as she made her way downstairs and outside, heading towards the rose garden, one of her many favourite places in Pemberley. She thought she would have it all to herself but one of the gardeners was already there, clipping and pruning, a basket of dark pink blooms by his side.

'Good morning. What a fine day,' said Kitty by way of greeting, bending her face down to smell a cluster of lilac-pink roses. 'What are these?' she asked.

The gardener, one of the newer members of the Pemberley household and one more at ease with horticulture than charming young ladies in white morning dresses who appeared out of nowhere, nevertheless managed to reply. 'Early Cinnamons we call those, miss. And them over there are Common Provence.'

Kitty resolved that one day, no matter what, she would have a rose garden and she would know the names of all the roses in the world. She flitted around the beds, asking more questions, her enthusiasm gradually wearing down the young gardener's resistance, so much so that he began to volunteer information. Kitty chatted on and by the time she was ready to leave, John – for she had ascertained his name – had selected a sizeable bunch of roses, of all the varieties she admired, for Miss Bennet to carry back to the house. 'Best pick them now,' he said, 'think it will storm later.'

'Do you really?' said Kitty sceptically, looking up at a brilliant blue sky.

'Too warm,' said John, by way of explanation, turning back to his work and leaving Kitty to skip – in a way she thought Elizabeth might skip, if no one was watching – back to the house in time for breakfast.

The party duly set off in two carriages, the road taking them through Chesterfield and a number of hamlets and then on to Sheffield, where they stopped to rest and refresh themselves. The sun was still high in the sky when they resumed their journey towards Doncaster but within an hour clouds had appeared on the horizon and Kitty, travelling with Mr Bingley, Colonel Fitzwilliam and Georgiana, began to wonder if the gardener had been correct in his prediction of rain.

They passed through the small village of Hazelton, with its Norman church, and soon after arrived at Hazelton Place itself, an imposing residence made largely from limestone ashlar and much larger than Dapplewick Hall. Two low wings flanked the house's seven-bay frontage. It was still smaller than Pemberley, Kitty realised, but excessively grand nonetheless.

A couple of carriages were stationed outside Hazelton's entry porch and Kitty recognised the stately figure of Sir Edward, evidently waiting for them.

'Good afternoon, to you all,' he boomed as, one by one, the travellers stepped down from their carriages. 'Mrs Darcy, delighted to see you again. Mr Darcy.'

'Bridgwater, my dear fellow,' he said to his son-in-law, shaking his hand with some vigour. 'Here we are again! Ah, here's the man for the horses. Now, who have you brought with you? My dear Miss Bennet, how well you look. I am very pleased to see you again.'

'And I you, sir,' responded Kitty, although her reply was lost as Sir Edward's roll-call of greetings continued, culminating in an introduction to Colonel Fitzwilliam. The civilities over, he looked around for the owner's steward, commandeered Mr Bingley, and the inspection of Hazelton Place began.

It was built on top of an Elizabethan palace, Kitty remembered as she and Georgiana stepped into the entrance, noting the palatial proportions and the fine iron balustrade on the main staircase. They paused at the huge library to the left with its Corinthian columns and then turned into the right wing to see the ballroom, which, like much of the house, was denuded of furniture although the windows still had curtains and, here and there, a sofa or table remained, marooned in a sea of elegant emptiness.

Kitty could hear Sir Edward praising Hazelton's architecture to Mr Bingley – 'James Paine, don't you know? Essentially Palladian' – and giving him chapter and verse as to Hazelton's history as well as recalling the times he had stayed there. The steward was no match to interrupt him. Mr Bingley, meanwhile, was nodding at everything Sir Edward said. 'Poor Charles,' she whispered to Georgiana. 'He will know every member of the family by name at this rate. I think he looks a little lost in this house but I am trying to imagine it with furnishings. I wonder how many rooms there are?'

'Do you think Mrs Bingley would approve?' asked Georgiana, looking over to Elizabeth and Darcy, who were moving towards Mr Bingley and Sir Edward.

Kitty followed her gaze. Lizzy was wearing an interested expression, one that Kitty knew she adopted when she wished to mask her real thoughts. The party reassembled and Sir Edward led the way to the second storey. Kitty had already made up her mind. She much preferred Dapplewick Hall and would say so if Jane asked her. It wasn't just that the house was so large – and, she felt, a little forbidding, almost Gothic – it was also its setting. It lacked charm, she decided, and charm was necessary for both Charles and Jane. She said as much to Georgiana and the pair drifted downstairs and into the gardens.

'It is going to rain,' said Kitty, looking at purple-blue clouds on the horizon. 'I think there may even be thunder.'

Georgiana looked at the sky and, ignoring Kitty's comment, remarked in a quiet voice: 'I heard Sir Edward tell Mr Bridgwater that his nephews and niece will be at dinner this evening.' Such a revelation eclipsed any predictions as to the weather or any finer point of detail about Hazelton's fireplaces or cornices, its stables and cellars. The pair exchanged conspiratorial smiles, linked arms, and walked around the house, ostensibly examining the gardens as they waited for the others to finish their deliberations.

In the carriage on their way to Doncaster to dine with the Fanshawes, Hazelton and its merits were under discussion. 'It is a fine house,' said Mr Bingley, as if trying to convince himself. 'Its architecture is impressive. The grounds are extensive. Not sure about the hunting.' He fell silent and looked troubled.

'Do you like it better than Netherfield?' prompted Kitty.

Mr Bingley looked surprised at the thought. 'Oh, no!' he said decisively. And Colonel Fitzwilliam and Kitty looked at each other, looked at Mr Bingley, and laughed.

'What?' said the would-be landowner, baffled. 'Oh, I see! I suppose there is nothing more to be said, then.'

CHAPTER 36

Three fine country homes in as many days, thought Kitty as the carriages slowed and stopped in front of Danson House, a magnificent red-brick and stone gabled residence approached through acres of woodland and the landscaped grounds of Danson Park. It was, she would learn, Jacobean in origin, dating back to 1616, although the downstairs part had been extensively modernised but fifty years before when a previous Fanshawe had inherited the property. Sir Edward was unstoppable on matters of architecture. As she stepped down from the carriage, Kitty began to wonder whether she should start compiling a compendium of the grand homes of middle England but her thoughts were interrupted by a clap of thunder, and Bingley, offering her his arm, hurried her inside before the inevitable rain began.

Lady Fanshawe, a petite, cheerful and somewhat rotund woman, carrying a small pug in her arms, appeared and welcomed her guests before each of the visitors was dispersed to rooms made ready for them. They would be expected at dinner in just over an hour.

Kitty, a little nervous at the thought of meeting Frederick and William Fanshawe again, was relieved that her arrival at the drawing room coincided with that of Elizabeth and Mr Darcy, and they entered to find their hosts and Mr Bridgwater conversing with a young woman of about two and twenty. Sir Frederick stepped forward to introduce, 'My daughter, Miss Felicia Fanshawe.'

Kitty saw before her a tall and elegant individual, striking rather than beautiful, whose blue eyes, high cheekbones and strong nose showed her family resemblance to her brother, Frederick. However, where his expression implied hauteur, hers hinted at merriment. Kitty saw all this as the ladies exchanged curtsies, but what shocked her – and shocked is hardly too strong a word – was Miss Fanshawe's hair. It was cut short! The style, Kitty knew – from her perusal of fashion plates in ladies' magazines – was called 'à la Titus', so named after that emperor's short and face-framing curls, and had become fashionable in France just a few years previously, but she had neither seen nor expected to see it sported here. She found herself transfixed and then wondered if Miss Fanshawe was carrying out a similar appraisal of her face and person. She almost blushed but, luckily, the arrival of Colonel Fitzwilliam and Georgiana diverted attention away from her.

'My brothers tell me you made their acquaintance in London,' said Miss Fanshawe, addressing Kitty and Georgiana. 'I hope they were not too tiresome! I shall do my best to make amends.' She laughed. 'You have been looking at Hazelton Place today, I understand. What are your opinions?'

Kitty and Georgiana made answers as tactfully as they could, not knowing Miss Fanshawe's views on the estate and aware that her uncle thought highly of it. 'You had best ask Mr Bingley,' said Kitty. 'As you are most probably aware, it is he and my sister, Mrs Bingley, who are seeking a property in this part of the country. I know not if any agreement has been reached. Your own home is quite delightful.'

Miss Fanshawe looked around, as if considering that possibility for the first time. 'Yes, it is. I like it best when I am outdoors, actually. There is some good riding to be had around here. You would have the same at Pemberley, no doubt, Miss Darcy?'

Georgiana agreed that was so but had little else to offer by way of conversation. One is as shy as the other is direct, thought

Kitty. She rather admired Miss Fanshawe's open warmth and firm manner; she was beginning to think that her cropped hair was not so bad either – it did not, after all, detract from her appearance. She imagined Mrs Bennet's reaction were any of her daughters to take so drastic a measure and touched her own hair as if to reassure herself that all was as it should be.

'Where is your family home, Miss Bennet?' enquired Miss Fanshawe.

Kitty's response was curtailed by the arrival of William Fanshawe, who made his way straight to his sister's side.

'Miss Bennet, Miss Darcy. Welcome to Danson Park,' he greeted. 'This is indeed a happy circumstance. I am most happy to see you here. You are both well I trust; not too fatigued from your journey?'

'They seem to have survived it quite well, William,' Felicia Fanshawe answered for Kitty and Georgiana. 'It is not so very far.'

'We met in one of the galleries in London,' William Fanshawe told her, 'just before the ladies were to journey to Derbyshire. I had thought we might have found some other galleries to visit in town but it was not to be.'

'I should have liked that,' said Kitty, wishing she could think of something more erudite to say to the young man now standing beside her. 'You have some interesting landscapes here,' she began.

'Ah, yes,' said Mr Fanshawe, looking around the room, 'some of the family heirlooms. I am afraid I don't take much notice of those but I can give you information about them all if you would like me to. You can also see the rogues' gallery that is the Fanshawe clan, but that may be asking too much. Ah, talking of rogues, here is my esteemed elder brother. Freddie, we are over here!'

Miss Fanshawe excused herself, saying she would rejoin them all shortly, and Frederick Fanshawe strode over, looking every inch the country squire. He bowed gracefully to first Kitty, then Georgiana.

'This is an unexpected pleasure,' he announced. 'We are most grateful to Bridgwater for bringing you here, and to Mr and Mrs Bingley for providing the reason. Neither my brother nor I knew you were residing so close to us. This bodes well indeed. We must show you around the park tomorrow before you go. I think, Miss Bennet, you are not so familiar with this part of the country?'

'Then we must remedy that too,' said William Fanshawe, looking to Kitty for acceptance of his proposal. 'What say you and Miss Darcy to taking a drive hereabouts tomorrow?'

'You are most kind,' said Kitty, who was pleased and favoured the idea, 'but I will have to refer to Mr Darcy. We arrived as one party and he may have other commitments. Colonel Fitzwilliam is with us, as well. Allow me to introduce you.' She looked around for him but he was talking with Miss Fanshawe and her father.

'Well, let us confer while we eat,' said William Fanshawe, dinner having just been announced. He offered Kitty his arm; his brother did likewise to Georgiana and the four proceeded, as happy and charming a quartet as anyone could wish to see.

It would be an exaggeration to say the conversation over dinner was particularly remarkable or especially enlightening. It did, however, serve in that the Darcys, Fanshawes and Bingley were pleased to find each other excellent company – in a way that people with like-minded opinions and wit will inevitably find themselves agreeable over the course of one evening – and Sir Edward was pleased to be the agent who had brought about this happy confluence. Hazelton was hardly mentioned, all but forgotten – and would be forgotten, except to show Dapplewick in a favourable light – but the Fanshawes hoped Mr and Mrs Bingley would be pleased to settle in this part of the country, the merits of which were discussed and lauded to further persuade him.

The attractions of Derbyshire and Yorkshire, though of some interest to Kitty and Georgiana, would not be uppermost in their recollections of the day. The Fanshawe brothers were amusing companions, well travelled, well educated and full of schemes for the entertainment of the young ladies and information as to the places they must visit. Kitty was quite delighted with both of them. Across the table, she noticed, Colonel Fitzwilliam was having no trouble engaging the attention of Miss Fanshawe. She was an animated conversationalist, not exceeding the bounds of decorum of course, but Kitty could see that she was lively and vivacious, clearly traits that were also endearing her to the colonel. Miss Fanshawe seemed as amiable and interesting a young lady as Kitty had ever met, even without the encumbrance of two charming brothers.

When the ladies withdrew after dinner, Kitty looked around her and wondered again at how quickly her life had changed. Here was Lizzy seated beside Lady Fanshawe in this wonderful old house, full of warmth and pleasant people with interesting things to say; and there was her dear friend Georgiana chatting to Felicia Fanshawe. She crossed the room to join the younger women in time to hear Miss Fanshawe lament their return to Derbyshire the next day. That lament was taken up by her mother, whose practised eye had noted the partiality her elder son had shown for Miss Darcy (and whose keen mind had estimated Georgiana's worth, both materially and physically) during dinner. The good lady was already formulating a plan. She was, she told Elizabeth, always glad of company; in fact, she had hoped to receive some cousins at Danson Park this very month but their arrival had been delayed. Perhaps – and she would be so delighted – Mr and Mrs Darcy and her charming relations would like to join them for a week? It was so hard on the young people when they were deprived of convivial company, was it not?

CHAPTER 37

The storm that had been threatening the previous afternoon vent its fury during the night, rattling the windowpanes in Kitty's bedroom. She lay awake thinking about Lady Fanshawe's invitation, which had been partially accepted. Elizabeth and Mr Darcy declined with thanks, citing other engagements (Kitty wondered whether they just wanted to be at Pemberley for a few days with only each other for company) and hoped, instead, that Sir Frederick and Lady Fanshawe would honour them with their presence at their summer ball in August. The alarm this polite refusal had excited in Kitty and Georgiana was doused by Colonel Fitzwilliam, who stepped in to gladly accept, and to offer his services to chaperone the young ladies to Danson Park. Thus, the remainder of the evening had been coloured by expectations of pleasurable pursuits in fine company and expeditions to local beauty spots. Kitty had listed these in her journal, along with other observations of the day, before she had climbed into bed. She had also tried to clarify her thoughts about the younger Fanshawe but had found it easier to discern what others were feeling.

Georgiana is a little in thrall to Frederick Fanshawe, although only those who know her well would see it. She did blush when he spoke to her after dinner, which would have vexed her excessively! And she was almost skittish at the thought of a week at Danson Park. Perhaps she is becoming less shy: lovely girl! FF is quite the beau.

As for Colonel Fitzwilliam, I do believe he is quite taken with Felicia. Then again, I do not know him well, so perhaps he is always this charming? I wonder why he has not married? Perhaps Georgiana knows. What does Miss Fanshawe think of the colonel? This will be an interesting week.

It is pleasant to see Sir Edward again. He is always so solicitous of me and so very kind. Avuncular, I think that is the word. He referred to his son tonight when talking to Mr Bridgwater; another man may have become bitter after such losses; I admire him for his fortitude.

As for William…

Indeed, what of William? Kitty liked him well enough but she could not shake the feeling that he was not so… Not so what? Not so handsome as Henry Adams? No. Not so artistic? Not so eligible? Certainly not that. William Fanshawe was far more eligible! What then? You are ridiculous, Catherine Bennet, she had told herself, and written,

…he is a most amiable and intelligent gentleman and I am looking forward to furthering our friendship.

'Well, that's insightful!' she had reprimanded herself, as she closed the journal and blew out the candle. Now, hours later, she was still awake. A furious flurry of rain made her look at the window. The room was dark but she thought she could discern the first glimmer of morning light. Yesterday they had spoken of a phaeton ride around the park; that seemed unlikely now. She shut her eyes and imagined the days ahead. She hoped nothing would go wrong. This was a constant worry in Kitty's life: something would go wrong. Why do I always think this, she wondered? When had it started? Perhaps it was because she had been ill when she was a child. 'But,' reasoned the calm voice in her head, 'you recovered; you are well now. You are happier than you have ever been. You have been to London. You are living at Pemberley.'

'But what is to become of me?' came the anxious reply. 'Where will I live? Who will I be?' All her sisters were married, all with their own lives; she had never imagined she would be the one left behind. In her mind that had been Mary. She turned over in her bed and rearranged the pillows.

'Silly and ignorant,' said her father's voice. 'Not so pretty as your sisters,' chimed in her mother. She had to marry, but who and when? If she didn't marry, she would have to stay at Longbourn... but Longbourn was entailed to the dreadful Mr Collins. She would have no home, just as Mama always said. Well, of course, she would have Lizzy and Jane; but she would not have her own home. Georgiana would marry and go away, just as Lydia had gone away... well, not just as Lydia had gone away. There would be nephews and nieces and she would become the useful aunt. At least she would not have to be a governess. But perhaps it was better to be a governess, lead one's own life, than be the aunt, travelling from Pemberley to Dapplewick – she supposed the Bingleys would take Dapplewick – and back again? No, she could not be a governess. What could she be?

'A wife, a mother,' said the voice in her head. Was that all? What else is there? No answers came, just more rain. 'Everything is so uncertain,' sighed Kitty, 'and I am so tired!' She pulled the quilt over her head and tried to get back to sleep.

***

The storm had worn itself into a fine drizzle when she went down to breakfast, and her night-time fears had subsided somewhat as well. She found everyone else already assembled and a lively discussion taking place at one end of the table as to the merits of visiting Conisbrough.

'It is just a lot of ruins,' Frederick Fanshawe was saying.

'Of course it is ruined,' rejoined his sister. 'It is a medieval castle. How could it be otherwise? It is romantic!' She turned to William for support but he had seen Kitty arrive. 'Miss Bennet, good morning!' he greeted. 'Join us, we value your opinions. We are trying to interest my brother here in the history of England. It is no easy task!'

Kitty smiled and Frederick Fanshawe shook his head, leaving the field open for his brother to continue. 'Conisbrough Castle is a fine relic, not far from here. The keep is massive, the walls crumbling as befits a medieval castle, and there are fine views from the top of the hill. It's been abandoned for centuries, since the Civil War at least.'

'I should like to see it,' said Kitty, whose recent reading had included the history of the Wars of the Roses, a period she found fascinating – more for the bitter and often murderous conflict between the families than for the battles. 'You are thinking of going today?'

'We cannot go today,' said Miss Fanshawe, indicating the weather. 'We are thinking about when you return. With or without you, Freddie.' She cast a disapproving glance at her elder brother.

'Oh, he'll come, won't you?' said William Fanshawe.

'I should not want to disappoint our charming guests, though I can think of better places to go.'

'The racecourse, I suppose,' said his sister. 'Lucky for us all that it is not the racing season.' There was an edge to her voice.

Her remark caused Sir Edward to look up from behind the *York Herald* and he opened his mouth to speak, but Lady Fanshawe, who thus far had been content to listen to her children squabble, broke in with: 'Miss Darcy, Colonel Fitzwilliam, should you like to see this castle? Perhaps you have already been there?'

Neither had; both expressed a wish to do so. Elizabeth also thought it would make a fine excursion one day and so Frederick Fanshawe was completely overruled. He took it well, of course, waiting a full three minutes before withdrawing from the discussions around him and finding refuge in his copy of *The Sporting Magazine*.

'Do you like riding?' asked Felicia Fanshawe of Kitty. 'I admit it is one of my favourite pastimes. It makes me feel free! And on horseback I am quite as strong as my brothers.'

'Though not as fast,' cut in Freddie Fanshawe.

'I didn't think you were interested in conversing with us,' rejoined his sister, addressing the back of his magazine. 'And in any case, that is only because I have to ride side-saddle. I should like to see *you* ride side-saddle!'

There was no response and Miss Fanshawe turned back to Kitty. 'Do try to forgive him,' she said.

Kitty smiled and then confessed she did not ride.

'Never mind. We will go out in the gig together when you come to stay. If you would like?'

'Be careful before you reply,' interrupted William Fanshawe. 'You might like to see how she drives the gig first.' It was a teasing warning, delivered without any spite.

'I am prepared to take the chance,' laughed Kitty. She was already looking forward to it.

At around midday, when the sun made a feeble appearance, a walk was proposed and everyone ventured outside. William Fanshawe took it upon himself to point out to Kitty the recent improvements to the wilderness area and she learned that he was interested in the new ideas about landscaping.

'We have pretty gardens at my home in Longbourn,' said Kitty in response to a question, 'but not so extensive as these.'

'I sometimes toy with the idea of landscaping myself,' said Mr Fanshawe, 'but I lack an estate of my own and this one has been designed without my help!' He pointed out the various vistas and prospects to Kitty, who admired everything he indicated as well as his knowledge of the subject. She was of a mind to admire knowledge in others, especially when the other was pleasant and eligible.

They had reached the formal gardens now, where they caught up with Lady Fanshawe and Elizabeth. 'At least your journey home will be more pleasant, Mrs Darcy,' her hostess was saying. 'The roads are generally good from here to Pemberley and I trust the rain will not have made them hazardous.'

Elizabeth hoped so, too, but opined the journey would take less than half a day. She had enjoyed her brief sojourn with the Fanshawes, and found much to like in her ladyship; she was pleased to have found another amiable neighbour within easy distance of Pemberley.

Mr Bingley and Mr Bridgwater were to remain at Danson Park until the following day when they would travel south together. The remaining visitors took their leave, full of thanks and promises to meet again soon, and in the case of three of the party, very soon indeed.

CHAPTER 38

'Four days will quickly steep themselves in night,' said Kitty to Georgiana, quoting from *A Midsummer Night's Dream*, which she had plucked from the library that morning and which now lay before her on the picnic rug. The summer weather had returned and they were lazing by the stream.

'Yes, I suppose it is wrong to count the days until we return to Danson Park,' said Georgiana, 'but I cannot help it.'

'You prefer Freddie Fanshawe to his brother, I think?'

Georgiana coloured and was about to protest no partiality but Kitty held her gaze. 'I do, but pray do not ask me why, for I have no explanation except that he is perfectly pleasant and of good family and' – she stopped to hide her smile with her hand – 'he is very handsome.'

'Well that is the beginning of an explanation,' teased Kitty. 'It will do for now.'

Georgiana, unsure if Kitty approved or not, did not ask for her opinions on either brother. Instead, she picked up the Shakespeare and started to read aloud from it. Kitty, for her part, resolved to keep a close eye on this incipient friendship with Frederick Fanshawe. It was her duty as the elder sister; a duty she would never have presumed in regard to Lydia.

Nearly a year had passed since she had seen Lydia. As Georgiana read, Kitty wondered what life was really like for Mrs Wickham, captain's wife. She found she did not envy her younger sister, which was something of a revelation. She remembered how very peeved she had been when Lydia went to Brighton; how she had railed against the unfairness of it all and cried and sulked. How she had been so jealous. 'I am no longer that girl,' Kitty noted, not without pride. 'I am content to be exactly where I am.' She wondered afresh at Mr Darcy's involvement in bringing about Lydia's marriage and how lucky it was for them all.

When they returned to the house, they found Elizabeth seated at a table in the drawing room, immersed in plans for the summer ball. 'An invitation list,' she said, handing it over for perusal.

'You have crossed out Lady Catherine and her daughter?'

'Darcy and I are still discussing it. I am all for a rapprochement, at the right time, but we feel this may not be the occasion.'

Kitty scanned the list for Mr and Mrs Wickham, but was not surprised to find the names absent. That reconciliation, if it ever took place, would also be at another time, and was unlikely to be at Pemberley. Among the names she recognised were those of Colonel Fitzwilliam's older brother, Viscount Mortlake, and his wife; Miss Bingley; Mr and Mrs Bridgwater; Mr and Mrs Hurst; the Fothergills; the Catchpoles; the Wintersons; Sir Edward and the Fanshawes.

'In the past, the summer ball has been attended largely by families from hereabouts,' said Elizabeth. 'It will be an opportunity to meet more of my neighbours.'

'Miss Bingley?' questioned Kitty.

'We expect her, the Hursts and the Bridgwaters at the end of this month. Apparently, it is another tradition – or has been for a few years past – that they stay here at this time of the year. I would not wish to overturn all Pemberley's traditions.' She made a face that only Kitty could see, and added, 'Not immediately.'

'We will have a house party then.'

'We will. Colonel Fitzwilliam has invited one of his fellow officers and the viscount and his lady are also likely to be with us,' said Elizabeth. 'I am minded to invite the Fanshawes, if your week with them goes well. And Georgiana, you must tell me if there are omissions, any friends of yours we have overlooked. The invitations will go out next week.'

'Pemberley will be so full of people,' said Kitty, as she passed the invitation list to Georgiana. She was imagining a moonlit night, windows ablaze with light, music playing, carriages and costumes, fashionable ladies and handsome young men. Perhaps Henry Adams would be among the musicians invited to play! An image flitted across her mind of him playing the violin, so intent and serious when he was performing. He would not be wearing that silly wig though; his hair would fall down over his forehead. Of course, if he were one of the musicians then he would be unable to ask her to dance, which rather dashed her reverie. As an alternative, she saw herself going down the room with William Fanshawe – he would be but one of many young gentlemen who would have asked her to dance – and wondered what she would wear.

'We will have formal dress?' she wondered aloud.

'Yes, it will be a fine excuse to wear my London gowns again. Georgiana,' continued Elizabeth, 'I hope you will forgive me but I have spoken with Fitzwilliam and my idea about this occasion signifying a coming-out ball for you now seems entirely wrong. Your brother thinks that should happen next year, and in London. Has he mentioned this to you yet?'

'No,' said Georgiana, 'but of course I agree.' Her relief was evident; the event was postponed and for that she was grateful enough.

Elizabeth made space for them at the table, interrupting Kitty's fantasies about summer balls and Georgiana's altogether less positive thoughts on coming-out balls, with more prosaic and practical questions. 'What do you think about flowers? And these supper dishes? We need to think about musicians. We need to think about a lot of things! We must arrange some baskets of provisions for the tenants too, I think, so they can have their own celebration. I saw Mrs Moore again yesterday – they are in their new house now – they all know about the ball. News spreads quickly!'

Kitty and Georgiana arranged themselves either side of Elizabeth and the three spent the next two hours discussing ways to re-establish Pemberley's summer ball as the ball of the county.

CHAPTER 39

Three things had become clear to Kitty after only three days at Danson Park: Georgiana evidently thought Freddie Fanshawe the most delightful man she had ever met (and he was happy to let her think this, behaving as a perfect gentleman should in the presence of a demure and handsome and – let us not forget – handsomely endowed young woman); Colonel Fitzwilliam very much admired Felicia Fanshawe's intelligence, candour and beauty, and this admiration was reciprocated by the young lady (whose own eligibility was in no doubt; what her personal fortune might be was unknown to Kitty but there was every reason to believe it was substantial); and that Freddie Fanshawe was quite an arrogant character, and possibly shallow, which was nothing so very out of the ordinary considering he was an eldest son and likely to inherit a large estate.

Kitty's dismissal of the elder Fanshawe did not affect her appreciation of the younger. Given the predilections noted above, William Fanshawe and Kitty often found themselves paired and, as each found the other good company and each approved the other's appearance and demeanour, a mutual affection would have been excusable. Kitty found him interesting and well informed, if sometimes a little too formed in his opinions and in no doubt those opinions were right. In this, he was like his elder brother, usually his chief combatant in verbal sparring – as long as the subject was not sport or hunting. The younger brother professed little interest in these pursuits, while the older thought them of paramount importance and this difference had been noted and needed no further discussion. In Kitty's company, however, William Fanshawe usually softened his stance and they could happily discourse on music and books; the decline in popularity of the minuet; the advantages and disadvantages of the phaeton; and the galleries in London; as well as discover a mutual interest in Tudor history.

This latter topic was under discussion as Kitty and he stood atop the hill, among the ancient stone walls of Conisbrough Castle, looking down at the tiny hamlets that dotted the fields, green meadows and darker woodlands. With the sky above blue and the breeze refreshing rather than robust, it was a scene straight out of a romantic novel mused Kitty. A short distance away, Colonel Fitzwilliam and Miss Fanshawe were examining the massive Norman keep that had survived six centuries of neglect, and Freddie Fanshawe and Georgiana were farther off, strolling alongside the castle's perimeter walls.

Kitty had found a book in the Danson House library that gave a history of Conisbrough. 'It was given to Edmund of Langley, first Duke of York, in the fourteenth century,' she told William Fanshawe, 'and it was through his son, who married Anne de Mortimer, that the Yorkists had a claim to the throne. Have you heard of the Southampton Plot?' He shook his head.

'Nor had I,' said Kitty, 'but this same son, Richard, who was the Earl of Cambridge by then, plotted to assassinate Henry V at this very castle and supplant him with one of the Mortimer relations. I forget which one, a brother-in-law, I think. At any rate, the plot was discovered and Richard was executed.

'They called it the Cousins' War, you know,' she continued, carried along by her enthusiasm. 'It lasted more than thirty years, before Henry Tudor took the throne. His claim was weak but nearly everyone else was dead by then.'

'My word, Miss Bennet, how very learned you are.'

Kitty stopped; she wondered if this was a criticism (she hoped she was not sounding too clever, behaving like Mary; it did not behove young ladies to be too knowledgeable, especially if male pride was at stake) and changed the subject. 'You were at Cambridge, were you not?' she asked.

'Yes, I followed in my brother's footsteps. As younger sons are wont to do, at least up to a point.'

'Did you like Cambridge?'

William Fanshawe shrugged. 'I enjoyed the camaraderie most, I think. I neglected my studies somewhat, although I applied myself more rigorously than my brother. My Roman and Greek history improved, as did my knowledge of Milton and Pope, though I have little use for any of it. Education is overrated in my opinion.' He noted Kitty's surprise.

'Perhaps you are one of those young ladies, like my sister, who disagrees? Felicia would have gone to Cambridge happily, or so she tells me. A ridiculous notion, of course.'

Kitty did disagree with Fanshawe's views on education in general but kept her views to herself. She had, more than once in the past few months, wished she had paid more attention to the masters who had been at her disposal as a child. As she tried to imagine Miss Fanshawe at Cambridge, a quote from the *Rights of Women* floated into her mind: '...both sexes ought, not only in private families, but in public schools, be educated together'. Is that what Miss Fanshawe thought? If so, she liked her better for it.

She looked back at her companion, who was himself deep in thought. 'Did your sister attend school?' she asked him.

'She did. In London. She went to a Miss Someone or Other's Academy in Kensington for a couple of years. Not sure it did any good, but Felicia was adamant she would go.'

Kitty was about to ask if he disapproved of schooling girls but decided against it; she thought she knew the answer. She reverted to a safer enquiry. 'Cambridge is a charming city, I believe. I imagine university life would have been an enriching experience?'

'It proved my ineptitude for law, and ensured my candidature for ordination,' returned the young man, somewhat dismissively. 'The racing at Newmarket was conveniently close.'

'Do you think of the Church, then?'

'Only as a last resort, I can assure you,' said Mr Fanshawe, turning to look at the view. He sounded bitter. 'I have no stomach for the Army or the Navy. Perhaps I may become a gentleman farmer. Who can tell?'

Or find an heiress, thought Kitty, who didn't think the fate of a gentleman farmer so very terrible. Mr Fanshawe turned back to her, an apologetic smile on his face. 'Forgive me, Miss Bennet. I am becoming a bore. Inexcusable.'

She smiled back. 'You only speak your mind, Mr Fanshawe. I am happy to listen.'

His attention was caught by Colonel Fitzwilliam, who was waving and beckoning them over. 'What are those two about?' he wondered aloud, as they drew near, nodding towards Georgiana and Freddie Fanshawe who were retracing their steps up the hill, their heads down as they studied the ground.

'They must have lost something,' said Kitty, and she started down to join them, the others following.

'My cameo has gone,' said Georgiana, her hand going to her throat. 'The clasp must have broken.' She looked most upset.

Kitty knew the pretty oval cameo had belonged to her mother. Lady Anne had worn it every day and Georgiana treasured it for that reason, not because it was rimmed with gold and diamonds. It was nearly always about her neck; Kitty had rarely seen her without it.

'It must be somewhere close by,' she said to Georgiana, who was now close to tears. 'Don't worry. We will find it.'

They all joined in the search, fanning out along the pathway, heads bent as they scanned the patchy grass. Georgiana continued to be anxious but everyone else was optimistic, reasoning rightly that the necklace could not be far, but a half hour passed without any success and the searchers began again, tracing a slightly different route. They ascended the hill once more, with no success, and sat down on the walls to rest. The afternoon was very warm and the conditions not optimal for climbing up and down hills. The ladies sat closely grouped on part of an old stone wall that was in shade.

'You're certain you were wearing it?' asked Colonel Fitzwilliam and Georgiana nodded.

'Then we will keep searching.' He went back to the keep and studied the ground at its base, walking around it in ever-larger arcs as he looked.

'I'm so sorry,' said Georgiana, pathetically. 'This is so much trouble.'

'My dear Miss Darcy. It will be our mission to find this heirloom,' declared William Fanshawe, placing his hand upon his heart. 'You must stay here with the ladies and allow us to reunite the necklace with its rightful owner. We shall not give up!' His theatricals produced a weak smile from Georgiana and the three gallants set off again. Miss Fanshawe began relating an anecdote about how once the nursery had been turned upside down when her elder brother, then about ten, had mislaid his favourite soldier, aptly a figurine of Frederick the Great.

'Was it found?' asked Kitty, hoping it was and that a similar outcome would be achieved today.

'It was indeed. One of the nursery maids found it inside one of Freddie's toy drums. He said he hadn't put it there of course, but no one believed him!

'Oh!' cried Miss Fanshawe, turning to Georgiana. 'I do not mean to imply that you had mislaid your cameo! Forgive me. I was telling the story only because it had a happy ending.'

Georgiana nodded her understanding.

They watched the gentlemen for a few minutes more. At one point, the colonel bent down suddenly to look at something on the ground and Georgiana stood up in nervous anticipation, but he straightened up again and, seeing them look across at him, shook his head.

Kitty regarded her friend anxiously, trying hard to remember when she had last seen the cameo. She was sure Georgiana had been wearing it when they left Danson Park that morning, and she thought it had been about her neck when they were in the carriage.

'We should help them,' said Georgiana, who was too fretful to remain seated, so the three started down the hill again, their eyes on the ground.

'Let us ask one of the gentlemen to go down to the carriage and see if it is inside?' suggested Kitty. 'Perhaps it fell off when we were travelling.'

'Good idea,' said Felicia. 'I will tell Freddie to go.' She strode off to give her brother this task, leaving Kitty and Georgiana together.

The afternoon wore on, but without trace of the cameo and, to everyone's surprise and regret, they had to admit defeat. Well aware of Georgiana's distress, Colonel Fitzwilliam took charge and declared they must all return to Danson Park, that the ladies needed rest and refreshment, and that he would organise a party of the groundsmen to come back and search the area before nightfall.

The return journey was a sombre affair. Everyone's sympathy was with Georgiana, of course (even if some thought and hoped that the cameo would be found safely in her bedroom at Danson House, or in the pocket of a dress, and there was indeed that possibility). Freddie Fanshawe was particularly solicitous, Kitty noted. He is quite the epitome of the knight helping the damsel in distress, she thought, and then scolded herself for being so uncharitable.

On reaching the house, Georgiana ran up to her bedroom, closely followed by Kitty, in the uncertain hope of finding the beloved cameo atop her dressing table. It was not there.

'Oh Kitty!' she sobbed. 'How could I have been so careless! My mother had it all her life, and now I have lost it!'

'You did not do it on purpose. As you said, the clasp must have broken. It is sad, I know, but it is not your fault.' Kitty held Georgiana while she calmed herself, wondering how she would feel in the circumstances. She wanted to say that there were other tangible reminders of Lady Anne's presence but knew that it was not the right time. She had not had to bear the loss of a parent and she felt ill-equipped to say anything.

When the pair went back downstairs they found Lady Fanshawe telling her brother of the day's turn of events. Sir Edward expressed his concern. 'Noticed it this morning, Miss Darcy,' he said. 'Thought how it became you. I do hope it comes to light. Lady Fanshawe has just been telling me that she has given orders for the house to be thoroughly searched.'

'Indeed I have, my dear,' said that lady, taking Georgiana's hand, 'and I have promised a handsome reward to the one who finds it. Not that they need one of course, but it may make their eyesight sharper!' She smiled, and bade them sit and have a glass of wine.

'Now,' she commanded Georgiana. 'Tell me about your mother; I hear she was a remarkable lady.'

Kitty was startled, fearing this would cause fresh pain, but then realised that Lady Fanshawe knew what she was about. As she spoke of her mother and recalled what memories she had, Georgiana's face softened and her manner became less agitated. Lady Fanshawe let her talk and when she eventually fell silent, patted her hand.

'Your mother will always be with you, dear,' she said. 'Pretty things are all very well, but their loss cannot take away Lady Anne's love for you.' Sir Edward nodded his head in corroboration.

Kitty looked at Georgiana, who was smiling at Lady Fanshawe. She wished she had known to say those words to her friend.

Chapter 40

Despite the best endeavours, the cameo remained lost. Colonel Fitzwilliam had reported that every inch of grass around Conisbrough Castle had been scoured but to no effect, and that searches had also been conducted along the road they had taken. Lady Fanshawe's housekeeper had informed her mistress that the house had been thoroughly searched but to no avail, excepting that everything was even cleaner and tidier than it was before.

To Kitty's surprise and relief, she saw that Georgiana, once she had overcome her shock at the loss, was quite composed, even stoic. At breakfast the next morning, she seemed her usual poised self and when Kitty quietly enquired how she was, she replied, 'Lady Fanshawe is right, I should not place such value on things. Besides, everyone has been so very kind to me, especially her ladyship, and you, and Mr Fanshawe.' Her eyes drifted to Frederick as she said this, and Kitty saw him return her glance with one of his charming smiles.

That morning saw the young people's arrangements divided. Freddie Fanshawe had already let it be known that a prior arrangement would take him to a property near Pontefract, about twenty miles away; the vague reason given out to his mother when she had enquired as to the purpose of this trip was that there were a couple of horses he was interested in buying. Sir Edward had immediately expressed an interest in seeing them and then decided it would be capital if all the young gentlemen rode out together – if, of course, the ladies had no objection to them leaving? Kitty, whose heart was not engaged, could easily bear the deprivation of their company for a few hours; Felicia Fanshawe looked as though she might speak against the plan but did not, satisfying herself with a cool glance towards her elder brother; and Georgiana, so grateful to all for their concern and kindness over her necklace, would not have dreamed of objecting – even in jest – to any of the gentlemen's arrangements. Accordingly, the four were ready to depart after breakfast.

'Good luck,' said Miss Fanshawe to Colonel Fitzwilliam. 'Try not to let them lead you into any duels or affrays!' He laughed at the thought, but promised to comply.

Lady Fanshawe proposed a walk, the better to get to know her young guests and a pleasant hour followed as they toured the park and learned more of the house's impressive history, and she gained more understanding of them. Discovering Georgiana played the harp, and that both she and Kitty were adept at the pianoforte, she pretended to chastise her daughter for keeping this knowledge to herself. 'You shall hear them play then,' replied Miss Fanshawe and it was to the music room the ladies repaired when they had tired of their outdoor exercise.

Kitty had already tried the Fanshawes' pianoforte and had not been surprised to find it an excellent instrument. The three took it in turns to play and sing, their music as pretty as the vignettes their performances presented. Lady Fanshawe spent the time smiling and clapping, and everyone was sure their afternoon was more pleasant than the one being enjoyed by the absent menfolk. Kitty liked Lady Fanshawe, who had a sharp mind but one that was ready to find delight rather than fault in the things around her. Her conversational enquiries were subtle and while Kitty knew that both she and Georgiana were being gently examined, she was comfortable enough in Lady Fanshawe's presence for this not to matter.

The gentlemen were not back by dinner time, which was a surprise only to Kitty and Georgiana, none of the Fanshawes seeming the least perturbed. 'They will have found some distraction or perhaps gone on to York,' opined Lady Fanshawe. 'My sons have so many acquaintance between here and there.' Sir Frederick expected them back before nightfall and saw no reason for concern.

Kitty, not sure of the distance to York but believing it to be not that far, accepted this news while Miss Fanshawe shrugged and suggested they set up the card tables after dinner. 'My brothers refuse to play vingt-et-un,' said she. 'They find such amusements a little tame, at least in this house. Our paltry stakes bore them, apparently.'

Her friends were happy to play and Lord Fanshawe happy to excuse himself, despite mild protests from his wife. He was, Kitty had realised, an affable but rather quiet gentleman and, like her own father, quite pleased with his own company. Sir Edward's absence had been notable at the dinner table; he was the one who kept the conversations robust, sparing his host the trouble of speaking too much.

The four played their game with much hilarity and some determination, and without losing any fortunes. Kitty was quietly relieved to find the stakes were not high, and by winning some deals, was left neither poorer nor richer at the end of the evening. They had just finished when the doors opened and in burst the travellers. The two Fanshawes were the most jocular, full of their day and expressing delight at finding the ladies still up. Sir Edward greeted everyone in turn, commenting on the excellent dinner they had had at an inn on their way back to Danson Park, and Colonel Fitzwilliam was a little quieter, hoping the ladies had had a pleasant day and apologising for their late return.

Having exhausted himself with his greetings, Freddie Fanshawe collapsed onto a nearby sofa and wondered about a glass of port. He is a little the worse for drink already, thought Kitty. She looked at the other gentlemen but saw nothing amiss.

'Did you buy your horse?' his sister enquired of him.

Mr Fanshawe looked nonplussed at the question. 'No,' he recollected. 'Wasn't any good. Waste of time.'

Georgiana was sorry to hear that; Miss Fanshawe wanted to know more.

'Was it a chestnut, a grey? I do like a grey myself. What was it like?'

'What do you mean, what was it like?' said her brother, annoyed at being questioned. 'You know what a horse looks like. It was a chestnut. You wouldn't have liked it.'

'You didn't like it either, it seems. You seem to have no luck in your quest for horses!' said Miss Fanshawe tartly, ending the topic. Sir Edward stepped in with an account of the market day at Pontefract, how busy it all was and so forth, and then turned the conversation to the ladies. How had they spent the day?

'Most enjoyably,' said Miss Fanshawe, and the others concurred.

'They all three entertained me delightfully at the pianoforte,' said Lady Fanshawe. 'It is a shame you missed it. They all sing like nightingales.'

The gentlemen looked suitably chagrined. 'If the ladies would honour us with a performance now?' asked Sir Edward.

'Too late for that,' announced Lady Fanshawe, getting up. 'That horse has bolted.' And laughing at her own little joke, announced she was retiring.

Kitty thought to follow her, and the ladies all took their leave. She went to bed wondering about Freddie and Felicia Fanshawe. She had picked up tensions between them before and couldn't decide whether this was just normal quibbling between brother and sister or whether some animosity existed. On the other hand, she surmised, nothing so very strange in siblings not enjoying each other's company; she had her own family to look to for evidence of that and perhaps brothers were different.

Sisters were different, too! Felicia Fanshawe was an adventurous spirit and would have put many a timid man to shame. Kitty found this out the next morning when the promised ride in the gig eventuated. They set off sedately enough, trotting along, and Kitty could see from the outset that Miss Fanshawe was confident and able in controlling the horse. She spoke to it, cajolingly and authoritatively, and Kitty, who had never been in a gig before, was completely at ease and enjoying herself.

'I have been told I do not comport myself as a lady should when I ride,' said Felicia, as they passed out of sight of the house and its occupants. 'I do like to ride fast when I can. What do you say?'

This was unexpected, but not entirely unwelcome. Kitty had seen young men hurtling about in gigs but never thought to be in that situation herself. A thrill of anticipation enveloped her. 'If you are sure it will be all right,' was her qualified reply.

'We will be fine!' cried Felicia, spurring on the horse and calling on it to 'Go! Go!' Kitty hung on to the side of the gig as they gathered speed and raced across the open ground. Her hair, bonnet and ribbons flew backwards and the wind was fresh in her face. It was fun and exhilarating and like nothing she had ever done before. Felicia was shouting out instructions and Kitty found herself laughing in pure delight. They covered quite a distance and she was still laughing when they cantered and then slowed to a trot.

'Oh, that was such fun!' declared Kitty, wiping her eyes and adjusting her clothing.

'As I said, not considered ladylike but where is the harm? If no one sees, then no one grieves – or more to the point, no one complains and forbids!'

'You have to keep it a secret?'

Felicia considered. 'Not a secret exactly. After all, when I was young Freddie would take me out in the gig and do just what we have done. He would be a fool indeed if he thought I had forgotten how to enjoy it! I exercise discretion. I think that is the best way of looking at it. Besides, it is tiresome to always behave so very decorously, don't you agree?'

This sort of indecorum was new to Kitty, and she had no ready argument against it. It had been so very enjoyable, after all. She was at once slightly alarmed and completely taken with Felicia Fanshawe's reasoning. Who determined what was ladylike anyway? No one could take her friend to task about her manners or appearance (even with her cropped hair), so did it matter if she enjoyed hurtling about in a gig?

'My brothers do more or less as they please, and are not called to account,' continued Felicia. 'It can be excessively vexing!'

Kitty wondered if this was an allusion to their arriving back so late the previous evening, but her companion did not elucidate.

'One day, Kitty – may I call you Kitty?'

Kitty nodded.

'Well, of course you must call me Felicia! One day, and do not tell anyone this, I am going to dispense with the side-saddle and ride my mare astride. Not in public, of course. But it cannot be so very shocking surely?'

Again, Kitty was not sure. It seemed to her the height of daring! Felicia, not needing a reply, had turned back to the house and quite soon Miss Fanshawe and Miss Bennet were back in the drawing room, taking tea and behaving impeccably. That too was pleasant, but Kitty could not easily forget the feeling of the wind in her face and the sensation of speed as they careered around the park. She smiled every time she thought about it.

They saw little of Sir Frederick except at dinner but Lady Fanshawe and Sir Edward were excellent company; neither was ever short of a word and could be very amusing when relating anecdotes from their childhood. More than once, Kitty found herself thinking that, for all his bonhomie and bluster, Sir Edward was lonely. He was always most attentive to her, but then so he was to Georgiana and his nephews and niece. Nonetheless, it was with Kitty that he held long discussions about literature and with whom he shared his knowledge of contemporary novelists. She never found her conversations with Sir Edward dull or uninteresting. In that he was unlike his nephews.

Their time at Danson Park passed quickly and pleasurably, picnicking and strolling around the grounds by day; music by night, and even charades after dinner on the last evening, when Miss Fanshawe, helped by Sir Edward, had shamed her brothers into joining the game. Kitty would have gladly accepted another ride in the gig, but the opportunity did not present.

Apart from the loss of the cameo, nothing else untoward occurred to cause distress or alarm and by the end of their stay, Kitty, Georgiana and Felicia had established themselves as dear friends and nothing, absolutely nothing, could prevent the three of them from meeting again soon. It was deemed fortunate indeed that Pemberley was fewer than fifty miles distant.

The menfolk, who had no need to express themselves so volubly, had rubbed along well enough and were content with that, leaving Sir Edward to sum up the week as 'Capital, capital!' Lady Fanshawe was pleased with herself for having thought to invite her guests and had cast a benign eye over the developing friendships between her daughter and the colonel, and her eldest son and Miss Darcy. Lord Fanshawe would be informed of her thoughts later.

CHAPTER 41

There was an air of expectation about Pemberley, thought Kitty on their return to the great house, as if it knew a house party and the summer ball were imminent. This intangible feeling was reinforced by a greater number of servants than was usual going about their duties, carrying supplies and making the guest wings ready. The first visitors would be arriving in a week.

There had, Kitty discovered, been no shortage of post during their absence. In addition to replies to invitations to the ball, Elizabeth had received correspondence from Jane, Mr and Mrs Bennet, Charlotte Collins and Aunt Gardiner. 'There is a letter for you from Miss Bingley,' she told Georgiana as they sat down on one of the terraces, looking out over the lawns to the lake, 'but nothing for you, Kitty. Oh, except Mr Darcy has received some music scores, sent to him from Mr Adams, who wrote he had ordered them on your behalf when we were all in London but that they had arrived after our departure. He hoped you would appreciate them. Most thoughtful of him, I think.'

Kitty agreed it was and hoped her face did not betray the feelings that this gesture generated. Not only was it unexpected, it meant that Henry Adams was still thinking of her. She had not dared hope for that.

'You will be more interested in Jane's letter and the one from father,' Elizabeth continued. 'Jane writes that she is in good health, and that Bingley intends to go ahead with the purchase of Dapplewick Hall. She hopes they will take possession at the end of the year.'

This was no real news to Kitty, who had anticipated such a decision. As such, she accepted it with equanimity. 'It will be wonderful for you and Jane to be so close,' said she, sincerely.

Elizabeth smiled back. 'And you will continue to visit both of us. Jane will insist on it, and so too will Georgiana and I.

'Jane also writes that Mary and Mr Gregory are gone to Portsmouth and are waiting on a ship to take them on their journey to India. She says their destination is Calcutta and that they think to be on-board by the second week of this month.'

'She really is going then,' said Kitty. 'I still can hardly believe it.'

'She is indeed. I have written to them, wishing them well and sent your good wishes. I did not want to wait for your return in case it was too late. Our mother, though, is not taking this news at all well. Jane tells me as much, and so too does our father.'

'Poor Mama. Has she taken to her bed?'

'Not entirely, for Jane says she visits Netherfield most days but your surmise is not inaccurate. Jane called in at Longbourn last week to see Papa and find out a little more about Mary's situation, and he told her that Mama often kept to her room and caused Hill much exercise in running up and downstairs to tend to her.'

Kitty began to feel a little sorry for her mother, although she suspected her concern for Mary, though real, was only part of the problem. Mrs Bennet had lost her favourite daughters to husbands; Mary had found a mission in life and her mother, whose sole aim had been to see her daughters wed, had lost hers. There is still me, of course, thought Kitty, but she seems to have forgotten that. 'Has Jane told her they are quitting Netherfield for Dapplewick?' she asked.

Elizabeth shook her head. 'She dreads breaking that news. She wonders about talking to Papa about it first, although I am not sure of the benefit there. Poor Jane. She does so hate to cause any concern and in this she is bound to disappoint.'

'And the other letters?'

'No other particular news from Mama, apart from a reference to Aunt Phillips calling in and wishing she heard more from Lydia. As for Papa, he writes that, as much as he would like to dance the night away at the ball and wear out his best shoes, he must decline our invitation. He referenced Mrs Bennet's disinclination to travel at this time as an excuse – a very convenient excuse! I did not expect otherwise!

'And Charlotte Collins wrote to say she has become mother to a baby girl, to be called Elizabeth.'

'Elizabeth!' exclaimed Kitty. 'After you? How lovely! But surely Catherine or Anne would have been Mr Collins's first choices. How very imprudent! Impudent, even! What does Lady Catherine think of this disregard?'

'That I do not know,' laughed Elizabeth. 'Perhaps Mr Collins can say it is his mother's name? In the event, I believe the little babe is to be christened Elizabeth Anne – that is Lady Catherine's daughter's name so there is some room for flattery!

'So now I have told you my news and you must tell me yours. How was Danson Park and are we to invite the Fanshawes to be our house guests?'

'Most definitely, yes!' replied Georgiana, uncharacteristically forthright. 'We have had a wonderful week, have we not, Kitty?'

Kitty nodded in agreement, although she was quite astonished that Georgiana's partiality for Frederick Fanshawe had eclipsed – at least for the moment – the loss of her missing cameo.

'Well,' said Elizabeth, 'I am going to ring for tea and you must tell me all about it.'

CHAPTER 42

To say Pemberley was bursting at the seams would be a wild exaggeration – in truth the house had capacity for ten times as many guests as now filled its elegantly decorated confines – but as house parties go, the one hosted by Mr and Mrs Fitzwilliam Darcy in the summer of 1813 was larger than in previous years. Kitty described it to herself as a London or (as she imagined) a Bath season in miniature. Where, just a week ago, she had Georgiana, Colonel Fitzwilliam, Elizabeth and Darcy for company, now there was an ever-changing cast of characters to be met every time she turned a corner or entered a room. Previously quiet salons were filled with lively discussion and chatter and, more often than not, music – some of the musicians engaged for the ball had been brought in to entertain the guests on one evening, and on other occasions there were plenty of opportunities for the ladies in residence to demonstrate their abilities on the pianoforte and harp. These days Kitty only needed the mildest persuasion to display her own musical skills.

The three Fanshawes had arrived, not at all concerned at the late invitation. Colonel Fitzwilliam had introduced his friend Captain Henry Morton, with whom he had served, a pleasant-looking man of middle height, noble bearing and twenty-eight years, who, it would soon be discovered, had been widowed a year previously. Mr and Mrs Bridgwater, Miss Bingley, and Mr and Mrs Hurst were happily ensconced in Pemberley once more, enjoying the prestige that went with the

Darcy hospitality. Last and certainly not least, Mr Darcy's eldest cousin and his wife, the Viscount and Viscountess of Mortlake, were in attendance, ostensibly adding an air of nobility to the proceedings.

In fact, the viscount and his lady were fine representations of the English peerage, wearing their titles with ease and without condescension. Elizabeth had met them previously, shortly after she had become Mrs Darcy, and had been quietly relieved and pleased to find them accepting of his cousin's choice of bride. She had since discovered that Lady Mortlake had once been plain Miss Mary (although of a much wealthier family than the Bennets), so perhaps that went some way to explaining their largesse, or maybe they were simply people too well bred to show their displeasure or surprise in public. Another disappointment to Lady Catherine de Bourgh, no doubt.

Colonel Fitzwilliam had introduced his brother to Kitty and she had found, as Elizabeth had already told her, that there was nothing to fear in talking to him, except perhaps remembering to address him as My Lord. As brothers, he and the colonel were very alike in their manner and appearance; only the order of their birth had marked them out to such different paths.

Caroline Bingley had been graciousness personified since she had entered Pemberley, playing her role as esteemed family friend to perfection. Kitty did her best to keep out of Miss Bingley's way, not because she was perturbed by her but simply because there were others whose company she preferred.

The day's activities had been discussed at breakfast and as a result some of the gentlemen were setting out for a little recreational fishing, while others sought to exercise themselves and their horses around the countryside. An impromptu archery competition had been suggested by Elizabeth, who assured everyone that she and Kitty would be vying for last place. Kitty could tell that Georgiana was a little disappointed that Freddie Fanshawe had chosen to go riding, depriving her of the chance to show off her prowess with a bow. Colonel Fitzwilliam, on the other hand, had waited to see what Miss Fanshawe wanted to do before committing himself elsewhere and was now escorting her towards the lawns where the range was being set up. Georgiana, acting as hostess with Elizabeth, followed with Lady Mortlake, Mr and Mrs Bridgwater, and others.

Kitty, who had begged a few minutes in order to complete and send an almost-finished letter to Jane, started out shortly afterwards. The day was warm, too warm to hurry, and to save herself time she took a shortcut on a path that led close to the stables. As she rounded the corner she saw Sir Edward and Freddie Fanshawe a little way off. She raised a hand and was about to call out but quickly realised they were in the middle of a heated argument. She could not hear what was being said but Sir Edward was clearly trying to reason with his nephew who, very agitated, was beating his riding whip against the stable door and remonstrating in return.

Kitty backed around the corner, unseen. She could not imagine what they were talking about so vehemently and didn't really want to find out. She made her way back to the lawn and happier people, where there was no opportunity to ponder, let alone discuss, what she had seen. 'Kitty! There you are at last!' Elizabeth called as she saw her approach. 'You are needed. I cannot be the only one who needs help reaching my target!' Kitty laughed and promised to be just as adept as her sister with a bow.

Georgiana won, of course, although Felicia proved a worthy opponent and Colonel Fitzwilliam was hard put to know whether to be pleased for his ward, who blushed prettily at her shocking temerity in besting her guests, or assure Miss Fanshawe that victory would be hers next time. The lady herself was not in the least bit disappointed; the colonel's attentions may have helped in that regard.

The afternoon drifted past, little knots of people wandering about the gardens or taking tea on the lawn, everything and everyone carefree. Mr Darcy and Captain Morton appeared at one point, having tired of their quest for trout. Kitty knew that Darcy was not overly fond of fishing. It was, however, a gentleman's accomplishment, she had told him, not unlike ladies having to embroider screens, and Lizzy had laughed. He proposed a walk before dinner, if his wife would oblige him? Captain Morton offered his arm to Kitty, and Colonel Fitzwilliam, forsaking Miss Fanshawe temporarily, sought Georgiana's company, and they all wandered off downstream towards the glen.

Captain Morton was full of admiration of Pemberley and the estate and found a keen listener in Kitty. His own home was in Dorset, where he said the countryside had a gentler character but one that was offset by the dramatic cliffs and seas that changed colour with the weather. He was also an admirer of Colonel Fitzwilliam, a fine friend and excellent officer, whom he had known for a number of years. Kitty turned to see what had become of the colonel and Georgiana; they were walking very slowly and engaged in what looked like earnest conversation. She wondered if he was talking to her of Miss Fanshawe; he certainly looked quite serious.

CHAPTER 43

Dinner the previous evening had been a jovial affair, everyone swapping stories of their day, interspersed with tall tales of large fish and speculation as to the ball, now just a week away. The August weather was uncommonly steady and Kitty thought everything more or less perfect.

She had woken early and gone to Georgiana's room, hoping to persuade her to take a walk before breakfast. With so many guests in the house, it had been days since they had had a proper tête-à-tête. As it turned out, Georgiana was wide awake and readily agreed to Kitty's suggestion. They were out of the house and taking the path up to the folly in no time.

'Isn't this all just heavenly,' declared Kitty, as she spun about on the grass, taking in the summer skies and inhaling the warm morning air. 'I hardly saw you last night, although I know you were at the same table as Frederick Fanshawe and his sister for most of it. His brother and I had you in our sights! And Colonel Fitzwilliam seems enamoured of our dear friend Felicia. What have you to tell me about it all?'

'Very little, as it happens.'

'Now Georgiana, you cannot be coy with me! First of all, I know you are partial to Freddie Fanshawe. Second, you must have noticed that Felicia and the colonel seem fond of each other. I wondered if he was speaking of her to you yesterday.'

Georgiana looked perplexed. 'No,' said she. 'I don't know what you mean.'

'When we were all walking near the glen,' said Kitty.

'Colonel Fitzwilliam would never speak of such things with me.'

'I suppose not,' agreed Kitty. 'Well, what of you and Mr Fanshawe, then?'

'I thought… I think, he likes me.'

'I think he does. What of *your* feelings, Miss Darcy?'

Georgiana twisted her fingers around her fichu. 'He is everything a gentleman should be. I find much to admire in him and he is so very charming.' She sighed.

Kitty supposed she must know the gentleman better than she did.

'Have you lost your heart to him?' she enquired in a gentler voice. She hoped not, but was ready to hear and advise, protect if necessary.

'We have no agreement,' said Georgiana. 'He has been most attentive to me though.'

And you to him, thought Kitty.

'He has asked me for the first two dances at the ball.' Georgiana smiled at the recollection. 'I think William Fanshawe will ask the same of you.'

Yes, thought Kitty, I think he will. The prospect, though not unpleasant, did not fill her with joy. She supposed it should. 'Do you think so?' she said. 'I had not thought so far ahead.' In fact she had, and those thoughts entertained the not unreasonable possibility of many young gentlemen asking her to dance, some of them as yet unknown.

Georgiana was looking pensive, and a little sad.

'You are out of spirits today?' said Kitty, holding out her hand. 'What is the matter?'

'Nothing.'

'Of course there is something. You are not yourself. Is there something you want to tell me? Can I help?'

Again, Georgiana shook her head. She freed herself from Kitty and kept walking. After a few minutes, she stopped and turned to face her.

'It is nothing and yet it is everything,' said she, earnestly. 'I try hard to do what is right. I do.'

'You do,' laughed Kitty. 'I have never thought otherwise. No one does.'

'But what one wants, what one should do, what other people want me to do… these are not the same things,' said Georgiana, shaking her head. 'It is all so confusing. Oh, do not look so alarmed, Kitty! I am not in any danger! I am just in a moral dilemma.'

'A moral dilemma? That I cannot believe! You, of all people! What can you mean?'

'I am not so good as everyone thinks.'

Kitty waited, a disbelieving expression her only response.

'Truly. I try to do what is right.'

'Well, your efforts have been entirely successful,' cried Kitty, at a loss to comprehend about what Georgiana – the very embodiment of everything a genteel, accomplished and clever young lady should be – could be reproaching herself. She linked her arm in hers again and they continued walking.

'Colonel Fitzwilliam does not approve of Mr Fanshawe,' Georgiana said at last. 'He is my uncle and I am his ward, so I must listen to what he says. He has not told me exactly why, but I know that is what he thinks. He has told me, in his kind way, that he feels he is not suitable for me. And he has spoken with my brother about him, too. I am certain of it.'

Kitty wondered how to answer. 'You do not know why they disapprove? Have they heard something against him?'

'They probably want me to marry a lord, someone of the nobility,' said Georgiana, looking very miserable and sounding peeved.

'You really think so?'

'We have not discussed it in detail, but why not? My brother has been more like a father than a brother in many ways and he and Fitzwilliam want only what is best for me, I am sure.'

'I do no doubt it, but he would not have you marry where you did not want to marry, surely? Not when he himself has married for love – and so disappointed your poor aunt, Lady Catherine, and possibly even her daughter Anne, into the bargain?'

'It is true he is very happy with Elizabeth. I cannot imagine he could have made a better choice.' Georgiana managed a small smile. 'He is quite changed, you know? He laughs more and sometimes he even laughs at himself!'

'Lizzy is adept at finding amusement in other people. Even her husband – especially her husband – would not escape her keen wit. I can testify to this, having been the recipient of it for as long as I can remember!' It was true, thought Kitty. Elizabeth was warmer towards her now than she had ever been, and she was glad of it, but she could be, had been, sharp.

'But why, Georgiana, would your brother wish you to marry someone you do not love? Why would he interfere with your happiness in such a way? As well, things are different now. Please forgive me if I speak out of turn but you have no need to marry. Not yet, anyway. There is no urgency to your situation. You are young and you have your own establishment in London; you have means enough to choose.'

'What you say is true. I should wish to be as happy as my brother and Elizabeth, if that were possible.'

'Well then, let us both presume that this is entirely possible, even probable. For you, and for me! If your brother and Colonel Fitzwilliam harbour misgivings about Mr Fanshawe, perhaps these will be overcome. Perhaps they simply want you to know your own mind, to not precipitate events. You have not known him for very long, nor they. Besides, you are not even officially out yet. You will have a season in London. I am sure they are just urging caution.

'And for my part, I shall make a full summary of all Mr Fanshawe's good points as well as all his flaws – from how he holds his spoon to his thoughts on weighty matters and everything else in between – and give you a full report.' Kitty said this more to lighten the mood than to convince herself or Georgiana of Freddie Fanshawe's inestimable character.

'You do not believe me? You are not convinced?' said she, when Georgiana failed to smile.

'I think it is easier for men to choose where to marry,' she replied. 'Women not only have to wait to be asked but they are also expected to marry where their families wish.'

'This is true,' said Kitty, 'but I cannot think that your brother would wish you to marry well for form or for material advantage or to please others. Would he not let your heart lead you? I am sure Lizzy would be your friend, too, in so serious an undertaking as marriage. You worry too much. In the end, you will choose well.' Although perhaps not Freddie Fanshawe, she thought.

Georgiana did not respond. When she lifted her head, she asked, 'Have you ever done something really wrong?'

Kitty shook her head, not at the question but in mild exasperation at her friend – although she could respond in the negative to the question also. She had not done anything *really* wrong, despite having felt otherwise for many years, and so she empathised with Georgiana while dismissing her fears.

'What have you done that you think is so very wrong? Tell me and then I can put an end to your concerns and we can both laugh them away. I cannot have you so upset.'

To her astonishment, Georgiana burst into tears. They were but a small distance from the folly and Kitty led her there, sat her down on one of the stone seats and held her until she became calm enough to speak. 'You will think me very foolish,' she sobbed, 'but I will tell you because I think of you as my sister, and I am sure you will not betray my confidence.'

'I would never do that,' Kitty assured her.

'I have thought myself in love before you see. I am so afraid of being wrong again! I was fifteen and living in London with Mrs Younge, my governess and chaperone. He was such a charming and handsome man. I had known him all my life. I trusted him completely. I thought I loved him. I *did* love him.'

Georgiana stopped and looked at Kitty, expecting some kind of censure. Kitty merely nodded.

'I thought I loved him, and he said he loved me. Mrs Younge and I were in Ramsgate for the summer and then suddenly he was there, too. I was so happy, and Mrs Younge approved of him, was always saying what a fine gentleman he was. Which of course I knew. We were planning to marry, to elope…'

'Elope!' exclaimed Kitty, in spite of herself.

'Elope,' sniffed Georgiana. 'Then my brother arrived unexpectedly and I could not keep so great a secret from him, I did not suppose he would so disapprove of my choice.' She shuddered, remembering how aghast Mr Darcy had been.

'Why was he so opposed that time?' asked Kitty, remembering the Mr Darcy she had first encountered, so cold and supercilious.

'My brother was not at fault,' said Georgiana. 'I was the foolish one.'

'You loved him though. And he, you?'

'I thought I did. His motives I now know were mercenary. My only excuse is my age and that I knew nothing of the world. I have better judgement now, I am sure I do, but my brother and Colonel Fitzwilliam do not think so. They have made that clear.'

'My dearest Georgiana, it was a lucky escape,' said Kitty, while silently agreeing with Darcy and Colonel Fitzwilliam on an alliance involving their ward and Frederick Fanshawe. 'This man was surely a scoundrel of the worst kind to take advantage of you.'

She saw Georgiana stiffen. 'There is one more thing you should know,' she said, resolutely. 'It will shock you but I cannot withhold his name now that I have confessed this much. He is known to you, Kitty. He is your sister's husband. Wickham, George Wickham.'

Incredulity, amazement and disbelief crowded for supremacy in Kitty's mind and rendered her speechless. This was astounding. Wickham! Lydia's Wickham had thought to marry – to elope!

– with Georgiana? No wonder Mr Darcy would not have him at Pemberley.

'Poor, sweet girl,' said Kitty, taking Georgiana's hand once more. Poor, reckless Lydia, she thought. What a practised liar and scoundrel Wickham was!

'Who else knows?' she asked.

'My brother and Elizabeth, Colonel Fitzwilliam, Mrs Younge, you. No one else.'

'None shall hear it from me. We will never speak of it again, if that is what you wish. It is in the past, Georgiana. It cannot affect your actions in future.'

Even as she spoke, Kitty's mind was in turmoil. For Georgiana of all people – sweet, shy Georgiana, so very well bred and nurtured – to fall prey to passion was almost unthinkable. And yet she had – and to Wickham! The very idea that Georgiana and Lydia had been in thrall to the same man was unbelievable. Georgiana was naïve where Lydia was forward, but it was still almost incomprehensible.

Georgiana sat slumped on the seat, her eyes closed. Kitty stood up, taking charge of the situation. 'We must get you back to the house and fit to be seen. We can go in by the east door. Some cold water for your face and all will be well. Will you go to breakfast or shall I say you have a headache?'

'I do have a headache!' cried Georgiana. 'But it would cause concern if I don't go in to breakfast.'

'I hope you are not going simply to see Freddie Fanshawe,' said Kitty, sternly.

Georgiana protested she was not; Kitty was unconvinced. Is this what it is like to be in love, she wondered? All reason lost? She remembered something Jane had once said about mixing prudence with passion. She held out her hands to Georgiana, forcing her to stand. She is so very young, she thought, suddenly feeling much older herself. Of course Mr Darcy and Colonel Fitzwilliam would want her to wait. She would have no shortage of admirers were she to come out in London.

Does Freddie Fanshawe intend to make her an offer, she wondered? Was he worthy of her? Kitty thought not, but it was not something she could discuss with anyone. She remembered the scene she had witnessed at the stables yesterday. She would have to make good on her promise – said in jest – to keep him under close observation.

Luckily for Georgiana, they gained the house and their rooms without interference and made a late entrance for breakfast. No one noticed anything amiss. Kitty's thoughts remained tangled, though. Georgiana and Wickham; Wickham and Lydia; Elizabeth and Mr Darcy; Georgiana and herself – she could hardly make sense of it. It was in the past, as she had said to Georgiana, and would remain so. How could it not? It would be too dreadful for all concerned – but especially for Georgiana and Lydia – were such a secret to be known.

CHAPTER 44

It was both fortunate and unfortunate that Pemberley was full of guests and activity. On the one hand, it left no time for Georgiana to be morose and on the other it allowed Kitty little opportunity to think and try to make sense of this new information. She realised that she wanted to speak with Elizabeth, who already knew about Wickham's treachery and with whom she could confide in safety. Elizabeth, however, was fully engaged in being hostess, and this was hardly the moment for unpleasant family history to be aired. She had, therefore, to do her best to put it to the back of her mind for another day.

Her surprise at Georgiana's revelations did not subside into criticism. After all, she reasoned, she had been even younger than Lydia – and more alone – when Wickham had planned his move. The more Kitty discovered about him, the more villainous he became. She was sure he had held no real affection for Georgiana; that his actions were purely mercenary. It was almost amusing, then, that he had been forced into marriage with an impecunious Bennet sister. It must have cost Mr Darcy dear, both in pride and in money.

Kitty had made excuses after breakfast, pleading the need to write a letter but in fact hoping to have an hour to herself, and was on her way to Georgiana's music room where she could enjoy some solitude. She had yet to properly look over the scores Henry Adams had so kindly sent; the least she could do was learn to play them. Her premise about the room being empty was wrong, however; when she turned into the passage she could hear someone else at the pianoforte but she was not unhappy to find the musicians were Felicia Fanshawe and Amelia Bridgwater.

'Ah, you have found us out!' cried Miss Fanshawe. 'We thought to have a quiet morning. It seems you have the same idea?'

'I would not disturb your plan,' said Kitty. 'Though I might become part of it.'

'Indeed you shall,' returned she. 'What shall we play?'

They made room for Kitty and music soon gave way to what some would consider idle chatter. They had not long been settled in this pursuit when a footman arrived, looking for Kitty. His mission was to inform her that Mrs Darcy would be obliged if she would join her in her private sitting room.

Kitty obliged, of course, wondering what her sister could want and surmised it must have to do with arrangements for the ball. She had almost reached Elizabeth's rooms when the lady herself appeared, saw Kitty, and walked quickly towards her.

'Is something the matter?' said Kitty, for the second time that day. Elizabeth looked pale and worried.

'We have a visitor,' said she, without preamble. 'Lydia is here!'

Kitty made the only possible response: 'Lydia?'

In the light of the morning's events, so very fresh and tumultuous, the idea of Lydia being at Pemberley was so preposterous it was beyond comprehension. What on earth could she be doing here? Where was Georgiana?

Before she could say anything else, Elizabeth had steered her into the sitting room and closed the door.

'Why is she here? Has something happened?' burst out Kitty, suddenly fearing bad news about Lydia or Wickham or Longbourn. Why else would Lydia suddenly arrive? What did she want? What would Georgiana do when confronted by her sister, Mrs Wickham?

'No need to alarm yourself,' Elizabeth was saying, outwardly calm. 'She looks to be in excellent health. She is here because she has found out that there is to be a ball.'

'She did not find out from me,' said Kitty firmly, detecting an undertone of accusation.

'No, of course not,' said Elizabeth, checking herself. 'It was not a secret. No doubt she heard it from Mama. However, it did not occur to me that she would presume to come without an invitation.'

This is terrible, thought Kitty. How could she do this? Then she remembered Lydia was ignorant of Wickham's designs on Georgiana. An even worse idea presented itself. 'Is Captain Wickham with her?'

'He is not,' said Elizabeth, sitting down. 'He would not dare to come to Pemberley. He knows very well that he would not be admitted here.' She paused. 'There are matters of which you are not aware.'

'Lizzy,' Kitty said quietly, joining her sister on the chaise longue. 'I know more about Wickham than you suppose. I know to whom we are indebted for arranging his marriage to Lydia.' She saw Elizabeth register surprise. 'This very morning, Georgiana told me how he had tried to take advantage of her.'

'This morning! Why?' cried Elizabeth. 'This is too much! Did she expect to see Lydia here? You had told her she would be coming?'

'Lizzy, no! I am as surprised as you at her presence here.'

Elizabeth was not listening. Agitated and upset, she was now pacing up and down the room.

'Lizzy!' tried Kitty again. 'I had no knowledge whatsoever that Lydia would come here today, or indeed any other day!'

'I know you and Georgiana are very close,' returned Elizabeth, her suspicions high, 'but why would she confide in you about… about that! Today of all days? It is unbelievable!'

'She was upset about something else. I don't think she planned to tell me but she did, and I know I am not breaking her confidence in speaking of it with you. I am as amazed as you are that Lydia is here now. Georgiana will be exceedingly alarmed. I am alarmed! Where is Lydia now?'

'I have put her in the Blue Room, on the floor above yours. Millie is helping her unpack.'

'So she will stay?'

'What else can I do?' said Elizabeth, with uncharacteristic bitterness. 'She is my sister, our sister. What else can I do.' The last was rhetorical.

'How long will she stay?' asked Kitty, at the same time thinking how strange it was that she herself did not immediately want to rush to see Lydia, to hear all her news.

'She says that Wickham is gone down to Birmingham with some fellow officers for a week and she thought it would be an excellent joke to come here and surprise us all. Apparently, it would be dull in Newcastle without Wickham. They parted at Lambton and she talks of being reunited with him there next Saturday.' Elizabeth sat down again.

'Does Mr Darcy know?'

'Not yet.' Elizabeth sighed and Kitty felt a wave of sympathy for her elder sister. Unless Lydia had undergone a radical change of manner and attitude, her presence would sorely test some and provide amusement and scorn for others.

'Kitty, I am going to need your help.' The request, contained in a statement, was nonetheless one that touched Kitty's heart. That she would render whatever assistance she could was not in question; that Elizabeth had asked for her help was at once surprising and gratifying.

'Of course,' said she. 'In whatever way you wish. I will go to Lydia now. We must let Georgiana know she is here.'

'Yes,' said Elizabeth, in a flat voice. 'I will take care of that.'

'Lizzy! It will be all right. Your guests know you and who you are. I understand you are concerned, but you are the same Mrs Elizabeth Darcy you were at breakfast.'

Elizabeth looked at her sister as if she had never seen her before.

'Yes,' said she simply. 'Thank you.'

CHAPTER 45

'Kitty!' cried Lydia, her arms outstretched. 'Are you not surprised to see me? Is this not the best joke?'

'It is indeed,' said Kitty, closing the bedroom door behind her and smiling despite herself as Lydia enfolded her in a hug. 'Everyone will be exceedingly surprised!'

'Lizzy's face was a picture when my name was announced,' said Lydia with some glee, as she released Kitty from her embrace and stepped back. 'To think, I have not seen any of you for a year! You are looking very elegant, I must say.'

'Thank you,' said Kitty. 'You look very well, too. You are not changed at all!'

It was true. Lydia, tall and well formed, was as handsome as ever, her complexion as fine and her face aglow with health and high spirits. Her self-assurance and confidence were evident and Kitty did not suppose that Lydia had learned tact or discretion since she had become Mrs Wickham.

'That is a very fine muslin you are wearing,' said Lydia. 'I see that things are done very well around here.'

She bounced down on the bed, a substantial piece of furniture replete with carved wood, a canopy and hangings. 'Look at all this brocade and this velvet! It's all rather old-fashioned but still rather splendid. I shall feel like a queen sleeping here! I don't much care for those paintings over there, although I suppose they were frightfully dear and done by someone I should have heard of. Lord! How big is Pemberley? I declare there must be a hundred rooms at least!'

'It is a beautiful house,' said Kitty.

'My dear Wickham has told me all about it of course, but I did not think it would be so very grand. And is this your home now? Lizzy and Darcy have taken you in? Have you quite forsaken Longbourn?'

'Not forsaken, Lydia…'

'Well, I could not blame you if you had. I should die of boredom were I at Longbourn. Life is so much more interesting in Newcastle, although the weather can be tiresome. But we have such excellent diversions at the Assembly Rooms and I usually win at the card parties because I am quite adept at loo and commerce, you know. Only Mrs Denton can come close to me…' She rattled on and Kitty found herself listening in a detached sort of way, as if Lydia were a distant acquaintance rather than the sister with whom she had once shared all. As self-absorbed as ever, she spoke only of herself and made no enquiries as to the health and happiness or otherwise of Jane or Mary; and, having seen Elizabeth and Kitty, any curiosity in that quarter seemed quite sated.

'We should go down?' said Lydia, at last. 'Lizzy told me there was quite a party of guests here already, including a viscount, if you please!'

'Mr Darcy's cousin. You will meet them all at dinner.

'Lydia,' she continued, trying hard to find words that would both convey her concerns and appeal to her sister's sensibilities. 'You should understand that the ball, this house party… It is the first time Lizzy has arranged such an event as mistress of Pemberley. It is important to her – to all of us – that everything should proceed well.'

'Oh, don't worry,' replied Lydia dismissively, looking at herself in the glass as she spoke and pinching some colour into her cheeks. 'Lizzy has already given me a lecture about behaving myself. I do know how to address a lord, you know! Besides, I am a married lady myself – don't forget! – and quite used to the ways of the world. What a pity my dear Wickham is not here with me to see all this.'

Kitty flinched at the thought and took her sister downstairs, wondering as to the whereabouts of Georgiana and also the Bingley sisters. There was no doubt in her mind that the latter would be as overjoyed as they were appalled to find Mrs Wickham in their midst. She led Lydia into a room near the library, one she thought would be unoccupied.

'There is a pretty aspect of the gardens from here,' she told her. 'Let me ring for some tea while we wait for the others.'

'Ooh, a pretty aspect!' mocked Lydia, but she was happy to comply and, after an inspection of the room and an evaluation of its contents, she dropped onto the sofa beside Kitty and announced, 'This is splendid! I am so very glad I decided to come. Wickham tried to persuade me otherwise, you know, but I told him I never could resist a ball! Do you remember how we persuaded Bingley to give us that ball at Netherfield?'

Kitty did, and not without embarrassment at the loud and public importuning that had accompanied their request.

'Jane should be very grateful to us,' continued Lydia. 'Were it not for that ball, she would not now be Mrs Bingley. And remember how we all looked for Wickham at that ball? How all the young ladies thought to dance with him. Ha! Who would have thought then I should become Mrs Wickham?'

She smiled at her good fortune. 'I am surprised you have not found a husband yet, Kitty. You were in London, too. Were there no dances, no suitors? There must be someone at Pemberley, surely? I shall have to help you.'

Kitty assured her sister she did not require any assistance in that endeavour and tried to change the subject. The tea arrived, and a message was sent to Elizabeth to let her know where they were. Lydia returned the conversation to eligible young men and Kitty gave up brief accounts of the Fanshawes and Captain Morton without giving away any of her own opinions of each.

When Elizabeth arrived a short while later she was accompanied by Colonel Fitzwilliam, who declared himself delighted to meet Mrs Wickham. Lydia, for her part, was pleased to find a soldier of higher rank than her husband and was soon telling him of the qualities and abilities of her dear Wickham, attributes that she considered unfairly underrated. The colonel bore this information stoically and then wondered if Mrs Wickham might care to take a stroll around the gardens. Within a few minutes, they were gone.

Elizabeth's strategy in managing Lydia's presence was a simple one: as far as was possible, they would contrive to keep her in the company of those family members they trusted, with the aim of containing her boisterous and more outrageous behaviour.

'Colonel Fitzwilliam, as you have seen, will be invaluable,' said Lizzy. 'We think it most unlikely that Wickham would have told Lydia anything about his involvement with Georgiana, so although the situation is awkward for her, and may cause some embarrassment, we think there is little to be feared there. Colonel Fitzwilliam says Captain Morton can be pressed into service if needed.'

'It is quite the military operation,' said Kitty, in an attempt to lighten the mood.

Elizabeth looked annoyed, then softened her face into a smile. 'I am sorry. Perhaps I am overreacting, but Lydia's behaviour is not always exemplary, as you well know.'

'She is a loose cannonball?' suggested Kitty, quite pleased with herself in continuing the military analogy.

Elizabeth ignored the remark. 'I expected we would receive her here one day, but not this week when we have so many other guests.'

Kitty understood perfectly. The rarified atmosphere of Pemberley would be blown about by Lydia, who was not so much a breath of fresh air but a hurricane, and a reminder of a different milieu, of relations that Elizabeth would as soon forget. She had not changed her character in becoming Mrs Darcy, but now she was in an unenviable position, her old world intruding on the new one she had been charting so very successfully. As someone who was trying to forge a new path for herself, Kitty could empathise. She wondered what Mr Darcy's reaction had been to Lydia's arrival; she hoped, for Lizzy's sake, he had borne it with his usual quiet dignity.

'Perhaps,' said Kitty, 'I could take Lydia on a tour of the grounds tomorrow. If there is someone to drive us, we could take a leisurely ride through the parklands and glades. No doubt Lydia would like to see the extent of the estate.'

'An excellent plan,' said Elizabeth, knowing that it was also one that would take Lydia away from the house and her guests for a few hours. 'I hope you will take some pleasure in it, too?'

'I am no stranger to Lydia's company and conversation,' said Kitty, 'and have been reminded of it often enough in the past.' She gave Lizzy a look that was at once playful and wry. 'Don't worry, I will give you a full account of it all! You are sure you would not like to accompany us?'

'No, I cannot,' said Elizabeth, who had not comprehended that Kitty was not serious in her request. In truth, she was too preoccupied to think clearly. Her old prejudices rose to the fore; Kitty and Lydia had always been inseparable; would Kitty revert to her old ways? She looked at her, a frown on her face.

'Do not look so concerned, Lizzy. I will take care of it.' Does she still not trust me, wondered Kitty, slightly irritated.

'Yes, of course,' replied her sister, although her tone betrayed a little uncertainty. 'Of course, you will. Thank you.'

Elizabeth need not have worried quite so much. Kitty was on her guard. Against Lydia, and anyone or anything that threatened her peace and enjoyment of Pemberley. Even so, Lydia was a force to be reckoned with.

CHAPTER 46

That evening, true to form, Lydia quickly identified the most eligible gentlemen in the room and commenced to flirt with them. Thus the Messrs Fanshawe were soon acquainted with Mrs Wickham, and Captain Morton was next in line for her attentions. Colonel Fitzwilliam made it his business to be at her side. This had the immediate effect of alienating Miss Fanshawe, hitherto the chief recipient of the honourable colonel's regard; and mortifying Georgiana, who could not bring herself to join any conversation of which Lydia was part and therefore watched from the other side of the room as Freddie Fanshawe paid court to the coquettish Mrs George Wickham.

Mr Darcy, seeing this, had moved to his sister's side as if to shield her from any unpleasantness, but they were soon joined by Miss Bingley, brimming with malevolent concern. 'I could hardly believe my eyes when I saw Mrs Wickham in our midst,' she exclaimed. 'How magnanimous of you to invite her, but of course she is part of the family now. And Mr Wickham, will he be joining us?'

'We will not have that pleasure,' replied Mr Darcy, tersely.

Caroline turned to Miss Darcy. 'A shame! He was such a favourite among all the Bennet sisters. He and all the other officers!'

Georgiana's startled expression was misread by Miss Bingley. 'Yes, of course, you would find that quite remarkable but…'

'Please excuse us, Miss Bingley,' interrupted Mr Darcy. 'We were just on our way to see the viscount. Feel free to accompany us if you so desire.' So saying, he took Georgiana's arm and led her towards his cousin, leaving Caroline temporarily marooned although far from desolate.

Kitty, acutely aware of Georgiana's feelings, thought to try and extricate the elder Fanshawe from Lydia and crossed the room ostensibly to chat with her sister. This action was misconstrued by Mr Darcy, who saw it as Kitty neglecting his sister by pandering to her own. She saw him frown and realised his assumption, but could do nothing about it. Meanwhile, Elizabeth, engaged in conversation by the Bridgwaters and the Hursts, was obliged to charm and be charmed, and was quite unable to see what was happening at her back.

Lydia, of course, was oblivious to all of this. At dinner, seated beside Captain Morton, Kitty could hear her telling him that Wickham had lived at Pemberley, that he was the son of the late Mr Darcy's steward and spent his youth here. Those within earshot who were aware of this circumstance politely ignored the reference; others, such as the Fanshawes and Mr Bridgwater, were left to wonder at this previously undisclosed family connection. Lydia, ignorant and devoid of tact, called across the table. 'Colonel Fitzwilliam, perhaps you knew my dear Wickham then? When he was a boy? To think that he must have once roamed in these very woods, fished in these very streams!'

Colonel Fitzwilliam answered that he had known Wickham, but not well and turned his attention back to Felicia, sitting to his right. Captain Morton broke the awkward silence that followed Lydia's loud enquiry by asking her opinion of Newcastle, which allowed conversation to resume around the table but did not promise much in the way of intelligent discourse for the captain. Mr Darcy's face was a mask of neutrality but Kitty marked the glacial expression in his eyes as he glanced towards Lydia, and also saw Elizabeth's attempt at a reassuring smile in his direction.

Despite the tensions felt by the immediate Darcy circle, the evening proceeded as convivially and almost as enjoyably as any other. So far Lydia was little more than a novelty to the Pemberley guests, not a wayward and unpredictable sister around whom clung the taint of scandal.

When the ladies withdrew, Kitty brought Felicia Fanshawe and Lydia together so that the former could quietly ascertain that her sister's behaviour was not specifically directed to Colonel Fitzwilliam. She had no doubt that Felicia would soon get the measure of Mrs Wickham. Elizabeth, she saw, had made sure Georgiana was seated with Amelia Bridgwater and Lady Mortlake. Someone suggested card tables be set up when the gentlemen joined them, an idea welcomed by a few and none more warmly than Lydia. Some deft manoeuvring by Elizabeth and Kitty saw their sister safely seated with Colonel Fitzwilliam, Miss Fanshawe and Captain Morton.

Kitty immediately looked for Georgiana, with whom she had not spoken at all since breakfast. She found her with the Fanshawe brothers, who had decided not to join the card parties, and looking calm if a little tired.

'Another renegade from vingt-et-un, Miss Bennet?' asked Freddie Fanshawe, by way of greeting. 'I thought you liked to play?'

'Certainly I do,' returned Kitty, 'but the card tables will always be available, whereas we are not so fortunate as to have your society every day. I hope you are enjoying Pemberley as much as we enjoyed our time at Danson Park?'

Answering for his brother, William Fanshawe assured her they were. 'We are deciding whether to ride or fish tomorrow, both of which will deprive us of your company' – he made an apologetic face to both Kitty and Georgiana – 'so I fear our plans have not been well thought out.'

'No indeed!' declared Georgiana, bestowing a sweet smile on Freddie. 'Well, we will have to bear your absence as best we can.'

'I am sure you will manage very well without us,' said Mr Fanshawe, who was not insensible to Miss Darcy's attentions. 'May I be of service in the meantime. A glass of wine, perhaps? Some other refreshment?'

Georgiana declined prettily – Kitty likewise, but her smile was less coquettish, her eyes less downcast – leaving the gentleman to fetch port wine for himself and his brother.

'What plans have you for the morrow, Miss Bennet?' asked William Fanshawe.

'I have promised Mrs Wickham a tour of Pemberley's grounds tomorrow so perchance we will see you somewhere along the way.'

Kitty knew the reference to Lydia would displease Georgiana and felt torn between her sister and her friend; she would have liked an opportunity to speak privately and explain that she was trying to do what was best for everyone, but it seemed the evening would not allow that possibility. When Frederick returned, it was clear that Georgiana intended to keep him in close conversation, and Kitty was happy enough to pass the time with William, who did indeed request the pleasure of the first two dances with her at the ball and amused both ladies, although not his brother, with diverting stories of their first dancing lessons and their lack of skill therein.

'Please do not be too alarmed, Miss Bennet. We have improved,' he concluded. 'Well, at least I believe I have. I am not sure about my brother.'

Kitty laughed. She liked William Fanshawe but often found that now the discussions on their mutual interests had run their course, there was little she had to say to him and vice versa. Moreover, his opinions, usually strongly expressed, where often at variance with her own with the result that she held hers in check. There would be more prudence than passion in any arrangement between them, she knew. Ever conscious of the need to marry, Kitty felt she *ought* to be encouraging him but her heart was not in it. She resolved to simply enjoy his company and try to clarify her feelings after the ball.

A shriek of laughter from the other side of the room reminded her of Lydia's presence. The card tables were breaking up and Kitty excused herself.

***

The next morning, as promised, Kitty and Lydia started out on a comprehensive tour of Pemberley and its grounds. The day was not without its pleasures. The natural beauty of the woods and parkland were unparalleled and they spent some time locating the herd of deer that had so enchanted Kitty on her first journey into Pemberley. Lydia was full of curiosity as to the extent of the land, the hunting, how many times the Darcys entertained, with whom they dined, how many servants were employed, where Lizzy had her dresses made, and all manner of material enquiries, which Kitty answered as fully or as vaguely as she thought fit. Anticipating a barrage of questions, she had also seen fit to bid the driver stop the carriage so that she and Lydia could stroll without being overheard.

'And these Fanshawe brothers,' her sister now asked. 'Is Miss Darcy out to get the elder one, Frederick? I would say so, what think you? He is most attentive to her, too.'

'They enjoy each other's company,' said Kitty.

'O fie! You must know more than that. You and Miss Darcy are firm friends, or so you told me!'

'That is true,' said Kitty. 'But she and Mr Fanshawe have not been long acquainted.'

'As if that counts for aught,' scoffed Lydia. 'From the moment I first saw my dear Wickham, I could think of no one else.'

This was a statement that required no comment.

'And you and William Fanshawe?' she teased. 'You are fond of him, I think? How very neat. You and Miss Darcy, both Mrs Fanshawes!'

The thought made Kitty excessively uncomfortable. 'I like him, Lydia. I am not *fond* of him. You overstate the situation.'

'And you, Miss Bennet, have become rather grand! I "overstate the situation". I say what I see. Are you blushing? Since when did we have any secrets?'

'Since you eloped with Wickham!' retorted Kitty sharply. 'I would say from precisely that point. And no, I am not blushing.' In fact, she was not.

'Besides,' she added, in a more conciliatory tone. 'I am keeping no secrets from you.' It was maddening, she thought, to be challenged like this.

'As you wish,' replied Lydia, quite nonchalant. 'I was merely asking. How are the Fanshawes acquainted with the Darcys?'

Kitty told her.

'I am sure I have heard the name before but I asked Freddie Fanshawe and he could think of no circumstance when we might have met. Perhaps he is known to my dear Wickham.'

Kitty thought this highly unlikely but held her tongue. Lydia enquired about Captain Morton. Was Kitty interested in that quarter? She was not; she thought the man was still grieving for his late wife. But it has been more than a year, insisted Lydia. Kitty began to talk of Jane and Bingley and their intended purchase of Dapplewick Hall, safer ground for discussion. That in turn led to Jane's impending motherhood and they amused themselves by naming the unborn baby. They had regained the carriage by now and were almost back at the house when Kitty remembered that Mr and Mrs Collins were now the proud parents of a daughter. 'Lord!' exclaimed Lydia. 'I hope the unfortunate child resembles her mother, not her father!'

'As do I,' said Kitty. 'Mr Collins came to see us at Longbourn, you know. Earlier this year. Mama was almost apoplectic!' She gave Lydia an account of the visit and followed it with an impersonation of their very dear cousin. As a result, both were rendered almost insensible with laughter as the carriage stopped at the house. Lydia misjudged her footing as they alighted, causing her to trip and clutch on to Kitty, which was further cause for mirth. Kitty was still laughing at Lydia when she looked up to see Mr Darcy coming down the steps. That he was unimpressed by their overt merriment was obvious to her.

'Mrs Wickham. Kitty,' he said coolly, by way of greeting, and continued on his way.

CHAPTER 47

Four days had passed since Lydia had irrupted into Pemberley, and the world still turned. Preparations for the ball were proceeding, quietly and without fuss. Chatter, music and genteel laughter emanated from the drawing and dining rooms and the summer continued fine. Underneath the surface, however, there were fissures and hairline cracks.

Georgiana had reacted by devoting all her time and attention to Freddie Fanshawe, in mute defiance of her uncle's caution. Mr Darcy, whose misgivings about Fanshawe's character and intentions were unvoiced and unchanged, thought him the lesser of the two evils presently under his roof and in dealing with one neglected to speak with Georgiana about the other; he would do so after the ball and Lydia's departure. Elizabeth, whose expectations of Lydia's gaucherie were only slightly diminished with each passing day, was making herself busier than was necessary in preparations concerning the ballroom, musicians and menus (all of which Mrs Reynolds had completely under control) and in entertaining her other guests. Colonel Fitzwilliam, enamoured of one Fanshawe and distrustful of another, was often beset and thwarted by Lydia's attentions. Kitty, who had spent more time with Lydia than anyone, was fatigued.

What am I to think and do? she wrote in her journal before breakfast. *Georgiana needs me and I have no opportunity to speak with her. I think she wishes she had not told me her secret about GW. I do not want that to come between us.*

Elizabeth asked me for help, now that is a miracle! She is tense, I can sense it. I hope she does not develop nerves, like Mama! How would I feel if I were Elizabeth? Would I be ashamed of Lydia or angry? Is it more that she is worried about what Darcy thinks? Lydia has broken into her perfect world. Is that world so very fragile?

Mr Darcy looked so cross when Lydia and I came back from our tour of the park. Very disapproving, just as he did when we first met him. As if it were wrong to laugh. Lydia has certainly ruffled some feathers. But when I think about Georgiana, how lucky for everyone that that event did not occur! Where would that Darcy pride be now? I cannot think about that. Georgiana is too dear to me!

And Lydia? She is dear to me, of course. I do see her differently now, though, I admit it. She thinks only of herself; and I suppose that was always so but I did not notice. How strange, how sobering, to think that at one time I thought she could do no wrong. Now – and I should not say this – I find she can be quite coarse and I wonder at myself for the criticism. I have changed, not she.

Lydia means no harm; she is just ignorant.

'Oh Lord!' cried Kitty. 'How can I say that? That is what our father says!'

She put away her writing and went to knock on Georgiana's door. There was no answer. She sighed; she really did want to talk to her and see how she was coping with Lydia's presence. It was still early and she made her way to the music room where she found the scores that Henry Adams had sent: two concertos by

Cramer, some sonatinas by Pleyel and the music for *Robin Adair*. Kitty's heart skipped. She knew the popular Irish song. 'What's this dull town to me,' went the first line, 'Robin's not here.' It was an ode written by a lady to the man her family had forbidden her to see. Kitty could not decide whether its inclusion was odd, deliberate or simply a way of varying the selection. Whatever the answer, she was pleased.

She sat down to sing and play the song, and to think about the last time she had seen Mr Adams. It was four months ago, she realised, but she could picture him so very clearly. Lost to herself, she sang the Irish air again and then turned to the other pieces, which were new and more complicated. An hour passed before she knew it. Left to her own devices, she would have stayed at the pianoforte all morning; it was a safe refuge from the tensions prevailing elsewhere.

On her way to breakfast she made another detour, this time curious to see how things were progressing in the ballroom. The large doors were open and at the far end she could see housemaids making sure the already clean windows and mirrors sparkled. A number of musical stands were in position on the platform to the east of the room, where another pianoforte – not the one that belonged to Georgiana – stood. The well-known John Gow band from London had been engaged. She counted the stands: at least three would be for violins, another for a violoncello, perhaps a French horn, but that still left two more. The crystal candelabra and girandoles, at present only reflecting sunlight, looked magnificent. Many other candles were piled on another table, waiting to be placed on smaller tables that had yet to be arranged along the sides of the room beside the chairs.

The most arresting sight, however, and the one which Kitty had come to see, was the chalked floor. The wooden floorboards, polished and in perfect condition, needed no disguise, but when she was in London Elizabeth had been delighted by the fashion for decorating ballroom floors. Instead of chalking feet to prevent dancers sliding, someone had thought instead to chalk the floors.

The two artists now on their knees at Pemberley were completely absorbed in covering the ballroom floor with an intricate pattern of repeating motifs of the sun, the moon, shooting stars and planets. They were three quarters of the way through their ephemeral task. Kitty marvelled at it, at the same time thinking it sad that such a beautiful work of art would disappear under whirls of dancing feet. She watched from the doorway for a few minutes more, revelling in the anticipation of being present at such a distinguished event as the summer ball. She intended to dance every dance.

When she finally arrived at the breakfast room, only William Fanshawe and Captain Morton were still at the table, both absorbed in newspapers but not displeased at being interrupted.

'Your parents arrive today, I think?' enquired Kitty of Mr Fanshawe, as she helped herself to some chocolate from the sideboard.

'Indeed, they do. With my uncle.'

'I look forward to seeing them again. Two other families are also arriving today, whose names are unknown to me. They, too, live half a day distant. I believe we shall be twenty-four at dinner tonight.'

'And after dinner, Miss Bennet. May we prevail upon you to sing?'

'Yes, indeed,' joined in Captain Morton. 'Please do say you will.'

'I shall consider your request, gentlemen,' said Kitty, airily. She would sing, she had already decided. She had new music to play.

CHAPTER 48

The day of the ball dawned and still the fine weather held. Everyone agreed it was a glorious summer, an excellent portent. Mindful of the activities ahead, most of the guests, certainly all the gentlemen, were content to pass the time quietly – reading, writing letters, playing chess or backgammon and perhaps venturing as far as tea on the lawn – but for some of the ladies there were more pressing concerns.

Kitty had already seen the dress Elizabeth would be wearing; she had been fitted for it when they were in London and had worn it but once. An elegant creation of cream silk trimmed with touches of emerald green, it perfectly complemented the jewels she would be wearing and there was no doubt in Kitty's mind that Mrs Elizabeth Darcy's appearance would command attention at the ball.

She had overheard Miss Bingley, Mrs Hurst and Mrs Bridgwater discussing the necklaces and gowns they had brought with them for the occasion and did not doubt there would be displays of finery from them. She and Georgiana had discussed their own gowns of course, but that was weeks ago and Kitty was most anxious to find her friend and examine the subject afresh, and in minute detail. Moreover, she felt that Georgiana had become a little distant with her and wanted to find out what was troubling her, to allay her concerns. She discovered her in a little-used morning room, alone and engaged in correspondence.

'At last! I have been looking for you everywhere,' cried Kitty. 'And you are by yourself! We have so many things to talk about.'

Georgiana looked at her a little warily, but relaxed when it became clear the most important subject to be aired was that of dressing for the ball that evening. Her letter was abandoned and the pair hastened upstairs.

'I have my new white gown, the one with the French lace,' said Georgiana, as they entered her room, 'but I have been thinking that the blue silk might be better. You shall give me your opinion.'

'Will you wear the pearls?' Kitty asked as she picked up first the white, then the blue gown, holding each in turn against Georgiana.

'Yes, I shall. And I have pearl and diamond combs as well.' She went to a drawer, found them and held them to her hair.

'This one then,' said Kitty. 'The white sets off your complexion so very well and with the pearls it will be even more becoming. Those combs are very pretty, I like them very much.

'Oh, it is good to be here with you,' she continued, sitting down on the bed. 'We have not spoken properly since that day at the folly. I cannot imagine how difficult it is for you.' She did not want to specify the conversation.

'You have been spending most of your time with Mrs Wickham,' said Georgiana, coolly.

Kitty looked at her. 'You are not reproaching me, surely? Do you not know that it was done for you? It would be strange indeed if I did not spend some time with her – and I am not entirely unhappy to see her, although I could wish she was not at Pemberley at this moment – but her arrival was such a shock to me, as it was to everyone. We – Elizabeth, Colonel Fitzwilliam, your brother, me! – have been most concerned for you. Especially me, after what you had told me only that morning! I have been seeking to protect, not exclude, you. Spending time with Lydia, taking her on tours of Pemberley, was done to spare you her company as much as possible.'

Georgiana coloured.

'Did you not know?' persisted Kitty, standing up.

'I did not think...' began her friend. 'I saw only you and Mrs Wickham chatting and laughing together. I thought...'

'You thought we were discussing you? How could you think such a thing of me?'

'But she is your sister so...'

'So therefore I would disregard my loyalty and friendship with you? I gave you my word, Georgiana. You are as dear to me as Lydia, perhaps even more so. I care for her, it would be unnatural if I did not, but we are not friends as you and I are friends. You have shown me nothing but affection and kindness since we met. I would never betray you!'

She stopped. The vehemence of her little speech, which had welled up and out of her heart, had taken her by surprise.

'Then I am sorry,' said Georgiana. 'I have been so concerned with my own difficulties, but I should never have doubted you.'

Kitty nodded, took Georgiana's hand and smiled. 'It has been a trying week for many of us, has it not? Let us leave it all behind and look forward to tonight. I am longing to dance.'

'What will you wear?' asked Georgiana, clearly thankful to return to the subject of the ball.

'My white silk gown, the one trimmed in pink. I have not worn it since I came to Pemberley. I like it very much, but will it be formal enough? Lizzy assured me it would do as well as any – and that I look very well in it.'

'I imagine some of the older ladies will have more elaborate gowns, and no doubt we will see a few bejewelled and feather headdresses,' said Georgiana, 'but I do not envy them those. So heavy! Your white dress is most becoming and hardly less formal than mine.'

'I had not thought about feathers!' said Kitty. 'Though I wish I had some pearls or something for my hair. Perhaps Lizzy has something I can borrow.'

'You can wear this!' said Georgiana, going to a velvet-covered casket on her table and bringing out a small yellow-gold tiara, set with brilliants and garnets.

'Oh, but this is beautiful, so delicate,' gasped Kitty.

'Yes, it is,' agreed Georgiana. 'It belonged to my mother. I like it but I never wear it. Put it on.'

Kitty did as she was bid, turning her head first one way, then the other and enjoying the way the light caught the diamonds.

'I feel quite the princess! Thank you, but I cannot wear this. I should be afraid to lose it.' She immediately thought of the cameo and wished she could take back the words.

'Nonsense,' replied Georgiana, unconcerned. 'What possible harm can come to it here at Pemberley.'

'But it belonged to your mother.'

'And now it belongs to me, and I would like you to wear it tonight at the summer ball, a ball that was such a favourite tradition of my mother's, one that is to be continued by our sister Elizabeth. It is all quite fitting. My mind is made up. I shall send Annie to arrange your hair just as soon as she has finished mine. You will find her better than your maid at such things. There!'

It was all settled. Kitty took the precious tiara back to her room and placed it carefully on the table. She could hardly believe she would be wearing something so very fine. She was sensible to a certain reserve in Georgiana's attitude to her, something that she had not experienced before, but now she had allowed her to wear this beautiful tiara. Perhaps it was her way of making amends.

Her gown was laid out on her bed, along with new white leather gloves; she had little pink roses on her shoes. Everything was in readiness, but there were still a few hours before the ladies needed to dress. She would have preferred to spend that time chatting with Georgiana, but she had said she must finish her letter, so Kitty went downstairs; she supposed she had better find Lydia.

Large bouquets of flowers were appearing on the landings of the staircases that led to the ballroom and supper room; even more floral arrangements were being carried hither and thither by servants Kitty had never seen before. The house smelled of lavender, roses and geraniums.

She heard Lydia before she saw her; she was in the drawing room engaged in a noisy game of backgammon with Captain Morton. 'We are playing the best of three,' Lydia told her. 'The captain here has just taken the second. It is not too late to wager on the outcome.'

'I am content to watch,' said Kitty. 'Although I do not know the rules of this game.'

'That is to your credit, Miss Bennet,' laughed Captain Morton. 'Your sister knows them very well, however. Please excuse me, I must have my wits about me if I am to win.'

Win he did, although Kitty was given to understand the game was close. Lydia was in excellent spirits and good-humoured in defeat, pushing across the few pennies that had been at stake. The captain made a show of protest but Lydia was adamant. 'It shall never be said that I do not honour my debts, sir,' said she, affecting a serious tone. 'Though given the opportunity, I shall try to recover my position in another game.'

She turned to Kitty. 'Shall we take a turn outside? I never saw so much activity in my life as I did earlier today. They are lighting the way from here to London, I think.'

Lydia's reference was to the lanterns being placed in the trees and along the curving drive that led through Pemberley's grounds. The sisters followed the path for a half hour, counting the distance between lanterns, before turning back.

'It will look exquisite,' said Kitty, as they neared the house. 'I can hardly wait to see it in moonlight.'

'It looks fearfully expensive as well,' returned Lydia. 'I suppose this is why Darcy has his ten thousand pounds a year!'

'Don't speak so loud,' chastised Kitty, looking around. 'Someone might hear you.'

'Ooh la la! Who is near?'

At that moment, Georgiana and Freddie Fanshawe came into view, perhaps bent on the same exploratory task, but then they changed course and wandered in the direction of the stream.

'Miss Darcy does not care to speak to me,' declared Lydia. 'She is monstrously proud.'

'I am sure you are mistaken.'

'I most certainly am not! Did you not see just then how she and Mr Fanshawe deliberately avoided speaking to us?'

Kitty had seen of course, but chose not to admit it. 'Perhaps they do not want any company at all, Lydia. I do not think they intend any slight.'

Lydia was unconvinced. 'They are both proud,' she insisted. 'That Mr Fanshawe as well; he thinks himself mighty important. Well, never mind. There will be plenty of others to dance with tonight, I am sure.' Kitty agreed, while thinking how much like their mother Lydia sounded. Her words were an echo of Mrs Bennet's sentiments when they had first been introduced to Mr Darcy.

They reached the house and met Elizabeth coming out of the drawing room. 'The house looks wonderful,' said Kitty, 'and the ballroom! And the lanterns! The flowers! Everything looks wonderful!'

'Thank you,' she smiled. 'I am happy to agree with you. I must look to my own appearance soon. And you? You have everything you need?' She looked at them and received nods of assurance. 'I was going to wait until tomorrow to tell you that I have just received a letter from Jane, but since you are both here I will do so now. She is well, she writes, but she is become concerned about Mama, who is tired and increasingly out of sorts. The physician has visited her twice in the past week but, according to our father, has no real explanation. Jane wonders if Papa is keeping some information from her, given that her confinement is so near, but she owns that this is speculation on her part.'

'Poor Mama,' said Kitty. 'I will write to her tomorrow. She will want to hear all about the ball. Perhaps she is just sad to be missing all the excitement.'

'More likely her nerves are plaguing her,' said Lydia, somewhat dismissively. 'She needs little encouragement to play the invalid!'

'That is enough, Lydia!' snapped Elizabeth. Turning to Kitty, she said, 'She will appreciate an account of the ball. That is a good idea. We should all write; there is nothing else we can do at present.'

'No indeed,' agreed Lydia. 'We married ladies can do no more.'

Kitty felt the implied comment that she, as the only unmarried daughter, might look to be at their mother's side.

'None of us can do anything more at present,' said Elizabeth firmly. 'I shall see you both at dinner. Excuse me. Oh, and Lydia, there is a letter arrived for you as well.'

CHAPTER 49

Kitty looked at her reflection in the mirror. As a result of Annie's ministrations, little curls now framed her face and the tiara sparkled, securely pinned into her dark brown hair, which had been swept up higher than she normally wore it and allowed to tumble in ringlets to the nape of her neck. She was most pleased with the result. She adjusted her bodice, smoothed her skirts and pulled on her gloves. The only thing missing was a necklace, which she did not have. Did that matter? She thought of asking Georgiana but hesitated. She had already lent her the tiara, she did not want to ask too much of her.

There was a knock on her door. 'Ha!' she called. 'The very person I need. Come in!'

'Well,' said Lydia. 'You look very fine. A tiara, indeed! Did you borrow it from Lizzy? I suppose she has plenty of Darcy jewels now.'

'No, it belongs to Miss Darcy,' said Kitty, recovering from the surprise of seeing Lydia rather than Georgiana in her room. 'Lizzy does have some splendid necklaces though. I saw them while we were in London and she will be wearing her emeralds tonight.'

Lydia feigned indifference.

'I have some news that should be of interest to you,' she said, a smug look upon her face, 'about your new and fancy friends. You remember I said I thought I knew the name Fanshawe?'

'I do remember,' said Kitty, wondering what Lydia could possibly know about the Fanshawes.

'I wrote to my dear Wickham,' she continued. 'He knows all about Freddie Fanshawe! It turns out they were at Cambridge together. He says he is the most prolific gambler, always at the races or at the card tables. A sharper, he calls him. And not at all concerned about leaving his debts of honour unpaid.'

'A sharper!' exclaimed Kitty. This was horrifying. 'That cannot be true!'

'Why? Because he is the son of a knight?'

'No, of course not,' said Kitty, struggling with the information and thinking that it would be another shock for Georgiana to bear. 'Surely, though, this was years ago? Perhaps he has reformed.'

'Reformed?' cried Lydia, scornfully. 'No, not according to my husband's letter. Fanshawe is a gamester and renowned for it. Everyone knows it.'

'But how can that be?' asked Kitty. 'His reputation would be ruined were it true.'

'Wickham says he has a wealthy old relation who is continually paying his debts,' said Lydia. 'His father, I suppose. Sir Frederick, isn't that his name? He is here now, is he not?'

'He is,' said Kitty, her thoughts racing. She had no doubt in her mind that it was not his father who was paying Freddie Fanshawe's debts; it was Sir Edward! She had no proof of course; she just knew it to be true. Poor Sir Edward, whose own sons had been taken from him, had become the most generous uncle, had taken it upon himself to protect his eldest nephew from scandal. She thought back to the scene at the stables and was even more convinced. He tries to keep him in check! The cruel irony of this information coming from a person such as Wickham was not lost on her.

'By all accounts, he is not a very clever gambler,' Lydia was saying. 'Hopeless, in fact. But he knows his debts will be paid, so he keeps on doing it.

'My dear Wickham saw him in London, not long before he came down to Meryton I suppose, and Fanshawe lost fifty pounds to him at faro. He had not thought ever to see the money but now that we are here under the same roof, I intend to ask him for it.'

'Lydia, you cannot! Not here!'

'Why not? He acts as though he were an honourable gentleman, therefore he should pay his debts. Why should my dear Wickham suffer at his hands.'

Wickham's suffering, such as it may have been, was of no concern whatsoever to Kitty.

'Lydia, you cannot confront him here. Have some care, please! Do not cause a scene.'

'I can, and I will if I wish,' retorted Lydia. 'All he has to do is pay, then there will be no unpleasantness.' She did not wait for Kitty's response. 'I will see you in the drawing room,' she called, as she opened the door and disappeared down the passage.

Kitty could not believe what she had heard. She had had misgivings about Freddie Fanshawe but she had not expected this. What should she do? The first guests for the ball would be arriving in an hour; Elizabeth and Darcy would be far too engrossed in receiving them to deal with such news. Colonel Fitzwilliam! He would know what to do, she would tell him.

She picked up her reticule and opened her door to find Georgiana about to knock.

'You will have no shortage of dance partners this evening, Miss Bennet,' said she, appraising Kitty as she stood back. 'The tiara suits you very well. Are you ready to come down?'

'I am,' said Kitty, taking a deep breath and forcing a smile. 'Let us go. You are looking very becoming yourself, Miss Darcy.'

Georgiana was all smiles again, no sign of her former reserve. Kitty could not tell her what she knew; she was afraid to be the bearer of such terrible news and perhaps – it was just possible – that Wickham was misinformed. No, she wanted advice from the colonel.

'I have never seen Pemberley look more enchanting,' said Georgiana, as they descended the grand staircase. 'Shall we step outside and see it as our guests will see it as they approach? I should like to see the lanterns lit.'

Despite, or perhaps because of, the turmoil in her mind, Kitty agreed. She too wanted to see the effect of the lanterns illuminating the trees and the drive. Careful of their dresses and dancing pumps, they passed through the entrance hall and stepped into the warm night air. In front of them, the lake reflected the house, its large windows ablaze with light, and the drive the carriages would soon be taking had become a golden serpentine leading up from the park and woodlands.

'Sublime,' murmured Georgiana, gazing around her and then up at a moon bright in the cloudless sky. They turned back to the house, where silhouetted figures were moving about in the drawing room.

'From here, it looks like a very large doll's house,' observed Kitty.

'Then let us go and play in it,' laughed Georgiana, taking her hand and pulling her along with her. 'Don't look so serious! This is going to be a wonderful night!'

CHAPTER 50

Entering the drawing room, Kitty could not see Colonel Fitzwilliam among those already assembled. Elizabeth, a picture of elegance in her cream silk and looking taller than usual, courtesy of a matching turban complete with an emerald brooch and small feathers, was standing next to an equally dignified Darcy. She beckoned Kitty and Georgiana over.

'You are perfect,' said she to them quietly. 'White becomes you both. Kitty, I see you have acquired a crown?'

'Only for this evening, Georgiana has kindly allowed me to wear it.' She gave her friend a gleeful look. 'I feel like Cinderella!'

Darcy, noticing the tiara, made an approving face, first at Kitty and then at his sister.

'Well, it won't disappear at midnight, even if you meet your Prince Charming,' teased Georgiana. 'When shall we go to the ballroom?' she asked Elizabeth.

'Very soon, the first carriages are expected at nine. The musicians are ready. Everything is ready.'

Darcy placed Elizabeth's arm in his own and smiled at her. 'You have made it so,' he said proudly. His expression as he looked at his wife said everything else.

Georgiana and Kitty moved away, one to speak with Felicia Fanshawe, the other to seek out Colonel Fitzwilliam. Lydia, Kitty noticed, was with Captain Morton. She was on her way to join them and ascertain Lydia's mood, when she was greeted effusively by Sir Edward, who was in the company of Sir Frederick and Lady Fanshawe.

'Miss Bennet. Enchanting as ever!' Sir Edward boomed. 'Is this not a splendid occasion? Quite the event of the summer. I hope I may not presume too much if I beg the honour of a dance this evening?'

'Of course not, Sir Edward. I should be delighted,' said Kitty, with sincerity. If only Frederick Fanshawe were more like his uncle, she thought.

'My younger nephew tells me he has claimed the honour of the first two. Rightly so!' he said, beaming at Kitty and the said gentleman's parents. Kitty smiled her best smile at all three, wondering at the innocence or otherwise of Sir Frederick and Lady Fanshawe in regard to the behaviour of their eldest son.

'Well, I shan't keep you, Miss Bennet, much as I might like to! A young lady such as yourself will be much in demand this evening. I shall claim you later! Off you go, off you go! Find the young people.'

Kitty thanked him and excused herself, looking again for Colonel Fitzwilliam and Lydia. Captain Morton, who was now grouped with Mr and Mrs Bridgwater, Miss Bingley and Mrs Hurst, saw her glance and bade her good evening. Kitty had no choice but to join them.

'We were just saying how little Mrs Wickham has changed since we last saw her,' observed Caroline Bingley. 'You must be so pleased to have your youngest sister here.'

'It was a pleasant surprise,' lied Kitty, calmly.

'She was earlier telling us about the assemblies at Newcastle. Quite riotous, they would seem! Louisa and I are in awe of her fortitude.' Mrs Hurst tittered and made an ineffectual attempt to hide a smirk behind her fan.

Captain Morton, whose manners were above those of Miss Bingley and her sister, and who was sensible to the insinuations being made, remarked to Kitty about the musicians he had seen setting up their instruments that afternoon, giving her a chance to expound on her knowledge of the band. She obliged, knowing it would be imprudent to enquire of him as to Lydia's whereabouts in the present company. Kitty had the uncomfortable sensation that she was the subject of some discussion between Miss Bingley and Mrs Bridgwater but was in no mood to find out what that might be about; she did not suppose it would be to her advantage to know. Her surreptitious glances around the room revealed neither Lydia nor Colonel Fitzwilliam, only that the three Fanshawe siblings had arrived and were in animated discussion with Georgiana. That caused her no surprise, just a dull sense of inevitability.

She became aware of a general movement towards the ballroom and saw Colonel Fitzwilliam arrive just in time to find Felicia Fanshawe and escort her there. Captain Morton offered Kitty his arm, and together they went in.

Unheard and unseen by those already enjoying the society and music in the glittering ballroom, a string of carriages clattered up to Pemberley's portico, where ladies in silk and satin accompanied by their elegantly attired menfolk alighted. Inside, having been relieved of their shawls and cloaks and made sure of the correctness of their appearances, their journeys up the regal staircase were checked only by their wonder of the scene about them and the necessity of waiting for their names to be relayed and announced.

Elizabeth, waiting near the ballroom entrance to welcome her guests, asked Kitty to stay at her side so that Darcy and Colonel Fitzwilliam could facilitate any introductions that might be helpful to those young people who wished to dance. Once again, Kitty marvelled at her sister, whose role as hostess and mistress of Pemberley seemed innate, and at the magnificence of the ballroom, now alive with expectation and the swirling movement and colours of myriad pretty gowns.

Lydia had reappeared, giving no outward cause for alarm, but was soon lost to Kitty's sight. Her attention was now claimed by

William Fanshawe, who had returned in readiness for the first two dances.

'You are looking very well, Miss Bennet,' he said, bowing. 'I am most honoured to be your first partner of the evening.' He looked around. 'I think I am just in time.' Kitty followed his gaze. A sufficient number of guests had arrived and the signal was given for the dancing to begin. The band struck up afresh and Mr Darcy walked across the room to escort Elizabeth onto the dance floor and the chalked celestial bodies, and lead the first set. The summer ball was in progress.

CHAPTER 51

It was approaching midnight and Kitty had not been without a partner for a single dance. Flushed but still full of energy, the exertions had done much to quieten and relax her mind. Her desire to speak with Colonel Fitzwilliam had been addressed by the gentleman himself when he asked if she would oblige him by dancing the third set with him, and although it had not been the time or the place she had gone so far as to tell him that she had something important that she wished to discuss with him in private. He had looked curious rather than surprised but readily acquiesced. The promise of relieving herself of the unwelcome burden of knowledge was enough for this evening, she thought, although Freddie Fanshawe had since asked Georgiana for the supper dance, thus signalling to all his interest in her.

That repast had been announced and nearly everyone was moving towards the supper room. Every source of nourishment needed to sustain and encourage further dancing was laid out upon the tables: mousses and pies, platters of meat and fish, artichokes in white sauce, small birds, large hams, the ubiquitous white soup. Kitty was content to be seated between Captain Morton and another young gentleman from a nearby estate to whom she had only just been introduced and who had proved himself a fine dancer. Not far off she could see Colonel Fitzwilliam and Felicia Fanshawe, both of whom looked very happy in each other's company. The conversation around her was of the excellence of the food, the skill of the musicians, the magnificence of the ballroom, of who was dancing with whom. Those who knew that there had been a tradition of a summer ball welcomed its renaissance; those for whom it was a new event hoped it would be repeated. Kitty was quietly proud to be part of the family providing such lavish entertainment.

Suddenly she became aware of Lydia. She was at a nearby table, seated next to Sir Edward, whose gallantry was conspicuous in the presence of attractive young women, and holding forth loudly about something or the other. Kitty could not hear what was being said but fervently hoped that Lydia would not humiliate herself, or more accurately, her host and hostess. Georgiana and Freddie Fanshawe were a small distance away, at one of the tables near the windows, as was William who had, not unexpectedly as far as Kitty was concerned, been an object of some admiration from quite a few of the young ladies present. She found she did not much mind.

The business of refreshment was soon achieved and, suitably revived, the belles and beaux were eager to return to the pleasures and potential conquests of the ballroom. She saw Georgiana depart in that direction and was about to follow when she noticed Lydia approaching Freddie Fanshawe, who was talking to his brother. Bereft of any other idea, Kitty hurriedly excused herself from the table and went to join them, in time to hear Freddie Fanshawe say that he was going to look for his father, whom he suspected was at the card tables. His brother preferred to go back to the ballroom and offered to escort the ladies but Lydia demurred, citing the need for some fresh air. Kitty said she would stay with her.

'What are you doing?' she whispered.

'I am going to talk to that Mr Fanshawe,' declared Lydia, putting down a glass of wine, and setting off in pursuit.

Feeling quite helpless, Kitty watched her sister follow Freddie Fanshawe, who appeared to be heading towards the gallery, which was not on the way to the card room. He stopped to light a cigar and had just begun to inhale when Lydia accosted him. His astonishment was equal to Kitty's embarrassment and she could only imagine what Lydia was demanding of him. He did not walk away, however, and Kitty wondered if he was perhaps a little the worse for drink again. Lydia's accusations were clearly having some effect on him; his expression changed from surprise to shock, and then something bordering on fear. He seemed to lose his balance slightly and had to steady himself. Lydia, her stance confident and her stare aggressive, stood before him waiting. She began to speak again, more loudly this time and Kitty saw Mr Fanshawe attempt to quieten her. She saw him reach into his pocket and hand her something. Was he going to give her money! Kitty looked behind her, thankful that no one else was witnessing this awful transaction. When she turned back again, it was to see Mr Fanshawe once again talking earnestly and quietly; he seemed to be imploring Lydia to secrecy. She stalked off, leaving him in quite a sorry state.

Kitty could only be thankful that this dreadful encounter had ended. Lydia came back to her, looking triumphant.

'Well, I hope you are satisfied,' hissed Kitty, furious and indignant. 'You are a guest in this house and you are behaving abominably! What is it you have there?'

'Quite a pretty little thing, a promissory note if you will.' She opened her hand to show what she had.

'No!' cried Kitty, who had thought the situation could deteriorate no further but now saw that Lydia was holding Georgiana's treasured cameo. 'But how…?' She looked across to where Freddie Fanshawe had been standing – her face expressing wonder and incredulity, her mind questioning his possession of the necklace – but he had gone.

She turned back to Lydia who was holding the cameo to her neck and preening at her reflection in one of the tall gold-framed mirrors that flanked the gallery walls.

'You cannot take this,' she said, in what she hoped was a quiet and reasonable tone. 'It does not belong to him.'

Lydia took no notice, merely bent in closer to the mirror to examine her appearance.

'It is not his to give,' repeated Kitty. 'Please, give it to me.'

'Have you lost your senses?' enquired Lydia, turning back to Kitty. 'Why would I do that? He can have it back when he pays his debt.' She looked at the cameo again. 'Unless I decide to keep it, after all.'

'Lydia, please,' remonstrated Kitty.

'No!' said Lydia, turning on her heel and flouncing back towards the ballroom.

Kitty ran after her, calling for her to stop. 'Please,' said she, catching her sister by the arm. Lydia shrugged her off with a violence that caused Kitty to stumble and in trying to regain her footing she caught at her sister's skirt, tearing it. Lydia rounded on her. She pushed Kitty, then slapped her. 'Go away!' she shouted. 'It is none of your business! You are so annoying!'

This, Kitty remembered with a sick feeling in her stomach, is just what she was like when we were young: always slapping and kicking when no one was watching. She stood stock still for a moment as the memory flooded over her.

'You and your silly tiara,' said Lydia nastily, pulling at it and dislodging it. Kitty watched it tumble to the floor. Incensed, she spun around and lunged at Lydia, catching her off guard. She dropped the cameo and Kitty swooped down to retrieve it. She stood back, her arm behind her, her fist clenched tightly around the necklace. She glared at Lydia.

'What is the meaning of this disturbance!' demanded a voice that was at once commanding and glacial.

Kitty turned to see Mr Darcy glowering at both of them. Behind him, at the entrance to the ballroom, a few of the guests were staring in amazement.

'I will not tolerate such vulgar behaviour under my roof.' Anger seared through the words. 'Kitty, what is that you are withholding?'

Crimson with shame, Kitty meekly handed him the cameo. He recognised it instantly, of course, looking afresh at both young women, surprise mixing with incomprehension and suspicion. 'How came you by this?' he demanded.

Kitty looked to Lydia, who was affecting nonchalance in the face of Mr Darcy's imperious authority, willing her to answer and explain. 'Ask Kitty,' she said, still angry and defiant. 'She seems to have acquired a penchant for pretty things.'

Kitty gasped, horror-struck.

'Very well,' said Mr Darcy, his expression exuding fury and contempt. 'We will discuss this tomorrow. For now, you will conduct yourselves with decorum or you will leave.' He looked from one to the other. 'Mrs Wickham,' he said, by way of dismissal. Then to Kitty, 'I had expected better of you.'

He bent down to pick up Georgiana's tiara. He looked at it and then at Kitty. After a moment's hesitation, he handed it back to her.

Kitty's mortification was complete. She hung her head and heard, rather than saw, both Mr Darcy and Lydia depart. Explanation would be both impossible and futile without Freddie Fanshawe's testimony. She stayed where she was for several minutes until gradually the gaiety and music spilling from the adjoining rooms filtered through to her. Forcing down her fears and foreboding, Kitty decided it would be better to return to the ball than retreat to her room; she could at least show herself in a polite and proper manner for the rest of the evening. She did not want to let Elizabeth down and, besides, the need to speak with Freddie Fanshawe had become paramount.

She walked farther down the gallery, found another mirror and spent some time adjusting her hair and the tiara – which continued to sparkle brightly as if in mockery of Kitty's devastation – and eventually made her way back into the ballroom.

A country dance was in full swing and Kitty watched in miserable isolation as the couples went down the room. Lydia, she noted with dissatisfaction, was among their number, laughing and unperturbed. With a start, she realised someone was saying her name and turned to find Lady Fanshawe.

'You are sitting this one out, Miss Bennet?' she enquired, fanning herself vigorously.

'Not intentionally, Lady Fanshawe,' answered Kitty, truthfully enough. 'I needed to get some air.'

'It is excessively warm,' returned her ladyship. 'Despite the hour! I wonder at my sons, neglecting you so. I am sure you will not be without a partner for very long.'

Kitty smiled at her kindness and, as if on cue, Sir Edward appeared before her. 'Miss Bennet, I thought I had quite lost you. May I claim the honour?'

'Oh, of course,' said Kitty, apologising for her absence at the beginning of the set. He chatted and commented throughout the dance, forcing her to become animated and sociable once more, although his compliments and obvious delight in her company nearly undid her composure. Here was her chivalrous Sir Edward, worried that she looked a little tired and hoping that she was not overexerting herself, oblivious to her confusion and distress and to his nephew's misdeeds. He is not ignorant of Freddie's gaming habits, she reminded herself, and looked up into Sir Edward's face. He beamed back at her, causing Kitty to blush and look away. It was all impossible, she thought, and nothing was more impossible than discussing or understanding the events of the evening whilst a ball was in progress and everyone but she was happy and carefree. At the conclusion of the set, Sir Edward bowed and made a show of reluctantly returning her to a group of young ladies containing Georgiana and Felicia.

'There you are!' cried Miss Fanshawe. 'We had been wondering where you had got to. I declare I have danced every dance and my shoes are in grave danger of wearing out! That shall not stop me though!'

Her companions concurred, each vying for the honour of the most threadbare pumps.

'Have you seen my brothers? William was here after supper but Freddie has quite disappeared. I have a notion that he has gone to find my father! It is remiss of him!'

'It most certainly is,' Georgiana agreed, 'but I am promised elsewhere for every dance so we shall do without him.' She is so secure of his affections, thought Kitty morosely, while the other ladies laughed benignly and looked around the room for their partners for the next set. The merriment was infectious but Kitty had quite lost her *joie de vivre*. She danced with vigour but not enthusiasm, and did her best to smile and look happy. Elizabeth caught her eye at one point and she could tell by the radiant expression on her sister's face that Darcy had yet to tell her what had transpired.

She did not see Freddie Fanshawe again until the close of the ball, when she and other lively souls who were determined to dance the night away were giving their all to the Boulanger. He was standing, his back to the wall, at the far side of the room and she was dismayed to see Lydia was with him again. Given the nature of the dance, it was difficult for Kitty to keep them in view. What was apparent, however, as she and the other dancers circled, was that Mr Fanshawe and Lydia were not merely exchanging a few pleasantries; their conversation, even to the most casual observer, would have appeared intense. She hoped Georgiana would not notice, but it was too late: at that moment, turning around her partner, she saw the pair and her expression changed from shock to alarm and bewilderment.

If only I could speak privately with Freddie Fanshawe and Colonel Fitzwilliam, Kitty thought wretchedly, knowing that the evening would present no such opportunity. As soon as the dancing concluded, she slipped away. She was upset and exhausted and could not explain Lydia's conduct to anyone, especially Georgiana.

CHAPTER 52

After a few hours of fretful sleep, Kitty awoke with a start. Her dreams had been littered with images of the ball and the dancing, which had somehow taken place around Conisbrough Castle and in full sunlight. Diamonds glittered on the ground in place of stones and Kitty had been watching everything unfold from atop the keep. No one had known she was there.

She deemed it too early to find either Freddie Fanshawe or Colonel Fitzwilliam but not too soon to disturb Lydia. She dressed quickly and without care, and went up to her room. To her surprise, Lydia was not there. Kitty sat down on the bed and wondered where she could be. She was anxious to discover what else she and Mr Fanshawe had been discussing. If Wickham's allegations were true, then Freddie would surely be feeling most uncomfortable; she had no doubt that Lydia would press home her advantage. How would he react to her demands? From what Kitty knew of him, he was a gentleman who expected people to do his bidding, not the reverse, but she was also sure he would not wish to risk losing Georgiana's esteem, or his reputation. As to the cameo, she knew not what to think but hoped he would provide a rational and reasonable explanation as to its mysterious reappearance. Georgiana would be very happy to have it once again in her possession.

Kitty waited for some time in the vain hope that Lydia would come back. Eventually she could sit still no longer and returned to her own room to prepare for the day ahead. It was past midday when, with some trepidation, she ventured downstairs. The house, still festooned with flowers, retained its festive air, and those in residence – those who had quit their rooms, that is – were scattered about the sofas and chairs in the drawing room and library, drinking tea and discussing the previous evening or, in some cases, gently dozing.

Elizabeth was the first to notice her arrival and looked across at her coolly, causing Kitty's heart to sink further. Darcy would have told her about the fracas he had witnessed, she knew that, but she could only imagine what he had said. Neither Lydia nor Darcy was in the drawing room; the ladies seemed to have claimed it for their own.

Only a few were present. Caroline Bingley, Amelia Bridgwater and Louisa Hurst were sitting on sofas near Elizabeth. Lady Fanshawe and Lady Mortlake were seated at a table by the window poring over magazines and discussing landscaped gardens and architecture.

Trying to maintain some semblance of normality, Kitty greeted everyone and took a seat on the sofa beside her sister. Elizabeth did not look at her. Mrs Bridgwater was complimenting her hostess on a wonderfully successful ball and Kitty sat silently, listening as the discussion veered into such important matters as the rise of the quadrille and the scandal of the waltz. Having exhausted such topics, the conversation lapsed until Caroline Bingley suddenly announced: 'Mrs Bridgwater and I were saying earlier how very elegant you were last night, Miss Bennet.'

Kitty thanked her, alert to whatever barb would inevitably follow. Miss Bingley was not in the habit of bestowing compliments on her, so there would no doubt be some sugar-coated insult on its way.

'Yes. We were particularly admiring your tiara. Such a lovely piece.'

Kitty agreed it was, feeling no need to declare its true ownership.

'Of course, one has to be careful. They do slip so easily.' She smiled one of her ingratiating smiles. 'Dreadful to lose one's crown!' Beside her, Mrs Hurst could barely keep her countenance.

'And now I understand we are losing dear Mrs Wickham today,' Miss Bingley continued, sparkling with petty malevolence. 'I had no idea she would have to depart so soon.'

Alarmed, Kitty turned to Elizabeth. 'Lydia is leaving today?'

'She is,' confirmed her sister. 'Events have called her away earlier than she anticipated. She will be leaving within the hour, I am afraid. I see she has not informed you.' Elizabeth regarded Kitty calmly, her face betraying no emotion.

'No, indeed,' said Kitty, her heart pounding. 'I will go and find her. I should like to see her before she goes.'

'Of course,' said Elizabeth smoothly, and turned her attention back to her guests as Kitty made her excuses and forced herself to walk rather than run from the drawing room. Once outside, she looked around wildly. Where was Lydia? She ran back up to the Blue Room, only to find the door open and its only occupant a housemaid, who could offer no information as to Mrs Wickham's whereabouts.

Kitty turned and hurried towards the main staircase that led to the entrance hall. Looking down from the gallery, she was relieved to see her younger sister below, talking to one of the servants.

'Lydia!' she called, almost out of breath as she drew near to her.

'You have come to see me off then?' said Lydia, sounding irritated. 'I suppose you know I have been given my marching orders?'

'Indeed I did not,' whispered Kitty in return. 'I have only just found out you are leaving. I have been looking for you! Where have you been? What has happened?'

'So many questions!' retorted Lydia. 'None of this would have happened if you had not interfered.'

Kitty took Lydia's arm and steered her outside into the grounds, where they could speak without being overheard. She saw one of the carriages was outside, no doubt waiting to take her sister to Lambton. When they had gained a little distance from the house, she again entreated Lydia to tell her what had happened.

'It appears I have made a spectacle of myself and must be sent away. Mrs Darcy has more airs and graces than I remember!'

'I saw you talking with Mr Fanshawe again last night,' said Kitty, ignoring the harshness in her sister's voice. 'Did he tell you where he found the necklace?'

Lydia laughed at her. 'Is that all that concerns you? All this fuss over a bauble! I told you, you should have let me keep it! Never mind, it is of no consequence now. Mr Frederick Fanshawe has seen fit, with a little persuasion, to pay his debt to my dear Wickham. Perhaps he is a gentleman after all. You may do what you will with the necklace.'

'It is not mine to dispose of,' said Kitty, increasingly exasperated in the face of Lydia's nonchalance. 'Neither does it belong to Mr Fanshawe. I would like to know if he told you how he came by it!'

'Well, he did not,' said Lydia, blithely. 'In fact, he knows nothing about it!'

'What can you mean? It was in his possession. You know that!'

'I am not sure I do.' She leaned in closer to Kitty and lowered her voice. 'We made a bargain,' she said conspiratorially. 'He gave me my fifty pounds and I agreed to say nothing about the necklace. My dear Wickham will be so pleased.'

'But,' remonstrated Kitty, 'Mr Darcy saw you with it!'

'He saw *you* with it, not me!' said Lydia, smugly. 'Oh, don't look so worried! You only have to say you found it.'

'I cannot!' cried Kitty, aghast.

'"Oh, I cannot!"' mocked Lydia, walking back to the house. 'Of course you can! Where is the harm? Your friend Miss Darcy will be delighted to have it back, and you will have all the glory. Oh, look!' she cried. 'There is our dear sister Elizabeth come to make sure I depart.'

Kitty looked up and saw Lizzy regarding them both from the steps of Pemberley. Once again, she felt she was being judged, and once again found wanting. She caught up to Lydia. 'Please, just tell Lizzy the truth!' she pleaded desperately. 'Please!'

Lydia made no answer. Instead she waved to Elizabeth, who was now walking towards the carriage, and quickened her step to join her. 'Such a wonderful ball, Lizzy! A delight!' she declared, her voice as loud and jolly as ever. 'I am sure I will always remember it!'

'As will we,' returned Elizabeth. 'Mr Darcy and I wish you a safe journey to Newcastle.' She stood back to allow Lydia into the carriage. Kitty watched as the door closed, saw Lydia arrange herself and let down the glass to say farewell, saw the coachman tighten his hold on the reins. She felt utterly powerless.

'Well, goodbye!' cried Lydia to her sisters. Then, as the carriage started off, added: 'I do hope Mama's health improves, Kitty. Longbourn will be so dull for you after all this!'

Chapter 53

As soon as the carriage turned into the drive, Elizabeth dropped all pretence of gracious civility and curtly instructed Kitty to go to her room; she would talk to her later. So saying, she went back into the house.

Defeated, Kitty went and lay down on her bed. Had Lydia planned the little piece of havoc she had created at Pemberley, it could not have been better orchestrated. I will be blamed for her behaviour, thought Kitty. I will be considered complicit, just as I was when she eloped from Brighton. She could not stop asking herself how Freddie Fanshawe had the cameo. The day at Conisbrough was vivid in her memory. They had all searched together; how could anyone have found it and concealed its discovery? Then she remembered. At her own suggestion, Freddie Fanshawe had been dispatched to the carriage to see if the necklace was within! Why would he keep it though, and relinquish his chance to be her hero? Her Frederick the Great! Her thoughts were interrupted by a knock at her door. Her summons had arrived.

She made her way to Elizabeth's rooms and sat primly on a small upholstered chair while her sister paced about, venting her spleen. She had never seen her so angry and upset.

'I am beyond disappointment,' she began. 'Darcy tells me that you and Lydia were brawling like fishwives outside the ballroom yesterday evening. How could you conduct yourself in such a reprehensible manner? Have you no respect, no decorum?

Lydia is wayward, that is understood. But I have a right to expect better of you. I did expect better of you.'

Kitty winced. Here again were the words that had cut through her yesterday when Mr Darcy had uttered them.

'I am told it was not the first time your behaviour has let you down since you came here. You were seen shouting and laughing in a most unseemly way when you returned from your excursion with Lydia. This is not the way things are done at Pemberley.'

Kitty opened her mouth to protest this crime, but Elizabeth silenced her with a gesture.

'If that were all it would be galling enough, bitter enough, but to think…' She stopped, closed her eyes as if to shut out her terrible thoughts. She took a deep breath and continued.

'You were fighting over a necklace, Darcy tells me. A necklace that belongs to Georgiana, a necklace that was believed lost. A necklace she held most dear. What we cannot understand is how you came to have it. You were giving it to Lydia?' Elizabeth shook her head, her expression even more severe.

'That is not true!' cried Kitty.

'Well what is your explanation?' demanded Elizabeth, turning to face her. 'That cameo was lost at Conisbrough Castle weeks ago. Georgiana said every effort was made to find it, extensive searches were carried out. And now it seems that you had it in your possession all the time! I cannot believe it, Kitty. I did not take you for a thief! How could you? It is heinous!' Elizabeth sat down, quite overcome at her sister's transgressions.

'A thief?' said Kitty, her face white with shock. 'Is that what you think?'

'I do not want to think it. I am horrified to think it, but you cannot expect me to believe you found it last night, here at Pemberley! Was Lydia to take it for you? What did you think to gain?'

'Lizzy!' she cried. 'You do not understand!'

'Unfortunately, I understand only too well. I am so ashamed!' Elizabeth turned her head away, wiped a tear from her eyes.

Kitty looked at her in horror. 'Lizzy,' she said, 'I wonder that you would think me guilty of such a crime. I would never do such a thing! Nor would I do anything to upset or abuse Georgiana. She is like a sister to me!'

'As is Lydia!' retorted Elizabeth.

'As are you!' returned Kitty, her voice rising. 'How dare you accuse me!

'It pains me, believe me!'

'You are right,' Kitty said, trying to regain her composure. 'Lydia and I were fighting over the cameo but I was trying to get it back…'

'Get it back!' cried Elizabeth. 'From Lydia? Why would she have had it? She has already told me that you found it. Really, Kitty! Do not think to blame Lydia for this!'

Kitty sighed, for herself and at the awful absurdity of her predicament. 'Of course,' said she, with a small laugh of exasperation. 'You would believe Lydia over me!'

'There is nothing amusing in all of this,' snapped Elizabeth. 'How could you be so base? So stupid?'

Suddenly, it was all too much for Kitty. Nothing she could do, nothing she tried to do, would ever be good enough. The injustice of Elizabeth's accusations, together with the revelations and confusions of the past few days simmered and boiled.

'Stupid?' she cried, jumping to her feet. 'That is all I ever hear from you, from all of you! Stupid Kitty! Silly, ignorant Kitty! You never ask, you never enquire – you only condemn! If I do something well, you do not notice. If something goes amiss – anything goes amiss! – it is all my fault. Stupid, silly Kitty's fault. You thought I had told Lydia about the ball, but I did not. Even if I had told her, would it be my fault if she took it upon herself to come here unbidden? You do not ask why I was arguing with Lydia, you only blame!'

Elizabeth lifted her eyes to the ceiling, and exhaled.

'And now I am base as well? Dishonest! Perhaps you should look to your necklaces and jewels, too. Assure yourself I have not taken them?'

'Oh, for heaven's sake! Please stop this pretence. I will not have it. You are exhausting.' Elizabeth finally sat down

'I am amazed,' continued Kitty, fiercely. 'Amazed that you would think so little of me! Since I came to Pemberley I have done my utmost to be a good sister to you, to be worthy of you! I have made new acquaintances who treat me with respect, treat me as an equal. Imagine that! People who listen to my opinions, who enjoy my company! It is just you – my own family! – who insist on my stupidity and ignorance. And worse!'

Elizabeth was unmoved. 'Kindly lower your voice,' she said.

Kitty had not finished. 'With regards to Georgiana, I would never abuse her trust. She is my friend, my confidante.'

'That has been noticed. Darcy feels your influence on her may be too great.'

'I beg your pardon!' cried Kitty, shocked at this new charge. 'This is intolerable. Am I to be blamed for everything? I presume you allude to Georgiana's friendship with Mr Fanshawe, about whom…'

'I allude to nothing in particular,' interrupted Elizabeth. 'We are not here to discuss Georgiana. She will have to be told, of course, that her cameo has been found and under what circumstances. She will be shocked and dismayed.'

Kitty blanched, imagining Georgiana's distress and her interpretation of the previous night's events.

'Darcy and I have discussed what to do and we agree this scandal need go no further than these walls. Accordingly, I will not inform our parents or Jane. For that you should feel most grateful. Meanwhile, I have a house full of guests, friends as well as guests, people to whom I owe hospitality and respect. I will not have the peace of Pemberley overturned by your conduct.' Elizabeth's expression was hard, her mouth set.

'Tomorrow,' she said, 'you will return to Longbourn. As Jane says, our mother is unwell and would no doubt be pleased to have your company. I will write to our father now. You may go.'

CHAPTER 54

Kitty spent the rest of the day feeling numb and pretending otherwise. News of her imminent departure to Longbourn, cloaked in a need to be close to her ailing mother, became known as everyone assembled before dinner, and was received with appropriate distress, most notably by Felicia Fanshawe and Colonel Fitzwilliam. They completely understood, or so they thought, why she must go, but lamented the fact and hoped they would meet again soon. They looked forward to seeing her in London for the season, if not before? How quickly the time would pass. William Fanshawe echoed their sentiments and was sure he could speak for Freddie. He would be most sorry to have missed her, Sir Edward told her, but his eldest nephew had had some business in Doncaster that had required his presence.

'Not to worry, Miss Bennet,' continued Sir Edward, oblivious to the fact that Freddie Fanshawe's absence dashed any chance of Kitty clearing her name or discovering his motives. 'We will get by very well without him. I think tonight is going to be a very special evening.' He tapped his nose and declared he should say nothing more. Kitty, too tired and upset to try to persuade him otherwise, let him talk on, barely listening. Georgiana swept by, affecting not to notice her, which cut her to the quick.

'Forgive me,' said Sir Edward, regarding Kitty more closely. 'You are thinking about your poor mother. What a sweet, compassionate young lady you are!' She felt her eyes fill with tears and struggled to contain her emotion in the face of kindness, which only made Sir Edward more attentive and Kitty more tearful. 'Come and sit down, sit down,' he bade her, leading her to an empty chair near an open window. 'Some fresh air, I think. Now, let me fetch you a little cordial.' He dashed off, returned with a small glass of wine and waited patiently for her to take a sip. He took a seat beside her and, aware of his concern, Kitty wondered if she could confide in Sir Edward. At the same time, she anticipated his disbelief and could not bear the thought of defending herself afresh.

Sir Edward was looking at her most thoughtfully. 'Your journey will be a long one, I fear,' he remarked. 'Please convey my best wishes to your parents. Hertfordshire, you say? Perhaps, I may have the privilege of calling when next I travel down to London?'

Kitty was too immersed in her own misery to read any significance into his remarks.

'Forgive me,' reiterated Sir Edward. 'You are upset. You do not need to listen to my rattling on!'

Before Kitty could manage a response, dinner was announced and, having ascertained she was well enough, Sir Edward escorted her in.

Everyone else was in high spirits. Elizabeth was playing the role of hostess to perfection and seemed to have not a care in the world; Darcy likewise. Neither as much as looked in Kitty's direction. Lady Fanshawe, seated to her right, seemed particularly cheerful and the reason soon became apparent. Colonel Fitzwilliam had sought, and been given, permission for Miss Fanshawe's hand in marriage and the announcement, when made, was greeted with pleasure and satisfaction by both her relations and his brother and cousins. Georgiana was clearly delighted by her uncle's betrothal to her friend Felicia, whose own happiness outshone all others. Kitty, at pains to conceal her melancholy, was effusive in her congratulations. She thought highly of both of them and thought theirs would be a successful union. She wondered if she would see either of them again.

When the ladies withdrew after dinner, Felicia's engagement was the subject of much animated chatter and Kitty was grateful for that diversion. Nonetheless, there were many who wished to speak to her, to wish her and her mother well, and regret both the reason and the fact she was called away. Although she had accepted her defeat and disguised disgrace, it took all Kitty's fortitude to smile and thank her well-wishers, alert as she was to Elizabeth's coolness to her and the unspoken animosity emanating from Georgiana.

She would be leaving early in the morning – Elizabeth had declared that best – so Kitty would be making her farewells that evening. It seemed an age before the gentlemen came to join them and allow her to say her last goodbyes. Everyone lamented her departure of course, and the supposed cause of it, and declared Pemberley would be a duller place without her. Lady Fanshawe and Sir Edward hoped to see her at Danson Park as soon as circumstances allowed; Felicia, also genuinely sorry to see her go, made her promise to write and was sure they would see each other again soon; William Fanshawe echoed his sister's sentiments, although Kitty knew, pleasant as it would be to see him again, he would never be anything but a good friend; Lord and Lady Mortlake had been delighted to meet her; Colonel Fitzwilliam likewise; others chorused their good wishes.

Saying goodbye to Mr Darcy was especially difficult. Outwardly both maintained a friendly accord: she thanked him for his excellent hospitality and he in turn made the necessary reference to expecting to see her at Pemberley again. Neither expected that to happen. Darcy's manner was as smooth as ice, and just as warm. Georgiana, with Elizabeth by her side, had the grace to wish Mrs Bennet well but would not meet Kitty's eye. She was not surprised, but deeply affected at the loss of so dear a friendship.

At last, Kitty was able to retire to her room, pleading a headache and the need to prepare for the days ahead.

She was up at first light. When she drew back the curtains she saw a summer storm had broken the previous night, drenching the countryside and breaking the weeks of fine weather. Now the day was damp and the sky sullen, but there was otherwise no impediment to travel.

Kitty made her way downstairs for the last time. As it would be neither right nor appropriate for any relation of Mrs Fitzwilliam Darcy to make such a long journey unaccompanied, a small escort of servants had been drafted to ensure Kitty's comfort and security. These would be her sole companions on the way to Hertfordshire. With her trunks aboard, she was ready to leave. If she had harboured hopes for some last-minute reprieve – that Freddie Fanshawe might at any moment gallop into view and take responsibility for his actions, absolving her of her perceived crimes; that her friend Georgiana would relent and come down to wave her goodbye – then she was disappointed. Only Elizabeth emerged from the house to perform that ritual, and it was done perfunctorily.

And so began the journey. Kitty was immensely sad as they passed through the glades and woodlands of Pemberley. The deer, so often capriciously absent when looked for, had grouped themselves picturesquely on a hillside, and she kept them in view for as long as she could. Her grief was not just for the house and grounds, of course, nor for her own tarnished reputation, but for all that she had enjoyed so briefly and then lost. Her sister's esteem, her friend's affection, a camaraderie that had seemed so strong and then vanished in an instant. Inconstant fortune, she thought to herself, but could not place the reference.

The maid who had been assigned to her was a pleasant girl called Jenny. She had never been outside of Derbyshire before and was exceedingly delighted and not a little nervous about travelling all the way to London, where she would become part of the retinue at the Darcys' Berkeley Square house. Her presence meant that Kitty could not give in to the sorrow and dejection that consumed her. She allowed Jenny to ask her questions about London and Hertfordshire and answered them graciously enough, and took a little pleasure at the wonder displayed on the girl's face at the thought of all that awaited her in town, but after a while she feigned sleep and they travelled in silence.

The journey seemed to go on for ever and was in stark contrast to the one she had made northwards just a few months previously, where the hours were spent in friendly conversation and the anticipation of Pemberley and all that it offered. Travelling in the opposite direction now, there was nothing to look forward to, just the familiarity and monotony of Longbourn.

Kitty lost count of the stops they made to change horses and took little notice of the inns they stopped at, except to know they were satisfactory. The maid and the other servant did all they could to provide for her comfort but Kitty, locked in her own melancholy and depression, was barely aware of her surrounds and it was not until midday on the third day of the journey that she recognised some fields and farmhouses and realised they were almost at Longbourn.

A few minutes later, the ivy-covered pale stone walls of her family home were in sight at the end of a short, gravelled drive. Kitty let down the side-glass to better see outside. A sudden gust of wind dislodged some leaves on the trees and blew a few on to her lap. They were turning, she noted dully; it must be nearly autumn.

The noise of the carriage had alerted Mr Bennet who appeared at the door to welcome his daughter home. 'There you are, child,' he said, not without affection. 'I am glad to see you safe and sound.'

Kitty walked back into Longbourn, its smells and sights so very familiar. She gave her cloak and bonnet to Mrs Hill, who was pleased to see young Miss Catherine again, and looked around her. Nothing had changed but everything looked smaller somehow.

'Is that Kitty arrived?' demanded a querulous voice.

'Yes, Mama. I am here,' said Kitty, unsure as to her mother's whereabouts.

'At last!' cried Mrs Bennet. 'I have been waiting.'

'She is in her room,' said Mr Bennet, indicating the staircase.

Chapter 55

S he went up, knocked on Mrs Bennet's door and entered her room. 'Mama!' It was as much a greeting as an expression of shock. It was seven months since Kitty had bade her mother farewell and then she had been in robust health, plump and pink-cheeked. The face she kissed now was drawn and pale, and through the layers of lace and wool that Mrs Bennet was wearing as she lay, almost lost in a sea of pillows, Kitty could see that she was much thinner. She sat on the edge of the bed, and took her mother's hand.

'It is good to see you, Mama,' said she, noticing how cold and light that hand seemed in her own. 'Jane wrote that you were not yourself. I can see that she was right to be concerned on your behalf.'

'It is very tiresome,' returned Mrs Bennet. 'No one can tell what is wrong. No one can give me any relief. I have told the physician that it is no good but does he listen to me? No, he does not. I have such a pain in my side some days. Such a sharp pain and I have to sit down. You cannot imagine. Oh, I do suffer but there is no use complaining. It just makes my poor nerves so much worse. Well, at least you are here now, Kitty. You will see for yourself how things are. Pass me that small bottle over there, dear. I cannot reach it myself.'

Kitty looked around and saw a small brown vial on the table. She gave it to her mother who unscrewed the top and took a small sip.

'What is that, Mama? Is it laudanum?'

'Laudanum mixed with some wine, dear. It is helpful for my nerves. The apothecary says I must not have more than this tiny amount. It is all very well for him to say so but I am the one who is in pain.' She sank back on the pillows, closed her eyes and seemed to relax a little.

Kitty waited, unsure what to do. 'Do you want to sleep, Mama? Shall I stay or shall I go and see Papa and come back in a little while?'

'You must do as you will. I will cope as best as I can here. There is no need to worry about me.' Her eyes were still closed as she spoke. Kitty looked at her mother, shook her head and made a sad smile. There was no doubting Mrs Bennet was unwell and that she had lost a lot of weight; she had not, however, lost the power of speech.

Kitty found her father in his usual chair in the library.

'What ails Mama?' she asked.

Mr Bennet sighed. 'The physicians are not sure. Various prognoses have been made but none are borne out by examination. Your dear mother complains of pain but it is difficult to locate its cause or indeed its exact location.'

'Physicians?'

'Mrs Bennet was dissatisfied with the first physician and so another was brought in. Both are of the same opinion, and that opinion is, to be frank, vague in the extreme. I am glad you are here, child.'

Kitty looked at her father and saw signs of fatigue. Mrs Bennet's nerves, exacerbated by pain, would be exacting for all.

'It is good to see you again, Papa.' She could not bring herself to say she was glad to be home. Mrs Hill bustled in with tea and the information that Miss Catherine's things had been put in her old room, just as before. She assumed, incorrectly, that this would be welcome news. Kitty thanked her and poured tea for herself and her father.

'Your mother will be wanting you,' he said, 'But stay here awhile and tell me how things go with Elizabeth. This summer ball of hers seems to have been a most grand affair.'

So she stayed and gave her father a brief account of life at Pemberley, which only increased her sadness, and then excused herself to go to her room.

Kitty closed her door, sank onto her bed and stared at her surrounds. The very sight of the room, its sameness, its contrast with the pretty and much larger bedroom she had had at Pemberley, taunted her. A great wave of panic and despair washed over her and suddenly she was gasping for air. She clutched at the bedpost to steady herself and forced herself to breathe. 'No!' she kept saying, over and over again. 'No. No. No. No. No!' She heard herself repeating the word and thought she would go mad. She would go mad and stay in this room for the rest of her life. Unloved, unwanted. Forgotten. Poor Kitty. She went mad, did you know? They say she stole that necklace!

She beat her forehead with the heel of her hand, as if to drive out the pain and anger. Catching sight of herself in the glass as she paced around the room, she asked her reflection, 'What am I going to do?' The distraught and crazed face in the mirror crumpled in front of her. 'Do not cry!' she instructed it. But the tears came, welling up into her eyes and down her cheeks. She felt the back of her throat constricting and she was convulsed by loud, wracking sobs. Kitty climbed onto the bed, covered her head with a pillow and cried and cried until she had no energy left.

She woke to the sound of Mrs Hill knocking on the door, asking whether she would be joining Mr Bennet for dinner. Having scant choice, Kitty got up, changed her dress, washed her face and tried, with little success and no great effort, to reduce the puffiness of her eyes with cold water. She gave up. What did her appearance matter here in Longbourn? If her father noticed she was upset, he would attribute it to concern about her mother.

Mr Bennet looked up as she entered the dining room, and asked her if she was rested? 'You still look tired. Unsurprising, after your journey,' he said.

'Mama does not leave her room?' asked Kitty.

'She has good days and bad days,' replied her father. 'This is not a good day. Although, of course it is good insofar as you are here,' he added, as an afterthought.

'She usually has dinner sent up?'

Mr Bennet nodded. 'It was good of you to come home, Kitty,' he repeated. 'Your mother will be pleased of the company.'

Kitty felt tears of self-pity threatening and managed to control them. She took a sip of wine.

'How is Jane? I must visit her soon.'

'She is looking well, quite well indeed,' said her father, brightening at the recollection. 'She will be pleased to see you as well.'

The rest of the meal passed in near silence. Mr Bennet had never been a great conversationalist, his wife took care of that aspect of their relationship. In her absence, he had taken to bringing a book to the dining table. One lay beside him now and, without thinking, he put on his glasses and opened it. Then he remembered Kitty.

'It's all right,' said Kitty, and he resumed reading. She finished her meal and listened to the sound of the clock ticking.

CHAPTER 56

It took less than a day for Mrs Bennet to start devolving the running of Longbourn to her daughter and soon Mrs Hill looked to and took her instructions from Miss Bennet. Over the course of the following few weeks a routine established itself, wherein Kitty tried to keep herself occupied as far as possible – which was not difficult, given the responsibilities and requirements of managing the household – while still being the dutiful daughter. It was not exciting but it was necessary and useful in keeping her from too much despondent reflection.

Every morning before breakfast she devoted at least an hour to practising at the pianoforte. After breakfast she went to her mother and, if Mrs Bennet's mood favoured it, she would read to her. This was Kitty's preference, although often the invalid preferred to talk, which invariably tried her daughter's patience and, ultimately, improved her forbearance. Aunt Phillips came to visit her sister regularly, three times a week, which gave Kitty respite for such delights as walking into Meryton or just going into the library to read – she no longer had any qualms about her father's reaction in that regard and, to his credit, he had not so much as raised an eyebrow.

Of course she wanted to see and talk to Jane, in whom she expected to find a sympathetic ear and perhaps a chance to explain some of the events at Pemberley, but she was thwarted in even that reasonable pleasure. Shortly after she arrived at Longbourn, Kitty had contracted a slight cough and cold, which had prevented her from visiting Netherfield. Then, just as that ailment had passed, Jane's physician had prescribed bed rest for his patient and also advised against visitors for the rest of her confinement. Jane was happy to see Kitty but the latter, mindful of the physician's instruction, wanted only to do what was best for her sister and the baby. So they continued to correspond even though Jane was but three miles away.

She had sought the company of Maria Lucas, but that was also denied her. She had lately gone to Kent, to be with her sister Charlotte and her new baby.

If Kitty and her father were dining *à deux*, as was usually the case, each would have a book as a companion, an arrangement that suited both. On the rare occasions Mrs Bennet and her nerves felt well enough to bring themselves downstairs, her husband and daughter had to mask their reluctance in favouring conversation over their books.

Her mother rarely required attention in the evenings; whether the result of her illness or the laudanum, she was often tired and drowsy. This allowed Kitty the genteel pursuits of playing music, reading and writing letters and, if she was really at a loss, of picking up some netting.

Once in a while, something untoward happened to vary the routine. The physician might call, or Lady Lucas might visit. Mr Bingley occasionally came by, usually at Jane's request, to enquire after everyone and apologise for his wife's inability to come to Longbourn herself. Such was the extent of the unexpected at Longbourn during those days.

Mrs Bennet's condition remained unchanged and Kitty reported as much when she wrote to Elizabeth. Those letters received polite but perfunctory replies and Kitty received more information as to what was happening at Pemberley through Elizabeth's letters to Jane, with whom she shared more interesting news.

Kitty had no intentions whatsoever of writing to Lydia, though she was once coerced into scribing a letter for her mother. Sometimes, Mrs Bennet handed over Lydia's letters for her perusal but Kitty did not deign to read them. It was galling to have to write on her mother's behalf, knowing that Lydia would recognise her handwriting and take pleasure in picturing her, the spinster sister, at Longbourn.

From Georgiana she heard nothing. Miss Fanshawe, however, had written a long letter, full of plans for her forthcoming wedding and the future and news of what was happening at Danson Park, including best wishes and kind enquiries from her mother, brothers and uncle. Kitty did not begrudge Felicia her happiness but the letter made her downcast all the same. The irony of receiving best wishes from Freddie Fanshawe, even at second-hand and imagined rather than genuine, was not lost on her. Nonetheless, she replied immediately, clinging on to the memory of a summer that seemed very long ago, and hoping to salvage at least one friendship from the debacle.

She remained sad but adapted to life at Longbourn, and there was, she discovered, some worth in being useful and helping care for her mother. She felt appreciated, by her father at least.

***

It was now October and the only thing that had changed at Longbourn was the season. The days were shorter and the trees were skeletal, devoid of leaves and colour. Kitty had been reading to her mother, who had now fallen asleep. She looked at her, such a shadow of the bustling and noisy woman she had been, and wondered what she could do to make her feel better.

Yesterday, Mrs Bennet had been quite voluble. She wanted to talk, she said, which essentially meant she wanted her views heard and validated by whoever was listening. Her subject range was narrow: Jane and the belief her child would be a son; this sometimes led to the observation that it didn't matter if Jane and Mr Bingley didn't have a son, because there was no spectre of a Mr Collins waiting to take everything from them; then there was the heady question of when Elizabeth and Mr Darcy would produce an heir, and really Elizabeth should not wait too long to do something about that; this led her to wonder when her dear Lydia and Wickham would give her a grandchild; then she might wonder vaguely about Mary, but never for long; and finally, inevitably, the conversation would turn to Kitty and when she was going to find a husband.

'It is hard to believe that you found no one suitable when you were in London, Kitty,' she had reiterated, irritated at her daughter's ineptitude in so simple a task. 'Jane wrote that you went to all the best places. You cannot be too choosy, you know.'

Kitty had agreed this was so.

'Was there no one who was interested in you? You are not a beauty, but you are handsome enough in your way. In fact, I think you are looking better these days.'

Kitty had thanked her for the compliment and Mrs Bennet had eyed her sharply. 'I hope you are not being smart with me, Miss.'

She had said she was not. The conversation rarely varied. Kitty could almost recite it, and sometimes she was almost amused by it.

Her mother turned in her bed, sighing loudly, but did not open her eyes. Kitty picked up the novel that lay open on her lap. It was not particularly good, certainly not good enough to keep her mother awake, and Kitty thought she could do better herself. A small voice in her head said, 'Well, why don't you?' It quite startled her. An idyllic afternoon on the lawn at Pemberley came into her mind. Georgiana had been painting and she and Elizabeth sitting on a great plaid blanket, reading. She remembered that one of the books had been authored by 'A Lady'. Was it a comedy of manners or a romance? Kitty wasn't sure, but the author had chosen to remain anonymous. Could she write a book? She wasn't sure about that either. 'That would surprise them all,' said the voice again. So it would, thought Kitty, the idea taking tenuous hold.

What could she write about? She thought about it for a long time, about the people she knew and their characters: the proud ones, the haughty ones, the downright ridiculous ones, the weak ones, the rich and the poor and the evil, grasping ones; about what she had seen and done in London and at Pemberley; about the places she had read about in other novels, places she had never visited but which she could imagine.

There was paper and writing instruments on the table. Kitty got up quietly so as not to disturb Mrs Bennet and went over to it. Yes, she could do this! Well, she could certainly try. She had already written a short story. She pulled out the chair gently to avoid making any noise, and sat down at the table. She could be 'A Lady', too! Or 'Miss Catherine Bennet, author'. She quite liked the sound of that. 'You haven't written anything yet!' said the voice. Kitty brought the little stack of paper towards her and started to scribble down ideas. She would work from the title *Town and Country*; it could be about a housemaid, perhaps, who went from a grand estate to work in London. She wanted to be something more than a housemaid. What could she be, thought Kitty. Perhaps a milliner? She could open her own shop, eventually. How would she find the money? Perhaps she had an admirer? An old, doting admirer with a booming voice. Kitty laughed. What a ridiculous idea!

'What are you doing?' Mrs Bennet had awoken.

'Writing a letter, Mama,' said Kitty, extemporising.

'To whom?'

'Elizabeth,' said Kitty. She put down her pen, and looked around at her mother.

'Well, remind her she promised to tell me how the new chairs suited, and tell her I look forward to receiving a letter.'

'I will, Mama.' Satisfied with her advice and this answer, Mrs Bennet drifted back to sleep. Kitty smiled and at the same time realised she was smiling. It was the first time she had felt anything approaching happiness for weeks. She picked up her pen again and started plotting.

It was one of Aunt Phillips' days and Kitty, hearing her arrive, bundled up her papers and went downstairs to greet her aunt. Then, instead of going out, she went upstairs to her room and continued writing.

CHAPTER 57

Mr Bingley had paid a brief visit that morning, bringing with him a letter for Kitty from Jane.

'How is she?' asked Kitty. 'If you think she is well enough, I wondered if I might call in to Netherfield tomorrow.'

'She is better than she has been for weeks, so it would seem the physician's advice was good. One would hope so, he came highly recommended. Jane is not so much tired now than tired of seeing no one. I think you will find that letter answers your question. She would be most pleased to see you.'

'Oh, that is excellent news, Charles! Mama will be glad to hear it as well. I think it will not be long now?'

Mr Bingley believed not and leaving behind that happy thought continued on his way. Kitty was delighted at the thought of seeing Jane again. She had visited Netherfield only twice since coming back to Longbourn, mindful of Jane's condition. Her confinement had not been an easy one and when Kitty had last seen her sister she had been surprised at how pinched and drawn she had become. She had been fearful, too, afraid of losing the precious life she was carrying, but that danger now seemed past. In consequence of Jane's fragile constitution, Kitty had quelled the urge to tell her sister of the injustices she had suffered at Pemberley. She still felt them keenly but had quickly realised that such revelations would cause Jane, who hated discord of any kind, especially between those she loved, much anxiety and distress. Now was not the time to unburden herself.

'Was that our dear Mr Bingley?' called her mother, as Kitty walked upstairs. She had her sewing bag with her, her chapters and notebook safely concealed within.

'Yes,' said Kitty, going in to Mrs Bennet's room. 'Jane is well. All is well; there is no other news yet. Shall I read to you?'

Her mother nodded, and Kitty picked up the book. Thus the morning passed and Kitty had little time to think about her own stories. Aunt Phillips arrived and Kitty went downstairs to greet her and let her know she would be going out.

'You are off to see your sister? That baby is taking its time to arrive.'

Kitty agreed and rang for the carriage to be brought around. She was plotting various scenarios and characters all the way to Netherfield but her imagination gave way to reality the moment she arrived. The housekeeper came running up to tell her the accoucheur and the monthly nurse had been with Mrs Bingley since the previous evening, and the baby was expected very soon.

'Good heaven!' exclaimed Kitty. The house seemed so quiet. 'Is everything well?'

'I believe so, madam. I hope so.'

'Who else is with her,' asked Kitty, handing over her bonnet and spencer.

'Just Mr Bingley, madam.'

'Shall I go to her? Please tell Mr Bingley I am here.'

The housekeeper started up the stairs, Kitty hurrying after her. They had just reached the second landing, when the thin wail of a newborn pierced the air. Kitty and the housekeeper both stopped, looked at each other. It was hard to say who was most delighted. At that moment, Mr Bingley appeared, looking dazed and supported by a small, dapper man who Kitty supposed must be the accoucheur.

'Charles!' cried Kitty. 'How is she? Is everything all right? Is Jane well?'

'Oh yes!' returned he. 'Yes! I have been sent outside by the nurse but, yes, all is well! I am so relieved. I had no idea…'

Kitty hugged him in response and Mr Bingley sat down on a nearby chair.

'It is all astonishing! I am quite amazed. Jane is so… so brave.'

'You are quite brave yourself,' returned Kitty. 'Not every man would be at his wife's confinement! But you have not told me whether you have a son or a daughter?'

Before he could answer, the nurse had opened the door and indicated that Mr Bingley could return. He jumped up, telling Kitty to come with him. She needed no further encouragement.

'Jane,' she cried. 'You should have sent word! I would have come sooner.' And then she stopped, taking in the sight of her sister propped up by pillows and cradling her tiny baby.

'Oh, Kitty,' said Jane, her eyes brimming. 'Look, we have a daughter!'

The little pink bundle in her arms took no notice whatsoever as her mother, father and aunt peered at her and marvelled at her tiny fingers and toes, her snub of a nose, her downy little head. Jane handed her to Mr Bingley, who paraded his daughter around the room, totally enraptured with both her and his wife. 'Her name is Elizabeth Charlotte,' he told Kitty. 'We had already decided. She is beautiful.'

'She is,' agreed Kitty, smiling at Jane, who was already half asleep.

Mr Bingley handed little Elizabeth back to the nurse and sank into a chair. He looked almost as drained as his wife. 'I confess I did not know it would be like this.' He made a vague gesture towards the various linens, towels and other paraphernalia that one of the maids was in the process of clearing away. 'I am not sure what I am supposed to do next.'

'Be the proud father!' laughed Kitty. 'Perhaps I can come back tomorrow and see what help I can be to Jane? I am sure Aunt Phillips will be happy to sit with Mama when she knows your news.'

'I would like that very much,' said Jane, her voice quieter than usual. They looked over to see her trying to sit up in the bed.

'I am sure you have been told to rest!' said Kitty, sternly, and Jane smiled and lay down again, giving up that struggle. 'I will go now so that you can sleep. I will come back tomorrow.'

'You have too much to do already,' argued Jane, feebly. 'Looking after Mama, I mean. I know how she can be. I have been no help. You have done it all. I have not had to worry about her at all.' She looked as though she might cry.

'Do not worry so, Jane,' said Kitty, kissing her goodbye. 'I will come back tomorrow. You will be unable to keep me away. Rest now, please.' She went over to have another peek at the sleeping baby and then Charles escorted her downstairs.

'She does appreciate your looking after Mrs Bennet so well,' said he. 'She often comments on it.'

Kitty, though pleased, was a little surprised at this information. How like Jane to be thinking of someone else, even after she had just given birth! She said goodbye to Mr Bingley, and looked forward to seeing him again on the morrow. The carriage started off towards Longbourn.

What more can be said on such a happy occasion, except to formally declare that the parents were happy and proud, the baby lusty and strong, the aunt delighted to be an aunt, the mother as well as could be expected.

CHAPTER 58

Happily for everyone, and especially the lady herself, news of her grandchild was enough to bring Mrs Bennet out of her stupor. When she received the glad tidings on Kitty's return to Longbourn, she called for her maid and insisted on leaving her bed immediately, at least some of her pains forgotten. She was not so strong as she would have liked, however, and it was some time before she was to be found downstairs and situated in her favourite armchair.

Mr Bennet was likewise delighted, both at the arrival of Elizabeth Charlotte and to find his wife in the parlour. A toast was in order, he declared, and a fine claret produced.

'Another Elizabeth,' said Kitty, remembering Charlotte Collins's baby daughter, Elizabeth Anne. She immediately realised her mistake in mentioning the name Collins in her mother's presence and expected a tirade, but Mrs Bennet was too pleased with Jane and Mr Bingley to notice.

'I shall go to Netherfield tomorrow,' she declared, and neither Kitty nor Mr Bennet attempted to caution her otherwise, though both thought it unlikely to happen given her health.

'Well, Kitty,' said her father, an hour or so later, after Mrs Bennet, fatigued by her excess of joy, had once more retired to her room. 'You are an aunt and I am a grandfather. Jane has worked wonders, not least for your mother.'

***

To everyone's surprise, Mrs Bennet did rally after this event. She still tired easily and kept to her bed most days, but she was more alert and more her old self. The physician, when applied to for his opinion, had no real wisdom or insight to offer.

Kitty's morning routine was quite severely disrupted by this change. Her nascent idea of writing suffered particularly as Mrs Bennet was now far more likely to want Kitty to read or listen to her. The constant haranguing to find herself a husband or become an old maid was now so predictable that it hardly had an effect; what Kitty found much more vexing was Mrs Bennet's praise of her dear Lydia and her admiration of the inestimable Mrs Darcy. One day, having exhausted herself in these areas, she began to talk of the next round of balls at the Meryton Assembly Rooms. Did Kitty have a subscription, with whom would she go? Was Maria Lucas back from Kent? What about Marianne Gregory?

Kitty let this topic air; she was not interested in dancing at the moment, it brought back too many painful memories, none of which she was about to share with her mother. She turned the conversation back to Elizabeth Charlotte.

'I have yet to see the babe,' said her mother, looking suddenly sad and very old. Kitty felt sorry for her. It would be another two weeks before Jane would leave Netherfield.

'When I visit next, if the weather is fine and not too cold, I will ask Jane if perhaps the nurse and I might bring little Elizabeth here to see you. Would you like me to do that?'

Mrs Bennet thought this was the most marvellous idea Kitty had ever had. She wondered at her ingenuity. She could not have made a better suggestion herself.

'Very well then,' said Kitty. 'Remember, I cannot promise, I can only ask. You should rest now.'

Mrs Bennet accepted this proposal and Kitty was soon rewarded by her mother's gentle snores. She went to the table and began to write. She now had more ideas in her head than she had put on paper about her poor maid about to turn milliner and the frightful bores and pompous gentlemen who surrounded her.

Kitty had become quite single-minded about her 'little novel' and worked on it in her room late at night and sometimes before breakfast. It diverted her greatly to lose herself in their ambitions and absurdities.

A couple of days later, Little Elizabeth – as she came to be known – was brought to Longbourn, accompanied by Kitty, the nurse and the proud father, and was received with rapture by Mrs Bennet and a quieter but no less heartfelt joy by Mr Bennet. Letters of congratulation had been received, a christening arranged and all the usual accompaniments that follow a wanted child's entry into the world.

Kitty continued her writing; it was her escape from the dreary monotony of Longbourn and, unlike real life, her characters could be made to do what she wanted them to in this fictional world. She was in charge of their destiny.

'You write a prodigious number of letters these days,' remarked her mother one morning, rousing herself and sitting back onto her pillows. 'To whom are you writing now?'

'Miss Fanshawe,' said Kitty, covering her papers and turning to face Mrs Bennet.

'If you say so,' said her mother, shrewdly. 'I am beginning to suspect you are writing to someone else. A gentleman, perhaps. An amour!'

'Why would you think such a thing?' asked Kitty, genuinely astonished.

'You have not been such an excellent correspondent in the past,' grumbled Mrs Bennet. 'I did not receive so many letters from you when you were in London and at Pemberley.'

'I am sorry, Mama.'

'What sort of a girl is Miss Fanshawe? What do you write to her?'

Kitty improvised and gave an account of Felicia Fanshawe, unwisely letting it be known that she had two brothers. Mrs Bennet seized on this information, wanting to know what sort of gentlemen they were, what were their incomes, where did they live? Bored with the truth, Kitty made some of it up: she made Freddie Fanshawe short and stout, with a droopy eye; she allowed William to have a distinguished military career. Her mother seemed satisfied.

Mrs Bennet was not entirely persuaded, however. As the days dragged by, she became increasingly convinced that Kitty was harbouring a secret, that she had a clandestine admirer. Once the idea was fixed in her head, nothing could shake it. One day she insisted on seeing Kitty's letter and when this demand was refused, she called for Mr Bennet to intervene.

'She is writing to a suitor, I am sure of it,' she shrilled. 'Ask her to show you her letter.'

'My dear Mrs Bennet. Kitty may write to whomsoever she chooses. You would surely not censor her correspondence.'

'Show your father your letter,' insisted Mrs Bennet. 'If you have nothing to hide, you will do as I ask.'

'I have nothing to hide,' said Kitty, 'but my correspondence is private.'

'You see?' cried Mrs Bennet. 'She is keeping something from me!'

'Kitty,' said her father. 'Do you have any objection to showing your mother your letter?'

'Yes,' said she. 'I do.'

If her father was surprised, he did not show it. 'Well then, Mrs Bennet. There is nothing more to be said.' He left the room. After that, Kitty was more circumspect. She wrote in her room, or in the parlour when she was sure her father was in the library, but she kept writing. The world of her imagination was far more exciting than the one in which she was living.

CHAPTER 59

Kitty and Mr Bennet were in the parlour together, having had dinner, and were comfortably arranged in chairs either side of the fireplace. The winter weather had set in, and the frosts were turning the fields white in the mornings.

A letter from Lydia to her mother lay on the table opened. It had arrived after Mrs Bennet had retired and Kitty eyed it with disdain, anticipating her mother's request to dictate a reply.

She turned back to her book, one of Samuel Richardson's novels. She had already read *Pamela: Or, Virtue Rewarded* (the title had ironic appeal) and was now working her way through the many volumes of his *History of Sir Charles Grandison*, which on the whole she found rather satisfying. She sensed her father's gaze and looked up.

'You do not hear from your sister, Lydia,' he observed mildly.

'No,' said Kitty, with some feeling. She had not meant to deliver the word with such venom.

Mr Bennet noticed of course. 'I have not heard from Lydia since she left Pemberley,' continued Kitty, making sure her tone was bland and reasonable. 'It was not so very long ago.' She did not want to discuss Lydia, the chief architect of her woes, but the mention of her presence in Derbyshire was greeted with incredulity by her father.

'Lydia was received at Pemberley?' said he. 'I am astonished.'

Kitty realised her mistake; he had not known. 'Everyone was astonished. She arrived in time for the summer ball. She was not invited.'

'My word,' said Mr Bennet, as he assessed the implications of Lydia's intrusion into the Darcy estate.

'Mr Wickham? Where was he?'

'Elsewhere. In Birmingham or somewhere, with his fellow officers,' said Kitty. 'Lydia thought it would be enormous fun to arrive at Pemberley, unheralded.'

'My word,' said her father again. 'And was it? Enormous fun?'

'It most certainly was not,' said Kitty, hoping to close the subject. Mr Bennet regarded his daughter.

'There has been a falling out, between you and Lydia?' he enquired. Kitty looked at him; she knew his sardonic humour only too well and she was not going to be made the butt of his amusement over something he might denounce as a silly, sisterly spat. Equally, she could not bring herself to air Elizabeth's condemnation of her as a thief. She said nothing more, but her steely composure only prompted more questions.

'And did Mrs Wickham comport herself well?'

The answering look of contempt and rage spoke volumes. Mr Bennet closed his book, 'Is there some fresh disgrace attributable to our dear Lydia?'

'It has been contained.'

'I should like to hear of it, nonetheless,' persisted Mr Bennet. Whether his desire for knowledge was prompted by concern for Elizabeth, a need to know whether yet more money had been expended on behalf of his youngest daughter, or even if it was a rarely exerted paternal solicitude cannot be known, but ask he did.

'It is a long story,' said Kitty, in one last attempt to fend off enquiry.

Mr Bennet gestured around him and sat back in his chair. 'I find I have no engagements this evening,' he said.

Kitty found it hard to begin. It would be gratifying to have her side of the story heard, but would her father hear it? He was wont to see little difference between her character and Lydia's and she dreaded this account being dismissed as yet another example of their joint stupidity.

'Very well then,' said she at last. 'I must begin with telling you about Miss Darcy.' She recounted her delight and surprise at her friendship with Georgiana and how it had culminated in her invitation to Pemberley, realising for the first time as she spoke that it was Georgiana and not Elizabeth who had made that possible. In speaking of her joy at being in London and in Derbyshire, her face became relaxed and the happy and confident Miss Bennet, who had been known to the likes of the Fanshawes, Sir Edward and Colonel Fitzwilliam, was once again in evidence.

Mr Bennet could not help but observe the change.

Gradually, the story went to Freddie Fanshawe and Georgiana's increasing affection for him and of Kitty's concern that he was not all he should be. She stopped at this point and looked at her father, suspecting he would tire of any tale that smacked of romance. He did not interrupt, however; he was waiting to hear what part Lydia would play. This Kitty disclosed. She spoke of Elizabeth's anxieties and how they had done all they could to keep Lydia's behaviour in check and of Lydia's revelation to her that Mr Fanshawe was a gamester. She kept it as brief as she could, but some detail had to be given to Lydia's inopportune attempts to coerce him into giving her money.

Mr Bennet looked grave, but stayed mute. So, Kitty continued her tale, calmly recounting the awful scene with the necklace and how she had tried to retrieve it; and how Darcy had witnessed what he saw as a vulgar brawl between herself and Lydia. How ashamed she had been and how unable to salvage her dignity. How Mr Fanshawe had been absent when Darcy had arrived and no blame whatsoever had been apportioned to him. How, as a result of all of this, her dear friend Georgiana thought she had been acting with Lydia and against her. How that friendship was now lost to her. How her attempts to find out more about Mr Fanshawe or share her fears with Colonel Fitzwilliam had come to nothing and that she feared no one would believe her in any case. She omitted all Elizabeth's accusations of theft. Her face had sunk back into sadness by the time she had finished her story.

There was a small silence, broken only by the clock chiming the quarter hour and the crackle of the fire, as Mr Bennet absorbed all this information.

'I see,' he said, finally. 'And Elizabeth knows?'

'Elizabeth knows what Mr Darcy has told her,' said Kitty, defensively. 'There was little opportunity for me to explain myself.' It was too painful to recount her audience with Elizabeth, but her expression gave away her distress.

'I see,' said Mr Bennet again.

'Well my dear,' he said, having sat in silent contemplation for a few minutes. 'It seems you acted with integrity and did yourself a grave disservice into the bargain. I fear there is nothing to be done about Lydia; she is as incorrigible as only the empty-headed can be.'

He tutted and sighed, then rose out of his chair. On his way out of the room, he laid a reassuring hand on Kitty's shoulder. She felt the sensation of that pressure for some time.

Chapter 60

In November, Jane and Bingley made it known that they intended to move to Nottinghamshire the following month. Their plans to announce this earlier had been delayed by Mrs Bennet's illness and Jane's fear of her mother's distress. As expected, Mrs Bennet took it badly. When she discovered that Kitty not only knew about Dapplewick Hall but had actually visited it, her daughter became complicit in the perceived plot against her mother. Kitty, who had become almost inured to calumnies and misrepresentation, was not inclined to argue. She had had more time to adjust to Jane's remove and had accepted it; she was, moreover, hopeful that she would be invited to stay.

Mrs Bennet could not let the matter lie.

'But my dears, you are so well settled here. Netherfield is such a fine estate. What need have to you to go so far away?'

'Netherfield is not ours, Mama,' said Jane, 'and Dapplewick is very fine, is it not, Charles?' She appealed to Bingley, who nodded in vigorous but grave assent. 'You and Father will come to stay with us, I hope, and see for yourselves.'

'I am very happy to see you in Netherfield, Jane,' replied her mother, obdurate. 'I do not find it easy to travel.'

'I should like it if you and Father and Kitty would come to us at Christmas,' persuaded Jane. 'We will invite Elizabeth and Darcy, of course. Would you not like that?'

Mrs Bennet would not countenance it. She was not well enough to travel. In the summer, then? Really, she could not think that far ahead. Her nerves were mentioned, and Jane retreated. Privately, she and Kitty agreed that their mother's health was improving: once her nerves became the principal ailment, all would be restored to normal.

Jane was not insensible to Kitty's loneliness. She was still unaware of the circumstances surrounding her departure from Pemberley; like everyone else, she attributed it to filial duty. She was, however, at pains to let Kitty know that she would be welcome at Dapplewick Hall, just as she would be at Brook Street when they were in town. She was sure they would all be together again soon.

Kitty held on to this hope, even more so as Mrs Bennet became increasingly demanding. Her only consolation was that her mother was regaining her vitality. Kitty's unmarried state continued to vex her. One morning, apropos of nothing, she said: 'It is my duty to see you wed.' Although this had been her mother's *raison d'être* for as long as Kitty could remember, when it was uttered thus Kitty found it quite touching. Mrs Bennet could be annoying and embarrassing – in the way of many mothers, as viewed by their daughters – but however misguided Mrs Bennet was, however shrill and nagging, Kitty realised that she had her best interests at heart. This, while not particularly soothing, added to her understanding.

***

It was a cold day but bright and dry, and when Aunt Phillips arrived Kitty decided she would walk into Meryton. She would look in at the draper's, perhaps find something pretty for her little niece. It was as good a reason as any and she set off at a brisk pace, enjoying the winter sunshine and the crisp air. The exercise restored her and she resolved to walk more often.

It was about three o'clock when she returned to the house, where she found Mrs Hill in tears. She could hear Aunt Phillips crying noisily in the parlour. Running in, she saw Mr Bennet by the fireplace, a stunned look on his face.

'Papa? What is wrong? What has happened?' She was truly alarmed now. 'Is it the baby?' Her heart jumped. Please, she thought, don't let anything have happened to Little Elizabeth.

'Your poor dear mother!' cried Aunt Phillips, holding out her arms to Kitty. 'Gone, dear. Gone!'

CHAPTER 61

The suddenness of Mrs Bennet's death shocked everyone, including her physician. He opined, with medical sagacity, that her heart had failed. Expresses were sent to Derbyshire and Newcastle, and to London to inform Mr and Mrs Gardiner of the sad news. At Longbourn, Mr Bennet was sunk in grief. Many a widower finds himself unexpectedly brought down by the death of his spouse, sometimes through genuine feelings of loss and sometimes by guilt for his previous treatment of the departed, but the acuity of Mr Bennet's grief was a surprise to all. It made him incapable of any decisions. Kitty organised the undertaker, made arrangements for the black drapes in the room in which Mrs Bennet's coffin lay, discussed the date of the burial and the sermon, and found suitable mourning clothes for her father, herself and the servants.

Aunt Phillips tried to help but, bereft of a sister and a life-long friend, she was rendered ineffectual. She kept vigil by Mrs Bennet's coffin, a tragic figure sitting stiff-backed in her chair, fingering the black wool of her shawls and lost in thought. Jane and Kitty consoled each other and their father as best they could; Mr Bingley offered his services. Nonetheless, the chief burden fell on Kitty's young shoulders. Her duties went from caring for her ailing mother to overseeing her final journey and looking after her father.

There is nothing like a death to bring a family together and Elizabeth had sent word that she and Mr Darcy would arrive at Longbourn within days. Mr and Mrs Gardiner were also expected. Lydia wrote with some feeling of her loss, but the long journey from Newcastle would prevent her, she said, from paying her respects in person. She cited other reasons, and validated them all to herself (if not to others), but the result was she could not, would not, be at Longbourn to say goodbye to her mother. From Mary there could be no response; the news of Mrs Bennet's death would take weeks to reach her.

Letters of condolence arrived, including one from Miss Georgiana Darcy. Kitty opened it with some trepidation, wondering whether it would go beyond the conventional forms of address in such situations. She need not have worried. Georgiana's regret at her mother's death was expressed exactly as custom and politesse dictated, neither a word more nor less than was to be expected. Kitty placed it with all the others. Meanwhile, the north-facing room in which Mrs Bennet's coffin lay grew chillier and chillier; in this, the winter weather was kind.

Kitty was making tokens of remembrance in the parlour when she heard Elizabeth and Darcy arrive. She did not get up to greet them, knowing that her father and Jane would be at the door. She chose instead to concentrate on the task at hand, fashioning sprigs of rosemary and tying them with black silk ribbons.

The door opened and the two sisters found themselves face to face. Kitty kept hers expressionless but the image of Elizabeth, severe in black, framed in the doorway etched itself into her mind. No one spoke. Then Jane appeared behind Elizabeth, causing her to move into the room. She smiled a sad smile and moved towards Kitty for an embrace. Without saying anything, she sat down beside her, picking up ribbon and scissors and wordlessly offering her help. Mr Darcy, Kitty supposed, was with her father and Mr Bingley.

Kitty found she had nothing to say to her sister. She did not resile from anything she had said in the sitting room at Pemberley; Elizabeth could, and would, think what she liked. The disbelief and shock she had felt in August had been supplanted by indignation and anger. With their mother gone, Kitty's concerns were for her father. Elizabeth had rejected her, accepted Lydia's lies, thrown her out of Pemberley, and she felt no need to make pretty conversation; she was saved from the pretence of trying by the arrival of Aunt and Uncle Gardiner, always a welcome presence at Longbourn, even and especially on an occasion such as this.

The melancholy congregation went about the formalities. Neighbours and friends called to make their condolences and farewell the deceased. Kitty oversaw it all, sparing her father as much trouble as she could and running Longbourn, which she had been doing in all but name while her mother lived. At one point, Elizabeth thought to offer assistance by giving some instruction regarding the dinner service but Mrs Hill looked askance at Kitty, who intervened with directions of her own. Mr Bennet had become used to dinner at a certain hour and that is what suited him; Kitty would not have it changed. Besides, she thought grimly, since they all think my place is here at Longbourn, I will at least have things done my way.

In a few days, everything was completed. The mourners had come to the house, the tokens of remembrance handed out, the coffin had processed to St Bede's, the sermon was read, the remains interred. Mr Bennet and the other gentlemen were soon back at Longbourn.

Aunt Gardiner took Kitty aside to ask if she could be of use to her. Kitty shook her head. 'We are as well as we can be,' said she. 'I am worried for my father, but I hope time will heal.'

'You must look to yourself as well, dear,' said her aunt. 'I see how well you are coping but do not make yourself ill. We shall invite you and Mr Bennet to come to stay with us in London shortly. I shall write and arrange it.'

Kitty nodded. She appreciated the invitation, but the prospect of staying in London, something that had once so enthralled her, seemed too far away to contemplate.

'Jane and Bingley will soon be gone?' said Mrs Gardiner, nodding to where Jane sat, cradling Little Elizabeth.

'Yes,' said Kitty. 'Next week. I will miss them most dreadfully.'

'Where is Elizabeth?' asked her aunt, looking around.

'In the library with my father,' she replied. The pair had been closeted for some time. Even in his grief, her father had been pleased to see Elizabeth, and Kitty knew that her sister had come to Longbourn as much to condole with him as to mourn their mother. She didn't blame her for that; she just knew it was so.

Aunt Gardiner embraced her and promised to see her soon. She and Mr Gardiner were the first to take their leave. The Darcys followed soon afterwards, en route to their London address rather than journeying directly back to Derbyshire. Kitty had heard them planning to travel north in convoy with the Bingleys in the next few days.

CHAPTER 62

Longbourn was a silent and empty place in the weeks following Mrs Bennet's death. Mr Bennet retreated into himself; Aunt Phillips visited regularly as before, deriving some solace from the continuity of her visits, but the atmosphere was melancholy and the clocks ticked on, louder than they had ever been when Mrs Bennet's nerves were there to be riled. Kitty was glad of her aunt's company. One afternoon they undertook the sad task of sorting through Mrs Bennet's clothes and treasures. Mrs Phillips would seize upon an item of clothing or some little ornament and remember when or how her sister had first worn or acquired it. The memories evoked were not all unhappy, occasionally bringing forth laughter as each remembered the Mrs Bennet they knew best.

Kitty was surprised and gladdened to find, hidden away in boxes in her mother's dressing room, little keepsakes of all her daughters. She found a forlorn doll, missing one arm, that had once been Jane's constant companion, and a notebook, its cover illustrated with flowers, which declared itself, in a large, childish hand, to be the property of 'Miss Elizabeth Bennet' and containing thoughts evidently important to its seven-year-old owner. For Mary, she had kept a wooden soldier and drum, of which Kitty had no recollection; for Lydia, a little cup that she must once have favoured; and then she found a child's silver-backed hairbrush that had been hers. Kitty exclaimed when she saw it, having forgotten its existence until that moment. Then she remembered her mother brushing her hair when she was little; she had been in bed and it was when she was ill, and she could almost feel the touch of the brush on her hair and her mother crooning that it would all be all right.

There were also some letters, very old and bound in ribbon, which Kitty realised with a small shock had been penned by her father in the early days of her parents' courtship. She would not have dreamed of reading anything so private; she bundled them up neatly and left them on her father's desk in the library. This sifting of things and memories gave Kitty a different perspective on her mother, helping her to understand parts of her that she had been unable to see when she had been alive.

Aunt Gardiner was as good as her word. Brooking no excuses, she insisted that Kitty and Mr Bennet, together with Mr and Mrs Phillips, come to London and stay with them during the Christmas season. It was a kind invitation, especially as it brought together Mrs Bennet's remaining siblings, her husband and daughter, and allowed for steady reminiscence in a household that was charged with a form of peaceful content.

For Kitty, it was also a welcome respite from the running of Longbourn, an unasked-for responsibility but one that she had managed well and without complaint. The party arrived on Christmas Eve and were welcomed with much excitement by the little Gardiners, animated by both the season and the arrival of their Meryton relations. Their exuberant spirits did much to dispel and prevent darker moods.

Mr Bennet, while in good health himself, was less inclined than usual to be sociable; even his love of books seemed to have forsaken him. At Longbourn he spent his time sitting in a chair, lost in thought. Kitty had spent much of their journey to the Gardiners talking of the British Museum in Bloomsbury as well as other places they could visit together during their stay in London and was rewarded by his cautious approbation of her schemes. 'The Cotton Libraries,' he said, brightening. 'I should like to investigate that collection further.'

'Hatchards, too,' reminded Kitty, referring to London's best bookshop. 'I am told the new premises in Piccadilly are larger than the previous establishment but I have not been there yet.' Her father nodded.

Their plans were thrown awry, however, by the weather. Two days after their arrival at the Gardiners, a thick, impenetrable fog descended on London, shrouding the city, turning day dark as night and making even short journeys well nigh impossible. The gas lamps, now lit in the daytime, provided only tiny pinpricks of light in the murky grey haze and, looking out of the windows, Kitty could hear rather than see pedestrians feeling their way through the streets, lanterns held in front of them as they tried to see what was ahead. London came to a standstill and the fog pinned down the city's inhabitants for nearly two weeks.

'It would be madness for anyone to go outside,' Mr Gardiner had declared at the onset of the fog. He had perforce to test his sanity on a couple of occasions in the ensuing fortnight, called forth on matters of business to his warehouses, but luckily for the Gardiners and their guests, their house was warm and well provisioned and the only real inconvenience lay in not being able to venture abroad. Those accustomed to playing loo and vingt-et-un improved their skills considerably during this period and there was plenty of opportunity for reading and, in Kitty's case, keeping up her writing and practice on the pianoforte. As before, when it came to her writing she was secretive in her task. She disguised her work as correspondence and her prolific letter-writing was noted but not a source of extraordinary comment.

There were actual letters, of course – both sent and received, although the postal service was severely hampered by the weather and it took much longer than usual for mail to arrive. Both Jane and Elizabeth wrote, enquiring as to their father's health and sharing their grief and, in Jane's case, providing news on Little Elizabeth. There was a letter from Felicia, apologising for her tardy reply to Kitty and hoping to see her in London very soon. She also made mention of Frederick, saying that he had suffered a bad fall from his horse and had taken some time to recover. Kitty was unmoved by this report but laughed at Felicia's way of telling it. 'He has been a terrible invalid,' she wrote, 'and we will all be glad of his being able to venture abroad once more!' She looked forward to seeing Miss Fanshawe again.

When the fog finally lifted, there was no respite. It started to snow heavily and to general astonishment did not stop for two whole days. 'Although,' as Kitty remarked, once again stationed by the window, 'it does make all the streets and buildings look very clean and pretty!'

Wrapped in her warmest cloak, Kitty, Uncle Gardiner and the two eldest children, all clad in greatcoats and scarves, braved the cold briefly and went outside to see icicles a yard and a half long formed on the roofs of the nearby buildings. The streets, normally chaotic with pedestrians and carriages, hawkers and coal merchants, were eerily quiet, what sound there was deadened by the blanket of snow. A baker appeared, weighed down by the heavy baskets on his shoulders, making his way carefully across the icy ground. He stopped when he saw them, volunteering the information that, 'The canal and ponds is all froze over. I reckon as we'll have a frost fair before the month is out.'

Mr Gardiner agreed he might be right, and wished him well as he continued his precarious journey down the street.

'What's a frost fair?' asked Kitty and her little cousins in unison.

'If the Thames freezes over, as it has only a few times in the past couple of hundred years, there will in all likelihood be a fair on the ice,' said Mr Gardiner.

Kitty found this idea quite enthralling but it was left to her cousins to vocalise their thoughts. 'May we go? May we go, Papa?' they asked. 'Please, Papa?'

'We will see,' said their father, chuckling. 'The river is not frozen yet and may not be so. The last frost fair was twenty years ago; they do not happen often. It was quite a sight, though. Enough now, we should go home before we freeze. Your mother will blame me if you take cold.'

Chapter 63

London, January 1814

The snow finally stopped but the temperatures fell even further. Everyone agreed it was the coldest winter in living memory. Mr Phillips, anxious now to return to Meryton and his work, made enquiries as to the state of the roads but was advised to wait for a day or two longer as huge drifts of snow, made even more solid by the frosts, were still a hazard.

Local journeys became possible though and Kitty and Mr Bennet took a carriage and covered the two miles from Cheapside to Bloomsbury without incident. Like so many other places in London, the British Museum was a wonder to Kitty. She duly accompanied her father to the Library Section, where they lingered for a couple of hours, he perusing old Anglo-Saxon manuscripts and she delighting in finding the museum housed a diary written by the young Tudor king, Edward VI. As was to be expected, this was undertaken in near silence: the other inhabitants of the Montagu House Reading Room – nearly all of whom were of a similar age to Mr Bennet – did not look to be the sort of gentlemen who would appreciate their concentration being broken by the smallest whisper.

By mutual consent, father and daughter eventually made their way to another part of the museum to look at the antiquities, more specifically to find the recently acquired Rosetta Stone. On their way to Bloomsbury, Mr Bennet had told Kitty what he knew of the stone's discovery in Egypt and of its potential importance as a tool to translate the ancient hieroglyphics. They both peered at the inscriptions wondering what they might mean, but had to content themselves with its mystery.

On the return journey, at Kitty's request, they took the road that passed alongside the Thames. She loved to see the river in all its busyness, its watermen, the barges and wherries weaving alongside the ships she imagined laden with goods and spices from the Indies, the constant water traffic around and under the arches of London Bridge.

A couple of days later, they bade farewell to Mr and Mrs Phillips, who were determined to brave the frosty roads and make their way back to Meryton. Their route was westerly, so Mr Bennet left with them and shared the carriage as far as Bloomsbury. He had made it plain that he intended to spend most of his mornings at the Reading Room in Montagu House. Kitty had fussed around him, exhorting him not to take cold and remember his scarf. 'Yes, child. I have it and I am confident of returning here none the worse for the experience. If I cannot retreat to my library in Longbourn, then the paltry offerings of the British Museum will have to suffice.' Kitty was pleased; this was more like the father she knew.

Although there were attractions enough in the museum – worthy and no doubt enlightening, and of which she had seen but a fraction – Kitty did not anticipate daily visits. For her, London held other charms – just being in the city interested her, and she was prepared to forgive it its terrible fog, smoke and noise in exchange for the grand buildings and the parks, and the sight of so many different people going about their different days. Besides, the days were clear now, if bitterly cold. Her aunt had some errands that would take her to Mayfair and Leicester Square and Kitty was pleased to have been asked to accompany her.

They set off, bundled up in cloaks and with a fur blanket covering their knees. 'I was minded to bring the foot-warmer,' laughed Aunt Gardiner, still stylish despite the extra layers, 'but I thought that might be thought excessive.'

'Time will tell,' answered Kitty. 'We are being very brave to go out at all, are we not?'

'We are not alone,' said her aunt, peering outside. 'The city is come back to life again. I am sure everyone is pleased to be out and about once more. I was worried for you Kitty, with all that fog. You were so susceptible to coughs when you were a child; I feared you may become ill.'

'I am stronger now,' she replied, feeling a little wave of emotion at her aunt's concern. 'The weather has done us no harm! On the contrary, your invitation to London has been such a comfort to me and to Papa. His spirits are lifting, I think.'

'I am glad of it and do not be in any hurry to leave. You will want to stay until your sister and Mr Darcy arrive, will you not? I imagine they will be down for the season, or part of it.' Kitty agreed that was likely, but how that reunion would be was a test even for her imagination. Georgiana would be with them, she supposed, and of course she would be received at Berkeley Square, but how different it would be, given all that had happened. Where once she had felt part of the Darcy household, she now anticipated being almost a stranger. She pulled herself back to the present, and once more thanked Aunt Gardiner for inviting them to stay. With or without her sisters, Kitty loved being in London.

Their first stop was at Leicester Square and a fashionable draper's called Newton's. 'I have not told your uncle we are coming here,' said Mrs Gardiner, conspiratorially. 'He would have me think he knows where all the best fabrics and trimmings are to be found, and at what cost, but I like to see for myself and, besides, the milliner's two doors down is a delight. You will see.'

Kitty, not at all averse to such an expedition, declared it was an age since she had been into a shop and both ladies soon found much to exclaim over. Purchases were inevitable and Kitty looked forward to trimming her bonnets with her new lace and ribbons. Although still wearing blacks, she could move into half-mourning soon and did not suppose anyone in her family would censure her for that. Her aunt certainly approved her purchases and they hurried off, arm in arm, to the milliner's.

'One more stop,' said she, as they returned to the carriage, and gave instruction to the driver to take them to Conduit Street, 'and then we will take some tea. You have been to Gunter's, I am sure?'

Kitty remembered the fashionable tea shop well. Not only had she and Jane been there, and partaken of delicious rose- and pineapple-flavoured sorbets on a day much warmer than this one, but it was within minutes of the Darcys' town house.

'That is an excellent plan. The only difficulty will be in deciding which of all those delicious pastries to try.'

'Well, if it all becomes too difficult, we will have to purchase some to take home. My children will be all the happier for your indecision, and I daresay your uncle and father will thank you as well.'

By the time they had visited two more milliners and looked into even more shop windows, both were quite ready to be seated at Gunter's, sipping hot tea from delicate gold-rimmed cups and savouring sugary pastries with Italian names.

They were getting ready to leave and had just stood up when Kitty's attention was drawn to the elegant attire of a woman just then coming in to the tea shop, on the arm of a tall gentleman. Her hand flew to her mouth as she recognised him as Henry Adams. Aunt Gardiner, seeing Kitty's reaction, turned to look in the same direction and so saw the pleased expression on the young man's face as he beheld her niece. He murmured something to his companion and the pair approached.

'Miss Bennet. How do you do? What an agreeable surprise. Allow me to present my mother, Mrs Adams.' Kitty saw a lady of middling stature but undeniable style, whose small, bright eyes conveyed both intelligence and curiosity and whose smile of greeting appeared genuine.

The ladies curtsied and the relevant introduction of Mrs Gardiner followed.

'I had no idea you were in London, Miss Bennet,' said Mr Adams, at the same time noting her mourning clothes. 'But

I see you have had sad news. May I offer my condolences to you and Mrs Gardiner.'

Kitty thanked him and let him know that it was for her mother she was in blacks. Her mind then refused to supply witty, clever sentences or even coherent ones, so surprised was she to see him before her. She made a bland and inconsequential comment about the weather and then remembered that her aunt would not know how she and Mr Adams came to be acquainted.

'Mr Adams and I met last March,' she explained. 'At a musical soirée at Brook Street; Mr Bingley introduced us. It was such a lovely evening. Mr Adams is a very talented musician and also a fine teacher. It is thanks to him that my performance on the pianoforte has improved.' She smiled at the reminiscence. 'His patience is exceptional.' She smiled again.

'Is that so, Henri?' observed his mother, wryly. 'I did not know you were known for your patience.'

'Miss Bennet is too kind,' returned he, shrugging off both ladies' remarks with easy charm. 'You reside with Mr and Mrs Darcy, I suppose?'

'No, the family is in Derbyshire still. My father and I are staying with my aunt and uncle in Gracechurch Street.'

'Is that so? What a strange coincidence! Only yesterday was I in that street. There is to be a concert at St Clement's at Eastcheap on Friday fortnight and our little ensemble has been rehearsing.'

'St Clement's is but five minutes away!' cried Kitty, delighted. It was where the Gardiners heard Sunday Service and where they had all attended at Christmas. How clever to think of holding a concert there! How clever to think of locating a church there! She was enchanted, and questions and answers flowed about the music, his part in the concert, for whom was it intended. The two older ladies meanwhile, both of whom were as aware as they were elegant, were independently fascinated by the animated conversation taking place in front of them. In turn, they exchanged a few pleasantries, each learning where the other lived and finding they shared a preference for a particular milliner in

Conduit Street, and it was left to Aunt Gardiner to gently suggest that she and Kitty should be thinking of returning home and allowing Mrs and Mr Adams to partake of their tea.

'Perhaps you and your family would care to come to the concert, Miss Bennet,' suggested Mr Adams, who, having at last seated his mother, saw them to the door.

Kitty looked to her aunt for approval. Mrs Gardiner did not dismiss the idea but was uncertain as to their engagements for the forthcoming week.

'Of course. Excellent,' declared Mr Adams. 'I will make sure you receive the programme in advance.' Then, in distress, 'Oh, but where shall I send it?'

Mrs Gardiner smiled and gave him the information, then she and Kitty took their leave. The afternoon air had turned even colder, presaging yet another frosty night, but the flush in Kitty's cheeks was not entirely attributable to the biting chill.

'An interesting young gentleman,' said her aunt, once they were ensconced in the carriage and on their way. 'You have not mentioned him previously.' Her eyes invited further comment from Kitty, who was looking a little bashful.

'It was not a deliberate omission, I assure you. I suppose I did not think to see him again.' She fiddled with her glove, fastening and unfastening the button.

'He was a tutor to Miss Darcy, you know?' she resumed, as if this would help her aunt's comprehension. 'He has a fine reputation as a music master.'

'I have no reason to doubt it, my dear. However, I think I detect a partiality that goes beyond music?'

Kitty coloured. 'It is true that I like him very well. More than I should perhaps, but he has not said or done aught to make me think there is a preference on his side.'

Mrs Gardiner allowed herself a small smile. 'His mother is French?'

'Yes, she is. I was a little surprised to hear her accent but that is foolish of me for Mr Adams had told me she is from Normandy and lived there until just after her marriage. He says they came to London because her parents did not approve of his father; it was a mésalliance as far as they were concerned.'

'It would not be the first time parents have disapproved of a match.'

'No, indeed,' agreed Kitty, warming to the subject. 'Her family was a noble one but Mr Adams says she does not like to speak of them much. They did not escape the Revolution.'

'Poor lady. That would be a hard cross to bear. But fortunate for her in that she was unharmed. What of Mr Adams senior?'

'He is a musician and composer of some note, I understand, although I confess I do not know any of his works. He will be the organist at the concert.'

Aunt Gardiner nodded. 'And Mr Adams? What do you know of his circumstances? He lives with his parents, I assume. He has no property of his own?'

'I think not. Mama would not have approved!' said Kitty, in what she hoped was a light voice.

Aunt Gardiner said nothing but patted Kitty's hand in reply. Unlike the late Mrs Bennet she would not take her to task about fortunes and prospects; but she had seen and heard enough to convince her of a keen mutual regard between Kitty and Mr Adams. She would discuss this young gentleman with Mr Gardiner.

Chapter 64

On their return to Gracechurch Street, Kitty and Mrs Gardiner found they had had a visitor. Colonel Thomas Fitzwilliam's card lay in the silver tray in the vestibule and, on further enquiry, they were told the gentleman had said he would call again tomorrow. 'Colonel Fitzwilliam!' Kitty exclaimed in delight, turning over the card to find the address. 'How did he know where to find me?'

'You forget we met the colonel last Christmas at Pemberley,' Aunt Gardiner reminded her, 'and your whereabouts are hardly a secret. Such a pleasant gentleman. I am sorry we missed him.'

'I wonder if Miss Fanshawe is in town,' said Kitty, and seeing her aunt's enquiring look told her of Fitzwilliam's engagement and a short history of her own friendship with the Fanshawe family. 'I like her very well,' she concluded, referring to Felicia Fanshawe. 'She is lively, witty and intelligent. I think theirs will be an excellent union.'

Aunt Gardiner could hardly disagree in the face of such enthusiasm and looked forward to meeting the lady. The housekeeper bustled up to claim her attention and Kitty went in search of her father. She found him in the drawing room by the fire. 'Here I am you see,' he greeted her, peering over his glasses, and putting down his newspaper. 'I have returned. Safe and apparently sound.'

'I am pleased to see it, sir. Aunt Gardiner and I have had an excellent day but one which you would no doubt deem frivolous in comparison to your own.'

'Ah! Am I to infer from that statement you would like me to enquire as to your day? Be aware, if you please, that my understanding of bonnets and tippets and suchlike will fall far short of your expectations.'

'Then I shall make no such demand upon you, Papa,' Kitty assured him. 'I will skip over the first part of our excursions and tell you naught of the fine brocades and Indian silks in Newton's, and the excellent displays and the new colours for the season, and the lace I have bought...'

Her father rolled his eyes.

'No, instead I will tell you about the milliner's in Conduit Street. Such an enchanting establishment. Such fine feathers. The lady who owns it has such an aristocratic bearing. You must come with me next time and—'

'Stop!' said Mr Bennet, in mock horror. 'You have made your point. I shall tell you about the fusty fellows in the museum, and then we shall be equal.'

'You are not suggesting that someone in the Reading Room actually spoke! Surely not?'

'It was an unusual and unwarranted occasion, I grant you, but it was done without detection so there was no retribution. A fellow whom I had not seen these twenty years took it upon himself to recognise me and, in tribute to his sharp memory, I allowed it – only because I knew him to be a man of some sense.' Mr Bennet looked at his daughter, daring contradiction.

'Of course. There are not many on whom you bestow such praise.'

Mr Bennet caught the nuance. 'Well, that is all,' he said. 'I suppose I may see him another time.' He picked up his newspaper.

'It is quite the day for unexpected meetings, then,' said Kitty. 'When Aunt Gardiner and I were at Gunter's, I met Mr Adams, who was my music master last year when I stayed with Jane.'

'Do I know this gentleman?'

'No, but you may meet him if you would like. He and his father will be performing at a concert in the church just around the corner in a fortnight's time.

'Just two minutes away,' Kitty added, by way of persuasion.

'I am little inclined for concerts, Kitty. I do not suppose this one would change my mind.'

'I think you will find Mr Adams to be an excellent musician. He plays the violin and the viola, as well as the pianoforte.'

'Do you have an interest in this person, child?' asked her father, his acuity taking her by surprise. 'Am I to brave the elements in order to see a young man whom you favour? If this is the case, could he not come to the house?'

'Oh, Papa! It is a concert! Perchance you would be entertained!' Kitty remonstrated, but she was in too good a humour to take offence. If her father would not go, she would persuade her aunt or uncle, or both.

She fetched some paper and was about to start writing a letter to Jane when Mr Bennet spoke again.

'I have today received a letter from your sister Elizabeth. It is dated but three days ago, so it seems the mail coaches are getting through once again. She writes to say that their journey has been delayed by the snow but they will be in London within the month. She thinks to call in on Jane and Bingley for a few days on their way to town. All of course is well in the grand estate that is Pemberley. I shall judge for myself later this year. Have you heard from Lizzy of late?'

'Lizzy?' asked Kitty. She shook head. 'No, my letter is from Jane.'

Her father made no comment.

'I forgot to tell you. Colonel Fitzwilliam called today when we were out. He says he will call again tomorrow.'

'Do give him my regards,' said Mr Bennet, unfolding his newspaper and retreating behind it. 'I regret I will be at the museum.'

CHAPTER 65

With the punctuality befitting a military man, Colonel Fitzwilliam arrived the next day at the time he had stated and was shown into the drawing room. 'Mrs Gardiner. My dear Miss Bennet,' he said warmly, clearly pleased to find both ladies at home. 'A delight to see you.'

The feeling was reciprocated and Kitty, especially, keen to hear his news.

'Miss Fanshawe arrives in London late this month, she is travelling down with her parents,' he told her in answer to her enquiry. 'She was to have been here before but our plans were set back by the snow. The roads were quite impassable. My way here today took me alongside the river. There is ice forming where the tidal flow is sluggish. Such weather we have seen, have we not?'

Aunt Gardiner agreed, and the weather having been duly noted, went on: 'Kitty tells me that you are to be congratulated on a certain happy event, Colonel Fitzwilliam.'

'Indeed,' said he, smiling. 'Miss Fanshawe and I plan to be wed in March in London. Part of the reason for my present travel is to facilitate some arrangements.'

'I am very happy for you both,' said Kitty. 'I am looking forward very much to seeing Felicia again. I have such fond memories of last summer.'

'As she is looking forward to seeing you, Miss Bennet, be assured. We all missed your presence at Pemberley, especially myself and Miss Fanshawe. Georgiana, too, you can be sure. She was quite out of sorts when you departed.'

'I was sad to go,' said Kitty truthfully, masking her surprise at the reference to Georgiana. She dearly wanted to enquire if she was still in thrall to Freddie Fanshawe but was at a loss as to how to introduce such a subject.

'How is Miss Darcy?' asked Aunt Gardiner. 'Is she out yet?'

'She is well, I thank you. There are plans afoot for a coming-out ball in London. No doubt she will tell you all about it,' he said, nodding to Kitty.

'And will she be presented?' continued Mrs Gardiner.

'She hopes not!' laughed Colonel Fitzwilliam. 'Court presentations have become rather sporadic since the King's illness and Georgiana is glad of it. She wishes such ceremonies be forgotten and, in truth, there is no real need.'

'Does Mr Darcy wish it, then?'

'I cannot speak for him but I do not think he would insist upon it.'

'No indeed.' Further inquiry was halted by the arrival of a servant bearing a message for Mrs Gardiner. 'Please excuse me,' said she, getting up. 'A minor matter. I will return shortly.'

The colonel resumed his seat. 'How long will you stay in London, Miss Bennet? Are you here for the season.'

'No, not at all!' laughed Kitty. 'We came at my aunt's kind invitation because she felt, and rightly so, that my father and I would be melancholy left to ourselves at Longbourn. My mother's sister and her husband, Mr and Mrs Phillips, were with us until yesterday. Their return to Meryton was much delayed by the weather.

'We will trespass on my aunt and uncle's hospitality for a few weeks more, I think. My father professes to hate London but he will be loath to leave until he has read everything the libraries in the British Museum have to offer! For myself, I would wish the next exhibition at the Pall Mall Picture Galleries was already open but, in truth, I am happy just to be in London.'

'Well, I am pleased that you are not leaving precipitately again. I hope you and your father and Mr and Mrs Gardiner will dine with us in Mayfair soon? My brother and his wife would be most pleased to see you.'

'Then we should be delighted, Colonel. I am sure I can speak for my father.'

A brief pause followed. Kitty realised Fitzwilliam was ignorant of the reasons for her expulsion – she could think of no better term – from Pemberley and of the rift between herself and Georgiana. She was wondering how to navigate the conversation when the colonel spoke.

'Sir Edward asked me to pass on his regards to you and your family. I saw him recently at Danson Park. That gentleman thinks most highly of you. You have made a conquest there!'

Embarrassed, Kitty smiled. 'I think highly of him also,' she returned. 'I trust he is well?'

'He is indeed,' said the colonel. 'Although he has been most concerned about his nephew Frederick. I think you know Freddie had a bad fall from his horse?'

'Felicia did mention it in one of her letters, but I did not know the injury was serious.'

'He broke a bone but the physician was confident that it would heal well in time. Unfortunately, he contracted a fever shortly afterwards and there were grave concerns for a few days.'

'He has recovered?' asked Kitty, out of politeness rather than concern. The mere mention of Frederick Fanshawe's name had disconcerted her.

'Very nearly. He is hobbling about the house now, although it has been some time since he ventured abroad. He is not a happy invalid!' Colonel Fitzwilliam laughed and then, noticing Kitty's somewhat stony face, apologised. 'Forgive me. I do not mean to be unkind, or speak out of turn.'

'I did not misunderstand you,' said Kitty stiffly, and, attempting to cover her awkwardness, asked: 'Does Georgiana still think well of Mr Fanshawe?'

'She has not confided in you?'

'There has been no correspondence between Georgiana and myself since I left Pemberley,' said Kitty, trying to sound nonchalant.

Colonel Fitzwilliam was all surprise.

'There was a misunderstanding,' she explained. 'More than one. Georgiana thinks I have wronged her. I cannot speak of that,' said Kitty, simply.

'However,' she continued, seizing the moment, 'there is something I feel it my duty to tell you because it concerns Georgiana. Unfortunately, it also concerns Mr Fanshawe and, given your alliance with that family, I fear I will cause offence. Mrs Wickham is also implicated.' She looked to the door, expecting Aunt Gardiner to return at any moment.

Without further prevarication but with some apprehension, Kitty relayed the information Wickham had given Lydia about Freddie Fanshawe's gaming and debts. She did not mention Sir Edward, but repeated Wickham's surmise that those debts were covered by an elderly relation. 'I was afraid for Georgiana,' said Kitty. 'This all happened on the night of the summer ball and I did not know who to tell but I sought you out, I thought you would know what to do – it was before your engagement was announced – but there was no opportunity.'

Colonel Fitzwilliam looked grave. 'Thank you for your candour,' he said eventually. 'I will make my own investigations. You may rely upon my discretion.'

'I would not lose your friendship, nor that of Miss Fanshawe over this,' said Kitty, distressed at the thought of forfeiting yet more amity and regard over such a wretched incident.

'Rest assured you will not,' returned he. 'You have my word. We need never speak of it again.'

Kitty was relieved. Colonel Fitzwilliam turned the conversation to lighter matters. When Mrs Gardiner came back into the room a few minutes later, they were discussing plays and a forthcoming performance of *The Merchant of Venice* at the Theatre Royal.

'I shall undertake to organise a box!' he declared. 'The last time I went to that theatre it tended to the rambunctious but it was diverting nonetheless.'

'I hope we can persuade you to sit down to dinner with us before then,' said Mrs Gardiner, an invitation he graciously countermanded with his own, but a date was put forward and agreed.

Shortly thereafter, Colonel Fitzwilliam bid the ladies adieu, leaving both with the happy expectation of seeing him again soon, and Kitty relieved to have finally shared her knowledge of Freddie Fanshawe's unfortunate predilection for gaming. Whatever happened now was in the colonel's hands.

Chapter 66

Whether Henry Adams had reason to believe the postal service fickle or unreliable, or whether he was simply unwilling to lose any time or spare any effort in securing a favourable response to his invitation is a matter of conjecture. Suffice to say that within a very few days of the happy coincidence of meeting Mrs Gardiner and Miss Bennet in Gunter's he found himself once more in the vicinity of Gracechurch Street – and with two of the concert programmes about his person. His card was sent up and he was spared no more than a few minutes' agonised wait before he was informed that Miss Bennet would receive him.

'My aunt is not home at present,' said Kitty, uncomfortably uncertain as to the propriety of Mr Adams' presence without the excuse of a music lesson. She had positioned herself near the pianoforte in order to reinforce his status as her music master; she hoped this would suffice. She had been alone with him before, she reasoned, and she could ring for tea. Besides, Aunt Gardiner was due to return at any moment.

Mr Adams presented Kitty with the concert bill as reason for his visit. She took the proffered programme and made to study it, catching at the names of those composers with whom she was familiar and hoping to be able to make erudite comments on others.

'You like living in London, Miss Bennet?' asked Mr Adams, breaking into her thoughts.

'I find I do,' replied she. 'Although I can say with equal sincerity that I was very comfortable staying in Derbyshire. I do not think anyone would find Pemberley anything other than delightful! London and Derbyshire are so very different but I find much to like in both.'

'And Hertfordshire?'

'I have lived in Meryton all my life, so perhaps it is only familiarity that renders it unexciting. Although everything is so much changed now, since my sisters have all married and my mother is gone.'

'Oh, forgive me! That was thoughtless of me,' apologised Mr Adams.

'There is nothing to forgive! Longbourn – my home – seems strangely empty now but it is still a fine house. I daresay that in the months to come my father and I will journey to stay with my sister Mrs Bingley, who has lately removed to Nottinghamshire. Mr and Mrs Bingley have a daughter now, called Elizabeth, after Mrs Darcy. I shall be the very picture of a doting aunt! And what of you, Mr Adams. You have always lived in London?'

'I have indeed. Well, of course you know that I was born in France, but my mother and father returned here when I was but a babe. Since then my family has always lived near Holborn.'

'And so you would never live anywhere other than London, of course!'

'Ah! That is not certain. You bring me to some news that I have been wanting to divulge.'

Kitty was disconcerted. Was Mr Adams moving away? Was he perhaps betrothed? Her expression remained of course perfectly placid. She waited.

'My father's music and connections with the church have brought him patronage from some influential people from time to time. Indeed, it was through one such gentleman that I was able to go up to Oxford. You remember that I went to that university?'

'I do.'

'It served me well, even though I was but a "commoner".'

'A commoner?'

'Yes, that is what I was called. The universities preserve rank, you know, and commoner was mine. Above me were gentleman-commoners, and above them the noblemen-students, a misnomer if ever I heard one as in general the sons of the nobility were not given much to study! I do not complain though; I am exceedingly grateful for the opportunity of such an education.'

'Not even a gentleman-commoner!' said Kitty, incensed on Mr Adams' behalf. 'I cannot think of you as a commoner!' She began to blush at the declaration and, much to her chagrin, felt her colour rising steadily.

'I thank you for your indignation,' said Mr Adams, pretending not to notice the flushed embarrassment of the lady before him. He smiled at her, which did nothing at all to alleviate the rosiness of her complexion. 'I was not offended, though, I assure you. Besides,' he continued, more to excuse Kitty from speaking than to expound on class distinctions at the universities, 'I could have been a servitor, in fact I think I was almost a servitor. Some of my friends certainly were. They enjoy an even lower rank, and must earn the privilege of education by serving those deemed their betters. Of all the scholars, the servitors study best, I think. Dr Johnson was a servitor. Some of us were fond of his quote, which was something like "the difference between us and the 'gentlemen' is that we are men of wit and no fortune and they are men of fortune and no wit".'

'Then I agree with Dr Johnson most wholeheartedly,' said Kitty, her equilibrium somewhat restored and all anxieties about this private interview completely forgotten. 'I have met others who have told me that there is more to do at the universities than study, and who have disparaged the notion of education. I am sure you are not one such.'

'I am sure I was not a perfect scholar,' laughed Mr Adams. 'There would be tutors who would happily attest to that. My father had thought I would join the clergy when I completed my exams, take ordination, but I had no inclination to do so. I wanted to pursue my music and do so without encumbrance. A young man's dreaming.'

'Why do you call it a dream?' asked Kitty. 'Your teaching and mastery of music is much admired. I think you have no want of students.'

'What you say is true, but I had not been giving much thought to the future and in time I began to see my father was right, that being of the clergy would be a good profession for me. Moreover, it is one that does not preclude in any way the teaching and practising of music.'

'Goodness!' was all that Kitty could find to say.

'And then, about a year ago, my father told me that one of his patrons had the gift of a living in Clapham, a village just a few miles from here. He had reason to believe that were I to be ordained, that I may get the preference of that living when it became vacant.'

Mr Adams paused, looking at Kitty.

'So I took the exams and began acting as deacon to the priest at the church where my father is organist. I will not deny that the thought of a valuable living in Clapham was absent from my deliberations. You are surprised! I can see.'

'Surprised, yes. I had no idea you were thinking of such a path, but I think you are as eligible a clergyman as any other I have known. Better, I venture, than some.' The egregious Mr Collins loomed into Kitty's mind, fawning and prating and oblivious to his inanity, and she suppressed a shudder.

'My role in that regard is yet to be tested,' said Mr Adams. 'Indeed, it may never be known for there is a corollary to my tale. Having taken all the necessary steps to secure myself a living and allowing myself to think of it as mine, my optimism and presumption were undone. A more suitable person was preferred.'

'More suitable!' cried Kitty. 'How so? In what way?'

'A young gentleman recently married was preferred. An excellent man, by all accounts, and with a fine wife the better to help him carry out his parish duties.' He looked thoughtful, a touch sad. 'I could not compete in that regard.'

'Oh, I see!' said Kitty, and indeed she did see. She saw Henry Adams looking at her ardently and she felt all the warmth of that gaze. Her own eyes locked onto his and she found herself unable to look away. This touching tableau lasted for a full minute, perhaps two or even three, with neither she nor he moving or saying anything but each understanding exactly what the other was thinking.

'I am, you see, Miss Bennet,' he said eventually, shifting in his seat, his rich dark voice quiet and full of regret, 'in no position to marry at present. I would that it were not so.'

'I understand,' said Kitty softly, as if speaking above a whisper would erase this moment. They lapsed into silence again, aware of every small creak and movement of the house and of sounds from the street that in other circumstances would have been but a little background noise.

At last Kitty could bear it no longer. She wanted to express her joy, to imagine herself as the wife of Henry Adams – musician, vicar, gentleman – and resident in a pleasant home in a village near London, but regretfully this could not be. That part was a dream. To break its spell, she stood and picked up the concert programme.

Mr Adams jumped to his feet. 'Miss Bennet, I hope I have said nothing to offend.'

'On the contrary,' she smiled.

'Then, I will see you and your family at our concert, I trust?'

'We are looking forward to it,' said Kitty. He bowed, gave her one last engaging smile and left the room.

Kitty fell back into her chair, cupped her face with her hands and did not know whether to laugh or cry. She found she could do neither. Her head was full of wonder. She marvelled at how much could be felt when so few words had been spoken; at how sure she was of both herself and of Henry Adams. The situation was quite hopeless, of course, just as hopeless as it had always been, but it had at least been acknowledged by them, and she was glad of that.

CHAPTER 67

By the third week of January, London had fully regained its bustling, noisy, chaotic and royally magnificent self, despite the persistent cold and frost. Those of the ton who had been at their country estates for Christmas had drifted back to the capital for the season, myriad lesser lights had arrived to revolve around them. Invitations to balls, salons and soirées were criss-crossing the streets of the wealthy and the fog, though never entirely absent for very long, was mainly confined to the cigar-smoke-filled rooms of gentlemen's clubs.

None of this affected those resident in the Gardiner household, where the social activity, neither dependent nor envious of goings-on in the fashionable part of town, was lively in its own way. 'We go out very little, you know,' Aunt Gardiner had said once. However, hardly a day passed without someone calling or those calls being returned; the little Gardiners were happy and cheerful children whose occasional remonstrances with each other were as noisy and short-lived as to make them almost perfect – even Mr Bennet had been seen on the rug with two of them taking a great deal of interest in a newly acquired spinning top; and the family dinners and the evenings that followed them were a mix of intelligent conversation, occasional card-playing and musical interludes. Kitty had not neglected her music and practised on the Gardiner's instrument most days, although she had been a little more assiduous since the chance meeting with her erstwhile music master.

That her thoughts dwelt on Henry Adams and his mute proposal was to be expected. Kitty had considered confiding in Mrs Gardiner, who was of course aware that Mr Adams had paid a visit to the house. However, when she imagined recounting their meeting to her aunt she could see that there would be little to divulge, other than the interesting news that the gentleman had become ordained and that she had shared. Of matters more intimate, nothing had actually been said – so she hugged the information to herself and if some of her emotions spilled onto the pages and into the hearts, minds and mouths of the fictional characters peopling *Town and Country*, then only someone who could read Kitty's thoughts would be any the wiser.

It was on one such routine day – Mr Bennet at the museum; Mrs Gardiner engaged in a morning call; Kitty alternating between writing or revising her prose and indulging in reverie – that two letters addressed to Miss Catherine Bennet were delivered to Gracechurch Street and brought up to the drawing room.

Kitty started when she saw them, seeing instantly they were from Pemberley, and recognising both her sister's and Georgiana's hand. She felt a frisson of anxiety, wondering what this portended. The Darcys would be in London soon, so she had not expected any correspondence; were they writing to say they would not receive her at Berkeley Square? Or perhaps to announce an engagement between Miss Georgiana Darcy and Mr Frederick Fanshawe? She hoped not! Though what business is that of mine, she asked herself. Agitated, she put down her pen and walked across the room, taking the letters with her and determining to read Elizabeth's first. She sat down on the sofa and opened it.

My dearest Kitty, it began – the affectionate salutation taking its reader by surprise.

Words cannot express the shame and contrition I feel in having so maligned you in regards to Georgiana's cameo necklace.

I know now that I was woefully mistaken and wrong to accuse you of so heinous a deed.

Kitty's heart jumped and her hand flew to her mouth. What had happened? She read on avidly.

Yesterday, we had an unexpected visit from Sir Edward Quincy. It was not a social call but a painful duty for that gentleman for what he revealed to us was indeed shocking. In short, he came to divulge that his nephew Frederick Fanshawe was a gambler and a thief, and that his crimes – and that is the word he used – included the theft of the cameo. It was an astonishing revelation, not least because Georgiana has the necklace, and so at first Darcy was perplexed and thought there must be some mistake. Sir Edward, however, was unaware of its return, still less the circumstances. He had, he said, discovered in his nephew's papers, pledges to a pawnbroker in Doncaster and had managed to retrieve two valuable items of jewellery – one, his own watch! – but not a third piece, described as a pearl and diamond necklace, which he supposed must belong to Lady Fanshawe or to his niece. His sister soon disabused him of that notion and it did not take them long to conclude that it must be the cameo lost at Conisbrough. He confronted his nephew, who at first denied, and then confessed that he had pawned it, but also insisted it had been returned to Georgiana. Sir Edward quite simply did not believe him. He came here yesterday to offer what reparation he could and to offer to have a copy of the necklace made.

This is a brief summary of what took place. There are more details and, indeed, more questions, some of which I think only you can answer. That is not important now. What is important is that you know how sorry we are. I speak here for Darcy as well as myself. We are both full of self-reproach and remorse for treating you so harshly, and for doubting your integrity.

How well I now remember you crying, 'I was trying to get it back!' and my disbelieving and dismissive reply. Kitty, I could not be more distraught and penitent! I hope with all my heart you can find it in yourself to forgive me.

We leave Pemberley today to go to Dapplewick Hall for a few days and, much as I would like to come direct to London and make my apologies in person, I can think of no excuse that would satisfy Jane for such a late alteration to our plans. For this, too, I ask your forgiveness and indulgence.

Your chastened sister
Elizabeth

Kitty sat completely still for several moments, staring at the letter. She had been exonerated! It was a shock, albeit a welcome one. Then, quietly, she began to cry. Tears of relief, of vindication, of elation mingled and fell and, were it not that one or two of these dropped onto Elizabeth's letter, threatening to blot and blur her liberating words, might have continued for some time. Kitty, however, saw that danger, and managing a small, triumphant laugh, wiped her eyes with one hand and held the letter away from her with the other.

Anticipating Aunt Gardiner's imminent return, and knowing that her tearful countenance would require explanations she was loath to give, Kitty picked up her correspondence and hurried upstairs to her room. Once there, she sat down on her bed and opened Georgiana's letter, written on the same date and evidently, given the untidiness of the writing, in some haste.

Pemberley
19 January

My dearest Kitty,

Can you ever forgive me? I should understand if you could not – you have good reason to wish never to see me again! – but

I rely on your kindness and compassion and hope fervently that you will read this letter and know how ashamed I am. Never has there been a less deserving friend than me! I can never be sorry enough, of that at least you can be certain.

I do not know where to begin, and have torn up three sheets of paper in trying to explain – in truth, in trying to find ways to excuse myself, but that will not do. So I write again, perhaps without sense, but from my heart.

When I look back, I cannot think how I arrived at my silly conclusions except to say I was jealous and afraid, and I thought you had played false with me – which I now know to be quite the opposite, and I am hot with shame. Mrs Wickham's arrival so soon after my admissions to you at the folly was what began it. I feared you would not keep my confidence and it made me uneasy. I cannot excuse my stupidity.

My preference for Mr Fanshawe blinded me and I became jealous when Mrs Wickham paid him so much attention, so often reciprocated. Then, when my brother returned my cameo to me and said that you had had it in your possession all the time! It was too much to understand, but I did not try to understand. We none of us did! It pains me to recollect my behaviour towards you, but the pain I have caused you is so much worse.

I hope you know that is true, thought Kitty. That pain was still fresh in so many ways. However, the relief of having it acknowledged was a balm. She read on.

I know Elizabeth is writing to you as I write this, and you will know what has happened and how distraught we all are. As for Mr Fanshawe! I can hardly bear to write of him! It is so hard to comprehend that he – who is from such a good family and who gives every appearance of being such a fine gentleman – is a gamester and a thief! Oh, I did not want to believe it when my brother revealed these truths to me, and at first I refused to do so, but as you know, Fitzwilliam would never deceive and neither does he act without evidence.

'That is not entirely accurate!' said Kitty, aloud this time. 'Darcy had no evidence against me but still I was accused.' She resumed reading.

I thought I was as wretched as I could be, but then my brother reminded me that Mr Fanshawe's deceit and cowardice had caused much more injury to you!

I have neglected to tell you how these events unfolded. You will wonder how Mr Fanshawe was exposed. I will write as plain as I can. His uncle was the means! Sir Edward called on Fitzwilliam yesterday and they were closeted in the library for some time. I saw him go in and thought he looked drawn and worried, which alarmed me a little as I thought it may have something to do with Frederick, but then I reasoned that was unlikely.

Eventually Sir Edward left, looking no less unhappy than when he arrived, and without stopping to take tea or bring me any news from Danson Park, which, as you would surmise, struck me as most odd and out of character. My brother returned to the library and soon afterwards I saw Elizabeth go in. By now I was in an agony of suspense, which was made worse when I saw your sister leave and run upstairs. I could see she had been crying.

Then my brother sent for me. He said he had grave and distressing news. At this my fears increased greatly, but what he then told me was more horrible than my imagination could have fancied.

Fitzwilliam says Sir Edward blames himself, that he believes himself culpable for having indulged his nephew for so long, lending him money to cover his gambling debts and pretending it was just a young man's folly. It all came out because Freddie's injured leg kept him abed at Danson Park and unable to meet with one of his debtors! Sir Edward undertook to act for him but in looking through his papers found that he had pawned jewellery and other valuables. He was aghast, as you would surmise, the more so because his own watch had gone missing and he realised Freddie had taken it. I am not sure what happened next but Sir Edward was at Danson Park when my cameo was lost at Conisbrough Castle and he must have recognised its description from the pawnbroker's pledge. Poor Sir Edward! I began to feel quite sorry for him.

Kitty felt the same. Sir Edward, undoubtedly an honourable man, who doted on his nephews, would hold himself responsible for Frederick's misdeeds. He would be mortified. She wondered how Sir Frederick and Lady Fanshawe had reacted to this terrible news and hoped some retribution would fall on their wayward son. She was not at all certain he would suffer the consequences of his actions. She turned back to Georgiana's letter.

He came not only to confess his nephew's wickedness but also to offer to have a copy of the cameo made, as he knew how much it meant to me. And here is mystery still to be solved! Frederick told Sir Edward he had retrieved it from the pawnbroker and planned to return it to me at the summer ball, having concocted a story about seeing it for sale in Doncaster. Sir Edward dismissed this as yet another falsehood, but perhaps part of it is true for how else did my cameo come to be at Pemberley? I do not know what to believe any more, except that I have done you a great wrong. My hand is shaking as I write this, I am so ashamed! I am most heartily sorry.

*I will call on you when we arrive in London and if you will
receive me it will be more than I deserve.*

*Your foolish, unworthy friend
Georgiana*

Such unexpected news and such swift turnarounds of emotion,
although gratifying in the extreme, raised mixed feelings. They
evoked many memories, sweet as well as bitter, although to
Kitty's mild surprise she did not feel aggrieved, only grateful
that the truth had at last surfaced. She read the letters again,
more slowly this time, noting Georgiana's misplaced concerns
and jealousies with regard to Lydia. Poor Georgiana, she thought.
so easily deceived yet again by a man of poor character. Both
Elizabeth and Darcy were full of remorse and self-reproach! She
tried to imagine Mr Darcy looking contrite. How strange that
Sir Edward should be her unwitting saviour in restoring her
reputation!

She paced about her room for a while, assimilating this new
information and unable to sit still. As her shameful secret had
been contained within Pemberley, there was no one with whom
she could share her exhilaration and relief. She was so lost in
her own thoughts that the knock at her door quite startled her.
Opening it, she found her two small cousins looking up at her,
slightly affronted. 'Kitty!' declared the eldest girl, sternly. 'You
promised you would play with us this afternoon!' Her sister
nodded vigorously.

'I can think of nothing that would please me more,' said Kitty,
laughing and taking their hands. 'You shall choose the games!'

CHAPTER 68

Colonel Fitzwilliam was expected to dine with the Gardiners that evening. Kitty surmised it was too soon for him to have been informed of Sir Edward's revelations to Darcy at Pemberley and resolved to say nothing to him about the contents of her letters. He and Darcy would have opportunity to discuss the matter, and her conversation with the colonel about Mr Fanshawe, soon enough.

When she came downstairs she could hear her father laughing, which was unusual but pleasing, and so she assumed that Mr Gardiner was home or that Colonel Fitzwilliam had arrived early. However, when she entered the room it was to discover Mr Bennet alone, sitting in the chair he favoured, and that the source of his mirth was his reading material. To her horror, Kitty saw that he had her unfinished novel in his hands. In her agitation at receiving the letters from Pemberley, she had completely forgotten her writing and left all the papers in plain view on the table. She closed the door behind her and leaned against it, watching him and wondering what to do.

Mr Bennet turned a page, scratched his temple and let out another small chirrup of laughter. Then, sensing another presence in the room he looked up and saw his daughter. 'Kitty!' he called, motioning her over to him. 'Did you really write all this?'

What could Kitty do but admit that she had? Her father knew her handwriting well enough; it could not be passed off as anyone else's. She stood, mortified, as Mr Bennet shuffled through the pages to find a particular passage. He began to read aloud:

> *Sir Reginald was as handsome as he was stupid, and he was a very handsome man. Nature had given him all the features so often pleasing to the fairer sex, but had counterbalanced this excess with a very meagre intelligence. The wonder was that Sir Reginald was unaware of his defects. He wore clothes well, but chose them badly; his opinions were ill-formed, but loudly spoken; his acquaintance was either well-born and as silly as he, or in need of his money and happy to do whatever was necessary to part some of it from him. Poor Sir Reginald could not distinguish between deserved praise and fawning flattery, and chief among those who fawned upon him was the egregious Mr Crawford.*

Mr Bennet paused, looked up at Kitty. 'Well, we know who that is, do we not?' Wishing herself invisible, Kitty stood beside her father's chair, her hands clenched together and her eyes shut. She said nothing. Undaunted, Mr Bennet continued:

> *Mr Crawford was tall and heavy-looking, with a grave yet pompous manner, and he had been called to God, something he would tell anyone who asked or anyone who did not. He affected very formal manners and seldom used two words when ten could be found. He thought of Sir Reginald as his own personal benefactor and hardly an hour passed when he was not congratulating himself or Sir Reginald on the felicity of that arrangement. 'Sir Reginald is the epitome of good grace and manners,' he opined to the lady sitting to his right. 'His manners and breeding are second to none.'*

'I have not got very far with this,' said Mr Bennet to the penitent author at his side, 'but I hope I will not find all our family so well described. Or indeed, if they are, that they are better disguised!

Luckily, Mr Collins would not recognise himself even if he were to get permission from his patroness or his God to read anything other than a sermon.'

'I am sorry,' mumbled Kitty.

'Sorry?' said Mr Bennet. 'For what are you sorry exactly?'

'For this,' said Kitty, gesturing at her work, her precious stories. 'It is just something to pass the time. I would not have them made public. I would not parody you or my sisters, I assure you. Let me take them.' She reached out her hands to take the pages from her father, but he held them aloft.

'You think I disapprove, child?'

'If you will just let me take them, I will destroy them,' said Kitty, distressed and not knowing whether her worst fear was her father's anger or his ridicule.

'I hope you will do no such thing. In fact, I shall forbid it!'

Kitty was dumbfounded. What did her father intend? Surely he would not humiliate her further by letting others see something he found so risible.

'My dear,' said Mr Bennet, seeing her concern at last and pointing to the papers in his lap. 'This is very good! I had no idea you had such a talent for prose. How long have you been writing this?'

A pause followed, wherein Kitty digested this strange information.

'I suppose it began when I was in London last year,' she said at last, unsure of her father's sincerity and well aware of his capricious tendencies. 'There were so many new things to see, so many new people to observe. I did not know many people, so it was easier to watch. It began as a journal, just a way of keeping a record so that I did not forget.'

'Well it has progressed well from there,' said her father. 'I would not have imagined it of you, Kitty. No, do not look alarmed! It is praise! Well meant, not like your Mr Crawford's! Praise and, I admit it, a fair degree of astonishment.'

'You really approve?' said Kitty, quite amazed herself.

'I do, child. Approve and applaud. And if you will permit me, I shall take these and I shall read the rest.'

'If you really wish it,' said she, still unbelieving.

'Now you are asking for more praise?'

'No, not all,' Kitty smiled at last. 'I am just surprised. I had not anticipated anyone reading my stories but me. The thought makes me feel uncomfortable. I would prefer it if you would not mention this to Aunt Gardiner, or anyone else for that matter.'

'An author who does not want to be read! Now there is a strange thing!'

'I am not an author,' protested Kitty.

'As you wish, Miss Bennet,' returned her father. 'But I am holding in my hand something that looks very much like a novel and someone must have penned it. Is that not so?'

'An anonymous someone.'

'Ah! Well that solves that riddle. Very well. I shall share it with no one else in this house without your permission.'

'Thank you.'

'Now as I imagine we will be joined at any moment by your aunt and uncle, let us secret these papers away and I will read them when I retire.' He looked at Kitty as he said this, and shook his head in happy disbelief.

'I think a little refreshment is in order. Please be so kind as to ring the bell.'

Kitty did as she was bid.

'Oh, and one more thing…' said Mr Bennet, as he picked up the newspaper on the table by his side.

'Yes?' said Kitty, nervously.

'Do keep writing.'

She sat down in a chair near the fire, once more in a state of confusion. Her father was opposite her, reading his newspaper as if the day were the same as any other, which of course it was excepting that the morning's post had brought her salvation, and in the afternoon someone – her father! – had read the beginnings of *Town and Country* and thought it worthy. Amusing, even. Her father! A man from whom praise was hitherto unknown. She had not thought about to whom she might have entrusted an airing of her writing, but her father would not have been among her first choices. He who was so liberal with his sarcasm rather than his advice.

She looked across at him again. That he appeared to have aged since Mrs Bennet's death was apparent, but his health was otherwise sound and, thought Kitty, he has regained his spirit, he no longer walks about as if he were wearing a coat made of lead. He is as content as he ever was, she realised, wondering – not for the first time – at the odd match her mother and father had made, at how he had so enjoyed deliberately misunderstanding Mrs Bennet for the sheer pleasure of vexing her; and how she had never understood that she was being provoked. She remembered Jane's advice about prudence and passion and smiled inwardly; no doubt there was as much prudence in Mary's marriage as there was passion in Lydia's. Prudence and Passion! A good title for a book, she mused, or was it too provocative?

She cast another glance towards Mr Bennet, still engrossed in his paper. Keep writing, he had said. It was almost too much to comprehend. Did this mean she was no longer silly and ignorant? Had something changed? She had no real need to answer her question. Even as she posed it Kitty knew the answer. Of course, something had changed. She had changed! The young woman sitting in this chair in a drawing room in London was quite different to the petulant child who, little more than a twelvemonth ago, had bemoaned her fate in the parlour at Longbourn. She could not have foreseen such an alteration in herself, known how events would have shaped the way she saw things, but despite her mother's death, despite Elizabeth's cold injustice, despite Georgiana's fickle friendship, even despite Lydia's malice, all these vicissitudes she had borne and overcome. It was quite an epiphany.

Epiphanies, however, will come when they want and pay no heed to social customs or the dinner hour, and this one was no exception. Unaware they were trespassing on momentous thoughts, Colonel Fitzwilliam and the Gardiners came into the room, discussing the events of the day, and curtailing further self-reflection on Kitty's part.

Afterwards, she would remember that dinner with a good deal of happiness. It was not just that the conversation flowed, that it was intelligent and that the subjects were of interest to all, it was more that she saw herself differently. She was the youngest person at the table by many years, but it did not matter. She felt taller, more substantial, and quite unafraid to put forward a reasoned opinion of her own, even in the presence of her father. With the possible exception of that gentleman, no one perceived Kitty any differently – she appeared to the same good advantage as she had at any other time since she had arrived at the Gardiners.

CHAPTER 69

The day of the concert at St Clement's arrived. On receipt of the programme so graciously hand-delivered, Aunt Gardiner had extended an invitation to Mr Adams and his family to take tea with them afterwards, thus assuring Kitty of both her aunt and uncle's intention to attend the concert. Mrs Gardiner had also invited a Mrs and Mrs Morris, who were near neighbours, so a cheerful little gathering was anticipated at Gracechurch Street later that evening. Mr Bennet had been persuaded to make the journey from house to church – despite the weather and despite his having little interest in Bach and Handel – and Kitty was more exuberant, though trying extremely hard to appear calm and almost disinterested, than she had been in a long while.

There were a number of people already assembled when the Bennet and Gardiner party took their pews in the capacious stone church of St Clement's. Kitty immediately sought out Henry Adams and saw him to the right of the music stands, in conversation with one of his fellow musicians. Hers may not have been an entirely unbiased view, but she thought he looked very well.

There was little difference in temperature between the inside of the church and the outside air, and while the audience had taken every precaution to be well wrapped some of the musicians, Kitty noted, were not prepared for the cold. It would be difficult, she supposed, to play the violin hampered by a greatcoat and scarf. From where she was sitting, it would be impossible to see the organist, so Kitty would have to wait until later to see whether Henry Adams bore a resemblance to his father; his mother she could see seated in the middle of one of the pews a few rows forward of her.

'I see we are to hear some Purcell,' noted Mr Bennet, looking at the concert programme for the first time. 'And some Maurice Greene and John Stanley. Well I am glad to see that our English composers are deemed worthy after all. I thought you said it was all Bach and Handel.'

'I said no such thing, Papa!' whispered Kitty.

'Purcell's Trio Sonata,' continued Mr Bennet. 'Ah, I see this Mr Adams plays the violin.'

'He does,' agreed Kitty, wishing her father would speak more quietly. 'As well as the viola and the pianoforte,' she added softly.

'His father is the organist?' said Mr Bennet conversationally.

'Yes.' It was not quite a whisper and not quite a hiss.

'One of Purcell's sons is buried in this church. Edward, I think.'

Kitty forbore to comment on this remark. No one else appeared to be speaking; all were waiting in near silence for the music to commence.

'That's right,' said Uncle Gardiner, leaning across from Kitty's right. 'He's buried near the organ gallery door.'

'Is that so?' Mr Bennet peered in that direction and Kitty, vexed beyond reason at such unnecessary and spoken observation, wondered what was wrong with her father and uncle. Why was her father not his usual quiet self?

'What do you think of Bach?' he now asked Mr Gardiner.

The reply was lost however, much to Kitty's relief, as the rich swelling notes of Bach's toccata and fugue filled the church and everyone, including her father and uncle, sat back to let the music envelop them. It was a promising start and she relaxed.

After the organ solo, the two violins and the cellist played a Vivaldi concerto, although of course Kitty had only ears and eyes for one violinist. Her father suffered two Handel compositions with no outward ill effect and nodded in what could have been construed as approval at the William Boyce sonatas, which were familiar to him. The music chosen was in general uplifting and even those who had nothing more than a passing interest in the musicians were buoyed by it. The audience showed their appreciation at the concert's conclusion and in the general stir of departures Kitty heard many complimentary comments passed about the individual performances. She could not have been more pleased had she been playing herself.

Mrs Gardiner went in search of Mrs Adams and the rest of their party waited at the porch for Henry Adams and his father. Kitty was duly introduced to a tall grey-haired man of pleasing appearance, who professed himself delighted to meet her. Mr Bennet was likewise introduced and once all such formalities were complete the party began the short walk back to Gracechurch Street.

'The concert was delightful,' said Kitty to Henry Adams as they walked side by side along the footway. She would have said the same had she found it quite odious, but happily the truth could prevail without compromise. He was pleased, both with her reaction and that of the wider audience, and they chatted on, only privately sorry that the journey was so brief. It was the first time they had spoken since he had visited Kitty at the Gardiners, when so much had been said and so much left unspoken, and she was relieved to find that there was no awkwardness between them. All, in fact, seemed exactly as before.

Kitty helped Aunt Gardiner with the tea things once everyone was settled in the warmth of the drawing room, cutting a pretty picture of elegance and charm as she attended to Mr Adams' parents and her own dear father. She was of course a little nervous, quite aware that both she and Mr Adams were the objects of veiled interest and scrutiny, but the conversation flowed, helped by the discussion of the concert all had just attended and, it should be noted, by Aunt Gardiner's easy manners and fine social graces. How different it would have been had Mrs Bennet been one of those present. That thought flitted across Kitty's mind. Poor Mama, she thought, without any bitterness. If you were here, we would have no need to wonder about Mr Adams' suitability. All would have been aired within a half-hour.

The conversation turned, as it invariably will, to the weather.

'I do believe there will be a frost fair this year,' opined Mrs Adams. 'There is much talk about it and Henri told me only yesterday that there is a lot of ice forming around London Bridge. Is it not so?'

'Indeed there is, madam,' said her son. 'I think the river will soon be frozen over. I confess I am hoping so, for I would dearly love the chance to skate again, and skating across the Thames would be something to boast of!'

'My children would be delighted to hear you say so,' said Mr Gardiner. 'Ever since I mentioned the possibility of such a thing, they have been eager to hear if it will happen. They ask me every day! They will be sorely disappointed if it rains.'

'What of you, Miss Bennet?' asked Mr Adams. 'What think you of skating?'

'I would like to try!' cried Kitty. 'Neither I nor my sisters have ever been skating, but I would try. Is it very difficult to master?'

'That depends on whom your partner is,' said Aunt Gardiner. 'It is a little daunting at first, but your uncle made sure I did not fall. I am not sure I would do it again. You will get your chance, Kitty, if the river does freeze, for I still have the skates and you are most welcome to have them.'

'Well, I will do my best,' said Kitty, resolutely, 'and hope not to become a laughing stock.'

'That could not be!' declared Mr Adams immediately. 'I should be happy to escort you, should you wish it.'

His announcement was heartfelt, and Kitty not the only person present to interpret it as so. 'It will be quite an excursion then,' said Mrs Gardiner, stepping into the breach. 'Mr Gardiner will have charge of our sons. They will no doubt want to skate and not be content till they have fallen! I am quite content to watch. Mr Bennet, will we see you on the ice?'

The question was so ludicrous – even those who had just made his acquaintance knew it to be so – and Mr Bennet's expostulation at such an idea so humorous, that the subject of skating was soon drowned in mirth. The chessboard on one of the side tables provided a more intellectual avenue for discussion between Mr Bennet and some of the gentlemen, the ladies had children and fashion to compare, and so the conversation subsided into general topics. As a result of this quiet conviviality, Kitty and Mr Adams were left to converse by themselves, and the evening ended in mutual satisfaction for all.

CHAPTER 70

A few days later, as Kitty was coming downstairs, a commotion in the breakfast parlour made her hasten her step and she entered the room expecting to confront some domestic disaster. Instead, she found the Gardiner children jumping up and down in excitement and their father regarding them, a bemused expression on his face.

'Kitty! Kitty! There is going to be an elephant!' declared the eldest boy as soon as he saw her.

'An elephant! An elephant!' chorused the others. Kitty, laughing at their wonder and enthusiasm, appealed to Mr Gardiner for an explanation.

'The Thames is completely frozen over,' said he, 'at least between here and Blackfriars. The word is that the rivermen are going to lead an elephant across the ice to show that it is completely safe. These four seem to want to see it happen.'

'We do! Papa, we do!' declared a cacophony of small voices.

'I should like to see that, too,' said Kitty to her little cousins. 'I have never seen an elephant. It would be a shame to miss such an event. When do we go?'

Mr Gardiner had not refused his children's request but had intended to confer with their mother. Kitty was their friend and saviour. They turned to look at him.

'In about half an hour if you can be ready by then,' he said, and never before had the little Gardiners been so willing and in such haste to make themselves fit for the outside world. They were on their way to the nursery and their outdoor clothes before their father had time to sit down.

'So there is to be a frost fair?' cried Kitty, quite as pleased as the children.

'It would seem so,' agreed her uncle. 'Provided the elephant does not sink!'

They were not the only ones keen to see such a spectacle. The city's great and good, dirty and disreputable, rich and poor and everyone in between were amassing on and near Blackfriars Bridge. Kitty and the Gardiners, who started their journey alongside the Thames near London Bridge, saw the great white expanse of ice, not as smooth as Kitty had imagined it but rather bumpy with little masses of chunky ice here and there. Liveried carriages were stopped by the river so their occupants could witness the scene and the elephant's progress. Gentlemen on horseback reined in their steeds and had the advantage of extra height, while those on foot simply edged as close as reason would allow to gain the best view. The watermen, their trade and livelihood stopped by a river frozen solid, were already improvising, guarding the steps down to the river and charging tuppence for entry onto the ice. Their cries and the anticipation and excitement of those assembled made for a noisy, chattering gathering and whenever the poor elephant, quite an aged beast by the look of him, so much as moved one of his great feet slightly or turned his head to gaze impassively at the raucous throng, a huge cry went up.

Kitty, who had charge of the two little girls, their hands firmly grasped by her own, while Mr Gardiner held on to his sons, observed it was fortunate that the elephant was tethered on their side of the river.

'It is so,' agreed Mr Gardiner. 'And it is a wonder none of these fellows has come around asking us to pay for the sight.'

'Not everyone is waiting,' said Kitty, nodding towards a band of men setting up a row of skittles on the ice, and writing up a tariff on a makeshift board. Elsewhere a printing press was being manoeuvred down steps and onto the frozen river.

'They don't waste any time,' laughed Uncle Gardiner. 'They'll be printing out souvenirs of this, just like they did last time. All manner of ruffians will be out there just as soon as that elephant makes it across. I think we can be assured of a frost fair, Kitty!'

'Can we play skittles, Papa?' asked one of the boys.

'Certainly not,' said his father. 'You may be able to watch. And see how the pickpockets help up those who fall down on the ice. There is plenty of trade to be had at a frost fair.'

Kitty instinctively tightened her grip on the little girls by her side. Then there was a great appreciative whoop and cries of 'Oh, look!' and 'There it goes!' and they saw the elephant being led on its plodding journey to the south bank of the river. It was nearly there when Kitty heard her name called and, turning, found Mr Adams a short distance away, in the company of two gentlemen. Detaching himself from them, he came to join her.

'I wondered if I might find you here, Miss Bennet,' said he, extending his greetings to Mr Gardiner and his progeny. 'This is quite a sight, is it not? We had to come and see for ourselves.'

They conversed for a few minutes and then heard, rather than saw, that the elephant had successfully reached Southwark. Mr Gardiner had no further wish to stay by the river and they made to return home – but not before Adams had sought permission to call on Miss Bennet within a day or two.

Although Kitty had said nothing of her feelings to Aunt Gardiner, that lady, sensible to the lack of any maternal influence on her niece, took it upon herself to raise the matter of Henry Adams. This happened shortly after Kitty's return that day.

'I think you are fond of this young man,' she began, gently.

Kitty coloured. 'There is no arrangement between us, Aunt, although…'

'Although?'

'Although,' said Kitty, drawing a deep breath, 'even though the words have not been spoken aloud, there is an attachment between us. We both feel it. But Mr Adams is an honourable man, and he has not said or done anything that is wrong or improper.'

'I do not doubt it,' said Mrs Gardiner, reassuring Kitty with a smile. 'There is a happy integrity to his character, one that will stand him in good stead now that he has taken orders. He seems to have no plans in that regard?'

'His father encouraged him to take ordination. Not that he has regretted the decision,' she added quickly, lest any negative mark should be imputed to Mr Adams. 'When he did so he thought to obtain a good living in the village of Clapham but, as it turned out, he was precipitate in his optimism as it was given elsewhere.'

'I am sure you are aware,' said Aunt Gardiner, with a well-meaning firmness in her voice, 'that such opportunities are very rare and usually given at the whim of those who have the power to bestow them. Mr Adams should not expect another living to appear. If such a thing were to happen, it may be years before such luck befalls him.'

Kitty shifted in her chair. 'He does not expect such a thing to happen. He wishes it were otherwise.'

'I would wish that, too,' replied Mrs Gardiner. 'I can see that a good living may open up very many opportunities for him but, my dear Kitty, one cannot live on hopes and wishes.'

'I understand you, Aunt, and I thank you for your concern. Truly I do.' Kitty paused for a moment, not really wanting to say what she knew she must. Eventually, she said: 'What you are telling me – what I already know but choose to forget – is that neither of us has any fortune and that this would be an imprudent match, one best forgotten. Is that not so?'

'I could not advise you otherwise,' said Mrs Gardiner, 'but that does not mean I do not understand your distress, my dear.'

So saying, she rose from her chair and went to Kitty, kissing her on the top of her head in the same way she kissed her own daughters. 'Do not despair,' said she, as Kitty looked up at her. 'I do not pretend to see a solution for this particular predicament but you are young, and with your sisters so well married you will find your way in the world. I am sure of it.' She laughed. 'I sound a little like your dear mother, do I not!'

Kitty watched her leave the room. She knew her aunt was right; there was nothing more to be said.

CHAPTER 71

Shortly after Mr Bennet left for his daily literary pilgrimage to the museum, a message was delivered at the Gardiners to notify the arrival of the Darcys to Berkeley Square. Elizabeth and Georgiana were therefore expected that day or the next.

Aunt Gardiner had some business to attend to around mid-morning but was confident that it would take but an hour, and so it was left to Kitty to receive any visitors that may call. If she was apprehensive about seeing Elizabeth again that apprehension was mild and tinged with a sort of curious excitement. She felt equal to any conversation with her sister.

Kitty was in the drawing room, immersed in one of the Grandison volumes, when she was informed that Miss Georgiana Darcy was downstairs. 'Please show her up,' she instructed, standing and gathering her thoughts. The door opened and Georgiana appeared, venturing just two tentative steps into the room before stopping and looking meekly towards Kitty, trying to gauge her reaction to her presence. If there was an awkward moment, it was very brief. Kitty smiled and opened her arms towards Georgiana, who ran across the room to embrace her with a most unladylike force. Kitty looked to the door to see if Elizabeth was following but Georgiana had arrived alone.

'I came as quickly as I could,' said she. 'I did not want to waste a minute. Please say you forgive me! I thought you might not receive me but I had to find out.' Kitty nodded, as these sentences, delivered at twice the speed normally deemed appropriate for elegant discourse, were followed by others in praise of Kitty and her gracious, forgiving nature and only stopped by the lady herself who insisted on a moment's silence and the chance to look properly at her errant friend.

She saw she was as demure and handsome as she ever was; if her heart was fractured there was no outward evidence. Georgiana, for her part, thought how well Kitty looked and within minutes they were seated and the conversation turned to all that had happened since last they had seen each other. Georgiana, still a little nervous and much more unsettled than Kitty, was the more voluble of the two.

As was to be expected, Freddie Fanshawe featured first and heavily in this conversation. Having castigated herself as unpardonably foolish for allowing her preference for Fanshawe to blind her to his faults and then absolving herself of some of this shame by remembering her disgraced suitor's deceptions, fine manners and covert betrayals, Georgiana gave Kitty her account. She had, despite the concerns that had been aired by the colonel, continued to bestow her affections on the Fanshawe heir. 'After all,' said she without much logic, 'it was a little strange for Colonel Fitzwilliam to raise objections when he was so obviously in love with Felicia!' Such different siblings, thought Kitty, but did not say so.

'Of course, I know better now,' said Georgiana sadly, 'but during last summer I thought my uncle's misgivings were more to do with my youth. You said as much yourself,' she continued, looking at Kitty a little defensively, 'and I had no reason to suspect such defects in his character. I think my brother and Colonel Fitzwilliam had supposed when the Fanshawes returned to Danson Park at the end of August that everything would be over, but they did not count on Freddie and William riding over when the weather was fine – Felicia as well, sometimes – so I continued to see him into the autumn months. Then he had his accident.'

'Yes, I heard about that,' said Kitty. 'What happened?'

'He was out riding on the estate and his horse threw him. That is all he said. In any event, he broke his leg very badly and it did not initially heal as the physician expected. Then he developed a fever and was very ill for more than two weeks, but eventually he began to improve. Felicia and my uncle were in regular correspondence of course, so we knew of his progress. Sir Edward postponed his trip to London to be with him, he was most concerned.'

'It must have been a dreadful reminder to him of his son's riding accident,' said Kitty. 'You remember his youngest boy died after a bad fall from his horse?'

'I do. It is very sad. At least his son did not disgrace him.' She fell silent.

'What did you think would become of your friendship with Mr Fanshawe?' asked Kitty gently, thinking how ironic it was, given her recent conversation with Aunt Gardiner, that she should now be the one listening and giving advice on matters of mismatched love.

'I do not really know,' said Georgiana, looking uncomfortable. 'He is handsome as well as eligible. Our family backgrounds were similar. I supposed myself in love. I wanted to imagine he was in love with me.'

'And was he not?'

'I do not know how gentlemen behave when they are in love! I do not know how gentlemen behave at all, it would seem! I have twice been so very wrong! He was always kind and solicitous to me. I do not know!' She looked to Kitty, as if she could supply the information she lacked. 'His parents – well, Lady Fanshawe, I am sure – want him to marry.'

'I cannot speak for Mr Fanshawe's feelings but I do not think his affection for you was pretence. Whatever else he has done, I do not think it was his intention to cause you distress, although his actions could not but do otherwise. I think he did not think at all, except of himself. As to Lady Fanshawe's expectations, Freddie is the eldest son and as such he must marry. You are a most eligible young lady, in every way. Of course she would approve. I like

Lady Fanshawe, although I do wonder how well she knows her son. Poor lady, she must be dismayed and disappointed.'

'He is adept at dissembling,' said Georgiana, once again looking very sad. 'I did not know him well either.'

'You were not the only one he fooled, take some comfort from that. It is easy for gentlemen to hide things from us. We are not privy to so many of the things they do.'

'I suppose so. My brother says I read too many romance novels. But at least in the novels the villains are always exposed! In life, it is not so easy.'

Kitty laughed, at the same time thinking how like Darcy to disapprove of novels.

'Have you seen Mr Adams since you have been in London?' asked Georgiana, suddenly remembering.

'Do you think him a villain, is that why you ask?' said Kitty, teasing.

'No, indeed! I ask because I know very well you like him,' returned Georgiana.

Kitty could not deny it; she and Georgiana had discussed the charming Mr Adams more than once when she had been at Pemberley, and although Kitty had concentrated on lauding his musical skills rather than his character or person, Georgiana had soon perceived her preference. It was one of their little secrets, albeit one rarely acknowledged.

'Well?' prompted Georgiana.

It became Kitty's turn to unburden her heart, and after some momentary misgivings about the prudence of disclosing what she felt, she gave way and described the recent events, even confiding that she thought he might have declared himself had he now been the incumbent of a rectory in Clapham.

Georgiana was all joy at this news and so Kitty had to explain that, flattering as it was and much as she liked Mr Adams, she had realised that nothing could come of their friendship. She finished this little speech by saying she did not expect to see him again once her father and she had left London.

Unable to avoid it any longer, Georgiana broached the subject of her necklace and what had happened on the evening of the ball.

'Ah,' said Kitty, 'I will tell you what happened. You will be the first to know! Where is your cameo, though? You are not wearing it. Like Sir Edward, I was surprised to learn that its reappearance was not widely known.'

'The clasp is still broken,' said Georgiana, 'and to tell the truth I have not been in a great hurry to have it repaired. We have it with us now, and it will be sent to the jewellers while we are in London, but when my brother gave it back to me and told me...' she faltered. 'When he said...'

'Go on,' said Kitty, mildly surprised at how calm she felt. 'I know what you all thought had happened.'

Georgiana blushed. 'Well, much as I love the cameo, after the ball and... and your departure.' She hesitated again. 'After the ball, it became a reminder of things that I preferred to forget.' She looked down.

'That I can understand,' said Kitty, but before she could say more, the door opened to admit a footman bearing Mr Adams' card. Moments later, the young man himself was allowed entry.

'Forgive me, I see I am intruding,' said he, after he had greeted both ladies in turn.

He was assured he was not. Georgiana was so pleased and amazed to see the so recently discussed Mr Adams that she was almost staring. Kitty was forced to catch her eye to make her aware of her blatant astonishment.

'Miss Bennet and I have been talking of ice-skating,' said Mr Adams, wonderfully oblivious to the effect he was having on Miss Darcy. 'I came expressly to ask if you still considered that plan as I have seen skaters on a part of the Thames near London Bridge, where the ice is quite smooth.'

'Such an adventure!' declared Kitty. 'Yes of course I still want to try it, though I admit to a little trepidation!'

'You are very brave!' said Georgiana. 'We are very close to the river here, are we not?' Is it really frozen over? I should like to see it.'

That was easily arranged. A walk was proposed, agreed on, and only when the three were in the vestibule on the point of departure did Georgiana remember. 'Elizabeth!' she exclaimed. 'I quite forgot to say. She was to have come with me this morning but I was too impatient to wait. I sent the carriage back for her when I arrived so that she could join us.'

'It is still early for morning calls. Do you know what time we should expect her?' asked Kitty. Georgiana had no firm answer and was afraid of making the wrong one. While she did not want to appear to be evading or deliberately avoiding Elizabeth, Kitty was in favour of walking out. 'We will not be above half an hour, I am sure. It is too cold to stay out longer.' Besides, she reasoned Aunt Gardiner would be back at any moment – Mr Bennet was, of course, poring over old books in Bloomsbury and would not be seen much before dinner. 'If you will wait a moment, I will leave a message with the housekeeper to inform her that Mrs Darcy may arrive and that we will return shortly.'

She was back within no time. Then there was another small delay while a muff was fetched for Georgiana and once more they prepared to depart. They stepped into the street at exactly the moment the Darcy carriage arrived at the door and Mrs Darcy was handed down. This time Kitty almost stared. Elizabeth seemed to become more elegant, more composed, every time she saw her. On this white-grey morning, Mrs Fitzwilliam Darcy was looking superb in black satin trimmed with jet beads, her matching cloak trimmed with black fur. She looked very serious as she alighted, her eyes straight ahead as she made her way to the entrance of the house. Only then did she become aware of movement to her right and looked around to see three people watching and waiting for her.

CHAPTER 72

The informality of the moment served both sisters well, each having anticipated their next encounter with some apprehension and, in Elizabeth's case, a little dread. Mrs Darcy's regal demeanour gave way to surprise and Kitty was not a little pleased to be flanked by Georgiana and Mr Adams. Elizabeth, however, was not concerned with formality or her dignity. She moved quickly towards Kitty and embraced her tightly, saying again and again how pleased she was to see her. Georgiana clasped her gloved hands together in delight and Mr Adams was left to wonder if Mrs Darcy and Miss Bennet were always so effusive in their greeting. He found it quite touching and wondered if perhaps he should show more emotion when next he saw his own sister.

Eventually, Elizabeth released Kitty and stood back, once more aware of their company.

'I think you have not met Mr Adams,' said Kitty, assuming responsibility for the introductions. 'Although you may remember me speaking of him. He is the musician and music master to whom I am indebted for my improvement on the pianoforte. Georgiana may have mentioned him to you, also.'

The last sentence was purely for Elizabeth's benefit. Kitty wanted to make sure that she knew Miss Darcy had received instruction from Mr Adams; she did not want him dismissed as some chance and suspect acquaintance of her own.

'We are on the point of walking down to the river,' she continued. 'Georgiana wishes to see it in its frozen-solid state. Will you come with us or do you want to see Aunt Gardiner? She will be home any moment and is expecting you. We do not intend to be gone long.'

'Yes, Elizabeth, do come with us,' said Georgiana. 'Do you not want to see it as well?'

Whatever Elizabeth thought of Kitty and Georgiana being escorted along the Thames by a music master she kept entirely to herself. She may have acquiesced to Georgiana's request because she felt she should chaperone; because she was curious to see the icy river herself; or because she wanted to speak with Kitty without any further delay. Whatever the reason, she did not hesitate. Of course she would go with them.

'We could take the carriage,' she suggested, but she was overruled. The others were ready to walk and the only confusion was in how to arrange themselves in pairs. Elizabeth thought to walk alongside Kitty, but as Mr Adams had already offered Miss Bennet his arm, she was left with no choice but to follow with Georgiana. Kitty turned around to see if this arrangement had irked her sister but was rewarded with a warm smile. She smiled back and they walked on.

The frost fair soon took up all their attention and Kitty saw the skating arena that had been cordoned off. They stood and watched the couples already on the ice, all of whom appeared graceful and worryingly proficient to Kitty. It was arranged that she and Mr Adams would venture onto the ice tomorrow morning; the weather looked steady.

It was the second full day of the fair and the attractions had increased. As they wandered along they could see a whole sheep being roasted on a spit under a sign that proclaimed it to be 'Lapland Mutton'. Makeshift booths had sprung up on the ice, selling beer, rum and other spirits; among the diversions advertised by small, scruffy boys and other hawkers were bear-baiting on the south side, fortune tellers and a roulette wheel.

The area between the Blackfriars and London bridges had been nicknamed 'City Road' and it was almost as busy a thoroughfare as the Thames was when it admitted waterborne traffic.

On the return journey, Elizabeth successfully gained Kitty's side, leaving Georgiana to walk ahead with Mr Adams. When a little distance had opened up between the two couples, she spoke.

'Kitty, I must talk to you. I am so sorry for judging you in the way that I have.'

Although she knew Elizabeth meant what she said, Kitty did not know quite how to react. This was unfamiliar ground and she felt a little tense.

Elizabeth misread her silence as indignance. 'You are quite right to be angry with me,' she continued.

Kitty opened her mouth to speak, but Elizabeth shook her head. She stopped walking and took her sister's hand. 'No, please let me go on. You were right to tell me that I did not question, I only condemned. A more rational being would have asked and wondered and come to a better conclusion, instead of lashing out and believing the worst.

'When Darcy told me that you and Lydia had been fighting at the ball, he was so very angry and it was easier – easier for me! – to believe that you were once again following Lydia's example. I should have remembered how much you had changed. I allowed myself to forget that you had been doing everything you could to help me contain her; how very sensible and selfless you had been in keeping her company. Darcy then revealed he had discovered you with Georgiana's missing necklace in your hand! He said you looked exceedingly guilty and shamefaced. I could not believe it of you but we could think of no explanation. I am ashamed to tell you that I thought of your delight in my emeralds and other jewels when we were in London. I thought – we both thought – the worst!'

She stopped, perhaps expecting some reaction or interruption. Kitty said nothing, however; her head was slightly inclined as if to better hear everything her sister had to say, but her countenance did not betray her emotions.

'In truth,' resumed Elizabeth, 'I was so alarmed when Lydia arrived at Pemberley, so very worried that she could make so much mischief – and perhaps make Fitzwilliam regret having married me! – that I could not wait for her to be gone. The scene at the ball, the fighting, was worse than anything I had anticipated. I lost my judgement completely. I did not discriminate; nor did Darcy. He saw only two young ladies behaving very badly and condemned you both. He, too, regrets that mistake.'

'He does?' asked Kitty, incredulous.

'He does,' said Elizabeth. 'He is capable of making mistakes, you know! We all are.' She allowed herself a wry smile. 'As I was saying, I did not discriminate. I judged you without asking what had happened.'

Kitty nodded. 'That is true,' she agreed.

'It was a terrible way to behave, especially to my own sister!'

'You would certainly not have believed such a thing of Jane,' said Kitty. 'Nor Mary, I wager. I do wonder still that you thought me a thief! That was very hard to bear.'

'Oh!' cried Elizabeth, her voice choked with emotion. 'I am so sorry!'

'I know,' said Kitty, gently. She had never seen Elizabeth cry before. 'You cannot take all the blame, you know?'

'Do not worry, Darcy knows he is at fault as well.'

'That is not what I mean. You have not considered Lydia's part in this fracas. None of this would have happened without her. I never want to speak to her again.'

Elizabeth saw Kitty's expression harden. 'What did she do?' she asked. 'Was she trying to take the cameo from you? What really happened?'

So, at last, Lizzy learned the truth of Wickham's dealings with Freddie Fanshawe, and of unpaid debts and Lydia's successful attempts at coercion. 'He gave her Georgiana's necklace to buy her silence until he could lay his hands on the fifty pounds she was demanding. He did not intend for her to keep it, but when she showed it to me, and I saw whose it was, I was horrified and asked her to relinquish it.' Kitty suppressed a small shudder at the memory of that evening.

'Of course, she refused?'

'She refused most vehemently! As you can imagine! I tried to reason with her but she became very angry and pushed me away. If she had not lost her balance, I would never have been able to wrest the cameo from her. Naturally, she retaliated and that is when Darcy discovered us! Brawling, as he put it.'

'You could not have explained this to Darcy then?'

'Mr Darcy was in no mood for explanations!' Kitty expostulated. 'Besides it was neither the time nor place. You have no idea how hard I tried to find Colonel Fitzwilliam that evening! Lydia had told me Freddie Fanshawe was a gamester just before the ball commenced and I wanted desperately to discuss the matter with the colonel. I thought he would know what to do for the best. I could not speak with you because you were too busy with your guests, but I soon discovered a ball is not the best time to try to have a private conversation. With anyone!'

Elizabeth was silent, remembering.

'The next morning, when I eventually found Lydia – just before she was sent to Lambton – she told me that Freddie Fanshawe had given her the fifty pounds on condition she say nothing about him having the necklace. She thought that was a fine bargain! She told me I could say I had found it! And then she left, leaving me to face the consequences. Freddie Fanshawe also left that morning, you may recall.' Kitty heard the notes of bitterness that had crept into her voice. 'It does not matter now,' she said in a gentler tone.

'I disagree,' said Elizabeth, moving closer to her sister and looking into her face. 'It matters a great deal and amends must be made, will be made. Darcy wishes to apologise to you in person. He wishes me to make that very clear.'

Kitty nodded. 'I am glad we are friends again, Lizzy,' she said, willing the tears behind her eyes to stay where they were. She could not properly express the emotions she was feeling.

'As am I,' said Elizabeth, giving Kitty a little hug. 'So very glad,' she whispered, as she took her arm and they walked on.

They could see Georgiana and Mr Adams a little way off. They were almost at Gracechurch Street but had stopped to wait for them at the Monument to the Great Fire of London. Kitty waved at them, and she and Elizabeth quickened their pace, once more aware of the chilly January air.

Having escorted the ladies back to the Gardiners' house, Mr Adams took his leave and pledged to return on the morrow, skates in hand. Aunt Gardiner appeared, all smiles and impatient to welcome Elizabeth and Georgiana inside and to hear all their news. She would not hear the half of it, of course, but she remained happily unaware of that.

Chapter 73

The following morning Kitty took to the ice on skates for the first time in her life, and did not fall down. That this, in large part, was due to the unfailing support of the young man by her side is undeniable but neither did her courage fail her. Having been steered along by Mr Adams and thus able to enjoy the peculiar sensation of gliding rather than stepping, she then found she could actually move her feet on the ice and make progress in that way also. They spent an hour or so going around in circles and she was satisfied with that. Clever turns and – heaven forbid! – any attempts at spinning or going backwards she was content to leave to more daring skaters. Hurtling around them at higher speed and with greater noise were the two smallest Gardiners. Their mother had been correct in her predictions about her boys. More daring in nearly every way than their elder sisters, they were fearless in their exploits and falling down was no impediment to their enjoyment. No one lost any fingers to rogue blades and no bones were broken, so Mr Gardiner accounted the excursion a success and one from which he could return home without recrimination.

'I do not think I have ever laughed so much in my life,' Kitty, her cheeks flushed with exercise and exhilaration, told Aunt Gardiner. 'Though I was not sorry to come off the skates and off the ice! It was such fun!'

Mrs Gardiner agreed that it was, then added, 'Your father is in the drawing room, he specifically asked for you on your return. Would you like me to have some tea sent in? Are you still cold?'

Kitty was not cold, she replied, though tea would be appreciated. She went in search of Mr Bennet.

'You are back early, Papa,' she observed. 'Are we expecting Elizabeth this afternoon?'

'Not to my knowledge,' said he. 'But I cannot predict my daughters' movements; I have long given up on such a futile exercise. However, you are the one to whom I wish to speak. Sit down, my dear. I have something to tell you that you may find interesting.'

Kitty sat, wondering why she had been summoned.

'Have you heard of a magazine called *La Belle Assemblée*?'

'I have. In fact, there may well be one or two copies in this very house. I am surprised to hear you speak of it, though!'

'Yes, yes,' said Mr Bennet, peering over his glasses. 'I suppose that was to be expected. Well, here is another one for you.' He fished along the side of his chair and produced a copy of the magazine.

'I had not seen it until yesterday,' he said, leafing through the pages of coloured fashion plates, 'but I understand it to enjoy a fine readership, especially among those ladies who wish to hold a discussion on something other than bonnets. It actually contains reading material, I see.'

'That is so, Papa. Again, I am a little surprised to see you with a copy, but there is always something worthwhile reading.' She smiled at him; he really was so much better.

'I am pleased to hear you say so, child. That will please one of the fusty fellows with whom I share the Reading Room. One of them is the publisher of this magazine. Fellow by the name of Bell. He helped set up the *Morning Post* too, though he doesn't have that any more. He isn't too popular with some of the other publishers in town, says they think he's a mischievous spirit. He tends to innovation and they don't like it. I do, of course.'

'Is this the gentleman who recognised you?' asked Kitty, somewhat bemused by her father's unlikely foray into the world of ladies' magazines.

'No. This is a friend of his. As I say, his taste is not solely given to fashion plates although clearly he knows his market. He has been complaining to me that some of his contributors are entirely unreliable; that the quality of their work is not always of the highest standard.'

He paused, seeming to examine one of the pages of the magazine and, without looking up, said: 'I showed him some of your chapters. He was impressed.'

This last sentence, delivered in Mr Bennet's laconic style and given as much importance as if he had been commenting on the weather, coincided with the arrival of the tea service.

'Ah, good!' said he. 'Let us have some tea, Kitty.'

'Papa, you are joking! This cannot be!'

'Joking, my dear? I am not known for my jocularity. I would like tea, I assure you.'

'Papa! I am not talking about tea! What are you saying? You gave my stories to this man, this publisher? To read?'

'Well, what else does one do with a story but read it? Do you disapprove? I know I said I would not share them with anyone else in this house but this man is a stranger to you.'

Mr Bennet took his tea and sat back in his chair, pleased with himself and the effect his revelations were having on Kitty.

'The publisher of *La Belle Assemblée* likes my stories! I cannot believe it. Which ones did you give him? They weren't ready!'

'He did say something about that,' said Mr Bennet, 'but he realised you could tidy them up. Those were his words, not mine. I take no blame for them.'

'Papa!' said Kitty again

'Yes, child?'

'Papa, are you serious? Please do not joke.'

'I am quite serious, Kitty. Look at me. Do I not look serious?'

Kitty got up from her chair and went over to her father. She looked at him very seriously. 'Papa. Swear to me you are not joking.'

Mr Bennet looked up at his daughter. He appeared to give the matter a lot of consideration. He scratched his nose. He sighed. He appeared disconsolate. 'Oh, very well,' he said at last. 'Miss Catherine Bennet, I swear that the proprietor of *La Belle Assemblée* not only likes your stories but wants to publish them. What do you say to that?'

CHAPTER 74

Kitty's elation at this unexpected turn of events was almost beyond words. She was incredulous; she was disbelieving; she was ecstatic; she was thankful; she was sure there had been a mistake. When a letter from John Bell, received the next day, professional and to the point, confirmed everything her father had told her, she stared at it as if it had magical properties. She longed to share the news and so far none but she, Bell and her father knew of her success. The person she most wanted to tell was Henry Adams and she did not know when he might next visit.

She wished she had organised a music lesson. That at least would provide an excellent reason for him to be at Gracechurch Street.

Elizabeth, Darcy and Georgiana were to dine with them that evening. What could she do in the meantime? She could write, it had after all become a daily habit and Bell had told her which stories he wanted her to revise, but her manuscripts were in his possession still so that was difficult. She sought out her cousins in the nursery but their governess was in the midst of a lesson. She went to the pianoforte and made herself practise some difficult sonatas. This last proved to be her salvation: as if in response to her pleas, some hitherto unknown god of music summoned Henry Adams to Gracechurch Street and into the drawing room.

'Good morning, Miss Bennet,' said he, in his pleasantly rich but otherwise non-celestial tone and quite unaware of the supernatural forces that had brought him to Kitty's side. 'I am come to say that we timed our skating well. There are signs that the ice is cracking and on my way here I saw one of the printing presses being moved nearer to the bank.'

'What will happen?' asked Kitty. 'Will the river flood?'

'My father says it is possible, especially if it rains – and it has not rained for weeks! But whatever happens I fear our frost fair is nearly over. The thaw begins.'

'The thaw begins,' said Kitty. 'That is quite poetic.'

'In what way?' asked Mr Adams, puzzled.

'Oh, just a reference to some family matters,' said Kitty airily, thinking of her conversations with Elizabeth and Georgiana, and her father's intervention on her behalf with a publisher she had previously never heard of.

'You are in very fine spirits today,' observed Mr Adams. 'If I may say so.'

'You may say so!' Unable to keep her news to herself a moment longer, Kitty told him that she had begun to write short stories, for her own amusement although she had secretly wished to be a novelist but did not dare hope that such a thing could happen, and then told him of the publisher's letter she had received only that morning.

He was delighted for her, not in the least bit surprised at her talent, and pleased at her success. That he was not at all familiar with a magazine called *La Belle Assemblée* was easily forgiven, and a copy produced to validate its existence. He looked at it dutifully while Kitty danced around. 'I so wanted to tell you,' said she. 'No one else knows, except of course father.'

'Why are you keeping it secret?' asked Mr Adams, not unreasonably.

'I don't know!' said Kitty. 'Perhaps it is news too good to share!'

'You are perverse, Miss Bennet!' said he, happy to find her so.

'The Darcys are dining with us tonight. If you are not engaged, would you care to join us?' This was daring behaviour for Miss Catherine Bennet; it was not her place to ask anyone to the Gardiners' table without first consulting her aunt, but she hoped she would be forgiven on this occasion.

Mr Adams was delighted to accept, so delighted in fact he excused himself shortly thereafter in order to return at the appointed hour. Perhaps he feared the invitation might be rescinded had he lingered. As soon as he had gone, Kitty went to find Aunt Gardiner to admit her impetuosity. Mrs Gardiner eyed her niece charily for a moment or two, and then said Mr Adams was most welcome.

As she was dressing for dinner, Kitty thought she would like to write a novel set in London; she could place her characters in the frost fair, she could imagine a fortune teller married to the manager of the printing press, there would be a child, a foundling left in the church of St Clement's and a miserly uncle. She had no miserly uncles, but she could invent one, of that she was sure. By the time she arrived downstairs, the miserly uncle was married to a young woman who deserved better and would soon find she had a mysterious benefactor. That will do, Kitty, she told herself, and went into the drawing room to find her father already there.

'Mr Adams is dining with us tonight, Papa. Did Aunt Gardiner tell you?'

'You have told me, Kitty. That is sufficient,' said Mr Bennet, without looking up from his book.

Kitty went to the pianoforte, played a few random notes, and turned back to her father. 'Should I tell the Gardiners? Elizabeth and Mr Darcy?'

'Tell them what, my dear?' asked Mr Bennet.

'About *La Belle Assemblée*, of course!'

'You would like them to know?'

'Of course!'

'It is just that you said you preferred anonymity.'

'Only outside our family, Papa!'

'Ah, I see! But you have just told me that Mr Adams will be here.'

'That does not matter. I mean…' Kitty faltered.

'What do you mean, my dear?' asked Mr Bennet, taking off his spectacles and inspecting them as if this would aid his comprehension.

'It does not matter, Papa! Only I would be pleased if you would tell them for me. I would like that.'

'You would like me to make an announcement?'

'Yes, Papa!' said Kitty, resigned to playing Mr Bennet's game. 'If you would tell them, please. No need to say a loyal toast to the King, or anything like that, just let them know that I am to be published. I would like that very much.'

'Well consider it done, child. It will cause me no pain whatsoever!'

Kitty sat down, smiling in mild exasperation at her father. Shortly thereafter, Mr and Mrs Gardiner arrived in the drawing room and then Kitty heard a carriage clatter to a stop and surmised, correctly, that it was the Darcys'. A few moments later she was face to face with all three.

She watched as Mr Darcy greeted his hosts and Mr Bennet. Then he turned to her.

'Kitty,' he said, 'I am so very pleased to see you again.' He took her arm and led her a few paces away.

'I know,' said Darcy, looking at her earnestly, 'you and Elizabeth have spoken and she has conveyed our deep remorse about our behaviour towards you last August. I heartily regret, and apologise for, my part in that injustice.'

It may not have been the most loquacious speech ever heard but, bearing in mind the speaker, Kitty knew it spoke volumes.

'Thank you,' said she, her tone sincere.

'I hope you will let us welcome you again, both to Berkeley Square and Pemberley. We are very much in your debt, Kitty.'

He smiled at her.

'I do not often see you smile, Mr Darcy,' said she, smiling back.

'I shall try to correct that,' returned he, his face solemn once again. 'Colonel Fitzwilliam called on me this morning. There is much more I want to say but on another day, I think?'

'Of course,' agreed Kitty. 'We should rejoin the others.'

He led her towards them and they were soon part of a larger conversation. Kitty was content to listen. She was thinking about Darcy, about how forbidding she had once found him. I am not afraid of him any more, she thought. I am not afraid at all! It was a most welcome realisation.

Georgiana came to claim her company. 'I have something to tell you,' said she, 'but I can't say what it is.'

'Well that is helpful,' laughed Kitty. 'Am I to guess?'

'You will never guess,' said Georgiana seriously, leaving her friend curious.

'Mr Adams is coming to dine with us,' Kitty told her. 'He should be here at any moment.'

'No?' said Georgiana, her eyes wide with wonder. 'That is remarkable!'

'Well, yes, I suppose it is. Remarkable is not the word I would have used, but it is remarkable in its way.'

'I only meant that it is remarkable that he will be here.'

'Yes,' said Kitty, wondering if Georgiana had temporarily taken leave of her senses.

'My brother will meet him.'

'He will,' said Kitty. 'He has met him before, has he not?'

This tortured exchange was ended with the arrival of the gentleman himself. He had met Elizabeth and Mr Darcy before but this was the first time Henry Adams had greeted Fitzwilliam Darcy in a purely social context. To Kitty's surprise, her brother-in-law detached him from the general group and walked with him to a far corner of the room, where he engaged him in private conversation. Such was the intensity and length of their discourse that it provoked mild interest but no interruption. Kitty wondered at it, but she could see that whatever was being spoken of was not a cause for consternation. They seemed to be enjoying each other's company. Georgiana, meanwhile, was watching her brother and Mr Adams intently. Something was clearly afoot, but Kitty had not the least notion what it could be.

Dinner was announced, bringing the two gentlemen's conversation to a close, and Mr Darcy rejoined Elizabeth in order to escort her into the dining room.

Mr Adams came hurrying over to Kitty. 'I am shocked beyond belief, Miss Bennet, but let me tell you what has just transpired! I can scarce believe it, but Mr Darcy has offered me a living, a parsonage in a village in Derbyshire that is in his gift. Not seven miles from Pemberley.'

Kitty was dumbfounded.

'It is a true,' said Mr Adams. 'He spoke in earnest.'

Kitty remained speechless.

'We should go in,' said the young man, offering his arm.

'We should go in,' she echoed.

'Miss Bennet?'

'Did you accept it?'

'I can only accept it if you will agree to be my wife.'

'Is that what you said?'

'It is.'

'Then you should accept it, Mr Adams!'

'You mean it?'

'I do!'

They went in. She held his arm as though she could not get to her seat at the table without his support and sat down as if seeing everyone around her the first time. Happily Mr Adams was placed beside her, so Kitty felt she had not entirely lost her grip on reality. His own grasp of the proceedings, he would later admit, was overlaid with a sense of wonder.

When, after the first course had been served, Mr Bennet rose from his seat and said he had an announcement to make, both Kitty and Mr Adams were quite startled until she remembered, and whispered to him, that it was about having her stories published.

Mr Bennet cleared his throat and said he would be brief. 'I have always known,' he said, 'that I had one daughter with a modicum of wit and sense.' He raised his glass towards Elizabeth. 'What I did not realise is that I have overlooked the talents of one of my other daughters. I can offer no excuse for this except my own dereliction of duty. Events, sad events, have shown me how wrong I have been. Ladies and gentlemen, you have here among you tonight, a writer and novelist. A lady who seeks anonymity outside this table, but who is known to you all. Her stories, which are clever and amusing, have been accepted and will be published in a magazine called – what is it again, Kitty? – *La Belle Assemblée*? I think it will be but the beginning for her. Ladies and gentlemen, Miss Catherine Bennet, novelist.'

Henry Adams led the applause whilst others around the table took in the news. Georgiana was first to understand and congratulate; only she apart from Mr Bennet had read Kitty's prose. The Gardiners and the Darcys followed in various degrees of happy amazement. Elizabeth, as surprised as anyone, smiled her delight to Kitty, a smile that conveyed pride and affection. Kitty, sitting next to Mr Adams and basking in the praise of those she held most dear, was nearly overwhelmed.

After a little while, Mr Bennet spoke again. 'A thought occurs to me,' he said, 'perhaps because Kitty's delightful prose has reminded me that I really must reply to a letter from one of our dear cousins, a man who is – most fortuitously – not with us tonight. A man to whom obsequiousness is all. I speak of course of our dear Mr Collins. I have been remiss in response to his letter – an excessively long missive – lamenting on the loss of my dear Mrs Bennet, a lady who, as you know, was most vexed by the laws of entail, and even more vexed by our dear cousin himself. Kitty has inspired me, so much so that I might try some fiction of my own. I could not replace Mrs Bennet of course, yet I feel certain she would forgive me if I were, at some point in the future, to write to Mr Collins to moot the possibility of my marrying again, to insinuate that there is yet time to beget an heir. Of course, it may disconcert the fellow! I cannot decide. What do you all think?'

His remarks left those at the table somewhat nonplussed. Henry Adams and Georgiana – who knew Mr Bennet least, and Mr Collins not at all – smiled politely, while others found themselves in need of a moment to gauge the seriousness of his intent. All except Kitty, who shook her head and laughed. 'Papa!' she said. 'Really I do think it would be best if you leave the storytelling to me.'

Acknowledgements

Sincere thanks to my friend and fellow author Christine Westwood, whose unwavering help at all stages of this book's development has been invaluable.

Thank you also to Selwa Anthony, whose feedback and belief in *What Kitty Did Next* encouraged me to look for a publisher in the United Kingdom.

The wonderfully enthusiastic and able team at RedDoor – Heather Boisseau, Clare Christian and Anna Burtt – has made me most welcome and I feel privileged to be part of the RedDoor catalogue. Thank you also to my editor, Nicky Gyopari, proofreader Matilda Richards, and to Clare Shepherd for her cover design, and patience.

Lastly, my heartfelt thanks to Jane Austen, who could not have imagined that her novels would have delighted and inspired – and continue to delight and inspire – millions of people all around the globe. Without her, this book could not have been written. She is incomparable, of course, and this novel a mere homage. I only hope that, were she able to read it, she would not be too vexed at this trespass into her world.

About the Author

*C*arrie Kablean began her career in London, where she was born, and now lives in Australia. Arriving in Sydney in 1990 (via eight years in Papua New Guinea, during which time she edited the local newspaper on Bougainville), she was with *The Australian* newspaper for more than twenty years, and was also a theatre critic for the *Sunday Telegraph*. *What Kitty Did Next* is her first novel; a second, also set in Regency England, is a work in progress.

www.carriekablean.com

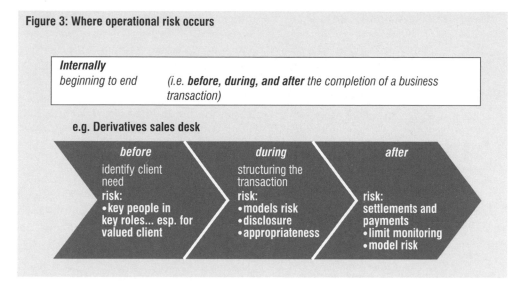

Figure 3: Where operational risk occurs

processes, aided by technology and external dependencies to achieve certain business objectives. Therefore it makes sense to define operational risk as the potential for loss due to failures of people, processes, technology, and external dependencies. This is a comprehensive definition. It includes the back-office risk, sometimes referred to as operations risk, legal risk, and reputation risk, fraud, systems failures, rogue trading, and so on.

This is similar to the industry definition that was synthesized from the BBA ISDA RMA survey[1] on operational risk.

Sources of operational risk

As we have said, it is important to note that operational risk is not limited to the risk associated with processing transactions by the back office, perhaps its traditional focus. Operational risk permeates the institution. It starts before the transaction, continues during and remains after the transaction is completed.

Figure 3 illustrates the operational risk in a typical derivatives sales desk. Before the transaction is actually negotiated, the firm is exposed to various operational risks. For example, the firm may be dependent on an extremely specialized sales force with special relationships with highly valued clients. If the key people leave, the valued clients may leave with them. The firm may also be exposed to risks associated with inappropriate soliciting, etc. During the transaction it may be exposed to model risk, which may wrongly price the transaction, and to inappropriate sales practices. Finally, after the transaction has been negotiated, the firm may be exposed to market losses due to failure in the limit-monitoring systems and processes. This is not meant to be an inventory of all the things that can go wrong, it is intended to emphasize that operational risk arises from beginning to end.

Additionally, operational risk can arise not only from the things that the firm does but also from things that others do, or fail to do, and on which the firm is dependent.

[1] *Operational Risk: The Next Frontier* by the British Bankers Association, ISDA, and Robert Morris Associates. The study is the first published report and analysis of operational risk technology, practice and management. The survey included more than fifty global financial institutions.

This flow of risk from the external to the internal is becoming increasingly important as firms focus on core competencies and outsource the rest. Outsourcing is often regarded as a way to take out the cost of delivering a service, and without due consideration of the new risks that have been taken on, a wrong decision may be made.

Who manages operational risk?

As a result of the fact that firms have been managing operational risk for a long time, many groups already have partial responsibility for managing operational risk. Any attempt to improve the management of operational risk must therefore take these various groups into account. So who are these groups (see Figure 4)? First, there are the risk takers, i.e., business management, who through their daily activities and decisions affect the level of risk. Then there are various functional or infrastructure groups which provide specialized services, such as legal, compliance, technology, etc. Risk management clearly has a role to play in the management of operational risk, ranging from risk control to tools development to proactive portfolio management, although traditionally this role has been very small. The increased attention to operational risk has led many firms to create operational risk management groups within risk management, and therefore the importance of risk management to the overall management of operational risk is increasing rapidly. Senior management is of course responsible for setting the risk appetite, and internal audit is responsible for ensuring the integrity and completeness of the entire risk management process.

With all these groups involved, who is actually responsible for operational risk management? Clearly, no one group has total responsibility. In another sense, all are responsible, but unless they are integrated into one process, i.e., singing from the same song sheet, there is potential for either under-management of certain risks and over-management of others, or both. Getting this right is important. Otherwise, instead of the structure contributing to the enhanced management of operational risk, it actually contributes to the amount of operational risk taken.

As Figure 5 illustrates, in most banks senior management receives various reports on aspects of operational risk, ranging from legal, compliance, system issues, audit reports, etc., and perhaps even an operational risk report, which may cover

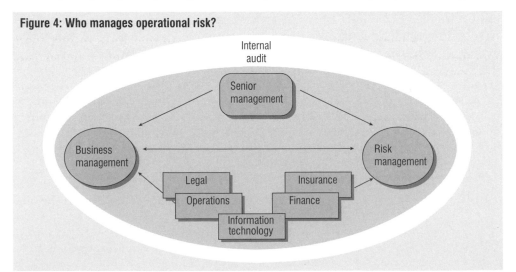

Figure 4: Who manages operational risk?

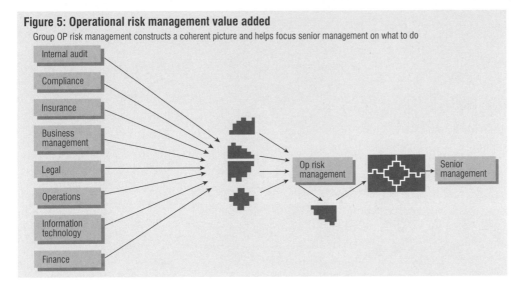

Figure 5: Operational risk management value added

Group OP risk management constructs a coherent picture and helps focus senior management on what to do

some of the issues already discussed in the other reports. Senior management is then left with the difficult task of creating a coherent picture of the operational risk taken by the firm.

Instead, the operational risk management group can assemble and synthesize the various components of the risk into a coherent risk profile. This frees senior management to add value by determining the maximum acceptable level of operational risk in the context of business strategy and by determining the degree of congruence between the potential rewards from that strategy and the risk taken. Senior management can also ensure that there is alignment between the various operational risk management strategies being executed in the various businesses and the overall business and risk management strategy of the bank. But to achieve this synthesis, the operational risk group must have appropriate enabling tools. For the picture to be synthesized, these tools must have the ability to measure all the different types of operational risks with a coherent and common basis.

Measuring operational risk: the qualitative approach

Operational risk managers often start by identifying the many key operational risk indicators in a bank or business line, and then try to find ways to link these indicators to loss levels and root causes. Although this has intuitive appeal, care must be taken. Otherwise an endless list of all the things that can go wrong is created, with no way of knowing what is important and what isn't. And if the firm's internal audit process is working well, the list has already been implicitly prioritized and only the material ones are reported. So what is the value in creating a new list? If the audit process is not working well, the firm is well advised to fix it, rather than creating a work-around process. Operational risk management must supplement the audit findings. We will explore how to do this later.

The same is true of root cause analysis. Rarely is the cause of an operational risk failure due to one major cause – it is often a confluence of failures in people, processes, technology, and external dependencies. No one factor on its own would have resulted in a material loss. As a result, without a coherent conceptual framework of the drivers of operational risk, root cause analysis often reduces to an arbitrary categorization exercise or to the endless list again. Take the Barings disaster, for example. It is easy to say that the root cause was the lack of separation of duties. But had management paid attention to the audit findings, or investigated the need for the very large funding by the relatively small operation, or had there been a different culture at the bank, and so on, the outcome would probably have been rather different. Perhaps the root cause was the Kobe earthquake, which led to the unsustainable losses. It is quite possible that without the earthquake, the positions could have come back and cleaned up. Barings would still be around, and no one would have known about it.

That is not to say that separation of duties is not an important mechanism for managing operational risk. What we are saying is that business management realizes that in a perfect world, with unlimited resources, every operational risk management process would be perfectly implemented, and every potential cause of an operational failure would be eliminated. However, in practice, management is about making the right tradeoffs. And to do that, a clear understanding of the potential rewards and the potential risks is needed. For example, suppose that not implementing separation of duties saves, say, $300,000, while the potential loss, as understood by management, is less. Clearly management should not spend the money to ensure separation of duties. This example is somewhat simplistic, but it illustrates the point about making the right tradeoff. Of course, the crux is as understood by management. So one of the most important value-adding contributions of operational risk management is to determine the financial impact of the risks taken and make these transparent to management – in short, to quantify the financial impact of the risk.

Measuring operational risk

The quantitative approach

The actuarial methodology borrowed from the insurance industry is the approach that has been the most fruitful for quantifying operational risk. The actuarial methodology is stochastically based and relies on creating frequency and loss given occurrence (severity) distributions for each type of operational failure. These are then combined using either Monte Carlo simulation techniques or various analytical methods to create the loss distribution. Once the loss distribution is created, the worst-case loss, to a certain confidence level, can be determined. One of the main attractions of this approach is that the results are directly comparable to the well-established market VaR models and to the various emerging credit VaR models. Throughout the remainder of this article, this statistically determined worst-case operational loss will be referred to as the operational value-at-risk, or Op VaR. Having a common measurement for each type of risk enables the firm to determine the total value-at-risk and makes portfolio management of market, credit and operational risk possible.

The actuarial methodology can be applied either within a top-down or a bottom-up framework. In a top-down framework, the methodology is applied to determine the operational value-at-risk at the firm level, and perhaps complemented with some allocation mechanism to determine the operational value-at-risk at the business unit level. The allocation mechanisms tend to be based on some measure of business activity, with expenses being one of the most popular. This top-down approach has limited use to business unit management, as it tends to ignore business-specific risk. Nevertheless, at the firm level it can provide a reasonable estimate of the overall operational risk.

In a bottom-up framework, the operational value-at-risk is determined for each business unit and then aggregated to obtain the firm-wide operational value-at-risk. This approach can be tailored to meet the specific operational risk management needs of each business, while preserving the overall methodology.

The statistical approach

Either way, the frequency and severity distributions must be created and the first thing to look at is the historical loss experience. Unfortunately, at least from the statistical perspective, there is a scarcity of internal loss data; fortunately, one might say from the management perspective, this must mean we have had very few failures in the past. However, the lack of internal data is not entirely due to the lack of frequent actual operational failures, but rather that the losses from these failures were not usually separately identified and reported. In most instances they would have been reported as part of other losses, such as market losses for rogue trading, and in higher expenses or lower revenues every time there was a system failure. Investing resources in desegregating historical losses may not produce sufficient data, especially the lower-frequency higher-severity losses, to be able to fit a statistical distribution. This is only natural, since those firms that experience those high-severity low-frequency events rarely survive intact.

The next step is usually to collect the loss experience of other firms and create the distribution with the combined internal and external data. The external data can be obtained from public sources such as news agencies, or from several commercial vendors. However, using external data to complete the data set surfaces three immediate obstacles that must be surmounted before the frequency and severity distributions can be created.

The first has to do with the relevancy of the external data to one's firm. No two firms have the same management, the same client, product, delivery channel, and infrastructure mixes, even though they are part of the same industry. Therefore the external data has to be modified using a relevancy factor to transform the external loss into a reasonable estimate of similar potential loss at one's firm. Determining the right relevancy factor is best done involving experts from risk management, business management, and the appropriate infrastructure management. Nevertheless, a high degree of subjectivity remains, and it is not certain that a different group of experts can reproduce the result.

The second obstacle has to do with the size of the loss. How are the losses experienced at one firm to be applied in estimating the potential for a similar loss at a similar firm, but operating at a different scale? For example, a firm with 1,000 financial advisers dealing with an average portfolio size of $5 million will experience a different frequency and severity of losses from a firm with 5,000 financial advisers and servicing an average portfolio size of $200,000. Although there seems to be very little correlation between the size of the firm and the size of the loss, as the example illustrates there have to be some distinguishing variables that connect the size of the loss to the characteristics of the firm.[2] Additional research is required to determine variables.

[2] Private discussions with external data vendors such as ORI, NetRisk, and Pricewaterhouse-Coopers.

The third obstacle has to do with the source of the external losses. These are typically available from news agencies or commercial vendors. Only the larger losses are reported and therefore using this external data may actually exaggerate the potential loss. There are now several initiatives to gather and share all internal operational losses, which once operational will correct the distortions of the current sources.

In addition, every time there is a big operational loss at some other institution, management asks for a review of activities within their firms. This is quickly followed with changes in either people processes, or technology, and a corresponding reduction or at least transformation of the operational risks. As a result, history may be not very reliable for predicting potential losses. So what to do?

The scientific approach

Let us begin with the end state and work backwards. The goal is to produce a loss distribution, which will allow the firm to determine the operational value-at-risk, and to identify the risk drivers (those variables) that determine the shape of the distribution.

Risk drivers are different from risk indicators. Risk indicators are a list of all the possible variables that may affect the shape of the loss distribution. Risk drivers are the variables that actually affect the distribution in a major way. They are the few variables (20 percent) which explain most of the risk (80 percent). This may sound confusing, so perhaps an analogy may help to clarify the distinction. Consider the operational risks associated with driving a car. Historical risk indicators about the driver, the car, and the driving environment could be collected. The list could include such things as the number of headaches the driver experiences in a year, the level of frustration with their job or family, the amount they drink, the number of miles driven, the state of the car's brakes. It may also include how many of the signal lights function, and how well, the age of the car, how often the car has broken down in the past. Other risk indicators concern when the driving is done, how often, during what traffic conditions, and during what type of weather conditions. This is only a small sample – the list can be as long as desired. However, the problem with the list being so long is that it is next to impossible to determine the level of risk or even the relative amount of risk between, say, two different drivers driving different cars in different driving environments. One has to be satisfied with simple, broad categories of high, medium, and low risks. There is, however, a better way.

The insurance industry has found it useful to develop a set of risk drivers, which capture the effects of a large chunk of risk indicators, and have a determining effect on the level of risk. For example, certain age and gender mixes (the risk drivers) are good proxies for determining the propensity to drive when having a severe headache, to drink and drive, to drive in bad conditions, etc. (the risk indicators). Similarly, knowing the few risk drivers allows the operational risk manager to measure operational risk with sufficient accuracy to be of value.

Another example of the power of risk drivers, or their equivalent, can be found in the scientific study of gases. The variables needed to determine the physical properties of the gas from the individual properties of each of the molecules that compose the gas are so numerous that no progress would have been made with this approach. Instead physicists created some macro variables such as temperature, volume, and pressure that summarize a great deal of information about the molecules that compose the gas. These macro variables allowed engineers to design all sorts of machines. The operational risk drivers are the equivalent of those macro variables.

The search for the risk drivers starts from recognizing that the operational loss distribution is itself a composite loss distribution, composed of individual loss types, each having its own characteristic loss distribution, and therefore characteristic risk drivers. Most operational risk can be classified into 11 loss types. These are:

- theft and fraud
- rogue trading
- transactions processing errors and omissions
- model risk
- lawsuits
- regulatory fines and sanctions
- loss or damage to assets
- market losses due to operational failure
- credit losses due to operational failure
- revenue management
- cost management.

These are exhaustive, but not mutually exclusive.[3] Rogue trading is a form of fraud, and model risk is a form of transaction processing error and omission, to name just a couple. However, these types of risk have caused some of the most severe and prominent operational losses, so it is worthwhile to separate them into their own distinct operational loss types.

A loss distribution for each of these loss types must be created, and as we have said, in order to do this the underlying frequency and severity distributions must be created. The distributions for each loss type can be determined from the individual people, process, technology and external dependencies risk drivers. Furthermore, each of these should reflect availability, capability, and capacity.

After all this, the question remains: how? Rather than approaching this as a statistics problem, where we know there is a scarcity of relevant data, a more fruitful approach is to apply the scientific method. In other words, begin with observations, develop a working hypothesis, and modify the hypothesis as data becomes available. Observations of distributions used by the insurance industry have revealed that many insurable failures follow the Poisson distribution for frequency and a lognormal distribution for severity. This is a good place to start. The working hypothesis for each of the 11 operational loss types is that their frequency and severity distributions are Poisson and lognormal respectively.

Having selected the distributions, the amount of data required is actually quite small. In fact, for the Poisson distribution all that is required is the expected frequency of the particular failure, and the full distribution is determined. For the severity distribution, all that is required is the expected severity and the variance of the loss given occurrence. The problem of obtaining the loss distribution has therefore been simplified to obtaining three variables. Sounds fantastic, but not really when the power of the mathematics is considered. How are the values for the variables to be obtained?

Where the relevant historical data exists, these three variables can be estimated

---

[3] Based on experiences at CIBC, all operational losses analyzed, including those contained in external loss databases, have been found to fit into one of these 11 loss types.

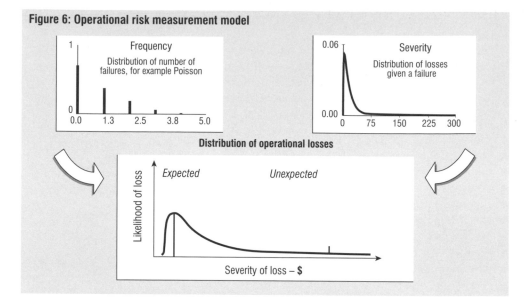

Figure 6: Operational risk measurement model

Frequency

Distribution of number of failures, for example Poisson

Severity

Distribution of losses given a failure

Distribution of operational losses

Likelihood of loss

Expected   Unexpected

Severity of loss – $

directly. For example, for credit card losses, most institutions have enough data to actually fit the distributions. Where there is insufficient relevant data, scenario analysis can be used to determine the values.

Scenario analysis works like this. First, create a set of expected frequency bands, for example once per year, once in three years, once in five, once in ten, and so on. These bands can be made as granular as required, although it is usually better to start with fewer bands. Otherwise much unproductive energy is spent arguing about the best fit among one of the very many bands, as opposed to moving on with the issue at hand, i.e., obtaining a reasonable first estimate of the loss distribution. To some, this approach may appear unrealistic, since in reality events rarely fit into neat buckets. However, bear in mind that the same approach has been found very useful in determining the value of risk of a bond. Although the interest yield curve is continuous, it is quite common to group cashflows into discrete time buckets and use the sensitivity of the cashflows at these discrete buckets to approximate the value-at-risk for a bond. The same approximation is being applied here.

Selecting the appropriate frequency band for a particular loss type can be achieved by determining the associated exposure base, exposure rate, and risk drivers. For example, the number of traders can be the exposure base for rogue trading and the exposure rate is the proportion of those traders that will potentially turn rogue. The number of transactions done per trader in a given time period, say a year, along with a variety of other risk drivers can be used to slot the expected frequency of a rogue trading incident into one of those frequency buckets. Once the expected frequency is thus determined, the entire distribution is determined since the Poisson distribution provides a reasonable approximation to actual distribution.

The expected severity of a rogue incident can be related to the average transaction size and the market VaR per average transaction. To complete the severity distribution, the variance of the severity is also required, and this can be obtained from the variance of transaction sizes.

At this point, the reader may be expecting a revelation of all the risk drivers and the mathematical function that relates the risk drivers to the expected values. The

Figure 7: Measuring operational risk by loss type for each business

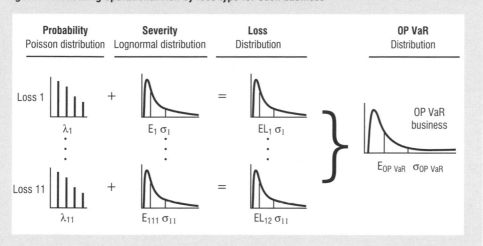

fact is that the functions are not known, and from a mathematical point of view this is a dead end. However, business management is not about having the right formulas. It is about making informed decisions with limited information. So the same principle is applied here. The relationship is determined through an iterative, disciplined, and rigorous process of testing out the implications of expert judgements. This may make the mathematicians cringe, but it is done regularly in business with much success. For example, most business plans, especially for new ventures, are created through an iterative process of refining the expert judgements through the rigors of balance sheet, income statement, and cashflow analysis. The rigorous process creates the risk drivers from expert judgement, and subsequent observations modify them.

This needs to be done for each of the 11 loss types and for each business line, and often for sub-loss types within each loss type. For example, in the case of credit card fraud the frequency and severity distributions for account takeover fraud may be sufficiently different from, say, no-card fraud that separate distributions are warranted. However, here too a balance must be struck between sufficient accuracy and sufficient timeliness and cost. A broadly correct answer, obtained at minimal cost, is much more useful than a very accurate answer obtained two years later and at much cost.

Making the most of the limited data, expert judgements from scenario analysis, and some reasonable assumptions about the nature of the frequency and severity distributions, a sufficiently useful model of operational risk can be built. However, the model needs to be continually tested against the reasonableness of its implications and against new data as it becomes available. As the model is used, imperfections will be revealed. And the assumptions should be modified to provide more and more accurate fits. It may be, for instance, that for certain loss types the negative binomial or the binomial is a better fit than the Poisson distribution. This improvement-through-use approach ensures that the time is spent on extracting useful risk management information from the imperfect model, rather than perfecting the model beyond the capability of the institution that will use it. Instead, the imperfections are fixed as required.

The individual loss distributions for each loss type have to be aggregated to get the operational risk distribution for a business unit. To do this requires knowledge of the correlation among the 11 loss types. As a first approximation, the correlation can be set at zero. This is probably not always the case, but it is a reasonable assumption as it is unlikely that multiple and distinct operational failures will happen at the same time. It is more likely that a certain operational failure will affect more than one business unit. For example, the technology group will often support many businesses, likewise for finance and other infrastructure groups, and a failure in any one of these will affect all the businesses they support, albeit with varying degrees of severity. Therefore in aggregating operational risk across business units, it is reasonable to use a correlation of one. This probably over-estimates the risk, and from a risk management perspective a slight overestimation is better than underestimation.

In addition, business units share the franchise value of the firm. If the operational failure of a particular business unit damages the franchise, the operational losses from that failure will be experienced by most if not all the business units that comprise the firm. For instance, continued unavailability of the internet banking service may cause some clients to transfer all their business to another financial institution, and this may have a substantial effect on, say, the wealth management group. This interconnectivity of risk goes beyond correlation. In fact, as the above example illustrates, it may magnify what is a small operational risk in one business unit into a large problem in another business. Scenario analysis is one way to take interconnectivity into account.

Figure 8 is a schematic showing how the various pieces discussed above fit into an integrated operational risk measurement process. Inputs such as scenario analysis, operational risk exposure bases, rates and risk drivers, internal loss history, and

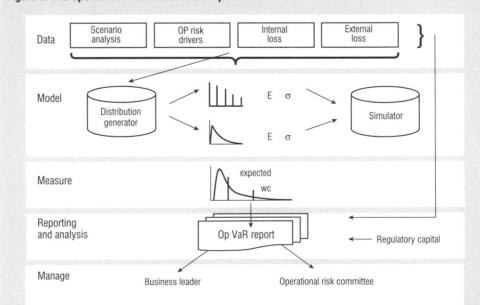

Figure 8: The operational risk measurement process

external loss history are factored into a distribution generating process that involves mathematics and expert business judgement. The outputs are the frequency and severity distributions, which in turn are fed into a simulator to generate the loss distribution. From the loss distribution and the various inputs such as the risk drivers, analytic reports are produced which help business unit management and senior management, as well as the risk committee, to understand more fully the nature of the operational risk they are exposed to and to better manage those risks. Should regulatory capital for operational risk be required in the future, the same process can be applied to either generate the operational regulatory capital or at the very least analyze its impact.

So far we have addressed the measurement of operational risks. Now we will explore how the measurement can be put to use in improving the management of operational risk. First, however, it is important to observe that the risk indicators that proved not to be terribly useful for measuring the risk are indeed important to the business unit manager. The car analogy may once again clarify the meaning. To the driver of the car, about to embark on a journey, the risk of that trip is very much dependent on the state of the car, the weather conditions, the state of the roads, and the state of the driver. Being aware of all these risk indicators allows the driver to adjust their driving. The risk manager is interested in determining what happens when those adjustments fail, and to do so requires knowledge of the risk distribution and its risk drivers, not the indicators.

Reporting operational risk

The above methodology allows the operational risk to be sliced and diced, to drill down and to aggregate as required. No one of these perspectives is sufficient to give a complete picture of the operational risk profile, but by viewing and analyzing these different perspectives, a sound understanding of the operational risk facing the firm can be gained.

As illustrated in Figure 9, the operational risk can be ranked in descending order

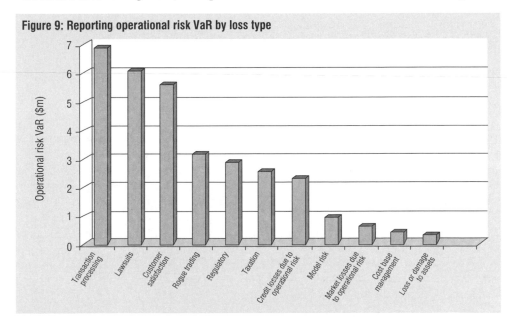

Figure 9: Reporting operational risk VaR by loss type

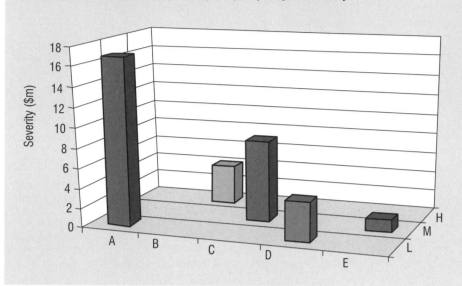

Figure 10: Transaction processing – analysis by frequency and severity

of exposure, which can focus management attention on the high-risk areas.[4] Also, the graph can readily show any concentration of risk, which management may wish to limit and monitor closely. Without a measurement of the risk, such management action would not be possible. And limiting a particular risk may have a profound effect on those new initiatives or expansion plans, which would add to that particular risk.

Although all the numbers have been created for illustration purposes, the value of such an actual operational risk profile is evident. For example, the graph shows that transaction risk is the highest risk, and a further drill-down (not illustrated here) would reveal that transaction risk accounts for about 25 percent of the total operational risk. The top three risks account for 70 percent of all the operational risk. Any one of these risks can be analyzed in terms of its exposure base, exposure rate, and risk drivers. To facilitate analysis, the risks can be aggregated into three broad areas: high, medium, and low risk, with actual numbers supporting the categories. This goes far beyond a simple intuitive ranking of risks into high, medium, or low.

Drill-down is possible. For example, transaction processing, the highest risk in this example, can be decomposed into its frequency and severity components, as illustrated in Figure 10. For illustrative purposes, the probabilities have been banded into high, medium, and low, but there are actual numbers behind them, reflecting the expected value of the underlying Poisson distribution. The value of the severity in the graph is the worst-case severity obtained from the severity distribution. Also mapped are the different business units, here identified as A through E. At a glance, it is quite clear that business unit B has a high frequency of transaction processing failures, but it also has a relatively low severity. By comparison, business unit A has a relatively high severity, but a low failure rate.

[4] The chart is based on actual results, although the values for each loss type have been randomly

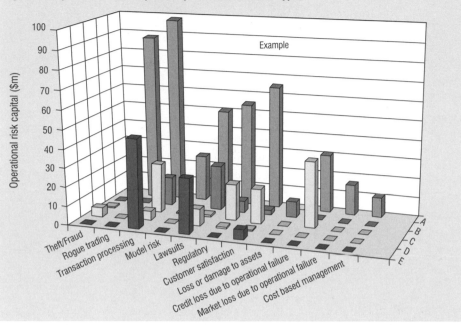

Figure 11: Operational risk capital – by business and loss type

The higher potential loss of business unit A may merely reflect that business A processes higher valued transactions, which is inherent to the business. In such a case little can be done to reduce the risk since the failure rate is already low. Business unit B, on the other hand, even though it has a lower absolute potential loss may require attention because it has a high failure rate. It is important to stress the "may" – the high failure rate may not mean poor risk management, it may simply reflect that the right risk-reward tradeoff has been made. In other words, management may have decided that it makes economic sense to have the higher expected failure rate, rather than spending the money to reduce it. Without such a model there would be no way of knowing that. Instead, pressure would likely be placed on the management of business unit B to fix the problem, even though in reality it may not be a problem.

The power of the model is further illustrated in Figure 11, which shows the capital that has been attributed to each business unit based on the Op VaR for each loss type. At a glance, management can determine which businesses are the biggest users of operational risk capital and for what reasons, and use this information to develop the appropriate management actions, such as actions to address the frequency or severity of a particular operational risk, or the entire risk profile.

Managing operational risk: economic capital

The operational risk profile for either a specific business unit or for the bank as a whole generally follows a distribution as shown in Figure 12. The operational risk profile can be divided into three distinct losses. There is the expected loss, the worst-case loss at specified confidence level (Op VaR), and the catastrophic loss. Expected losses should be built into the business plan as a cost of doing business, and whenever possible incorporated into the pricing of the products or services offered. That is not to say that these should not be managed down, but it should be

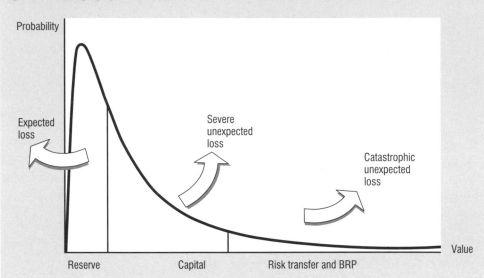

Figure 12: Managing operational risk

recognized that beyond a certain point the benefit of a further reduction is outweighed by the cost.

Capital should be set aside to absorb unexpected losses up to a pre-selected confidence level, the Op VaR level. This recognizes that, despite excellent management, failures will occur and capital is there to absorb the losses, and ensure that the firm continues as a going concern.

Catastrophic losses cannot be supported by capital. These are low frequency, high severity losses, which can be managed much more effectively through other means. In fact, capital is expensive, and allocating enough capital to support these rare and extreme events would make the entire business uneconomical. This is similar to what is done for credit and market risk. For example, capital is allocated to support unexpected credit losses up to some confidence level, and not to support the extreme event that the entire credit portfolio goes into default. There simply isn't enough capital, and even if there were, all loans would have to be priced so high to recover the return on the capital that no business would be done. Therefore if capital were allocated for extreme events instead of acting as a buffer to ensure the survival of the firm, it would in fact kill the firm. Of course, the potential for catastrophic losses needs to be managed, but the arsenal of management tools required to manage this risk is different from that required for non-catastrophic risks. Catastrophic risk is managed by having effective business recovery plans and through various risk-transferring alternatives, ranging from insurance to some of the emerging capital market solutions. Even the actuarial model may not be sufficient to measure these risks accurately and may have to be substituted by extreme value theories.

Proactive portfolio management

Active portfolio management of operational risk should be integrated into the day-to-day and strategic business decisions. This involves reengineering business activities by changing people, processes, technology, and external dependencies so as to achieve the desired risk profile, consistent with the business strategy and the firm's tolerance for risk. This means:

- identifying and measuring the operational risk under normal and stressed conditions;
- incorporating expected operational losses into the business plan, and pricing for this risk whenever possible;
- allocating economic capital for unexpected, non-catastrophic losses;
- implementing loss management programs that
  — avoid certain risks altogether, and for other risks
  — reduce the frequency of a loss and
  — reduce the severity of the loss should the loss happen;
- managing concentration risk by reengineering activities to ensure that the business is not exposed to simultaneous multiple losses due to a single event. This is a well-known method for controlling credit risk, now being transferred to operational risk management;
- implementing effective business recovery plans;
- buying loss protection in the form of insurance and other effective risk-transfer solutions, such as captive-reinsurance combinations and capital market insurance securities, such as Catputs.

These actions should be carried out not only for ongoing business activities but for all new products and initiatives before they are launched.

Important future developments

The quantification of operational risk will proceed rapidly over the next few years. As with market and credit risk, there will soon be several vendors that will provide bottom-up operational risk measurement systems to complement the existing top-down systems. There are already several industry initiatives developing standards for classifying operational risk losses and for sharing internal loss data. As these initiatives take hold, the current actuarial models will be made more robust and will have much wider application. In a few years' time, many firms will be actively using operational risk measurement models to proactively manage their operational risk. These same models can form the basis for the regulatory capital requirements for operational risk at sophisticated firms.

Causal models which help business management implement risk management strategies will be developed further and will be expanded to include a wide variety of activities, beyond the current transaction processing focus.

As illustrated in Figure 13, the integration of operational risk and insurance management within firms is another exciting development. Traditionally, these have operated in silos, rarely exchanging information even though they are addressing many of the same risks. As a result, insurance is probably purchased for risks that are already supported by capital, and capital is being allocated to risk that is already covered by insurance. Regulators impose the purchase of insurance even though provisions against these risks may already have been made through capital.

The future will show an explosion of the traditional corporate insurance market, which has included as the major categories property and casualty, professional liability, and bond insurance. Already some insurers are expanding their offers to cover other forms of operational risks such as credit card fraud, rogue trading, and some legal liabilities. It is early days, but as operational risks become more widely

Figure 13: Where do we go from here?

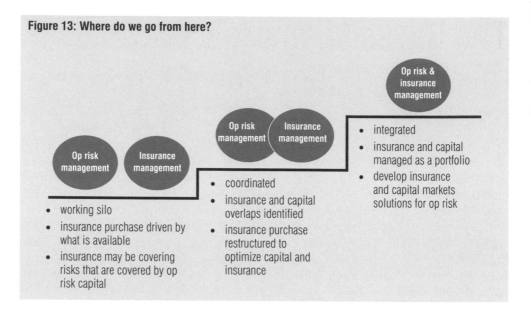

measured, these types of coverage will expand rapidly. Looking even further into the future, it seems that firms will manage capital, insurance, and operational losses on an integrated basis. This will also spur the evolution of insurance derivatives, which will greatly improve the management of operational risk, in much the same way that credit derivatives have done for credit risk management.

Conclusion

Some doubt that operational risks can be measured, or even if measurable, some question its use. After all these people would say operational risk management is all about good business management. To those that doubt that it can be done, I say look at the insurance industry. It has been successfully measuring some operational risks for years. And besides how do we know that it can't be done until we try. That is what science is all about. To those that doubt the usefulness of the measure, I ask them if they would not like to know the magnitude of the financial impact of the inevitable operational failure that will occur despite the best efforts of good management. Finally to those bankers that say that earnings should cover operational risk not capital, I wonder what they would say to a borrower who asks the banker for 100 percent financing, without collateral or any other form of capital cushion, and instead ask the banker to rely only on the future earnings stream of the business venture.

Summary

Tony Peccia examines the design of an operational risk framework, which incorporates the quantification of operational risk at the business unit level, including business-specific risk drivers, and integrating into a RAROC framework. The chapter demonstrates how operational risk management can be incorporated into the business management process, including setting aside appropriate reserves for expected losses, capital for unexpected severe losses, and business recovery and risk transfer strategies for catastrophic losses. It also explores issues surrounding organizational structure for the effective enterprise-wide management of operational risk. It concludes with a look into some promising early developments, which point the way for future developments, in particular the integration of insurance and operational risk management.

The Bayesian approach to measuring operational risks

by Carol Alexander

The imposition by regulators of minimum standards for capital to cover "other risks" has been a driving force behind the recent interest in the quantification of operational risks. When the 1988 Basel Accord imposed a minimum ratio of qualifying capital to risk weighted assets of 8 percent, the capital was intended to cover "other risks" in addition to the credit risks used in the risk weighting. Credit risks will now be assessed by separate internal models and the "other risks" element might be thought of as the additional capital required to restore risk capital to the original level. However, this rather crude view of operational risk capital gives little indication of how capital charges might be pegged to the activities of individual banks in a level playing field.

The Basel 2 Accord that is due in 2001, for implementation in 2004, will outline a three-stage approach to the assessment of capital charges for operational risks:

- in stage 1, operational risk capital will be a proportion of a simple volume indicator such as gross revenue;
- in stage 2, the charges will be disaggregated according to business lines;
- in stage 3, the charges for each business line will be internally calibrated according to the type of operational risk.

By the time the amendment is implemented it is expected that many banks will be using the stage 2 or stage 3 models; a fourth stage is under discussion that will allow banks to define their own business lines, risk types and loss distributions.

Operational risks include many different types of risk, from the simple "operations" risks of transactions processing, unauthorized activities, and system risks to other types of risk that are not included in market or credit risk, such as human risks, unauthorized activities risks, legal risk and information risks.[1] If banks are to measure operational risk capital using stage 3 models it must be clear which risks should be included in operational risk capital charges, and which risks should be the primary focus for developing good operational risk management practices. The first section of this article argues that regulators should focus on low-

---

[1] Transaction processing risk is the risk of loss arising from incorrectly executing or funding a transaction or not receiving funds or securities. Systems risk is the risk of loss arising from computer failures or system infiltration, and the risk of breakdown of other systems. Unauthorized activities risk is the risk of loss arising from individuals operating outside their authority. Human risk is the risk of loss arising from inadequate staffing for required activities due to lack of training, poor recruitment processes or working culture, loss of key employees or poor management. Information risk is the risk of loss arising from inappropriate decision making due to erroneous data such as on client quality. Legal risk is the risk of loss arising from financial disclosure errors, or change in regulations or legal incompetence. After much discussion, "reputational" risks will not be included. Reputational risk is the loss arising from reputational events or external events such as political upheaval and involvement in legal action.

frequency high-impact risks for capital adequacy; on the other hand, high-frequency low-impact risks should be the main concern for internal risk management. If the capital charges from a stage 3 model include charges for high-frequency low-impact risks, the capital charge will be a percentage (gamma) times the expected loss. These risk types may have larger expected loss than low-frequency high-impact operational risks, but their standard deviation of loss is generally much lower. Therefore the gammas that should apply to high-frequency low-impact risks should be relatively small.

There are several types of operational risk and within each risk type a variety of quantitative data could be used to assess the extent of operational risks. At the "top-down" level, quantitative data may be based on gross income, or expenditure, or average asset holdings; at the "bottom-up" level, quantitative measures may be based on errors, failures and other performance indicators, internal or external risk ratings or risk scores and direct and indirect financial losses.[2] The problem with any model for operational risk is that these data are inadequate. For example:

- gross revenue or annual settlement throughput data have a tenuous relationship with operational loss. Consequently, the proportional charges that regulators plan to introduce in stage 1 may be very inaccurate;
- internal loss event data for low-frequency high-impact risks such as fraud may be too incomplete to estimate an extreme value distribution for measuring the tail loss. However, augmenting the database with external data may not be appropriate;
- internal risk ratings are based on assessments of the size and frequency of operational losses, or the percentage of errors, from all the different activities in a business line. These data are likely to be inaccurate when they are based on only a few observations.

The inadequacy of the data means that subjective choice is much more of an issue in operational risk than it is in market or credit risk measurement. Unlike market risk, there is limited scope for quantifying operational risks using observable, and therefore "objective", data. Even when hard data are available it will be necessary for the modeling process to incorporate decisions that result in subjective choice. For example, internal risk-rating models are based on subjective estimates of the probabilities and the impacts of events that are thought to contribute to operational loss.

Whenever subjective choice on model parameters influences estimates, one must

---

[2] In the same way as with market and credit risk, if operational risk capital is to be assessed by a profit and loss distribution, it may be thought of as the cover for unexpected loss, the distance between the expected loss and the tail loss. For regulatory purposes, profit and loss distributions are based on a ten-day risk horizon and a 99 percentile for market risk, and a one-year horizon with a 99 percentile for credit risk. It may well be that the 99 percentile is also taken as the generic "tail" loss measure for operational risk. Any higher percentiles would compound the measurement difficulties associated with scarcity of data, but any lower percentile would include too many events that the firm will have to control with internal processes. The appropriate risk horizon for operational loss distributions is not easy to determine. There is even less uniformity here than there is with different market and credit risks. For example, a fraudulent trader could be fired within a day, whereas indirect financial losses that arise from a poor working culture could take years to turn around. The current consensus opinion is that about three months might be a reasonable time-horizon for most operational loss distributions.

employ a Bayesian analysis. In fact, any model that incorporates subjective data or prior beliefs is a form of Bayesian model. These models therefore have a crucial role to play in modeling operational risks. The aim of this article is to introduce Bayesian methods and outline their applications to the measurement of certain operational risks. The first section distinguishes between high-frequency low-impact and low-frequency high-impact operational risks and the Bayesian methods that are relevant for modeling each type. The second section introduces Bayes' rule and Bayesian estimation. A simple application of Bayesian estimation to operational risk scores is mentioned, but the main purpose of this first section is to lay the foundations for the next two sections. The third section explains how Bayesian methods are applied to simulate loss distributions for high-impact low-frequency risks where data are sparse; a combination of an extreme value distributions and Bayesian simulation is emerging as the preferred internal model for high-impact low-frequency operational risks such as unauthorized activities risk.

The fourth section of this chapter explains how Bayesian belief networks (BBNs) and influence diagrams may be used for measuring and managing high-frequency low-impact operational risks, such as transaction processing risks and human risks. Bayesian networks have long been used for the modeling of an operational process:[3] if the attributes of certain types of operational risks can be identified, the Bayesian network will model the relationship between these attributes and their contribution to the performance of the process. In simple terms, a Bayesian network is a model for a multivariate distribution. As with every model, it not unique; it is a picture of the mind of the modeler. There is no single Bayesian network that is capable of modeling an operational risk for all institutions; the network must be specific to the institution.

Although there is no generic Bayesian network, they have many advantages. They:

- increase transparency of the process and often provide insights that would otherwise be obscured;
- facilitate scenario analysis and stress testing, whereby the manager may identify maximum operational losses;
- may be used for the integration of operational risks with market and credit risks;
- can incorporate management decision processes; indeed, Bayesian networks have been used successfully in the management and decision sciences.[4]

Frequency and impact: implications for management and regulation

Ensuring that firms have sufficient capital to cover risks other than credit and market risk is not the only purpose of regulation. Supervisors should be open and accommodating to market innovations that enable certain operational risks to be insured, or securitized, or mitigated in some other way. Most banks view capital

---

[3]The extensive literature on Bayesian networks goes back over a decade: see Pearl (1988), Neapolitan (1990) and Jensen (1996). Duncan Wilson (1999) of Ernst and Young, London first drew my attention to the potential for Bayesian network modelling of operational risks. Applications of Bayesian networks to modelling operational risks are also described in King (2001).

[4]See Howard and Matheson (1984), Geoffrion (1987), Morgan and Henrion (1990), Heckerman et al. (1995) and Henrion et al. (1986). Other important applications of Bayesian networks and influence diagrams include reliability analysis – see Fenton and Littlewood (1991) – and the design of expert systems – see Henrion et al. (1991) and Neapolitan (1990).

charges as secondary to good risk management practice, so it is most important that regulators provide the correct incentives. Understanding the models of different types of operational risks, those that are likely to jeopardize the ability of the firm to function at all, and those that have their primary effect on the daily mark-to-market, is the first stage.

Statistical models of financial risks are often based on the calculation of a (profit and) loss distribution;[5] and if not the whole distribution, at least certain parameters such as the expected loss and the upper 99 percentile "tail" loss. In market and credit risks the expected loss is taken into account in the mark-to-market, in the pricing or provisioning for the portfolio. By the same token, operational risks that have a direct and measurable effect on the balance sheet should be quantified by both expected loss and tail loss. Control procedures and provisioning should be required for the expected loss; risk capital could be required to cover the tail loss.

Some high-frequency low-impact operational risks such as settlement risk have an expected loss that is much larger than the standard deviation of loss. The tail loss for this type of operational risk may have a relatively small impact on the ability of the firm to function, but the expected loss may have a relatively large impact on daily profit and loss. Therefore the important issue to address is the establishment of a good risk management processes. On the other hand, low-frequency high-impact operational risks such as fraud have a relatively small expected loss but a tail loss that could have an enormous influence on the firm's ability to operate. Therefore regulators should be concentrating on these operational risks for capital charges.

Under stage 3 models the capital charge for each risk type in each line of business will be a multiple (gamma) of the expected loss given by $PE \times LGE \times EI$, where EI is an exposure indicator such as the volume of transactions. Internal models for calculating the probability of a loss event (PE) and the loss given the event (LGE) will require quite different approaches: low-frequency high-impact operational risks are amenable to the use of Bayesian estimation using external data for priors, and classical statistical distribution fitting (perhaps with Bayesian simulation for parameter estimation); high-frequency low-impact risks are amenable to modeling with either a classical distribution fitting method or a Bayesian belief network. The main focus of this chapter is to demonstrate the advantages of the Bayesian methods.

In the fourth stage that is currently under consideration the bank may be able to calculate the expected loss directly under its own definitions of business lines and risk types. Even with stage 3 models banks will be able to define their own gammas, using a "risk profile index," if their loss distributions are demonstrably far from the industry-wide norm. A comparison of the gammas that should be applied, for different types of operational risks, is given in Pézier and Pézier (2001).

Bayes' rule and Bayesian estimation

A basic assumption in a classical statistical model is that at any point in time there is a "true" value for a parameter. Given that there is a "true" (but unknown) fixed value for each parameter in the model, the model gives the probability of the data. The Bayesian approach to statistical inference was introduced by the Reverend

---

[5] Operational risks can of course lead to profits and not losses. For example, a delayed time stamp on a ticket might result in an inflated mark-to-market, and a settlement delay might lead to a profit instead of a loss.

Example 1: Human risk

Operational losses that are incurred through inadequate staffing for required activities are commonly termed "human risks". These may be due to lack of training, poor recruitment processes, inadequate pay, poor working culture, loss of key employees, bad management, and so on. Some operational risk score data on human risks might be available, such as expenditure on employee training, staff turnover rates, numbers of complaints, and so on. But human risk remains one of the most difficult operational risks to quantify because the only information available on many of the important attributes will be subjective beliefs.

A simplified example illustrates how Bayes' rule may be applied to quantify a human risk. Suppose you are in charge of client services, and your team in the UK has not been very reliable. In fact, your belief is that one-quarter of the time they provide unsatisfactory service. If they were operating efficiently, customer complaint data indicate that about 80 percent of clients would be satisfied. This could be translated into "the probability of losing a client when the team operates well is 0.2". But your experience shows that the number of customer complaints rises rapidly when a team operates ineffectually, and when this occurs the probability of losing a client rises from 0.2 to 0.65. Now suppose that a client of the UK team has been lost. In the light of this further information, what is your revised probability that the UK team provided unsatisfactory service?

To answer this question, let X be the event "unsatisfactory service" and Y be the event "lose the client". Your prior belief is that prob(X) = 0.25 and so

$$\text{prob}(Y) = \text{prob}(Y \,|\, X)\, \text{prob}(X) + \text{prob}(Y \,|\, \text{not } X)$$
$$\text{prob (not } X)$$
$$= 0.65 * 0.25 + 0.2 * 0.75 = 0.3125$$

Now Bayes' rule gives the posterior probability of unsatisfactory service, given that a client has been lost, as:

$$\text{prob}(X \,|\, Y) = \text{prob}(Y \,|\, X)\, \text{prob}(X) / \text{prob}(Y)$$
$$= 0.65 * 0.25 / 0.3125 = 0.52$$

Thus your belief that the UK team does not provide good service one-quarter of the time has been revised in the light of the information that a client has been lost. You now believe that they provide inadequate service more than half the time.

Thomas Bayes (1702–1761) in his "Essay towards solving a problem in the doctrine of chances," published posthumously in 1763. Bayesian models give the probability of the model parameters, given what is observed in the data; the approach is one of continuously revising and refining our subjective beliefs about the state of the world as more data become available.

The cornerstone of Bayesian methods is the theorem of conditional probability of events X and Y:

$$\text{prob}(X \text{ and } Y) = \text{prob}(X \,|\, Y)\, \text{prob}(Y) = \text{prob}(Y \,|\, X)\, \text{prob}(X)$$

This can be rewritten in a form that is known as Bayes' rule, which shows how prior information about Y may be used to revise the probability of X:

$$\text{prob}(X \,|\, Y) = \text{prob}(Y \,|\, X)\, \text{prob}(X) / \text{prob}(Y) \tag{1}$$

When Bayes' rule is applied to distributions about model parameters it becomes:

$$\text{prob}(\text{parameters} \,|\, \text{data}) = \text{prob}(\text{data} \,|\, \text{parameters}) * \text{prob}(\text{parameters}) / \text{prob}(\text{data})$$

The unconditional probability of the data "prob(data)" only serves as a scaling constant. Denoting the parameters by θ and the data by X, the generic form of Bayes' rule is usually written as:

Figure 1: The posterior density is a product or the prior density and the sample likelihood

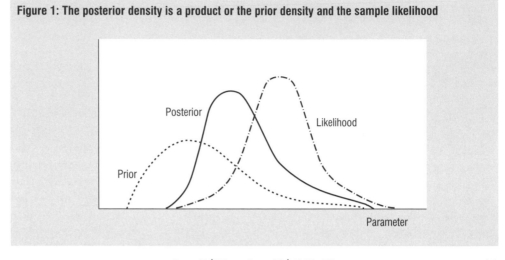

$$f_{\theta|X}(\theta|X) \propto f_{X|\theta}(X|\theta) * f_\theta(\theta) \qquad (2)$$

Prior beliefs about the parameters are given by the *prior density* $f_\theta(\theta)$ and the likelihood of the sample data $f_{X|\theta}(X|\theta)$ is called the *sample likelihood*. The product of these two densities defines the *posterior density* $f_{\theta|X}(\theta|X)$ that incorporates both prior beliefs and sample information into a revised and updated view of the model parameters, as depicted in Figure 1.

If prior beliefs are that all values of parameters are equally likely, this is the same as saying there is no prior information. The prior density is just the uniform density and the posterior density is equivalent to the sample likelihood. More generally, the posterior density will have a lower variance than both the prior density and the sample likelihood. The increased accuracy reflects the value of additional information, both subjective as encapsulated by prior beliefs and objective as represented in the sample likelihood.

Subjective beliefs may have a great influence on model parameter estimates if they are expressed with a high degree of confidence. Figure 2 shows two posterior

Figure 2: The posterior density for (a) uncertain prior beliefs and (b) confident prior beliefs

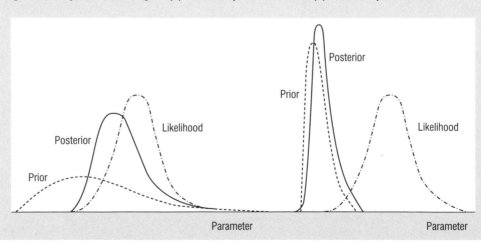

densities based on the same likelihood. In Figure 2a prior beliefs are uncertain and this is represented by the large variance of the prior density. In this case the posterior density is close to the sample likelihood and prior beliefs have little influence on the parameter estimates. In Figure 2b, where prior beliefs are expressed with a high degree of confidence, the posterior density is much closer to the prior density and parameter estimates will be much influenced by subjective prior beliefs.

It is not just prior expectations that have an influence: the degree of confidence held in one's beliefs also has an effect. Bayesian analysis simply formalizes this notion: posterior densities take more or less account of objective sample information depending on the confidence of beliefs, as captured by the variance of prior densities. There is no single answer to the question of how much sample information to use and how confident prior beliefs should be. As with any statistical model, the only way one can tell which choices are best for the problem in hand is to conduct a thorough back testing analysis.

Classical estimates of model parameters are optimal according to some given criterion, such as minimum variance or maximum likelihood. When available, the maximum likelihood approach is commonly regarded as the best of the classical methods because it will produce consistent estimators under fairly general assumptions. However, when viewed from the Bayesian perspective, maximum likelihood estimation (MLE) is rather a crude method. To see this, note that Bayesians regard the process of finding a point estimate of a parameter as a decision. A loss function is defined on the parameter estimate. Standard loss functions are:

- *zero-one*, where the loss is zero if the estimate equals the "true" parameter value, and one otherwise;
- *absolute*, where the loss equals the absolute value of the difference between the estimate and the "true" parameter value;
- and *quadratic*, where the loss equals the square of the difference between the estimate and the "true" parameter value.

Having chosen a loss function, the expected loss under the posterior distribution may be calculated; then the Bayesian estimate is the parameter value that minimizes the expected loss.

It can be shown that with the zero-one loss function the Bayesian estimator will be the maximum (mode) of the posterior; with the absolute loss function the Bayesian estimator will be the median of the posterior; and with the quadratic loss function the Bayesian estimator will be the mean of the posterior. Now it is clear that MLE corresponds to a Bayesian estimator that is rather crude: with no prior information, so that the posterior is the likelihood, and a zero-one loss function so that the estimator is the maximum of the likelihood. Therefore Bayesian estimators are far more general than classical estimators and contain some of the best classical estimators as simple special cases.

Maximum likelihood estimators are not always "no information and zero-one loss" Bayesian estimators. Consider, for example, the MLE of a proportion or percentage. If n "occurrences" are observed in a sample size m, the MLE is n/m and the accuracy of this estimate as measured by its standard error will depend on the sample size. Contrast this with the standard Bayesian estimator of a proportion or probability p;

normally this will be based on a beta prior of the form $f(p) \propto p^a(1-p)^b$ for $0 < p < 1$. With a quadratic loss function a few calculations show that the Bayesian estimator will be $(n + a + 1)/(m + a + b + 2)$. Now, if viewed from this Bayesian perspective, the MLE of a probability is based on the prior $f(p) \propto p^{-1}(1-p)^{-1}$. Therefore the use of the MLE of a probability has the implicit belief that the probability is highly likely to be very near zero, and equally likely to be very near one. It is hard to think of practical applications where prior beliefs of this form would be appropriate.

Banks that wish to qualify for stage 3 models under the Basel 2 proposals will need to estimate, for each risk type and each line of business, the probability of a loss event. These probabilities will be very difficult to estimate for low frequency high impact risks, since very few internal loss events will be available. Bayesian estimation techniques may therefore be considered as a way of smoothing these probability estimates (e.g. by using external data for the beta prior).

Operational risk scores often take the form of simple proportions or percentages: the percentage of failed trades, of system downtime, employee turnover rates, of errors in transactions processed, and so on. A problem arises if these risk scores are to be estimated with the usual MLE when little data are available. Point estimates may be produced from the hard data available, but the reliability and robustness of these figures will be open to question. The standard errors of the estimates will be high, but a standard operational risk scoring method will not include this standard error.

For example, suppose a percentage error, such as the percentage of failed transactions, has been recorded over many weeks. The total number of transactions per week is usually of the order of 10,000 and the number of failed transactions is usually between 300 and 500, so the MLEs of the percentage of failed transactions are usually between 3 percent and 5 percent each week. Let us suppose that the mean number of transactions and the mean number of fails per week are 10,000 and 400 respectively. Now suppose that for one week there were only two trading days during which only 3,000 transactions were recorded and 150 of them failed. Then the MLE for this week would be 5 percent, which is on the high side but still within normal bounds. However, the Bayesian estimate of the same thing would be 4.11 percent. It differs because it takes into account the data from previous weeks in the prior density; the fact that the current estimate is based on less data than usual is captured by the imprecise sample likelihood, relative to a fairly confident prior, so that the Bayesian estimate will be closer to the prior mean than the maximum likelihood of the current sample.

This section has aimed to introduce the reader to basic concepts in Bayesian statistics. The next two sections describe the two main approaches that have useful applications to the quantification of operational risks using internal models.

Extreme value distributions and Bayesian simulation

Extreme value distributions are a class of distribution that only applies to extreme values (see Fisher and Tippet, 1928). They have useful applications to risk capital allocation methods that focus on extreme values of returns or exceptional losses. Exceptional losses over a high and pre-defined threshold u are extracted from the loss data X.

The 'excesses over threshold' $Y = \text{Max}(X - u, 0)$ are often modelled using the generalized Pareto distribution (GPD), one of the extreme value distributions that has found useful applications to the measurement of significant but rare events. The point-process of exceedances has a Poisson character. Leadbetter at al (1983) give the theoretical background and results on convergence to the Poisson process in detail. The combination of a GPD distribution for loss impact and a Poisson process for frequency is called the 'Peaks over Threshold' (POT) model. It has been extensively studied in many papers by Smith (1987) and other references in the suggested further reading. O'Brien, Smith and Allen (1999), Ceske and Hernandez (1999), Cruz (1999) and King (2001) have all explored the use of extreme value theory for the measurement of operational risks. The frequency of exceptional loss events is modelled by a Poisson distribution and the loss severity is fit by a GPD. These are combined in a Monte Carlo simulation to generate the exceptional loss events that should contribute to the risk capital provision.

Exceptional events occur with very low frequency, by definition. However the classical (MLE) approach to fitting the parameters of the GPD model is only applicable when sample sizes are large. Estimation procedures for the POT model have been developed by Pickands (1975) and other references in the suggested further reading. An alternative, Bayesian approach to estimating the GPD parameters has been advocated recently: see Bernardo and Smith (1994). Following Medova (2000) a conceptual overview of hierarchical Bayesian methods is given in this section.

The distribution function G_u of excess losses Y over a high and pre-defined threshold u has a simple relation to the distribution $F(x)$ of X, the underlying loss. In fact, the distribution of $Y = \text{Max}(X - u, 0)$ may be regarded as the conditional distribution of X given that $X > u$:

$$G_u(y) = \text{prob}(X - u < y \mid X > u) = [\, F(y + u) - F(u) \,] / [\, 1 - F(u) \,]$$

For many choices of underlying distribution $F(x)$ the distribution $G_u(y)$ will belong to the class of generalized Pareto distributions given by:

$$G_u(y) = \begin{cases} 1 - exp\,(-y\,/\,\beta) & \text{if } \xi = 0 \\[2mm] 1 - (1 + \xi y\,/\,\beta)^{-1/\xi} & \text{if } \xi \neq 0 \end{cases}$$

In the peaks over threshold (POT) model the frequency of excess losses is modeled by a Poisson process. The Poisson distribution has one parameter, λ, called the intensity of the process. It represents the average number of excesses over the threshold u during the sampling interval. This parameter is related to the shape parameter ξ of the GPD: for $x > u$, $\lambda = (1 + \xi\,(x - \mu)/\sigma)^{-1/\xi}$ where μ and σ are the mean and standard deviation of X. It can be shown that $\beta = \sigma + \xi(u - \mu)$ so the parameters of the POT model are $\theta = \{\xi, \mu, \sigma\}$.

The threshold must be predefined. Medova (2000) suggests that an appropriate value for θ would be the integrated market and credit value-at-risk quantile. The excesses over threshold are calculated and then Bayes' rule may be applied to obtain a posterior density for the POT parameters. The parameter estimates are then obtained using an absolute loss function, i.e. taking the median of an empirically generated posterior density.

The simple form of Bayes' rule $f_{\theta|X}(\theta\,|\,X)\propto f_{X|\theta}(X\,|\,\theta)^*f_\theta(\theta)$ is extended so that the parameters θ are assumed to be normally distributed random variables whose density function $f_{\theta|\psi}(\theta\,|\,\psi)$ depends on a set of "hyper" parameters ψ. The hyper parameters are therefore the mean and variance of normally distributed random variables. A further layer of the hierarchy is added so that ψ are assumed to be bivariate normal-gamma random variables with density function $f_{\psi|\varphi}(\psi\,|\,\varphi)$ determined by a set of hyper-hyper parameters φ. Bayes' rule becomes:

$$f_{\theta|X,\psi}(\theta\,|\,X,\psi)\propto f_{X|\theta}(X\,|\,\theta)^*\,f_{\theta|\psi}(\theta\,|\,\psi)^*\,f_{\psi|\varphi}(\psi\,|\,\varphi)$$

By Bayes' rule: $f_{\theta|\psi}(\theta\,|\,\psi)^*\,f_{\psi|\varphi}(\psi\,|\,\varphi)\propto f_{\psi|\varphi,\theta}(\psi\,|\,\theta,\varphi)$ therefore Bayesian updating of the posterior density $f_{\theta|X,\psi}(\theta\,|\,X,\psi)$ takes the form:

$$f_{\theta|X,\psi}(\theta\,|\,X,\psi)\propto f_{X|\theta}(X\,|\,\theta)^*\,f_{\psi|\varphi,\theta}(\psi\,|\,\theta,\varphi)$$

Initially values for $\theta=\theta_0$ are chosen so that the hyper parameters $\psi=\psi_0$ have a high variance, to reflect the lack of information on these parameters before the loss data are taken into account. Combining these priors with the sample data in the form of the likelihood $f_{X|\theta}(X\,|\,\theta)$ and applying Bayes' rule gives the posterior density $f_{\theta|X,\psi}(\theta\,|\,X,\psi)$.

It will be necessary to simulate the posterior density. Analytic forms for posteriors exist only in special cases, when priors are said to be "conjugate" with the functional form of the likelihood. The Bayesian updated parameter estimates $\theta=\theta_1$ are obtained by taking the median of the empirical density. The process is repeated many times. After sufficient iterations the Bayesian simulation forgets the initial state of the parameters and converges to a stationary posterior distribution. However, the computations are extremely burdensome because computational intensity has been substituted for the low-quality of the data.

This type of hierarchical model has been applied to statistically dependent operational losses across business types. Alternatively it may be applied to a specific business unit or firm across different types of risks. In principle the method applies to the full matrix of operational losses by risk factor and business unit (see Dempster et al., 2001)

Bayesian belief networks

Over recent years there has been increasing interest in the use of Bayesian belief networks to model operational risks.[6] Reasons for this interest include:

- a BBN describes the factors that are thought to influence operational risk, thus providing explicit incentives for behavioural modifications;

[6] A commercial Bayesian network package for measuring operational risks has been developed by Algorithmics in consultation with Jack King (Genoa, UK). It is available from www.algorithmics.com. There are several software packages for Bayesian networks that are freely downloadable from the internet. The examples in this article have been generated using an excellent package called Hugin lite (downloadable free for research purposes from www.hugin.com). Microsoft provides a free package for personal research only that is Excel compatible at www.research.microsoft.com/research.dtg/msbn/default.html and a list of free (and other) Bayesian networks software is on http.cs.berkeley.edu/~murphyk/Bayes/bnsoft.html

Figure 3: A simple BBN for the client services problem

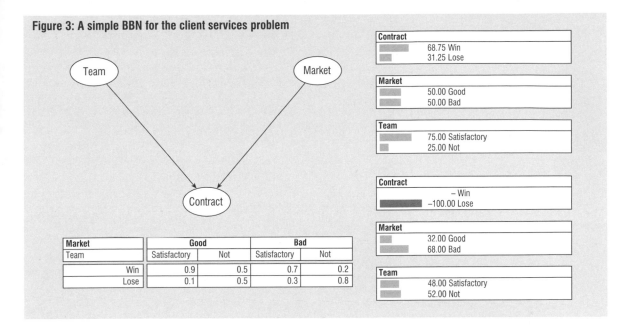

Market	Good		Bad	
Team	Satisfactory	Not	Satisfactory	Not
Win	0.9	0.5	0.7	0.2
Lose	0.1	0.5	0.3	0.8

- BBNs have the ability to perform scenario analysis to measure maximum operational loss, and to integrate operational risk with market and credit risk;
- BBNs have applications to a wide variety of operational risks. Over and above the categories where available data enable the modeling of operational risk with standard statistical models, BBNs have applications to areas where data are more difficult to quantify, such as human risks;
- augmenting a BBN with decision nodes and utilities improves transparency for management decisions.

The basic structure of a BBN is a directed acyclic graph where nodes represent random variables and links represent relationships between the variables. There is no unique BBN to represent any situation, unless it is extremely simple. Rather, a BBN should be regarded as the analyst's view of process flows, and how the various factors interact. In general, many different BBNs could be used to depict the same process.

A simple BBN that models the client services team of Example 1 is shown in Figure 3. The nodes "Team", "Market" and "Client" represent random variables, each with two possible outcomes, and the probability distribution on the outcomes is shown on the right of the figure. It is only necessary to specify the probability distribution of the two parent nodes (Team and Market) and the conditional probabilities for the contract. The four conditional probabilities, "prob(win | market = good and team = not satisfactory)" and so on, are shown below the contract node. The network then calculates prob(win) = 68.75 percent and prob(lose) = 31.25 percent, using Bayes' rule. Then the BBN may be used for scenario analyses. For example, if the contract is lost, what is the revised probability of the team being unsatisfactory? The bottom right box in Figure 3 shows that the posterior probability that the team is unsatisfactory given that the contract has been lost is 52 percent, as already calculated in Example 1.

More nodes and links should be added to the BBN until the analyst is reasonably

Figure 4: Network architecture for settlement loss

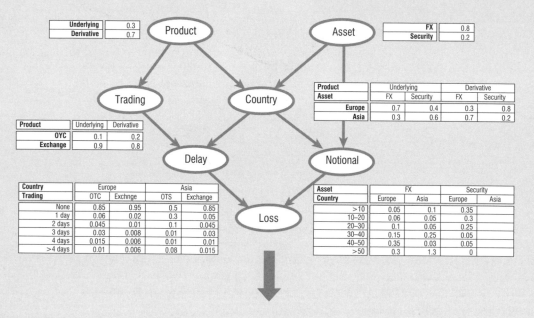

Underlying	0.3
Derivative	0.7

FX	0.8
Security	0.2

Product	Underlying	Derivative
OYC	0.1	0.2
Exchange	0.9	0.8

Product	Underlying		Derivative	
Asset	FX	Security	FX	Security
Europe	0.7	0.4	0.3	0.8
Asia	0.3	0.6	0.7	0.2

Country	Europe		Asia	
Trading	OTC	Exchnge	OTS	Exchange
None	0.85	0.95	0.5	0.85
1 day	0.06	0.02	0.3	0.05
2 days	0.045	0.01	0.1	0.045
3 days	0.03	0.008	0.01	0.03
4 days	0.015	0.006	0.01	0.01
>4 days	0.01	0.006	0.08	0.015

Asset	FX		Security	
Country	Europe	Asia	Europe	Asia
>10	0.05	0.1	0.35	
10–20	0.06	0.05	0.3	
20–30	0.1	0.05	0.25	
30–40	0.15	0.25	0.05	
40–50	0.35	0.03	0.05	
>50	0.3	1.3	0	

Delay	None					
Notional	<10	10–20	20–30	30–40	40–50	>50
0	1	1	1	1	1	1
0–1,000	0	0	0	0	0	0
1,000–2,000	0	0	0	0	0	0
2,000–3,000	0	0	0	0	0	0
3,000–4,000	0	0	0	0	0	0
4,000–5,000	0	0	0	0	0	0
5,000–10,000	0	0	0	0	0	0

Delay	3 days					
Notional	<10	10–20	20–30	30–40	40–50	
0	0.4	0.4	0.4	0.4	0.4	
0–1,000	0.6	0.3	0.2	0.1	0.1	
1,000–2,000	0	0	0.2	0.1	0.1	
2,000–3,000	0	0	0.2	0.1	0.1	
3,000–4,000	0	0	0	0.3	0.1	
4,000–5,000	0	0	0	0	0.2	
5,000–10,000	0	0	0	0	0	

Delay	1 days					
Notional	<10	10–20	20–30	30–40	40–50	>50
0	0.2	0.2	0.2	0.2	0.2	0.2
0–1,000	0.8	0.4	0.2	0.2	0.1	0.1
1,000–2,000	0	0.4	0.2	0.2	0.1	0.1
2,000–3,000	0	0	0.4	0.2	0.1	0.1
3,000–4,000	0	0	0	0.2	0.1	0.1
4,000–5,000	0	0	0	0	0.4	0.1
5,000–10,000	0	0	0	0	0	0.3

Delay	4 days					
Notional	<10	10–20	20–30	30–40	40–50	
0	0.5	0.5	0.5	0.5	0.5	
0–1,000	0.5	0.3	0.2	0.1	0.1	
1,000–2,000	0	0.3	0.2	0.1	0.1	
2,000–3,000	0	0	0.1	0.1	0.1	
3,000–4,000	0	0	0	0.2	0.1	
4,000–5,000	0	0	0	0	0.1	
5,000–10,000	0	0	0	0	0	

Delay	2 days					
Notional	<10	10–20	20–30	30–40	40–50	>50
0	0.3	0.3	0.3	0.3	0.3	0.3
0–1,000	0.7	0.3	0.2	0.1	0.1	0.1
1,000–2,000	0	0.4	0.2	0.1	0.1	0.1
2,000–3,000	0	0	0.3	0.2	0.1	0.1
3,000–4,000	0	0	0	0.3	0.2	0.1
4,000–5,000	0	0	0	0	0.2	0.1
5,000–10,000	0	0	0	0	0	0.2

Delay	>4 days					
Notional	<10	10–20	20–30	30–40	40–50	
0	0.6	0.8	0.8	0.6	0.6	
0–1,000	0.4	0.2	0.1	0.1	0.1	
1,000–2,000	0	0.2	0.1	0.1	0.1	
2,000–3,000	0	0	0.2	0.1	0.05	
3,000–4,000	0	0	0	0.1	0.05	
4,000–5,000	0	0	0	0	0.05	
5,000–10,000	0	0	0	0	0.05	

confident of his prior beliefs about the parent nodes. In the client services example the factors that are thought to influence team performance, such as pay structure, appraisal methods, staff training and recruitment procedures, can all be added as parent nodes to the Team node.[7] Later in this section we shall see how decision nodes and utilities can be added to a Bayesian network to facilitate management decisions.

Settlement risk

Settlement risk is the risk of loss arising from interest foregone, fines imposed or borrowing costs as a result of a delay in settlement. It does not include the credit loss if the settlement delay is due to counterparty default, but it may include any legal or human costs incurred when settlement is delayed. A complete process model of settlement failure could include client information, details of counterparty confirmations, valuation matching between front and back office, legal entity confirmation, trade capture, window dressing, remote booking, and so forth.[8] The model presented in Figure 4 uses a simple macro perspective, but it is sufficient to illustrate the important points, namely how BBNs:

- specify the attributes of an operational loss distribution;
- back test against historical loss event data to revise the network parameters;
- employ scenario analysis to identify maximum operational loss.

Data from the trading book provide the probabilities for each node in Figure 4a. For example, the probabilities assigned to the "Country" node show that 70 percent of spot FX trades are in European currencies, and 20 percent of derivative securities trades are in Asia. Similarly, the "Delay" node shows that only 50 percent of over-the-counter trades in Asia experienced no delay, 0.6 percent of exchange-traded European assets experienced five or more days' delay in settlement, and so on. The "Notional" node shows that 35 percent of European FX trades were in deals in the $40m–50m bracket, but just 5 percent of trades in European securities fell into this bracket. Obviously this picture of the settlements process is not unique.[9]

The loss is calculated as a function $L(m,t)$ of the notional m and the number of days' delay t. This function depends on many things, including the settlement process (delivery vs payment, escrow, straight-through, and so on), and whether legal and human costs are included in settlement loss. In the example, the notional of a transaction is bucketed into $10m brackets, and the loss distribution is given in round $000s. So for example the loss distribution in the initial state, shown in the

---

[7] If a node has many parent nodes, these conditional probabilities can be difficult to determine because they correspond to high-dimensional multivariate distributions. An alternative approach is to define a BBN so that every node has no more than two parent nodes. In this way the conditional probabilities correspond to bivariate distributions, which are easier for the analyst to visualize.

[8] Source: Personal communication with John Hedges, Financial Services Authority, London.

[9] For example, the analyst might wish to categorize trades not just by country and asset type but also according to whether the trades were in derivatives or the underlying. In that case the architecture of the network should be amended by adding a link from the "Product" node to the "Notional" node. Alternative architectures could have the "Country" node as a root node, or other nodes could be added such as the settlement process or the method for order processing. Most nodes in this example have been simplified to have only two states, so "Country" can be only Europe or Asia, "Asset" can be only foreign exchange or security, and so on. The generalization of the network to more states in any of these variables is straightforward.

Figure 5: Scenario analysis for settlement loss

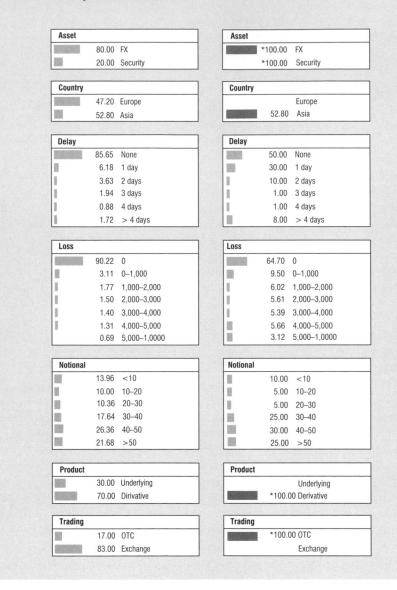

left column in Figure 5, gives an expected loss of \$239.3 per transaction and a 99 percent tail loss of approximately \$6,750 per transaction.

Which is the best of many possible specifications of a BBN for settlement loss will depend on the results of back tests. A number of network architectures for modeling settlement loss should be tested and for each the initial probabilities[10] should be based on the current trading book. The result of the network in this initial state could then be compared with the current settlement loss experienced. A basis for back testing is to compare the actual settlement loss that is recorded with the

[10] That is, the probabilities from the initial propagation of the network, before it is propagated again for scenario analysis.

predicted loss, using a simple goodness-of-fit test. By performing back tests over suitable historic data – perhaps weekly during a one-year period – the best network design would be the one that gives the best diagnostic statistic in the goodness-of-fit test.

Scenario analysis

BBNs lend themselves very easily to scenario analysis. The operational risk manager can ask the question: "What is the expected settlement loss from over-the-counter trading in Asian FX futures?" The right column in Figure 5 illustrates this scenario: per transaction, the expected loss is $957.7 and the 99 percent tail loss is approximately $8,400. Similarly, the manager might ask: "What is the expected settlement loss from an FX trade in the $40m–50m bracket?" By setting probabilities of 1 on FX in the "Product" node and on $40m–50m in the "Notional" node, the answer is quickly calculated as $303.9m.

BBNs are not the only models that will generate a settlement loss distribution; after all, if historic data are available for back testing the BBN, they could be used to generate a simple, empirical settlement loss distribution. One might therefore ask, why bother with the BBN? To take the view that there is no need for a BBN misses the whole point, which is that BBNs improve transparency for internal management: they identify the attributes or factors of an operational loss and how they inter-relate. BBNs also lend themselves easily to scenario analysis so that operational risk managers can identify the types of trades and operations where the settlement process is likely to present the greatest risk; and by simulating scenarios on market risk factors such as interest rates and exchange rates, and credit risk factors such as credit ratings, managers can judge how operational risks could be integrated with market and credit risks.

Human risk

Human risk has been defined as the inadequate staffing for required activities, due to lack of training, poor recruitment processes, loss of key employees, poor management or poor working culture. Models of human risk may be based on key performance indicators rather than on direct loss event data. It is not essential to establish global standards for performance indicators for the purpose of internal management, but management will need to clarify which indicators are used.

The balanced ccorecard approach developed by Kaplan and Norton[11] examines performance indicators across four dimensions:

- financial (e.g. percentage of income paid in fines or interest penalties);
- customer (e.g. proportion of customers satisfied with quality and timeliness);
- internal processes (e.g. percentage of employees satisfied with work environment, professionalism, culture, empowerment and values);
- learning and growth (e.g. percentage of employees meeting a qualification standard).

Process models of human risk may be based on the balanced scorecard. Alternatively, Table 1 illustrates possible key performance indicators for measuring human risk in an investment bank.

[11] See Olve, Roy and Wetter (1999). Also www.bscol.com (The Balanced Scorecard Collaborative) and www.pr.doe.gov/pmmfinal.pdf (a guide to the balanced scorecard methodology).

Table 1 Possible key performance indicators for measuring human risk in an investment bank

Function	Quality	Quantity
Back office	Number of transactions processed per day	Proportion of errors in transactions processed
Middle office	Timeliness of reports Delay in systems implementation IT response time	Proportion of errors in reports Systems downtime
Front office	Propriety traders "information ratio" Quality of contacts	Proportion of ticketing errors Number of time stamp delays Number of sales contacts Number of customer complaints

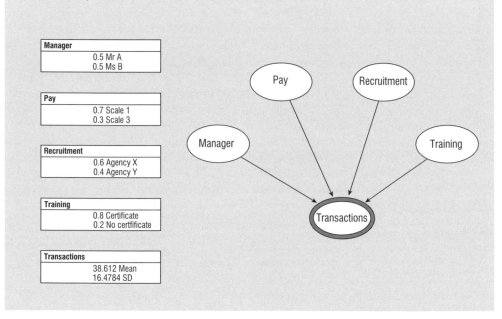

Figure 6: BNN for number of transactions processed per day

Manager	
	0.5 Mr A
	0.5 Ms B

Pay	
	0.7 Scale 1
	0.3 Scale 3

Recruitment	
	0.6 Agency X
	0.4 Agency Y

Training	
	0.8 Certificate
	0.2 No certfificate

Transactions	
	38.612 Mean
	16.4784 SD

We will now look at a BBN that models the human risk in transactions processing. The architecture shown in Figure 6 uses the number of transactions processed per day as the key performance indictor. The node probabilities on the left of Figure 6 are obtained by indicating the relevant manager, their pay scale, the recruitment process and the level of training of each person involved in transactions processing. To keep things simple the network illustrated has only binomial variables for the parent nodes, but they could of course have many states; for example, there could be more than two possible managers, or certain attributes such as pay could be regarded as continuous variables.

The conditional probabilities for the key performance indicator (transactions) node are calculated under the assumption that all conditional distributions are normal; then, for a fixed time period, the mean and standard deviation of the number of transactions processed per day for all employees managed by Mr A, on pay scale 1, recruited from agency X and with a certificate of training, are estimated. Continuing in this way over all states gives the multivariate distribution of the number of transactions processed per day; in the initial state of the network

Figure 7: A simple Bayesian decision network for managing human risk

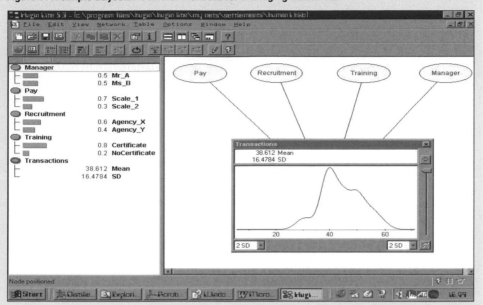

this is the mixture of normals shown in Figure 7. A scenario analysis over the managers, pay, recruitment and training can be employed to see how this distribution changes as the states of these nodes are changed.

Management decisions

The BBN approach has a great advantage for modeling human risks: the management decision process may be modeled by augmenting the BBN with decision nodes and utilities. This article ends with an example to illustrate how management decisions can be accommodated in the BBN framework. Figure 8 illustrates a BBN for a key performance indictor (KPI) that takes the states excellent, good, average and poor; variables that have a relationship with this indictor are pay, management and training, and to illustrate the framework it is sufficient to assume that these are binomial random variables. A (positive or negative) benefit is then attached to each state of the KPI; it is only necessary to ensure that benefits decrease as the KPI deteriorates from "excellent" to "poor". The rectangular node is a decision node that represents the choices of restructuring the pay scheme, the management and/or the training program. A utility, which can be thought of as the expected cost of restructuring, is assigned to each choice.

When a BBN is augmented in this way it is called a Bayesian decision network or an "influence diagram". In the simple influence diagram in Figure 8 the costs and benefits have been assigned in such a way that, in the initial state, the highest utility would be gained from giving employees more training.

Figure 8: A simple Bayesian decision network for managing human risk

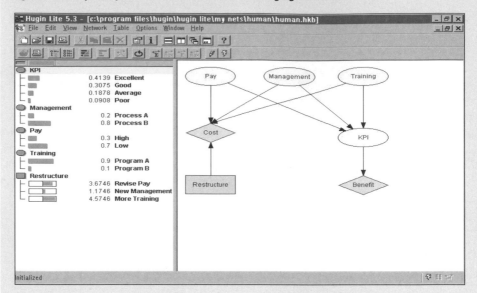

Conclusion

This chapter has surveyed a number of applications of Bayesian analysis in operational risk measurement. At the most basic level, Bayesian estimation of the probability of a loss event and the loss given event can be employed. For example, external loss data can be used in a beta prior; this will have the effect of smoothing the internal expected loss estimates over time and allow for more effective risk budgeting.

Bayesian updating of parameters of the POT model may be applied to simulate empirical loss distributions that are much more robust than those obtained using classical methods such as maximum likelihood. These models are relevant for low-frequency high-impact operational risks where there is little data availability (Medova, 2000). They have important applications to the measurement of tail risk and the allocation of operation risk capital.

Bayesian belief networks have applications to high-frequency low-impact operational risks, with a view to developing internal control procedures. A Bayesian network improves transparency for efficient risk management, but it is also possible that risk capital provisions from a stage 3 model (as outlined in Basel 2) will be reduced for the risk types that are well modeled by a Bayesian network. Bayesian networks are useful in scenario analysis, both over the attributes of operational risks and over market and credit risk factors. This is useful for the integration of operational risk measures with market and credit risk measures, moreover "maximum operational loss" scenarios can be identified to help the operational risk manager focus on the important factors that influence operational risk.

Management of operational risks may be facilitated by the use of a Bayesian decision network, in which the belief network has been augmented with decision nodes and utilities. Bayesian decision networks increase the transparency of senior management decisions. They also improve understanding of the managerial process; a simulation over the states of parent nodes will allow the decision maker to base choices on "what if?" scenarios.

Summary

The stage 3 models for measuring operational risk capital charges that are in the proposals for the Basel 2 Accord will require the assessment of expected loss for different lines of business and risk types. The capital charge will be based on a "tail loss" that is generated as a multiple (gamma) of the expected loss. At the moment there is little idea of the appropriate values for the parameter gamma; it is likely to be quite different for the different risk types in different lines of business. The first part of this paper argued that the gammas should be much lower for high-frequency low-impact operational risks than for low-frequency high-impact risks.

Capital charges will be designed so that they are less under stage 3 models than under stage 2 (standardized approach) or stage 1 (basic indicator). At the time of writing only a handful of banks are thought to meet the rigorous criteria for stage 3 model implementation. Therefore there is bound to be enormous interest in developing models for calculating operational loss and many banks are currently investigating the statistical models that might be used. **Carol Alexander** has shown how Bayesian methods may be applied to a variety of operational risks, including those that are difficult to quantify, such as human risks.[12]

Suggested further reading

Alexander, C. (2000) "Bayesian methods for measuring operational risks," *Derivatives, Use Trading and Regulation*, Vol. 6, No. 2, pp. 166–186.

Bernardo, J.M. and A.F.M. Smith (1994) *Bayesian Theory*. John Wiley & Sons.

Ceske, R. and Hernandez, J. (1999) "Where theory meets practice," Operational Risk Special Report, *Risk Magazine*, November 1999.

Cruz, M. (1999) "Taking risk to market," Operational Risk Special Report, *Risk Magazine*, November 1999.

Dekkers, A., Einmahl, J. and de Haan, L. (1989) "A moment estimator for the index of an extreme-value distribution," *Annals of Statistics* 17: 1833–1855.

Dempster, M.A.H., Kyriacou, M.N. and Medova, E.A. (2001) "Extremes in operational risk management," *Risk Management: Value at Risk and Beyond*. Dempster, M.A.H. and Moffat, H.K. (eds) Cambridge University Press.

Drees, H. (1995) "Refined Pickands estimators of the extreme value index," *Annals of Statistics* 23: 2059–2080.

Fenton, N.E. and B. Littlewood (eds) (1991) *Software Reliability and Metrics*, Elsevier.

Fisher, R. and Tippett, L. (1928) "Limiting forms of the frequency distribution of the largest and smallest member of a sample," *Proc. Camb. Phil. Soc.* 24: 180–190.

Geoffrion, A.M. (1987) "An introduction to structured modelling," *Management Science* 33 pp. 547–588.

Heckerman, D., Mamdani, A. and Wellman, M. (1995) "Real-world applications of Bayesian networks," *Comm ACM*, 38(3) pp. 25–26.

Henrion, M., Breese, J.S. and Horvitz, E.J. (1991) "Decision analysis and expert systems," *Artificial Intelligence Magazine* 12(4) pp. 64–91.

Henrion, M., Morgan, M.G., Nair, I. and Wiecha, C. (1986) "Evaluating an information system for policy modeling and uncertainty analysis," *Journal of the American Society for Information Science* 37(5) pp. 319–330.

Hoffman, D.G. (ed.) (1998) *Operational Risk and Financial Institutions*, Risk Publications, London.

Hüsler, J. and Reiss, R.-D. (eds) (1989) *Extreme Value Theory*. Lecture notes in Statistics 51, Springer, New York.

ISDA/BBA/RMA survey report (February 2000) "Operational Risk – The Next Frontier" available from *www.isda.org*

Jensen, F.V. (1996) *An Introduction to Bayesian Networks*, Springer Verlag, Berlin.

King, J. (2001) *Operational Risk: Measurement and Modeling*, John Wiley, Chichester, UK.

Leadbetter, R., Lindgren, G. and Rootzen, H. (1983) *Extremes and Related Properties of Random Sequences and Processes*. Springer-Verlag NY.

Medova, E. (2000) "Measuring Risk by Extreme Values," *RISK Magazine*, 13:11 pp. s20–s26.

Morgan, M.G. and Henrion, M. (1990) *Uncertainty: A Guide to Dealing with Uncertainty in Quantitative Risk and Policy Analysis*, Cambridge University Press (reprinted in 1998).

---

[12] Many thanks to Telia Weisman of Randloph-Macon Women's College, Lynchburg, VA for enthusiastic research assistance.

Neapolitan, R. (1990) *Probabilistic Reasoning in Expert Systems: Theory and Algorithms*, John Wiley, New York.

O'Brien, N. Smith, B. and Allen, M. (1999) "The case for quantification," *Operational Risk Special Report, Risk Magazine,* July 1999.

Olve, N-G., Roy, J. and Wetter, M. *Performance Drivers: A guide to using the balanced scorecard*, John Wiley, New York.

Pearl, J. (1988) *Probabilistic Reasoning in Intelligent Systems*, Morgan Kaufmann.

Pézier, Mr and Mrs (2001) "Binomial gammas," *Operational Risk*, April, RISK Publications.

Pickands, J. (1975) "Statistical inference using extreme order statistics," *Annals of Statistics* 3: 119–131.

Reiss, R.-D. and Thomas, M. (1997) *Statistical Analysis of Extreme Values*, Birkhäuser, Basel.

Smith, R. (1987) "Estimating tails of probability distributions," *Annals of Statistics* 15: 1174–1207.

Wilson, D. (1999) "Is your operational risk capital adequate?" *Operational Risk Special Report, Risk Magazine,* July 1999.

Operational risk and regulatory capital

by David Murphy

It is rather unfortunate that any article on operational risk and regulatory capital should make an attempt at defining both terms – unfortunate because operational risk is a relatively immature field, and regulatory capital is an area which arouses strong and sometimes contrary views. While there is a natural tendency to allow the considerable efforts of the industry on operational risk measurement to mature into a widely accepted praxis, early conclusions will be needed. The reason for this is the currently proposed revisions to the Basel Capital Accord.

Recently the Basel Committee of Banking Supervision has published its plans for an overhaul of bank regulation. The original 1988 Basel Accord introduced the idea of risk-weighted assets and required capital to be based on them. This set the capital framework for all internationally active banks. The framework has been revised since – most notably in the market risk amendment which gave permission for banks meeting appropriate standards to calculate market risk capital using Value-at-Risk (VaR) models – but the current revisions are the widest ranging revision to the framework since its inception. They introduce:

- more sophisticated capital rules for banking book (chiefly loan) exposure;
- significant changes in the handling of credit derivatives and financings;
- proposals covering the enhanced supervision of banks and the use of supervisory discretion;
- extended disclosure; and, crucially for our purposes,
- charges for operational risks.

The Basel Capital Accords are also highly significant away from banks, as they are implemented (often with little modification) in the European Union for all investment firms. This community includes securities dealers, asset managers, and various non-bank financial firms. Since EU investment firms are a more heterogeneous community than internationally active banks, and have a much more diverse set of activities and financial structures, one of the real challenges of the EU implementation is to ensure that the Basel banking rules remain appropriate for this wider community. Moreover, the European legal process can constrain the speed of innovation of the capital regime: a full directive can take three or more years to pass into law.

Various procedural mechanisms exist that could potentially ease this burden and allow capital adequacy legislation to keep pace with developments within the industry, but it is not clear that these will be applied to the new Capital Adequacy Directive. Hence we are in the unenviable position of having to write capital rules dealing with operational risk for a wide range of firms while the area is comparatively underdeveloped and with the knowledge that these rules may persist, in Europe at least, for ten years or more.

These operational risk charges are likely to be significant for many institutions and, as presently constituted, highly onerous for some. At the time of writing, the proposals are still in consultation, and radical changes are possible before the full Accord is implemented in 2004. Unfortunately, moreover, complete clarity on the proposals has not been granted; some of the crucial parameters, particularly in the area of operational risk, are not precisely stated in the consultative documentation. Nevertheless, we can hope to glean some understanding of the proposals, their impact, and possible alternatives to them.

Operational risk and operational risk losses

A commonly accepted definition of operational risk (OR) reads: "The risk of direct or indirect loss resulting from inadequate or failed internal processes, people, and systems or from external events..." The Basel Committee then goes on to add: "Strategic and reputation risks are not included...", but legal risk is.

Within this broad definition, various risk types have been identified:

- write-downs;
- loss of recourse;
- restitution;
- legal liability;
- regulatory and compliance (including taxation);
- loss of or damage to assets.

This typography is helpful, but it does cover some definitional ambiguities. For instance, are fraudulently obtained loans that subsequently default operational risk or credit risk?

These risk types can give rise to losses. A definition of operational risk loss would include the cost of rectifying an operational risk, payments to third parties and write-downs. The Basel Committee goes further and suggests that operational risk includes near misses and latent losses, presumably including opportunity costs. There is also the interesting matter of operational risk profits: an FX exposure which should have been levelled can generate a profit as well as a loss, for instance. While such events clearly point towards weaknesses that may give rise to genuine operational risk losses, it is not clear that an operational risk loss history should contain such events.

There is a balance to be struck here. It opposes definitional precision – always necessary for an area of risk management to fully mature – with a laxer definition which does not invalidate the use of the currently available data sources. Given that operational risk management must necessarily concern itself with high-severity, low-frequency events, and that modelling such events requires large amounts of data, compromising for the moment may allow the industry to progress further than attempting to impose a definition before the data is available to validate it.

However, it is important to understand in this context that there are limits to the usefulness of industry-wide loss data. Not only can an individual firm's losses differ almost arbitrarily from the average inferred from pooled loss data, but that pooled data is itself not only inconsistently gathered but also necessarily incomplete: disclosure of operational risk loss events to industry data pools may leave firms open to legal discovery processes and/or civil litigation based on that disclosure. Thus in some circumstances there are incentives for firms not to disclose data to industry pools.

What is capital for?

At its simplest, regulatory capital is used for two purposes: reducing systemic risk, and protecting clients of the financial system. By requiring institutions to have a level of capital appropriate to the risk they are running, supervisors can ensure that failing institutions do not affect the health of the financial system as a whole and that the insurance that governments have sold via deposit protections schemes is at worst infrequently called upon.

Traditionally, banking and securities regulators have differed somewhat in their perceptions of the aims of capital, with banking supervisors sometimes tending to take the view that any bank failure is undesirable, whereas securities regulators have tended to view capital more as a buffer, which ensures that defaults, when they do occur, are orderly and do not pose risk of contagion. This comes down to a view of how secure a firm should be: should capital protect risk to the extent that a typical large firm is expected to fail once in 100 years, or once in 100,000 years? Clearly the lower the default probability supervisors wish to have, the more capital will be required against unexpected loss, and the higher the entry barrier for new firms. Also, of course, as size brings diversification benefits, higher capital standards benefit large institutions at the expense of smaller ones and hence tend to produce a smaller number of very large firms. This lack of diversification and concentration of risk capital does not necessarily promote the stability of the system.

Discussions about regulatory capital, then, often come down to a position on the extent to which a firm should be protected against unexpected loss. Many of the large losses in the financial system have had elements of operational risk, so it is clear that operational risk has the capacity to produce firm-threatening events in some cases. Hence it is understandable that supervisors wish to see capital to cover unexpected operational risk losses. Indeed, it is arguable that "expected operational risk losses" are already priced into many products: fees and commissions, for instance, typically are set to cover the expected cost of the product.

The Basel Committee intends to set a capital charge for operational risk based on expected and unexpected losses and allowing some recognition for provisioning and loss deduction, although it accepts the proposition that in some activities where expected operational risk loss is priced in (e.g. credit card fraud), capital could be based on unexpected loss alone. There is also some acceptance of the desirability of recognizing provisions for operational risk losses; however, little consideration has been given to the acceptability of such provisioning within the accounting framework.

The committee has used a small sample of banks to calibrate its proposals and has concluded from this sample that operational risk typically accounts for an average of 20 percent of total economic capital. Given the absence of industry-wide loss data, it further proposes to use this figure to calibrate the proposed charges. This approach, of course, is fraught with difficulty.

Firstly, it is not clear that economic capital is the appropriate risk driver: there seems no reason *a priori* to believe it is well correlated with operational risk. Secondly, the sample is small, and hence while 20 percent of economic capital may, by happenstance, come to the right amount for this population of banks, it may not serve the whole community of all Basel banks, let alone the much wider collection of EU investment firms. Finally, there is a lingering suspicion that 20 percent of economic capital does not represent a real estimate of the operational risk capitalization of Basel banks but rather an estimate of the size of the charge leaving the system through changes to the credit risk charges for banks in the Accord.

These considerations suggest that a more extensive calibration exercise is necessary before we can determine the magnitude and form of a charge appropriate for the whole community of firms to which it will be applied. This is particularly the case since the charges are, as we shall see, penal for some institutions and can fall rather far from the stated goal of risk sensitivity.

We will discuss first the proposed capital charges in some detail. We will then look at the implications of these proposals for the industry and for European competitiveness. Finally, we will suggest some alternatives which may meet the supervisors needs better than the current proposals.

Stages in the operational risks proposals

The supervisors are proposing three approaches to the calculation of an operational risk charge:

- the *basic indicator* approach: this will be very simple, with a capital charge produced as a fixed percentage of gross income;
- the *standardized* approach: this is somewhat more sophisticated, with the capital for the institution being the simple sum across a number of regulator-specified business lines of a volume indicator times a supervisor-specified percentage or haircut. Most sophisticated firms will start here, with the expectation on the supervisor's part that those with significant operational risk will eventually migrate to:
- the *internal measurement* approach: Here the firm uses its own internal data to calibrate the haircut, perhaps with a supervisor-specified multiplier.

In the future, a *loss distribution* approach, in which the firm specifies its own loss distributions, business lines, and risk types, may be available.

The committee anticipates that a firm may have some business lines in the standardized approach and others in the internal measurement approach. It will not be possible to retreat to a simpler approach once a firm has been accepted for a more advanced approach.

The committee has stated that it intends to calibrate the approaches so that the capital charge for a typical bank would be less at each progressively more sophisticated approach. This is welcome, but the implication is clearly that institutions significantly different from a typical Basel bank may not find an incentive for moving to a more sophisticated approach – this appears to be true for the current calibration as far as it has been revealed.

The basic indicator approach

Here the charge is currently proposed to be 30 percent of gross income (meaning net interest income plus net non-interest income). This figure may change, as it is calibrated on a limited amount of data: in particular, the committee has stated that it may be desirable to set the haircut at a different level to encourage progress towards the more sophisticated approaches or in the light of better calibration data. There is good evidence to indicate that 30 percent of gross income is typically greater than the 20 percent of economic (or regulatory) capital discussed above, so there may be movement here.

The standardized approach

Here the charge is based on a number of business lines, with an indicator of volume for each line serving as a proxy for operational risk. The specified lines and indicators are currently:

Investment banking	Corporate finance	Gross income
	Trading and sales	Gross income
Banking	Retail banking	Annual average assets
	Commercial banking	Annual average assets
	Payment and settlement	Annual settlement throughput
Others	Retail brokerage	Gross income
	Asset management	Total funds under management

For each line, an exposure ("EI") indicator is multiplied by a supervisor-determined haircut and the results summed. The haircuts have not been specified precisely in the current proposals which makes precise quantification impossible at this stage. Ranges have been suggested, but even using the low end, it is not difficult to find institutions which, because of their size in a particular business line, have a larger charge under the standardized approach than under the basic indicator approach. Part of the problem here is that the haircuts in the current proposal were calibrated to a very small sample and hence may not be representative of the wider industry experience.

The internal measurement approach

In this approach, firms will use their own internal loss data to calibrate the charge. The firm's activities will be split into a number of business lines, probably the same set as above, and for each business line a set of loss types will be identified. The supervisor will specify an "exposure indicator" for each loss type within a business line. The firm will then calibrate both the probability of loss due to this event (PE), and the loss given the event (LGE). The product

$$EI \times PE \times LGE$$

will give the expected loss for this loss type. This expected loss will then be scaled up to cover unexpected losses by a supervisor-determined gamma factor: the intention being to "conservatively" cover losses to a high percentile, perhaps 99 percent, of the loss distribution. Finally, the capital charge will be obtained by summing

$$\gamma \times EI \times PE \times LGE$$

across all business lines and loss types. Historical loss and exposure data will be used to determine the firm's measures of PE and LGE, perhaps in combination with pooled industry data.

The committee hopes to develop an industry-wide OR loss distribution. Clearly an individual firm's distribution may differ significantly from the industry-wide distribution, either due to its own particular features or due to sampling effects. The committee suggests that a firm's capital charge may be adjusted for this by the use of a "risk profile index" which would adjust for differences between the unexpected loss level of a firm's distribution and that of the industry-wide calibration distribution.

Finally, beyond the internal measure approach lies the loss distribution approach. This will not be available for regulatory capital purposes when the current revisions to the Accord are introduced. However, in due course, the committee will encourage the industry to enter into a dialogue concerning the use of internal models of the whole-firm operational loss distribution with a view to the use of such models for capital purposes – once they can be appropriately validated.

Implementation of the operational risks proposals

In addition to the proposed capital charges, it is worth touching on their implementation. Supervisors will set entry criteria for the more advanced stages; they are proposing a floor on the benefit obtained by the more advanced capital calculation methods; there is some discussion on the role of risk mitigation techniques such as insurance; and the operational risk charges in pillar one also interact with the other pillars of the Accord.

Entry criteria for the stages

Each of the approaches above the basic indicator have entry criteria. For instance, to qualify for the standardized approach, firms must demonstrate:

- involvement of senior management in operational risk management;
- a robust qualitative operational risk management control process and robust operational risk information systems, including both independent risk control and internal audit functions;
- specific, documented criteria for mapping current business lines and activities into the standardized framework.

In addition, to qualify for the internal measurement approach, firms must demonstrate:

- the accuracy, consistency and completeness of internal operational risk loss data over "a number" of years;
- regular review of this data and comparison with external data to ensure its continuing appropriateness;
- knowledgeable, independent and empowered operational risk management staff;
- the use of loss data in the firm's OR reporting, and full integration of the internal measurement methodology into day-to-day activities and major business decisions including capital allocation.

Given the comparative immaturity of operational risk measurement as an area, this requires a considerable commitment by a firm.

The floor

The potential benefits from the more sophisticated stages of the OR capital calculation have been explicitly capped. The committee has proposed a limit on the capital benefit obtained by moving from the standardized approach to the internal measurement approach. The level of this floor is not clear at the time of writing, and the committee proposes a review of the need for its existence and possible level two years after the implementation of the Accord.

Two possible techniques are suggested for setting the level of the floor. One is to take a fixed percentage of the standardized approach capital charge. Alternatively, the committee could set a minimum level for expected loss based on industry-wide data.

Risk mitigation

The potential for certain risk mitigation techniques to be recognized for capital purposes is offered in the proposals. This does not mean operational risk management techniques, but rather the use of mechanisms such as insurance or outsourcing to transfer OR to third parties (or other group companies). The criteria for the recognition of risk mitigation are aimed at ensuring a clean break, i.e. that risk has been effectively transferred.

While the principle that techniques such as insurance can transfer the risk of low-frequency, high-impact events has been accepted, this replaces operational risk with counterparty risk to the mitigation provider, and hence does not necessarily remove all capital requirements. Furthermore, the committee notes that these techniques can give risk to concerns of enforceability, scope, and moral hazard, and these will have to be addressed before complete recognition of risk mitigation can be granted.

Pillars 2 and 3: supervisory discretion and market discipline

The Basel Accord envisages the use of supervisory discretion and market discipline as supporting pillars to capital adequacy. Supervisors will be expected to apply their judgement on the overall adequacy of capital in each institution compared with its control environment and, if necessary, take prompt action, including increasing capital requirements, to correct perceived risks. The committee intends to publish guidance and criteria to facilitate such an assessment process.

Moreover, the qualitative supervisory judgements necessary to approve the more sophisticated stages of capital calculation will require supervisory assessment of a bank's strategies, policies, procedures, and practices. These two threads – supervisory discretion and the approval of the later stages of capital calculation – will between them involve the assessment of:

- a firm's process for assessing OR capital adequacy and allocating OR capital by business line;
- the effectiveness of the operational risk management process, including data quality issues;
- the integrity of the interlinked processes of OR internal control, review and audit;
- the efficacy of any operational risk mitigation.

Not only will any issues identified during this process potentially hamper access to sophisticated capital treatments, they could also trigger capital requirements above the minimum or remedial action, including required enhancements to processes and/or management.

The third pillar of the Accord addresses the use of market pressures to encourage firms towards best practice. These pressures will be exerted through the use of enhanced disclosure. Specifically, the following core disclosures are recommended semi-annually for all firms with regard to OR:

- the capital calculation approaches chosen for each business line;
- details of the OR management framework, policies, reporting and organization;
- summary of operational risk mitigants such as insurance used;
- operational risk exposure by business line;
- OR regulatory capital charge as a percentage of the total minimum capital charge.

The test is that any material of interest of a "reasonable investor" should be disclosed. Moreover, firms in the internal measurement approach must disclose:

- annual experienced OR losses by business line.

Implications

There is much to welcome in the proposals outlined above. In particular, the committee has recognized the importance of operational risk in firms, and has stated the intention of producing a capital charge to cover it that is both risk sensitive and offers incentives for better operational risk management. However, there are some highly problematic features of the proposals. In this section we look at five features of concern and highlight their possible implications for the industry.

Redistribution and capital inadequacy

In their current form, the proposals as a whole will lead to considerable redistribution of capital requirements from lending institutions to other firms. Studies by the Financial Services Authority (FSA) indicate, for instance, that some monoline asset managers and corporate finance advisory firms would be capitally inadequate under the proposed new regime. Given that neither class of firm has hitherto been seen to be a dominant source of systemic risk, it is hard *prima facie* to justify such an outcome. Moreover, since these charges would be applied to European non-banks, the net effect may be to make Europe's non-bank financial services industry less competitive than that in the United States.

Outsourcing

Supervisors have already accepted that operational risk mitigation, whether via insurance or outsourcing, can result in reduced capital. If the capital benefits of outsourcing certain classes of operational risk are significant enough, there will be a strong incentive for risk to leave the regulated system. Consider, for instance, clearing and settlement. If the operational risk charge is proportional to volume with a haircut which results in an onerous charge, then large firms will consider outsourcing their clearing and settlement to third parties. Providing that outsourcing is done under a robust service-level agreement which clearly transfers OR, the firm will obtain a significant capital benefit. Since there is no requirement for the firm undertaking the outsourced function to be regulated, it is unlikely that it will choose to shoulder this burden.

The net result will be that a number of clearing, custody and settlement firms will appear, and that risk will have left the regulated system. It is unlikely that such firms would have anything approaching the capital of the banks which originally carried out this function. Moreover, there are clearly economies of scale in such activities, so the market may be dominated by a small number of specialist firms. The result is arguably an increase in systemic risk.

Prescription

The current proposals are highly prescriptive, both of business lines and of operational risk indicators. Many firms, particularly away from the continental universal banks, are organized very differently from the prototypical business lines of stages 2 and 3. The costs of gathering data and slotting it into this arbitrary pattern purely for regulatory purposes will be considerable.

We are still in an immature stage of quantitative operational risk measurement: operational risk management, of course, has been going on for as long as banking has, through the activities of functions such as legal, operations, internal audit, and management. Given this immaturity, it is hard to believe the prescription of exposure indicators is appropriate, especially given they may be fixed until European law can next be revised. Over time, firms will find leading indicators of operational risk that are appropriate for their businesses: some have already done so for some businesses. These indicators will serve not as a crude indicator of volume, but as a guide to possible changes in the size and shape of the operational risk loss distribution. Firms must have the freedom and the incentive to develop these indicators as they see fit.

A similar argument applies to the entry criteria for the various stages of operational risk capital. While it is certainly appropriate to reward more sophisticated firms with a better capital treatment, it may not be appropriate to define in detail what we mean by sophisticated operational risk management today in the knowledge that we may have to live with the result for ten years. Supervisors have in the past waited for an industry consensus to develop on modelling before imposing it via entry requirements for a capital treatment. Here the laudable desire to do something quickly on operational risk may prejudice the eventual development of a framework which most agree reflects best practice. The danger is that sophisticated firms will eventually evolve their internal operational risk measurements so far from the supervisor's framework that there can be no confidence that the regulatory numbers are used by management – they could become a sop, far from the bank's practice.

Statistical issues

One interesting issue arises in the proposed internal measurement approach. By asking firms to estimate PE and LGE by business line and risk type, supervisors are asking firms to make a number of statistical estimates. Since there are at least seven business lines proposed, and presumably some will have more than one risk type, one might assume that at least 20 estimates in total will be necessary. Clearly, in each case the data can be dominated (or not) by one low-frequency, high-severity event. The statistical challenge of the internal measurement approach is greater than that for the full loss distribution approach: at least there only one number (the 99 percent expected loss, say) is being estimated rather than 20 or more parameters. Thus while the internal measurement approach is superficially simpler than measurement of the firm's loss distribution, it may well be more problematic in practice.

Double counting

There is significant double counting between the operational risk proposals in the Basel revisions and other areas of the Accord. For instance, the 3 (or more) times multiplier for VaR in the market risk provisions, the w factor for credit risk mitigation, and the use of supervisory discretion to set higher capital requirements could all be justified due to risks covered by the supervisors' definition of OR. These superfluous capital requirements risk warping the risk sensitivity of the Accord.

Alternatives

The current Basel and EU timetable places severe constraints on feasible alternatives for operational risk capital charges. Nevertheless, there are some routes forward that appear to be more practical, prudent, and risk sensitive than the current proposals.

Linearity

A common feature in all of the committee's proposed methodologies in stages 1, 2 and 3 is that the charge is linearly proportional to an indicator of volume. This implies that operational risk is directly proportional to volume. This does not match industry experience in a number of areas.

Perhaps the best place to test this is in the area of transaction processing, as many internationally active firms have a considerable history of steadily increasing volumes in both equity and debt instruments. In contrast to the linearity assumption, here industry experience has been that operational risk losses have risen much more slowly than increases in volume. This is principally due to investments in improved controls: often as volumes rise, so does income, and this supports improvements in process. Furthermore, additional volume is often caused by improved liquidity, and this can tend to mitigate the effects of OR, both because increasingly timely systems are required to monitor more liquid markets, tending to decrease the time to discovery of operational risk losses, and because liquidity is available to support trading should that be necessary to neutralize a position caused by an operational risk event.

Areas of relatively large volume for a firm are typically its core areas. The incentive to invest in controls here is often largest, and the firm's core competence is highest. Whereas the linearity assumption indicates operational risk is largest in these areas, firms' experience is instead often that it is typically in non-core or new areas where it is highest. New markets, products or risk classes, if not entered into with care, can generate considerable operational risks despite their low volume, whereas high-volume areas are often well understood, monitored and managed by firms. While the scale of new product innovation and controls around it is a pillar 2 area, it does show the dangers of assuming operational risks are borne by participants in the market in proportion to their share of it – they may instead be borne in proportion to their investment in controls.

There is folklore evidence that the current industry OR loss databases invalidate the assumption of linearity. This, combined with the observations above, lead us to suggest a re-exploration of the data with a view to determining the real empirical relationship, if any, between indicators of volume and operational risk. Without wishing to pre-judge the results of such a study, intuition would suggest a much more shallowly rising function than a linear one would give a better fit.

Calibration

If the standard approach is to be retained, albeit in a modified form where the charge is proportional to some sub-linear function of volume, it is vital that it is calibrated to the best available data. Moreover, since it will be applied to investment firms as well as Basel banks, this calibration should not be confined to the Basel community. It may well turn out, for instance, that the addition of many more firms to the sample significantly changes the calibration, or that a widely different calibration is suggested for investment firms.

Forward-looking indicators

We have already touched on the need for indicators of OR that look forward. There is a natural tendency to lock the door after the horse has bolted – after an OR event, firms often invest in controls to ensure that an event of the same types become much less probable. Therefore almost by definition, the existence of a significant event in a firm's loss distribution ensures that that loss type is unlikely to be significant for the firm again. Capital charges should clearly focus on the current loss distribution – after investment in controls – hence the need to ensure that if indicators can be developed that reflect the likelihood of future OR losses, these are used in preference to those which reflect the past (historic loss distributions) or the industry average (haircuts of volume indicators). While there is clearly little agreement today on what these indicators might be for many risk types and investment businesses, firms should be incentivized to search them out and convince supervisors of their veracity.

Conclusion

Let us return to the purpose of capital, simplistically, it seeks to ensure that a firm can survive unexpected losses. The model here is of a loss distribution: expected losses are (typically) priced in or reserved for; capital supports unexpected losses to a given percentile. Unfortunately this model assumes we can get a good sense of what the loss distribution for a given firm looks like. This is by no means clear for operational risk: perhaps the historic industry-wide distribution can be derived, although there are some problems there, as we saw in the section "What is capital for?". Some sophisticated firms may derive observations of their individual historic distributions. But there is doubt that these historic distributions reflect current reality given a changing business environment and changing controls around it. The history of mathematical modelling is full of examples of the folly of attempting to model non-stationary fat-tailed distributions with only sparse observations available.

This is not to say that operational risk cannot be quantified, simply that it is a young field, and operational risk management, at first at least, will rely as much on the development of pragmatic indicators of OR, good controls, and management oversight as it will on complex statistical methods.

The proposed Basel framework has some good features, notably the stated desire for incentives for firms to better manage operational risk, and to provide capital benefits for those that can convince their supervisors of their success here. However, we believe that some modifications to the current proposals would enhance success:

- the standard approach should have a charge that is non linear with volume and is appropriately calibrated for a wide range of firms;
- the framework should allow for the development of forward-looking indicators of operational risk and for benefit to be given for the quality of a firm's control environment;
- the elements of double counting in the Accord should be eliminated.

Summary

David Murphy discusses the current Basel Capital Accord proposals regarding operational risk as they apply to Basel Banks and EU Investment Firms. Some fault lines in the proposals are analyzed, and the consequences for the overall market discussed. Modifications to the proposals are suggested which may be less problematic.

Further Reading

The New Basel Capital Accord: Second Consultative Package (2001). The Basel Committee on Banking Supervision. Available from www.bis.org

The views expressed in this article are those of the author alone and should not be construed as the view of any other individual or body corporate.

Subject index

Note: following a page number f = figure; n = footnote; t = table; all placed after textual references.

Organization index

Name index